Helix - The Second Renaissance

The second book in the Helix Dreams series

by

Michael Davies

Helix – The Second Renaissance

For information address
mickiedaltonbooks@lycos.com

First Printing 2018

ISBN: 978-0-9876304-0-7

Published by The Mickie Dalton Foundation
NSW
Australia

Acknowledgement

This book could not have been developed without the extraordinary collaboration with Greg Dickson.

Greg came to my house several times during the year for two and three day brainstorming sessions which took up almost the entire day from breakfast through to retirement and left us astonished, delighted and somewhat wrung out with what we had created.

The process enforced my belief in the synergy of multiple minds working on a problem and left me grateful for the creative experience.

Similarly, sincere thanks to Penny le Couteur for her detailed, professional editing of the manuscript at several stages of the development.

And now to Book III of the Trilogy!

Other Works by Michael Davies

The Janus Conspiracy
Accounts of a Killing
A Friendly Killing
Dreamkill
Ready, Steady, KILL!
The Nightmares of God
Helix Dreams

For the Young Adults (12-18)
The Many Worlds of Mickie Dalton
The Many Galaxies of Mickie Dalton
The Many Universes of Mickie Dalton
The Strange World of Mark and Anna

For the 8-12 age group
The Julie Malloy Gang and the Smugglers
The Quest for the Locket
The Secret of Yuri Kirilenko
The United Nations and the Extra-Terrestrial
The Secret of Charlotte's Cello
The Star of the Yshan Kings
The War of the Yshan Empire
The Star of the New Yshan Empire
The Red Fog of Time
The Mysterious Recorder and The Door to Elsewhere
Prisoners of the Picture
A Step Back in Time
What Can't be Seen Can Exist
How I Spent My Evening

For the Little Ones (3-5)
Mary's World

And in non-fiction
The Business School Approach to Writing Your Novel

In the Beginning

Karen Petrova was considered the finest pharmacologist in the world. Entering Moscow University at fourteen, her family transferred to England when her father, a Nobel Prize-winning physician was awarded a post at Cambridge University. Karen graduates at sixteen from Cambridge with first class honours, going on to complete her doctorate and then a fellowship at Harvard and she returned to England as a lecturer at Oxford University. There she met a renowned geneticist, Hector Forbes whom she married soon after. The marriage was intensely happy.

Karen began designing new drugs, set up Life Technology, a business designing and licensing drugs to drug manufacturing companies and became immensely rich, possibly the richest woman in the world. Hector died of cancer, but had told Karen of his own dream, that human DNA contained something far more critical than just the blueprint for the human body.

In his honour, Karen set up a subsidiary company, Blueprints to investigate the nature of DNA to the greatest possible extent. She provided essentially unlimited funding.

She hired Garry Lawson, a manager in the pharmaceutical business with a reputation for management of complex operations. The greatest acquisition though, was Bill Askins, a genius with a doctorate in genetics and also an extraordinary electronic instrumentation engineer.

The brilliance of Bill Askins and the genetics researchers began to pay off. At first, the team was only able to find short visual episodes from the DNA record as seen through the person's own eyes.

Even at this primitive level, some extraordinary finds were made. The most powerful was the sight of a woman being brutally murdered as seen by her killer.

Bill was able to find the audio tracks to the images and another geneticist was able to find the tracking system that enabled them to see the whole of the person's life from the start to the point at which the DNA sample was taken.

Then came the world-changing development. The researchers find that the DNA contains not only a complete record of a person's life up to the moment of the sample being taken, but also the record of the person's parents from birth to the point of procreation when their DNA is passed to the child. Further investigation shows that the same is true for the parents' DNA and further back through the generations. It becomes possible to look back through time and see historical events and ordinary daily lives.

Massive changes begin in the justice system, in historical research and religion.

The issue arises of why this feature exists in humans – it is not a Darwinian survival factor and seems unnatural.

A fanatical religious mob attacks the offices with heavy weapons. A bomb is shot through the front doors and many people are injured. When Karen arrives, a bomb under her car is set off and she is killed.

Garry finds that Karen has left him a billion pounds to maintain the companies and their work. In addition, Karen has set up a backup company in Australia and all arrangements have been made to Blueprints' staff to emigrate there, should they wish.

Garry advises his staff and arrangements begin for the move.

Chapter 1 - January, 2022

"What on earth is going on?" Garry's voice was harsh with tension and bewilderment. He stared round the room at the people who had stood up as he walked in. Not one of them fitted his ideas of what he had been expecting.

Fifteen minutes earlier

"You have reached your destination, Number 211, Hartsbourne Road."

The woman's voice with the strong Australian accent sounded from the little global positioning satellite device on the dashboard of Garry's rental car.

"That's a more symbolic statement than you realise," Garry muttered aloud and stopped. He switched off the engine and looked at the three-storey, elderly terrace with white, wrought-iron railings on all three balconies.

"Lovely," he said, got out and stretched, feeling a little stiff after the three hour drive from Sydney. He locked the car and walked up to the dark blue front door which opened before he had the chance to press the bell.

The face that had confronted him on the few Skype

calls they had held with each other was familiar, but the rest was not. Mary Hennessey was well over six feet tall and most imposing. She wore a long grey skirt with a brown sweater to counter the rather chilly Spring day that had not yet warmed up in the bright sunshine. Dark hair fell to her shoulders, framing a strong face with rimless glasses over brilliant blue eyes.

"G'day," she said with a wide grin. "Lovely to meet you at last!"

A shade off balance, having to look up to her commanding face, Garry took a breath.

"Same here," he said.

She flung the door wide open. "Come in, coffee's on." She turned and led the way into a room immediately on her right. Garry's first impression was of a large crowd. There must have been at least seven or eight in the spacious room that went some fifteen metres from the bay windows at the front to the French doors at the back. A large conference table filled the front of the room. All the occupants were standing.

"Here's the new boss," proclaimed Mary cheerfully. "As you all know, this is Garry Lawson. Garry, let me present Blueprints Two."

Still feeling off balance, Garry let the men and women introduce themselves and at the end he smiled and said, "I'll never remember you all right away, so please forgive me. But it's a great pleasure to meet the Australian end of Blueprints."

"Let's sit down," said Mary and pointed at the head of the conference table. "Yours," she said shortly and sat down at his right as the others took seats.

A young man appeared at the other end of the room and began filling coffee cups, loading them on a trolley and wheeled it up to the table. There were three desks at that end of the room as well, all with the scanning equipment that was so familiar to Garry.

Garry counted the seated members and there were, as he had estimated, seven of them, eight with Mary. Five of them were men, all of them looked at least forty years old. It was not at all what he had expected.

"This is my house," said Mary in reply to Garry's unasked question. "I live on the top two floors, this is the office."

"And where is the main laboratory?" asked Garry.

"Should be complete by next week," she said.

"Next week?" Garry was starting to feel deeply uneasy. "My people will start arriving next week and will want to start work. They're all in the middle of some deep research projects."

"I suggest they may want to get organised first," said Mary. "Accommodation, cars, driving licences, phones, medical coverage, all takes time."

"I suppose," said Garry. "I know that I was told in Reading that this was a different sort of operation, but have you not had any geneticists or pharmacologists working on the equipment?"

"No geneticists. No pharmacologists. No scientists of any kind, just some historians and linguists from universities here in Australia who use the facilities but are not on staff."

"I think you need to explain to me just what your role is, then." Garry was feeling confused and worried. Despite the briefing in Reading, he was sensing such a different operation that he felt out of his depth.

Mary touched his arm. "Let me show you," she said and pointed at each of the people at the table.

"Brad Robertson, futurist," she said, starting at Garry's left and the tall, thin man smiled lightly.

"Salmaan Basrai, statistician," Mary continued

round the table and the short, stocky, bespectacled man waved a hand.

"Jennifer Soo Ling Chan, international legal expert," continued Mary, and the petite Chinese woman smiled gently.

"Robert Swann, crisis manager." The tall, man in his fifties with greying hair nodded with a smile.

"Annabelle Calvert, historian." A middle-aged woman with unnaturally red hair made a small wave.

"And Mark Craymer. Mark is a military historian, has lectured at West Point, the RAF College at Cranwell and our military college at Duntroon."

The middling height, athletic man in his forties nodded at Garry.

"And that's your team," concluded Mary. "Me, I'm a retired spook, ASIO experience in Afghanistan and Europe and my task is to scare the crap out of people if they don't do what I tell them. And I pay their salaries."

"This is beyond me," said Garry, his voice harsh with tension. "What on earth is going on?"

"Garry, calm down," said Mary. Her personality shone out and she had an air of command about her that cut through the anger in him. "This is exactly what Doctor Petrova asked for and she approved of everything we were doing."

"She's been here?" Some of the frustrated anger in Garry was declining as he heard that Karen's wishes were being followed. The anger was replaced by bewilderment.

"Several times. She came with some interesting ideas that had been suggested to her by one of her best friends..."

Chapter 2 – August, 1990

"Isaac, my dear, you are not looking well."

"Nor feeling it, Karen."

She was right. Asimov's distinguishing muttonchop sideburns had faded to a light grey and thinned out from their previous healthy growth. He looked tired.

"What is wrong with you? You have never looked so unwell in all years we have known each other."

"You know I had a triple bypass a couple of years ago after my heart attack?"

"Of course I do. Wasn't it successful? It's usually operation that leaves you stronger than before."

"It should have done. Karen, this must not go beyond us." Asimov looked round the coffee shop and saw nobody within hearing distance. Still, he leaned forward in his armchair and hid his mouth with the magazine he had been reading.

Alarmed, Karen did the same until their faces were just a small distance apart.

"Karen, during the surgery, I needed a blood transfusion. Some time later, I began to feel unwell and they tested my blood. It turns out it was infected with the HIV virus from the transfusion."

Karen sat back in horror. "Oh my God! Isaac! How bad?"

"It's bad. Now, I repeat, this must not get out. The nastiness attached to this disease could cause real unpleasantness for me and for my family."

Karen felt tears in her eyes and took a deep breath. "Can anything be done?"

"The usual cocktail of drugs. They don't work."

"How is family taking it?"

"Janet is being her usual strong self. The kids are being adult about it. So we'll manage. My teaching load has been sharply cut anyway to allow me to write pretty well full time and that's what I'm doing."

He sat back. "Enough on that topic. So, tell me Karen, how is the new business venture going?"

She took a deep breath. "Isaac, I never dreamed how this could be. Hector and I set up this company, "Life Technology" and I began selling licences to my drugs. We have made *Millions!* Money keeps pouring in!"

He smiled at her enthusiasm. "You always said you and Hector would change the world."

"This is only start. Hector told me once that what he really wants to do is investigate DNA."

"For what?" Asimov looked interested.

"He doesn't really know. But he says scientists are wrong when they say DNA is mostly junk from evolution."

"And what are you thinking of?"

"When we have more time and few more millions, I want to set up research group to investigate his idea."

"What do you think you will find?"

"Isaac, I do not know. Nor does Hector. But when mind like Hector thinks like this, he is almost certainly right. There is something."

He laughed. "You remind me of something Arthur C. Clarke once said. It was something like, *'If an elderly but distinguished scientist says that something is possible, he is almost certainly right; but if he says that it is impossible, he is very probably wrong.'* This sounds like something where a distinguished scientist could be right!"

"I think so. And then we will most certainly change world."

"Yes, you will. And what happens then?"

She looked curiously at him. "Meaning what?"

"Karen, massive changes will always cause consequences. These could be destructive and lots of forward thinking is essential."

"We haven't got that far. We don't even know what changes could be."

"Have you read my books in the *'Foundation Series?'*"

"Of course I have! When you told me about these when we first met, I read them almost at once."

"Then you will recall that the great scientist, Hari Seldon developed a sort of epidemiology on steroids called 'Psycho-history' that could accurately forecast human events once he had a suitable number of people, in this case many billions to work with. He forecast the end of the Galactic Empire and this would cause chaos."

"I remember that."

"So he set up 'The Foundation' to try and counter the coming tens of thousands of years of chaos by accumulating all human knowledge to help shorten the dark ages."

"And he also set up Second Foundation," she said. "I always liked that idea. It was totally different from First Foundation."

"Indeed. And you might want to think along those lines. Whatever it is you find in human DNA might well change our very concept of what it is to be human. What do you think will happen?"

She paused for a few seconds.

"Enlightenment. Fear. Chaos. New forms of humanity."

"All those things," said Asimov. "And what steps are you taking to reduce the impact of those issues?"

She sat still, her mind whirling.

"Isaac, dear, you have always made my mind work overtime. I have read all your books. Now I must go back and read Foundation series again."

"I hope you do. Let's have another coffee."

As their cups were being refilled by the waitress, a woman approached the table with a small child walking alongside, holding her hand. Asimov looked up and smiled then held his arms out to the child who ran to him and jumped on his lap.

"This is my niece, Tatiana," he said to Karen who exchanged nods of greeting with the woman. "Tatiana, this is Karen Petrova, a pharmacologist visiting from England. And this gorgeous little moppet is Galina. She's two."

"Uncle Isaac, you said you'd look after Galina for an hour while I had my hair done."

"Of course, Tatiana," said Asimov. "Have you got her books with you?"

"Never travel without them," replied Tatiana and put a shopping bag on the floor next to Asimov. "See you in an hour." With a small wave to Karen, she left the coffee shop.

Asimov bent down, picked up a book from the bag and showed it to the little girl who shook her head.

"The other one," she said clearly.

He repeated the move and brought out a second book. The little girl immediately opened it and began looking at the pages. Peering over, Karen saw only text, no illustrations in the book.

"She's reading?" asked Karen. "At two years old?"

"And you should see what she's reading," said Asimov with a tiny grin. "Galina, will you show my friend Karen your book?"

The child looked up and studied Karen with a disconcertingly direct stare, then smiled and turned the book so that Karen could see it.

"She reads French?" said Karen, startled.

"And English," said Asimov.

"Good grief," said Karen.

"That's the usual reaction," said Asimov, a proud grin on his lips.

The child resumed reading the book.

"Something else I just thought of," said Asimov. He tapped his coffee cup with one finger, looking down in concentration. "It's probable that at some stage you will start accumulating lots of DNA samples, thousands and thousands of them. You will need electronic automation to store the data, at least as much as the big mainframe computers being used in corporations and governments. You could even find yourself with many millions of samples if this research proves fruitful."

"What are you thinking, Isaac?"

"Data on many millions of human beings will start to give you the sort of information processing power that I wrote about with Hari Seldon's psycho-history. This can be very dangerous and very productive. You may be astonished by what you find."

"I'll remember that, Isaac. Now, tell me more about what this remarkable grand-niece of yours can do."

Chapter 3 – January, 2022

"So playing the role of Asimov's Second Foundation, that's our job." Still touching his arm, Mary sat back in her seat.

"You'd better explain." Garry still felt bewildered and lost, but the references to Isaac Asimov and his close friendship with Karen at least gave him some assurance that there was logic in this situation.

"Change can be frightening," Mary said. "And the greater the change, the more frightening it can be. But if the changes or the effects of the changes can be anticipated, it might be possible to prepare for it and put in place some actions that will counter the effects, or at least minimise them."

"And that's your role," said Garry, at last understanding.

"And that's our role. There's no need for any more geneticists, your team is clearly superb at what it does and they will no doubt find out even more startling abilities in our DNA in coming times. But is the world prepared for what you discover?"

"It's been pretty calm so far," said Garry. "I thought the churches would throw serious hissy-fits but it's all been peaceful."

"So far," said Mary.

"You think that will change?"

"We're certain of it. Major changes in religious philosophies have always resulted in upheavals. Just look at the development of Christianity in Europe. Look at Henry the Eighth and what he caused by splitting away from the Catholic Church. And now your discoveries have taken away the entire underpinning of Christianity, probably the biggest event ever. The firestorm is just waiting in the wings."

Garry was silent in thought for a few moments.

"That's pretty well what Cardinal Jackson told me," he said finally. "There's a schism brewing in the Catholic Church and it might explode at any time."

"We're expecting it," said Mary. "And the same with the Church of England."

"And what can anyone do about it? Is there anything you can advise anyone to do something?"

"In this case, not a lot," said a man a few places down the table. He was a little overweight but looked healthy, late forties Garry estimated, but almost completely bald. "Ben Fuller," said the man and smiled. "Sociology, got my degrees from several places around the world. I met Hector Forbes during my post-doc at Oxford and I met Karen the next day. The news of your discoveries and the first reactions of the main Judeo-Christian religions have already been released, so there's not much we can do now to prepare governments. They and the Churches have been worrying and planning for a while now and they have as much expertise as we do."

"So is there anything at all to be done to prepare for it?" Garry was still feeling a sense of having been let down by this new group. "By the way, my memory for faces and names could be better! Would you reintroduce yourselves at first?"

"There is a lot of possible preparation, and that's coming into my territory," said the tall man on Garry's right. He looked exceptionally fit and intelligence almost shone from his eyes. Garry put him in his late fifties. "Robert Swann," he said with a smile and reached over to shake Garry's hand. "Crisis Manager."

"Robert's under-stating his talents," said Mary. "He's the most highly regarded expert in crisis management, disaster recovery planning and business continuity planning in the country and several other countries also."

"That's impressive," said Garry with a smile. "So what have you done about all this?"

"We brainstormed it round this table first," said Swann. "Then I wrote the recommendations. Here's a copy for you." He reached down to his briefcase and took out a spiral-bound document, sliding it across to Garry. The cover said, "Action Plan for Civil Unrest."

"And what did you do with this?"

"First, we talked with the Government in Canberra. Both the ruling party and the opposition are fully aware of the work your group has done and they know of Karen's reputation. Of course, they learned of the discoveries regarding the Christian legends when they were announced by both the Anglican and Catholic Churches, so they have had a lot of time to absorb it. This document was well received and the Ambassador to the United Nations was also there and is raising the topic in New York this week."

"Can you give me a potted summary?" asked Garry, seeing more than two hundred pages in the document.

Swann nodded and began to speak in a calm, measured manner.

Chapter 4 – Mary Hennessey
November, 1992

November, 1992

"Mary, we're so proud of you, both of us."

Mary Hennessey looked at her father seated across from her in the settee and thought he looked absolutely smashing in his army uniform with the crown and two stars on his shoulders.

"Yes, daddy Colonel," she said, smiling. It had been a joke between them since she was seven and had understood what her father did and became so proud of his senior officer rank.

"Those exam results, a place at Sydney University, we're just delighted," said her father.

"And you're younger than I was when I went to University," added her mother. As always, she was smartly dressed, something she had once told Mary was essential as she never knew when one of the officers under the Colonel's command would come to the house and meet the Commanding Officer's lady.

"Any thoughts on what you'll do when you graduate?" asked Colonel Hennessey.

Mary shook her head. "Not yet," she said. "I might want to go on for a doctorate. Or I might follow my daddy Colonel and join the army."

Her parents laughed.

"Don't let me influence you in any way," said the Colonel. "One thing we've learned about you is that you'll give a hundred percent to anything you try."

Mary smiled and stood up to give her parents a hug,

* * *

September, 1996

"Mary, we're so proud of you, both of us."

Mary Hennessey looked at her father standing in the reception room next to her mother and thought he looked absolutely smashing in his army uniform with the crown and three stars on his shoulders.

"Yes, daddy Brigadier," she said, smiling. She was well aware that her parents were drawing a lot of attention from everybody. They were both such imposing figures.

"First class honours, eh?" said the Brigadier. "I always wanted to see you in a cap and gown holding that degree. I tell you, I had to wipe some tears away when I saw you walk up to get it from the Chancellor."

"Me too," said her mother, and wiped another drop from her eyes.

"Any decisions about the next step?" asked her father.

"I'm going to be a spook," said Mary. "I got the offer from ASIO yesterday."

"Oh my!" said her mother.

"Probably a better choice than the army," said the Brigadier with a laugh. "Can't have two military geniuses in the family, can we?"

"You're sure you don't mind?" asked Mary. She didn't want to tell him how many hours she had spent worrying about her choice, really concerned that he might be offended.

"You have always followed your own path," said her father. "And we have always supported you, whatever you chose."

Trying to suppress her own tears, Mary moved to her father and hugged him, burying her face in his shoulder. He responded and kissed the top of her head.

"We're very close to seeing a senior army officer break down in tears in public," he whispered.

Mary pulled away and smiled.

"I don't think anyone would care," she replied.

* * *

The post graduation holiday in England was something she had been promising herself since she was a little girl. Now she was here, taking full advantage of the month between graduating and joining ASIO as an Intelligence Officer.

"Somebody I want you to meet," said Jill Featherstone, an old school friend of her mother's and welcome guide to London. They were near the famous Harrods store and Jill had led them to a little restaurant for lunch.

At the door, she waited for a moment, looking around and finally selected a booth by the window. A waitress approached, accepted orders for coffee while Jill said they were waiting for a third person and brought them a few moments later.

Curious, Mary sipped at her coffee, aware that Jill appeared excited by the prospect of the meeting with somebody.

The whole restaurant changed suddenly as the air of electricity seemed to run through the place. Startled, Mary looked at the entrance where a tiny woman had appeared. She was dressed in a beautiful blue silk dress, carrying a white handbag, no hat and her jet black hair was tied in a ponytail. What pulled the eyes irresistibly was the bright scarlet lipstick on a wide, generous mouth.

Mary could see that every person in the restaurant was staring at this vision as she looked round the room, settled on Jill and smiled, beginning to move to their table. Every eye followed her as if she was a royal personage performing some nationally critical function and there was not a sound anywhere.

The woman took a seat next to Jill, opposite Mary and smiled.

"Hello," she said. "I'm Karen Petrova."

Mary realised her jaw had dropped, so imposing was the presence of this tiny woman. Around her, the sounds of conversation slowly grew again.

"She does have this effect on people," said Jill with a light laugh. "Karen dear, can't you tone it down a little?"

Mary swallowed, feeling a little easier.

"Mary Hennessey," she said.

Slowly, the three of them eased into a friendly conversation and Mary found herself charmed by the speech of Karen Petrova, with its Russian intonation and style with no direct or indirect parts of speech.

She had no memory of ordering or eating lunch and was astonished to realise two hours had passed when Karen rose to her feet, said quick farewells and walked out, again causing a complete silence to envelope the restaurant until she was outside.

"She likes you," said Jill.

"How on earth can you tell?" said a bemused Mary.

"She'd have gone after fifteen minutes otherwise," replied Jill. "And by this evening, she will know everything about you, your father, your first-class honours degree, your new job, everything."

"Good grief!"

"And between her and her husband, she's well on her way to becoming the richest woman in the world and most likely, the most influential. As she has always said in her own particular way, she will "Change world." I believe her."

Mary sat still, somehow aware that she had encountered a highly influential figure in her life.

"Tomorrow, we're heading to the Lake District," said Jill. "I think you'll fall in love with the place. Everybody does."

* * *

April, 1998

Mary stood quietly as the young sergeant standing in the doorway of the office threw a smart salute to the occupant.

"Intelligence Officer Mary Hennessey reporting as advised, sir."

"Show her in, Sergeant," said the voice inside.

"Sir!" snapped the sergeant, threw another salute and retreated. "All yours, Ma'am," he said as he walked away leaving Mary to enter.

"Hello, Daddy Major General," she said with a cheerful grin.

Her father stood up and returned the smile, walked round his imposing desk and enveloped her in a king-sized hug.

"You have no idea how proud of you your mother and I are," he said.

"I've had good role models to follow," she said as he waved her to a seat by the coffee table in the spacious office. She looked at her father and thought again how marvellous he looked with the crossed swords and star on his shoulders. His promotion had been rapid and he was now in command of the Australian troops in Afghanistan.

"Can you tell me what your job here is?" he asked.

"Simple really," she replied. "Monitor the communications that we can intercept between the Taliban, military people and any government officials foolish enough to be caught talking to them."

"You have enough support from Farsi and Arabic speakers?"

"Canberra made certain of that," she replied.

For a while they chatted about her training and life in Canberra for the last three years and then the General stood up.

"Military duties call," he said and she stood up alongside him. "But we'll see you at home whenever possible," he added.

"Yes, Daddy Major General," she said with a grin and left him to his job.

Over the following two years, her days and evenings were crammed. She followed the communications between the Taliban, the Afghan rebels and just occasionally caught connections between government officials and the enemy forces. These were passed to the Afghan military and she preferred not to think about what happened to the officials.

And then she was posted back home.

May, 2000

Soon after returning to Canberra, the next move occurred.

"You've shown an astonishing aptitude for the work," said her supervisor, a middle-aged woman dressed in a dull, unremarkable business suit, a face that showed nothing and as Mary knew, a mind like a super-computer.

"Well, thank you," said Mary in surprise. It was the first compliment she had ever received at ASIO.

"Few people have the flexibility to live in such a different world as you have."

"I'm an army brat. We moved every two years, all over the world."

The supervisor nodded. "And your father's influence has shown. I want you to run a few projects in Europe."

Mary said nothing, but her excitement grew.

"You'll have twelve people reporting to you, they'll be based all over the place. Be careful, all of them are older than you, it will take great diplomacy to supervise them."

"What exactly are we doing?"

"Very sensitive stuff," said the older woman. She slid a solid envelope over the desk. "This will explain it. Let me stress, absolute secrecy is required."

Mary picked up the envelope and returned to her office. A week later, she flew to Geneva where an apartment had been found for her.

For the next two years, she travelled all over Europe, meeting other agents, sometimes the governments of the countries as she and the group tracked down terrorists, following even the smallest signs, working with security groups of many countries and often watching as these silent, professional men and women cauterised the ugly sores of international terrorism. Twice, she had to fly back to Australia in an RAAF Hercules, escorting the bodies of one of her agents and talk to grief-stricken relatives without revealing the exact nature of what their loved ones had been doing.

And once again, she was posted back home.

* * *

February, 2016

"Mary, dear, I think we should have coffee and talk about world," said the soft voice when Mary picked up her phone. The voice and the accent were immediately recognizable even though not heard for over six years and Mary laughed with delight. They had not met again since London twenty years before, but Karen had occasionally called her on her infrequent trips to Australia

"Karen, are you in Australia again?" she said.

"In Australia, in Canberra," said Karen. "Talks with government people which might concern you."

"Concern me? Karen, how could that be?"

"Perhaps I can come round and talk about it?"

"That would be lovely. I'll put the kettle on."

Mary was sure she felt the moment when Karen turned into her road and stopped outside her house in Curtin. The energy level seemed to rise, even the birds sensed it as the magpies intensified their musical warbling as a celebration of wonderful things happening.

It was no taxi that stopped outside her house but an official government car and a uniformed chauffeur got out and opened the rear door. Karen emerged, dressed in a royal blue silk dress, white shoes and a white handbag, walked up the driveway and was unsurprised when Mary opened the door for her before she could knock.

"I think half the street is watching this," said Mary, struggling to control her laughter.

"It is common event," said Karen. Her face was expressionless, but Mary was certain there was a gleam of humour in her perfect features framing the bright red lipstick of her wide, generous mouth. "I do not understand reason for it."

"Come in before everybody rushes outside," said Mary and led the way to her lounge room. Making tea, she served her visitor seated in her armchair and sat down across the room.

"Mary, I have been talking to government about setting up some businesses here."

"What sort of businesses?"

"It is unimportant. Just businesses. Only one business is important and I want you to run it."

Mary took a deep breath.

"Karen, I have never run a business of any sort. Why would you pick me?"

"Back in England, I have small group of very brilliant people researching DNA. What they are finding will change world. One day, I am sure, they will have good reasons to leave England and settle somewhere else. That will be here. What I want here before that is small group of extraordinary men and women who will think about what people in England are doing and how it will affect world. I want somebody to direct them and prepare them for future events. I believe you are right person."

"How many people in this small group?"

"Maybe seven or eight. Up to you."

Mary knew immediately that there was no analysis, no thought to be applied. Working for Karen Petrova would be, she knew absolutely, an amazing experience.

"Of course I will do this."

"Good. My people in England, you and your group here, we will change world."

Mary had no doubt about it.

"This afternoon, I am meeting young man called Ben Fuller," continued Karen. "I will ask him to join you so he will call you and talk about it. He is sociologist at National University. I think you will get on well."

"If you approve of him, Karen, I am certain of it."

Chapter 5 – February, 2022

"Looks like we're both on," said Mark Craymer as he drove the golf cart along the path to the par-three fourteenth hole.

"Only just," said Ben Fuller, observing the putting green. "I think that's me on the far fringe, you on the near one, just about directly opposite each other. Not easy putts at all."

They got out of the cart and selected their putters from the bags strapped to the back.

"I'd say you go first," said Mark after eyeing the locations of the two balls.

Ben walked round the green to the far edge, knelt down behind his golf ball and peered at the route to the pin.

"Looks like a bit of a right curve," he muttered, took his position and hit the ball. It moved along the ten metre curve but slowed and drifted further right than he had intended, heading for a position about a metre from the pin. But the ball appeared to speed up a little and began to curve back towards the pin where Mark was standing. Astonished, Mark quickly lifted the flag pole and watched as the ball trickled into the hole with a distinctive rattle.

Mark stared at Ben who was standing still, looking stunned.

"How the hell did you do that?" he asked.

"Buggered if I know," replied Ben, kneeling down again and studying the green. "I can't see any gradient to make that happen."

"Must have been the grass angle, or something," said Mark. "Bloody fluky putt, I must say!" He laid the pole down a short distance away and went back to his ball. "I think your first reading was correct, though."

He struck the ball which followed a gentle curve, gradually moving left and stopped a hand's width from the hole. He walked up and tapped the ball in.

"Good putt," said Ben, picked up the flag pole and replaced it in the cup after Mark had removed both balls and tossed one to him.

They climbed back into the cart and marked their score cards. "Par for me and a weird birdie for you," said Mark. "I've never seen a ball do that before!"

"I'll take anything I can get," replied Ben with a laugh. "On to the fifteenth, driver!"

As they moved along the roadway, they chatted with the ease they had always known in the decade of their friendship.

"That Garry Lawson bloke seemed a bit shattered when he came last week," said Mark.

"I think he was expecting another group of young geneticists and assorted boffins," said Ben, smiling at the memory. "And instead, he finds a middle-aged bunch of academics in the soft sciences."

"Well, you have to admit, it must have been quite a shock. He'd already had to cope with a mob of historians and linguists when they descended on his laboratory a few years ago," said Mark, slowing at the side of the fifteenth tee.

"Seems a good bloke, though," said Ben as they got out and consulted their cards. "Now, what have we got here?"

"Par five, 450 metres, dogleg left," said Mark. "Your honour, I think."

Play proceeded normally with both players hitting down the fairway, making decent second shots towards the green and then Mark's third shot ending in the short grass by the side of the green.

Ben took position for his third shot and struck the ball. It landed in the greenside bunker.

"Shit!" he said and climbed back in the cart.

Mark appeared to be further from the hole, used his putter and managed to get his ball within a metre of the flag. Ben climbed down into the bunker, peered up at the green and could just see the pin and the flag. He swung his sand wedge and swore again as the ball leaped out of the sand and raced off to one side of the green. But then it swerved, changed direction back to the pin and rolled straight at the hole, hit the pole and dropped.

"What the hell?" exclaimed Mark. He walked up to where the ball had changed direction and examined the grass. "There's nothing here that could have caused that," he said. "Ben, what did you do? That was impossible."

Ben took his time raking the bunker sand and then came up to him. His face was white.

"I have no idea," he said. "I know I felt a bit angry seeing my ball flying off like that and then it swung back to the pin."

Mark walked back to the point where Ben's ball had changed direction.

"You have a look, maybe I missed something. Is there anything there that could have caused that?"

Ben walked to the same spot, knelt down and carefully examined the green surface.

"Not a thing. I can only think that maybe it struck a worm or an insect and the culprit has gone."

"Okay, as good an explanation as I can think of. I'll mark it as another fluke. Let me finish and we can move on."

They stopped by the par four sixteenth and selected their drivers.

"Okay, Ben, just golf, eh? Plain and simple, no flukes," said Mark.

Ben nodded, took his stance and drove the ball a good distance down the fairway. Mark followed and saw his ball run just a few metres past Ben's.

Ben's iron shot landed just short of the green, Mark's did much the same.

"All right, no funny stuff," said Mark as they reached the green and selected wedges for the pitch onto the green. Mark's shot was clean, rose high and landed an arm's length from the pin.

"Neat," said Ben, made his shot and muffed it. The ball went off at an angle, hit the right hand edge of the green, stopped and then began to roll back onto the green and approached the pin. It struck the pole and dropped into the hole with a subdued rattle.

Mark stared at Ben who was standing motionless, his face white.

"Okay, mate," said Mark, "two flukes in a row is just amazing luck. Three is something else and it's not natural. What the hell are you playing at?"

"I did that," said Ben, his voice harsh.

"What do you mean, you did that?" asked Mark.

"I just know that somehow I made that bloody thing go to the hole. Maybe I'm going insane."

Mark went quiet for a moment. "Or maybe not.

Bear with me a moment, 'cos I'm getting a crazy idea. You know those reports we read from the researchers that they were developing some form of telekinesis? They reckoned it came from working with the DNA all the time. There's something in the process that's modifying the brain. It's not strong, they couldn't manage more than move little foam rubber balls around, but it was definitely telekinesis."

"But I..." Ben stopped. "I was going to say I don't work with the scanners all that much. But the last few weeks I've been doing a lot of work with various samples looking at societies going through great changes. I've concentrated on Britain after the First World War."

Mark pointed at his ball still sitting a metre from the pin. "Make that ball roll to the pin," he said.

"Mark, this is daft," Ben said, but looked at the ball and went quiet. The ball twitched and then rolled smoothly to the hole, hit the pole and dropped into the cup.

"Holy Tapdancing *Christ!*" said Ben.

"The people in Reading only managed very light objects, nothing as massive as a golf ball," murmured Mark. "You seem to have got it in a big way, Ben."

Ben walked to the pin, bent down and removed both golf balls. He stared at them in disbelief.

"I'm not playing with you again," said Mark, making a joke out of the situation. "You have an unfair advantage."

"I need a drink," said Ben. "Let's get back to the club house."

"Seriously, mate," said Mark as they set off back to the club house. "You'll need to be careful. You've got something very powerful there."

"I know. But do you realise, if this becomes

widespread, the game of golf is fucked? Who's going to play with somebody who can control the ball like that? The game's dead."

"And not just golf," said Mark. "Depending on how powerful somebody can get, it'll kill off snooker, tennis, archery, hell I can probably think of any number of sports that could collapse."

They parked the golf cart, retrieved their clubs and put them in the car, then went for the drinks.

"We'd better get the council together," said Mark. "We're probably changing Karen's world in a way she never thought about."

* * *

"Something very strange happened yesterday," said Garry to the faces round the conference table. "You have all read the reports of the researchers in Reading developing very low-level telekinetic powers as a result of working so many hours on the scanners with DNA samples. We have for now decided that the molecules are somehow teaching our minds how to find and use this power, but we have no idea how."

He looked round the table. All of them were listening intently.

"As you have also discovered, the ability is almost entirely focused on moving the perspective of the timeline in the molecule to focus on a particular location. None of you so far has reported on wider abilities, which in the Reading team resulted in some of them being to move very light, small objects with their minds. So far, it's been limited to moving tiny foam rubber insulation balls and the ability extends no more than two metres. But yesterday, Ben and Mark played golf and Ben found something. Ben?"

He nodded at Ben who put his mobile phone on the

table and sat back in his seat. After a second or two, the phone lifted a few centimetres into the air, hovered for a second, moved a short distance across the table and gently settled down in front of Mark sitting across from him.

"What the hell?" exploded Annabelle Calvert, the middle-aged historian. Her face had gone white and she stared at the phone as if she feared it would explode. The others round the table displayed reactions varying from dropped jaws, shocked faces to hands clasped before their mouths and some deep breathing.

"Let me tell it as it happened," said Ben calmly. "Three times in a row, I sank impossible putts that could not have been made under normal circumstances. My golf ball diverted from absolutely wrong directions going nowhere near the hole, changing direction to the hole and dropping in it. Mark was the one who raised the idea of telekinesis to a level far greater than the Reading people ever had and we proved it when I moved a stationary ball about three metres into the hole."

"It looks like Ben has developed this wild talent by a factor many times greater than any of us have before," said Garry.

"You said your people in England couldn't do it at more than two metres," said Robert Swann, the crisis manager. His face was calm, but his eyes were wider than usual, the whites showing all the way round. "How far does it extend with you, Ben?"

"Let's see," said Ben and stood up. He walked round the table to a point about two metres away and stared at the telephone. It did what it did before, lifted up a few centimetres, moved through the air and settled down in front of his chair. There was a slow outlet of breath from everybody at the table. Ben moved another two metres and tried again. This time, the phone just shifted slightly, rose up a tiny distance and fell back on the table with a small clatter.

"That may be about it," said Ben. He moved another metre away and tried again. Nothing happened.

"Looks like about four metres," said Ben, returning to his seat. "That phone is heavier than the golf ball and I think I was affecting the ball from about five or six metres, so there's a correlation between telekinetic power and the weight of the object being moved."

"Ben, how are you *doing* that?" asked Jennifer Soo Ling Chang, at 35 the youngest of the group, a tiny woman from Singapore, a lawyer with degrees from Singapore, Cambridge and Sydney.

"I really don't know," said Ben. "I just somehow *will* the object to move and it does. Somehow, I get the sense of wrapping my mind round it."

"Can any of the rest of us do this?" asked Mark. "Ben has spent a lot of hours at the scanner in recent weeks, how about the rest of you?"

Murmurs ran round the table indicating that nobody else had spent major amounts of time with the equipment.

"We've been more concentrating on imagining the effects of all this technology and working out what to do," said Mary. "Not a lot of reason for us to get into the scanning process except for some research into history and I know most of us have had a look at our ancestors, but no more than that."

Garry took a small plastic bag out of his pocket and extracted one of the tiny foam rubber balls on which the people in England had first tried their new powers.

"Each of you in turn," he said. "Would you put that in front of you and see if you can move it?"

One by one the people at the table took the ball, placed it in front of them and concentrated. When nothing happened, they passed it on to the next person. Nothing happened until it moved to Brad Robertson, the second futurist in the team, a journalism graduate from the University of Western Ontario in London, Canada and renowned for his perceptive commentaries on world affairs. He stared down at the ball and it twitched, moved sideways a hand's width and stopped.

"Holy shit!" exclaimed Brad. His hands were trembling.

"Can you lift it?" asked Ben.

Brad stared down again, concentrated and beads of sweat appeared on his brow. The ball lifted a centimetre and dropped again. Brad looked like he had just finished a marathon. He was breathing hard and his mouth was open as if struggling for breath.

"Interesting," murmured Ben.

Nobody else in the room was able to cause the ball to move.

"I wonder why just Ben?" asked Salmaan Basrai, the statistician with major specialisations in epidemiology.

"I think I read somewhere a comment from some famous author, can't remember who, who said that whatever field of activity, even completely new ones, there are always people who seem born to it, who have that special talent that puts them head and shoulders above everybody else without trying too hard. We see it in sports men and women, science topics and similar." Mary smiled at Ben. "Maybe Ben is the first one we've discovered who had this talent very close to the surface and the work has brought it right up."

"So the issue becomes one of what will happen if more people develop this talent to the level that Ben has," said Salmaan Basrai.

"It raises another issue," said Robert Swann. "Does this talent only develop from using the equipment and working on the DNA modules? And does everybody eventually develop it?"

"All the researchers in Reading developed it to some extent," said Garry. "Some more than others, but nobody to the extent that Ben has and they have spent many hundreds of hours working with DNA."

"So is it possible that only people who have to study the DNA and move the timelines will develop it?" asked Jennifer.

"For a time, at least," said Mary. "That seems the way to learn it. But it must surely be that the power is there in everybody, probably to greater or lesser extents as with the researchers in Reading. And like all other barriers, it will become more widely found just because people will hear that it's possible, see it demonstrated and start to believe that they can do it as well."

"Probably right," agreed Garry. "One of the researchers who first came up with this cited the example of the four minute mile by athletes. It was long considered impossible until a medical student called Roger Bannister did it back in the fifties. Almost immediately, other runners began doing it and soon it became commonplace. Athletes realised that it *was* possible and so they found they could also do it."

"Yes, I think we have to accept that the talent will become more common over the coming years," said Mark. "But it could be twenty, thirty or more years before we see it."

"The worry then, is how it affects life," said Ben. "My first reaction when I realised I was doing this was to think that the game of golf is screwed. Then Mark suggested it could also cause a problem with other games where a relatively low mass object at a short distance could be affected, like billiards, maybe darts."

"Garry," broke in Annabelle. "Did you find any changes in the brains of the researchers? Could the telekinetic ability be located in any specific part of the brain?"

Garry shook his head. "We didn't try that."

"Then we should," said Annabelle. "I'm not the neurosurgeon here, but can we do brain scans of Ben, while he's at rest and while he's actually moving an object? Maybe one of those EKGs or something, maybe we can find out how he's doing it?"

"Ben, how do you feel about that?" asked Garry.

"I'd say it's essential," replied Ben. "It means bringing a neurologist into the circle and getting him or her to advise us and then carry out the tests. It'll cost money."

"That's the least of our concerns," said Garry with a smile. "I'll arrange a meeting with the hospital, I think Karen's name will facilitate that, and see if I can get a neurologist to come in and talk to us."

"And what should we do about the possible effects on games like golf, billiards, darts and anything else that could be affected?" asked Mark.

"I think we can safely leave it," said Garry. "I would suggest Ben's astonishing wild talent is for now unique. The chances of anybody else finding it to his level for some years are very low."

"I'm not so sure," said Mary. "The equipment is now installed in many universities and people are spending hundreds of hours researching history, languages, population movements and stuff like that. They all know they have to use some sort of unexplained technique to more along timelines in the DNA and most of them will probably develop some sort of telekinetic abilities, even if they don't recognise them at first. There are bound to be others with Ben's latent powers and they may prove even more powerful. This will come out in time."

Garry looked at her and thought hard.

"You're right," he finally said. "Robert, this seems to be in your field of expertise. Can you develop a plan for what to do? Do we advise the world authorities of golf and others of an impending crisis, how do we do it and what advice do we provide?"

Robert nodded. "I'll do that," he replied. "And thinking about what Annabelle has said and what you're planning to do. Supposing we do find the part of the brain that controls this ability? Maybe there's a way of blocking it. Maybe there's a way of blanketing an area, like the putting green with some sort of field that suppresses the mental abilities?"

"Good thinking," said Garry. "Let's see what the neurologist says after we find one and brief him or her on the issue. This could be interesting."

"Changing the subject," said Mary. "When do your people arrive, Garry?"

"Over the next few days," replied Garry. "They're all in Australia but they're all taking a week off to locate living space then we'll formally meet at the new corporate premises."

"We'll be ready for you," said Mary.

Chapter 6 – February, 2022

"I'll drive you to the new building and explain the security features," said the man after Mary had introduced him to Garry as the architect. He was in his seventies, Garry knew, but he was slender and looked extremely fit. He walked briskly and spoke with the authority of a senior executive or military office. Mary had introduced him as Connor Shackleton.

"Sure," said Garry and followed him out of the house to a black Toyota Landcruiser. Both climbed in and Connor drove the vehicle away, handling it with the sure touch of a professional driver.

"About twenty minutes," he said. "We found a nice block far enough away from town to give us space, near enough for convenience."

He looked across to Garry in the passenger seat.

"I know about the attacks on your building in Reading. It was a pretty awful business."

"Mary said you're qualified to design buildings for that sort of thing," said Garry. Something about this man was inspiring confidence.

"I've done a bit of work for the British military as well as the Australian."

"The British?"

"Actually, I lectured at the Royal Military Academy at Sandhurst on building security."

"That's quite a recommendation," said Garry, his confidence rising.

"And I built a couple of blocks in Riyadh and Teheran as well."

"Even better."

Garry's mobile phone rang and he recognised Mary's number.

"Yes Mary?"

"Thought I'd let you know," she said. "Because he won't tell you himself, but that nice old bloke you're with is Colonel Connor Shackleton, Royal Fusiliers. Retired, of course."

"That's encouraging."

"He's also known as Sir Connor Shackleton. Knighted by the Queen in 1986 for services to architecture and to the military."

Garry looked at Connor with respect.

Two hours later, the respect had grown to strong admiration after being shown the new Blueprints building. The ground floor didn't have any windows and the only entrances were a secure front door and a steel panelled loading dock.

It was the rest of it that gave Garry great comfort.

* * *

Moving the staff from the Reading offices to their new location in Newcastle on the mid-north coast of New South Wales, Australia took a week. There was general approval of the new offices, more space for everybody and Garry set up the same canteen facilities that had existed in the old place. Revelling in the financial power which Karen had given him, he bought a block of apartments south of Newcastle near the sea and provided free accommodation to anyone who wanted it. Some used that facility just long enough to find houses to buy but the rest cheerfully took apartments in the block, delighting in the large heated swimming pool and the short walk to the beach. The Blueprints Australia organisation was in full operation a week after the staff arrived in Australia.

The only thing that marred the process was a serious accident to Avram. He was using the workshop in the apartment building to build a bookshelf for himself. He had the circular saw installed on the work bench and was slicing along a length of pine to make one of the shelves when his hand slipped.

Screaming pain shot through his hand and blood gushed all over the work bench. Avram shouted in shock and agony and luckily, Bill was passing by the workshop entrance. He ran to Avram who was sobbing and clutching his hand while blood poured all over his clothes.

Bill took out his mobile phone and pressed triple zero, the emergency number in Australia. When the voice answered, he said, "Ambulance, serious hand injury with a saw," and gave the address. Then he spotted something on the ground under the bench, half covered by sawdust and caught his breath. "It looks like an amputated little finger," he said into the phone.

"The ambulance is on its way," said the operator. "Try and get that finger, wash it and pack it in ice. It may be possible to re-attach it. Put a tourniquet on the wrist."

Torn between conflicting pressures to follow that instruction and to try and support Avram, Bill first found the finger, wrapped it in his luckily clean handkerchief then went back to Avram who was barely conscious.

"Avram, hang on!" said Bill loudly. "The ambulance is coming. Try and hold the hand up above your shoulder, reduce the blood loss. I'm going to wash the finger and pack it in ice."

He ran to the exit and raced to his own apartment, washed the finger as well as he could, feeling a pressure to be sick, then took several cubes of ice from his freezer and packed them with the finger into a plastic bag before running back to the workshop. He arrived just as the ambulance pulled up and handed the bag to the medic as they helped Avram into the ambulance.

"We're going to John Hunter Hospital," said the medic, climbed in after Avram and shut the door behind him.

Helplessly, Bill stood and watched before returning to his apartment, climbed out of his blood-stained clothes and took a shower before calling Garry to tell him the news.

That afternoon, Bill, Garry and Penny drove to the hospital and enquired about Avram at the Emergency Ward.

"He's awake, you can go and see him," said the woman at the reception desk after consulting her computer monitor and directed them to the emergency section.

They found Avram sitting up in bed, looking very pale and weak. He smiled when the visitors walked in.

"A pretty rough introduction to Australia," said Garry.

"Avram, you poor soul," said Penny and stooped over him to kiss his cheek."

"I'd say I was lucky," replied Avram. "Only my little finger of my left hand. It could have been half the hand or more."

Penny shuddered. "Don't say that, Avram, dear."

"What did they do?" asked Bill. "Were they able to re-attach the finger?"

Avram shook his head. "Too much damage, the surgeon said. And the nerves were also too mangled up. It looks like I have to go through life missing a pinky."

"But is the hand usable?" asked Garry anxiously.

"Not a problem," said Avram. "They said they'll bandage it up leaving the other fingers free, so I can still use a keyboard. What else does a man need these days?"

He smiled, but the pain and sadness were obvious.

"I'll be back at work in a week," he continued. "I'll be on some pretty major-league painkillers for a while, so that may slow up the brain cells a bit."

"You mean you may be reduced to simply genius-level operations?" said Bill.

"That's about it," said Avram then lay back. "You know what, I think..."

But he was asleep. The trio walked quietly out of the ward.

* * *

"Garry, there's a young lady to see you."

The receptionist's voice broke into Garry's thoughts as he sat at his desk, the day after moving into the new office building. He shook himself out of the dreamlike state, already forgetting what it was that had put him there.

He took advantage of the new security systems and switched his computer to viewing the monitor in the lobby. The receptionist's desk was behind a bullet-proof glass wall and on the other side of that wall was a young woman. Something niggled at Garry's memory at the sight of her but he couldn't place the cause.

"Does she say what she wants?" he asked.

"She said that it's in reference to Karen Petrova's will."

That was enough for Garry. "Send her in," he said.

A few minutes later, he rose to his feet as a tall young woman walked in. She was clearly an athletic, fit woman, judging by the clear skin of her face, the trim shape under a blue blouse and black skirt. Garry estimated she was in her mid-twenties, but thought she could look younger than her years, given her extreme fitness. He still couldn't place where he had seen her before but he was sure that he had.

"I am Galina Volkova," the woman said.

Garry moved round his desk, shook her hand and pointed at a chair by the coffee table. Both sat down. There was no smile on the woman's face.

"What can I do for you, Ms Volkova? I understand you have something to share about Karen Petrova's will?"

"We have met before, Mr Lawson."

"We have? I believe you're right, I think I remember the face, but I can't place where."

"I was one of Madam Petrova's assistants. I met you when you first came to see her and another time I drove you back to Reading."

Now Garry remembered that first meeting with Karen and how this woman had shown him to Karen's living room. Another time, she had driven Karen's Rolls Royce to take him back to Reading after a meeting with the Prime Minister. On neither occasion had she spoken a word or allowed a smile to show. He quickly revised his estimate of her age. She must be in her late thirties, he decided. She displayed a slight Russian accent, much like Karen had always affected.

Now he smiled. "Yes, of course! How nice to see you again!"

She didn't smile back but opened the leather note book she was carrying, extracted a letter and handed it over. "Madam asked me to give you this."

Curiously, Garry looked at the envelope. It was addressed to him and he recognised Karen's distinctive, beautiful handwriting. Carefully, he opened it and his heart began beating a little faster as he saw the same script in a letter. It was dated July, 2020, a year before her murder.

My Dearest Garry,

At some time, I must assume you have moved Blueprints down to Australia after something serious has occurred. This was all arranged after meeting with Isaac Asimov who advised me to follow the ideas he had created in his wonderful "Foundation" series.

One thing that the lawyers who handled my will did not tell you at the time was that there was a codicil, an additional request which I am now making of you.

I want you to hire Galina Volkova. It doesn't matter what roles you assign to her, I assure you she will be of immense value. You will have no legal issues. Her immigration and permanent residence were guaranteed along with all the other Blueprint staff.

This is my last gift to you. I am sure you are still enjoying your Islay scotches and changing the world in ways that perhaps I never anticipated.

I will never forget the immense debt I owe you for making my dream and Hector's come true and I will always love you for that.
Until we meet again in Heaven
Yours always,

Karen

Garry noted with amusement that Karen had not followed her normal habit of using Russian grammar features, but felt tears come to his eyes at reading the note. He didn't try hiding them from Galina and he wiped his eyes.

"What an amazing thing you have brought me," he said. "I shall always treasure it. Do you know what she has said here?"

Galina nodded. "You will hire me."

"Of course. But please tell me about yourself. How did you get to meet Karen?"

"I met her when I was two and I remember it. She was having a meeting with my Great-Uncle Isaac."

"Isaac? Isaac Asimov?"

She nodded.

"And what have you done since then?"

"Learn languages. I have always been good with languages."

"And what do you speak?"

"Russian, of course. English, naturally. French, German, Italian, Spanish, Japanese and Mandarin."

"That's very impressive. Given how many countries we are starting to deal with, I have no doubts you will be very useful to us."

Despite the assurance, Garry felt uncertain about this woman. She had displayed not a trace of warmth or friendliness though she must have known just how close he had been with Karen and the role he had played in her life. He felt worried that she might not fit into the highly informal, unstructured world of Blueprints.

She opened her handbag and extracted a small wooden box.

"Karen also asked me to give you this," she said and placed it on the coffee table.

Garry picked it up. It was beautiful, painted in black lacquer and decorated with an artistic mosaic in gold. He had no doubt that this was pure gold, not any imitation. He opened the lid and found six flash memory sticks. There was no note. He raised an eyebrow at Galina.

"Karen never stopped working and thinking about new drugs. That box contains all her unknown work of the last ten years. There are formulations that will do a great deal of good. They should of course go to the other company, but she had no way of knowing whether you would both be in Australia or not."

"Thank you, I'll make sure they go to the British operation."

"Please be very certain of whom you can trust before you do," said Galina. For the first time, Garry sensed some insecurity in her.

"I will, I promise. Now, apart from those amazing language skills, what else do you do?"

"I kill people."

The response was so totally unexpected and shocking that Garry felt unable to speak for a second or two.

"But not more than two or three a month," she added.

This shook him even more. He remained speechless. She stared firmly into his eyes, not a trace of humour in her face.

"Just kidding," she said.

Garry found his voice. "I'm relieved to hear it."

"Usually just one every two months."

"Oh, well that's all right then."

Before he could say any more, there was a tap on the door.

"Come in," he said, grateful for the break in what was becoming a most confusing situation.

Bill poked his head in.

"Garry, can Avram and I...?" He broke off as he saw Galina. "Sorry, I'll come back."

"No, come in," said Garry. "Meet a new member of Blueprints. Galina, this is..."

"Village Idiot," she said before Garry could finish.

Bill stared at her and she met his gaze firmly. Garry was startled. Only he, Bill and Karen knew of that nickname Karen had created for Bill.

"The world's finest Village Idiot," said Bill. There was no anger in his voice. "There has never been a Village Idiot like me and there will never be a better one."

"That's what Madam said," said Galina. "For some strange reason, she thought you might be almost intelligent."

"This is Galina Volkova," said Garry. "She was Karen's personal assistant when I first met her. And she's a great-niece of Isaac Asimov."

"And now I will be Garry's Personal Assistant," said Galina.

Bill's eyes widened.

"She speaks lots of languages and she kills people," added Garry, recognising the absolute inevitability and great value of Galina's announcement. "But no more than one every two months."

Only because he had known Bill for so many years did Garry see the first signs of a grin on his face.

"No shit?" said Bill.

"None at all," she replied. "Shall we go and have a coffee?"

Without a word of farewell, she stood up and walked out. Bill looked down at Garry.

"We've got a right one here," he said.

As the door closed behind them, Garry started laughing. But after a while reflecting on the renewed memories of Karen, he took the first of the flash memory sticks and inserted it into his computer. The first file was a document and he opened it.

My Dearest Garry,

This is one more gift to you and to both my companies. I have been working on some new drugs to tackle some of the worst afflictions that hurt humans so much and these could do much good.

If Life Technology still continues its work after my passing and you are certain that the management is as wonderfully ethical as it was with Greg Mullaney, then pass these files to them.

I shall look down from Heaven and be happy that my work still helps people.

All my love,

Karen

Garry saw that the next file was an index. He opened that and stared for several minutes at the contents. At the end, he let out a slow whistle of astonishment.

"Good grief, Karen, will you ever get tired of changing the world?"

That evening, he placed a call to Greg Mullaney, still the CEO of Life Technology in Reading.

Chapter 7 – February, 1998

"Ben Fuller," said the young man. "I'm doing a post-doc here."

Hector Forbes had deliberately moved towards the man, having heard him talking with other faculty members at the "get to know you" gathering in the faculty lounge and perceived an unusual intelligence. At a break in the discussion, Hector had introduced himself.

"In what?" asked Hector.

"Sociology. I've had a grant from a United Nations educational body to work on international relations."

"That's impressive," said Hector. "What path has led you to Oxford?"

"A long and winding road," replied Ben with a smile. "I'm Australian, did primary and some high school in Melbourne, then my foster-parents sent me to finish off my high school in France because my French had been fairly good."

"So university in France?" asked Hector.

"Scholarship to Humboldt in Berlin. I'd learned good enough German and this was a good chance to get fluent."

"Really cosmopolitan!" said Hector. "So I suppose a Master's in Tokyo?"

Ben laughed. "Toronto, Canada."

"And I don't dare try and guess where you did your doctorate."

"Witwatersrand, South Africa."

"Okay, Ben I'm very impressed indeed, but why this nomadic, globe-trotting education?"

"I just wanted to see the world," said Ben. "I wanted to try and understand how different societies work and relate to each other. So I applied for places almost everywhere and my grades were good enough for me to win a place and get financing at all of them."

Hector had been studying the young man the whole time. He had always had an excellent sense of people's characters and in this one he felt sure there was something exceptional though he couldn't put his finger on what it was.

"I'm having lunch with my wife tomorrow," he said. "I think she'd be interested in meeting you. Would you like to join us?"

"Karen Petrova? I'd be honoured, Doctor Forbes."

Chapter 8 – May, 2023

The phone call Garry received a couple of weeks later was not really a surprise.

"Garry, it's Eamon Jackson."

"Your Eminence! What a surprise!"

"Cut the Eminence crap, Garry! Those titles are rapidly fading. It's Eamon, right?"

"Okay, thank you, Eamon. I have a sneaky feeling that this may not be good news. Are you in Rome?"

"I am," said the Cardinal. "And Rome has become a trifle tense in recent weeks."

"So the initial easy acceptance of the new realities has begun to fade? You did indicate that you expected it."

"I did. For a time I had high hopes that the peace would continue. I've maintained communications with Canterbury and the Church of England has taken an easier path. They have simply allowed each diocese to run as it wishes. Those churches and congregations that went along with the new concepts have done so, others who wished to retain traditional beliefs have done so and there has been no stress between the two. The former have simply called themselves "New

Churches." The nicest thing is that congregations have increased in both organisations."

"That's what has been happening here," said Garry. "The Anglican Church announced complete freedom of choice for all its churches and it seems to be working well."

"Unfortunately, the Catholic Church has always been a bit more rigid in its policies," said the Cardinal. "Initially, that's how it seemed to be going, but I could feel the tensions rising among the Cardinals here and it blew up last week."

* * *

"You weren't elected to throw everything away that we've built for two thousand years!" Cardinal Joseph Maguire of Dallas was on his feet, his face red with rage and spit running down his chin. He was a tall, thin man, almost bald with remaining outcroppings of hair above ears that stood out almost horizontally. He had small eyes, close-set over a thin, aggressive nose and little could be seen of his lips. Several people who disliked the man had referred to him as looking like a snapper turtle.

The Cardinal's fury was directed at the Pope who was sitting in one of the three seats facing the rest of the conference room. The other two seats were empty. In front of him, the rows of seats were almost filled with over two hundred Cardinals of the Catholic Church. Among them were just ninety members of the College of Cardinals who had elected the Pope. More than twenty of the original group had already left the Church after the shocks of recent discoveries.

"You are quite correct, Joseph," said the Pope calmly. "I was elected to lead the Catholic Church according to the convictions I had, and these were formed and came from a time very different from now."

"There is no difference!" shouted Maguire. "Just because some atheistic lefties pretended to find that Jesus didn't exist doesn't mean it's true. You're destroying the Church based on that rubbish?"

On the front row, Cardinal Eamon Jackson rose to his feet. He looked for permission to speak from the Pope and received the small nod.

"It's not rubbish, Joseph. You know very well that I tested the technology on myself by having a sample of my own DNA scanned by the system and seeing episodes from my life and that of several of my ancestors. You also know that we repeated the tests that the professor from Cambridge University conducted in Israel, with thousands of DNA samples. We scanned hundreds of lives from around the time of Christ and found absolutely nothing to verify the stories by which our church has lived for so long."

Maguire's fury did not reduce.

"It's all lies," he shouted. "How can anyone believe such rubbish about seeing the lives of one's ancestors?"

"You were invited to take part in the same test I took," said Jackson calmly. "Most of us here did just that and came away convinced."

"I certainly did and I agree entirely," said a tall, black speaker, rising to his feet. Cardinal Zul Thobani from Kenya had been one of the first to test the scanning equipment and had wept profusely when he saw his grandmother through the eyes of his father as she was shot by a British game hunter. His voice was beautifully deep and sonorous. "Joseph, you really must try the experience. You will change your mind."

"I will do no such thing," the American retorted, waving his arms as if waving away a wasp. "That is the

Devil's work and I will not risk my immortal soul by touching it."

"So what do you intend, Joseph?" The Pope did not raise his voice but he brought silence on the room. "It would seem your choices are limited. Either you accept the leadership of the Pope or you reject the Church."

"I will not live with the heresy that you have brought upon us!" The American's face was even brighter red than before. "And there are many here and around the world who will agree with me."

"So are we to have to have another split?" asked the Pope. "Are you planning to set up a competing Church in France like the last time? Will there be a new Vatican in Avignon with you as the opposition Pope?"

"Not Avignon," replied Maguire. "It's time the one true church made its home in the United States."

"The one true church?" said the Pope with a smile. "And no doubt with you as the Pope? You may wish to review your history, Joseph, because I fear you are falling into the trap that those who not know their history are doomed to forever repeat it. No doubt you will begin a series of American-only Popes, just as your French examples did with their countrymen. How did that work out?"

"I don't care what happened back in 1309," snapped the American. "We're Americans, we'll do it properly this time. I reject all this heresy, I reject your leadership in taking the Church down this cowards' path."

The Pope nodded sadly. "And who will follow you?" he asked.

He was answered by several other Cardinals rising to their feet. The Pope recognised all the other seven Americans in the Curia. He sighed in resignation and looked across to Eamon Jackson who gave a half smile in support.

"We were expecting something like this," he said and turned back to the men in front of him. "Then go with God, Joseph and your followers. I have no doubt many of your countrymen will also reject the new realities and stay with the traditional structure. I pray it does not lead to violence."

"America will reject all this heresy," said Maguire. "The government will ban the use of this Satanic equipment and America will be the leader in Christianity as it always has been."

He walked along the row to the aisle and out to the main doors at the back of the hall, followed by the other seven Americans. Complete silence accompanied the departure.

"Anyone else?" asked the Pope.

Three more men rose to their feet. All were dark, bearded and wore black robes.

"The Coptic Church of Egypt also rejects your heresy," said one. "All discussions about returning to the Catholic Church are now ended." The Pope recognised him as the Patriarch of that group, Halim Khalifa.

"As does the Maronite Church of Lebanon," said another, recognised as the Patriarch Emeritus of Antioch, Fawzi Abu Jamra. The third man, recognised by the Pope as the second Patriarch of the same Church, Issam Salloukh did not speak.

"Then go with God, also," said the Pope and watched in silence as the three men walked out.

* * *

"We did expect this, but it was painful for all of us," said Jackson.

"I imagine so," said Garry, hearing the sadness in the Cardinal's voice. "But was that it? Ten out of over two hundred Cardinals seems a small number?"

"No, more have since followed," said Jackson. "Most have been from the African countries, a few from South East Asia and the final number seems to be that we have a hundred and fifty three Cardinals out of the original two hundred and fifteen. Better than it might have been."

"I suppose so," said Garry. "I must say, the American response doesn't surprise me after my experience in Chicago."

"Agreed," said the Cardinal. "And we were not surprised by the departure of the Coptic and Maronite Churches. The Christian Churches have had their problems too, with all the Greek, Russian, Serbian and other Orthodox groups going their own way in rejecting the new developments."

"What happened in 1309?" asked Garry, remembering the comment from Cardinal Maguire that Jackson had reported.

"The first big schism in the Church," said Jackson. "Strife had broken out between the papacy and the French king, Philip the Fourth for a number of political reasons. It had started with Pope Boniface the Eighth and continued with Pope Benedict the Eleventh who died after only eight months. The conclave to elect a new pope got badly deadlocked and finally the Curia elected a Frenchman, Clement the Fifth."

"I bet that went down like a train smash," said Garry. He heard the muted laugh down the phone line.

"Pretty well," said the Cardinal. "Clement refused to move to Rome and eventually declared his home town, Avignon as the new seat of the Church. It started what is known as the Avignon papacy and it lasted nearly seventy years. There were seven popes in that time, all French, and they were all under pressure from the French crown to submit to French authority. Finally, the last one returned to Rome and abandoned the Avignon period."

"And did that restore peace?"

"Not at all. Rivalries continued and another Pope did the same as before and established a Papacy in Avignon again. His successor finally gave in and although there were disputes again, it finally got resolved in 1417 with a single Pope once more. I hope you haven't minded the history lesson, Garry?"

"Not at all," replied Garry with a laugh. "I never realised the Church had gone through so much turmoil. But I can see where all this appears to be happening again. A Dallas Papacy, eh? How do you think that will work?"

"Not well," said Jackson. "Politically, he might get more support, because I understand that the Congress in America is about to ban the use of this equipment and that means the New Churches might have a hard time of it, even though the majority of Americans seem in favour of what we have discovered."

"So what do you expect, Eamon?"

"Trouble. The Catholic Church is split into several groups, those around the world who accept the new realities and those who don't. The Americans are setting up their own Papacy and many of the traditionalists around the world are looking to Maguire to maintain the traditions. I fear some violence. We have been holding discussions for years now with the Eastern Orthodox Churches about ending the ancients splits, they have broken away, too, but I think there is more tolerance between the old and the new churches within the non-Catholic world."

"What are you planning then?"

"Oddly enough, we are trying to preach classic Christian philosophies of tolerance. We are talking to most of the traditional churches and asking them to exercise the teachings of the Jesus Christ that they still insist was the Son of God. That catches them in a bit of a bind, because if they claim to be true to those teachings, they must do just that. But the governments of all countries have been asked to watch out for violence directed against the New Churches."

"We're doing that here," said Garry. "My group has prepared a detailed disaster plan and the government has taken it as national policy."

"Would you send me a copy?"

"I have your email address, I'll send it at once."

"Thank you, Garry. I'll pray for peace."

"Sometimes, Eamon, I worry about what my group released on the world."

"You shouldn't. I believe that in the end, all your work will be hugely beneficial. Removing false mythology from the world's religions will end much conflict, but the transition might be difficult."

"I hope not too much. I suspect we still have much to learn about our DNA and what it is to be human."

"I'm certain that is the case. And I'm certain that as a man of God, this is the mission that God has set us."

"I bet Karen is up there right now arguing with God about that!"

The Cardinal laughed. "I have no doubt," he said. "We must stay in touch, Garry."

"I'd like that, Eamon."

Garry replaced the phone with a sense of unease about future world events.

Meanwhile, Avram returned to work and Blueprints Australia began to adopt its normal routine of detailed, highly disciplined research into the nature of DNA.

Chapter 9 - May, 2024
The World Changes Again

Nearly twelve months passed in a steady hum of work by the researchers and the brainstorming sessions of the councillors.

And then the world changed again in a way that nobody had foreseen.

"My God, Avram, your face is white as a sheet!" Penny stared at Avram as he sat at the coffee table in the canteen. "What's wrong?"

"My hand. It's hurting like hell." Avram lifted his left hand and placed it on the table. He still wore the protective glove specially made for him that covered the palm and the stub of the little finger he had lost in the circular saw accident but left his other four fingers free.

"When did it start?" asked Penny, the concern and worry showing in her face.

"About two days ago," Avram said, returning his left hand to his lap and holding the wrist with his right hand in a vain effort to stem the pain. "But it was fairly mild, it just got really bad this morning."

"Can I have a look?" she asked.

"Hey, I'm the doctor," said Avram, making a weak joke, then he flinched and let out a small gasp. "That just got worse again," he mumbled through the tension in his jaw, but he carefully removed the glove.

"Oh ye gods!" exclaimed Penny. "That looks terrible!"

"Like it feels," said Avram.

The stump of his little finger was red and raw.

"It almost feels as if there's a lump of something under the skin," he said. "I'm wondering if some sort of tumour is developing under the scar tissue."

"We need to get you to hospital," said Penny, standing up decisively. "You doctors are all the same, refusing to get treatment long after you'd have made your patients get some." She called across to another researcher a few seats down. "I'm taking Avram to John Hunter Hospital," she said. "Tell Garry, will you?"

She walked around the table and placed her hand under Avram's arm, urging him to stand and led him out of the building.

The drive to the hospital was difficult. Avram's pain was growing and he was having difficulty controlling his breathing, letting out moans of distress on occasions. At the entrance to the Emergency Room, Penny carefully eased Avram out of his seat, walked him to the Triage Desk and spoke quickly to the nurse.

"This is Avram Fischer, recent loss of finger, developing severe pain." Then she raced outside to move her car and park in the public parking area before returning, just as Avram was being taken to see a doctor. She joined them as the doctor led them into a small office and carefully removed the protective glove.

"Looks bad," said the doctor economically. A few questions gave him the history of Avram's accident and he nodded. "Could be a swelling from the scar tissue, could be infection. Let's get a couple of pain killers down you first, then we'll X-Ray that hand."

He walked out, returning minutes later with a small plastic cup and a glass of water. The cup contained two tablets and Avram swallowed both of them with the water.

"Endone," said the doctor. "It might make you a bit drowsy or dizzy."

"Avram's a doctor," Penny said with a smile. "We're both working at the Blueprints Company."

"The Karen Petrova operation?" said the doctor, his interest obviously roused sharply. "I've been reading all about that! Are you a doctor, too?"

"Geneticist."

"It's amazing what you people have come up with. It's changing the world dramatically."

"Sometimes it worries us," said Penny. She looked at Avram who seemed to feeling some easing of the pain. "Avram? Any better?"

Avram let out a long sigh. "Getting better."

"Okay, let's get you into radiology," said the doctor. He suddenly smiled. "My name's Brian Harcourt."

"Penny Barstow."

"And Avram Fischer."

"Glad to meet you both, though sorry about the circumstances," said Harcourt and led them out of the office to the Radiology Laboratory a few doors down. He seemed perfectly happy to let Penny join them.

A young woman was waiting for them and she smiled as they entered.

"Good morning," she said. "I'm Norma, the radiographer."

She was about thirty, Penny estimated and had the dark, classical features of a New Zealand Maori. Privately, Penny thought she was quite beautiful. She smiled and introduced herself and Avram who by now was looking sluggish and half asleep.

"I'll take him from here," said Norma and sat Avram down at a table, spread his hand over the protective covering and drew the X-Ray machine over and down to within a few centimetres of his hand. Then she joined the others behind the protective screen, pushed the button, waited a few moments and then returned to reposition Avram's hand and took a second picture. Twice more she did that, nodded at Harcourt and waved them goodbye as they all returned to the doctor's office.

"They'll be on my monitor in a few seconds," Harcourt said and turned to his screen just as the first of four images appeared.

"What the hell?" Harcourt spoke loudly, obviously stunned and leaned forward to stare hard at the images.

"What is it?" demanded Penny, shaken by the violence of Harcourt's reaction. She also stared hard at the image and even though she was far less experienced in looking at such X-Ray images, she could see that there was something, a small object in the area of the base of the amputated finger.

"I just don't believe it," the doctor said. "And I'm not going to try and conjecture until we'd had a proper look at this."

"I think I know," mumbled Avram. "But you'd better open it up."

"Damn right," said Harcourt. "And we can do that right here. I'm giving you a local anaesthetic first."

He took a jar from his cupboard and carefully swabbed Avram's hand then slid on surgical gloves before filling a hypodermic needle from a small bottle and injecting Avram's hand near the base of the lost finger. After a few minutes of tense silence, he opened a case and extracted a scalpel.

"Ready?" he asked Avram who nodded. He slowly sliced the skin away over the stub of the little finger and already the stub had grown by about a centimetre, standing up from the hand. In a few seconds, he sat back and all three stared at the sight.

"My finger's growing back," said Avram.

Chapter 10 – November, 2024

The young woman seated at the monitor took a deep breath and pressed the button at her side. Nothing was heard in the large room lined with similar monitors, each tended by an attentive watcher, mostly young, but within seconds, an older woman in police uniform with the single crown of a Superintendent on her shoulders appeared behind the operator.

"Where is it, Grace?" she asked quietly.

"Saint Jude's, Stoke on Trent," replied the young woman.

The police officer watched the monitor intently for a few moments. She saw the large crowd of people, many carrying banners marching purposefully down the main street of an industrial town.

"Home in on one of those banners," she said and the operator moved her controls until one of the cameras mounted high on a building focused on a banner being carried by a middle-aged man in working overalls and a flat cap.

"God will punish the Christ-deniers," read the Superintendent aloud. "Not much doubt there, I'd say. Hit the button, Grace."

Immediately the woman pressed the red button

next to the computer monitor. The computer system read the location of the cameras pointing at the scene, selected the appropriate location and transmitted a signal.

"The third one this week," muttered the police officer. "And it's only Tuesday. It seems to be getting worse."

At a police location in the Potteries town of Stoke on Trent in the Midlands, a low-pitched siren sounded all through the building. About thirty men and women in black protective clothing, seized helmets, shields and batons and raced to the waiting windowless trucks. Once all were inside the two vehicles, they moved out of the large parking space, followed by a third vehicle with what looked like an anti-aircraft gun on the roof.

The man in the left-hand seat of the lead vehicle watched the screen in front of him as information was fed to him from the Controller. He wore the two stars of an Inspector on his shoulders

"St Jude's, Stoke," he said to the driver. "Estimated two hundred marchers, usual banners, so far looking harmless."

"That what we were told the last time," said the driver. "And look what happened then."

"And it looks like the boss is aware of it. He's raised the choppers."

"Let's hope we don't need them," replied the driver.

"And the blue light's flashing," said the Inspector.

"Shit!" said the driver.

In the rear of both trucks, a blue light was flashing a subdued signal. In each truck, one of the squad stood up, took a heavy key from around his waist and opened a large, steel container. He took out a series of viciously functional guns, one at a time and handed one to each of the fifteen-man team.

"Three minutes," said the man in the left-hand seat.

As the three vehicles arrived at the front of the church, they stopped and all the riders leapt out, carrying their guns and shields, taking positions along the entire front of the building where the sign proclaimed it as *"The New Church of St Jude's."* The third vehicle positioned itself further to one side and the gun barrel moved back and forth a few times as the operator inside checked the controls.

Overhead, the "whop, whop, whop" of the rotors of two helicopters was the only noise to be heard. The aircraft circled slowly round the entire area.

"Marchers approaching, two hundred metres," said the voice of one of the pilots into the earphones of all the armed squad. No obvious movement could be seen in any of them, but somehow the tension rose a notch.

A few minutes later, the lines of people appeared and began to crowd into the street in front of the church. A voice erupted from the police squad as a loudspeaker came into life.

"COME NO NEARER," said the voice. "THIS ACTION IS CONSIDERED A THREAT TO CIVIL PEACE AND ORDER AND WE WILL TAKE WHATEVER ACTION IS NEEDED IF YOU CONTINUE."

The protesters were also carrying loudhailers. Although at a much lower level of sound, one came to life.

"This church is the agent of the devil," shouted a voice. **"It denies Jesus Christ, Our Saviour and we demand that it be shut down and no services allowed."**

Loud cheers came from the crowd and it surged forward a few metres. Nobody moved in the police lines.

"THIS IS ENGLAND," said the police speaker. "WE HAVE FREEDOM OF RELIGION. NOW, DISPERSE, GO HOME AND STOP BEING SILLY."

People in the crowd began looking at each other as if in doubt. But the loud hailer user started again.

"We speak with the voice of God. You cannot stop us making sure the voice of God is heard. You will all be condemned to everlasting hell."

With that, the forward surge started again. The gun barrel atop the third vehicle moved and began a blast of water, the stream moving along the front ranks of the crowd. It was not hard enough to knock people off their feet but many of them turned away, tried to avoid the stream, some lost their banners.

But two hundred people behind the front line were still moving. The water cannon increased the power of the blast and this time, people fell over and were knocked into the feet and legs of the rows behind. The heavy flow of water began playing over the rest of the crowd until all were soaked, many of them lying on the ground. Already, people could be seen leaving the area and heading away.

The water cannon stopped and for a moment, silence reigned. But then, with shocking abruptness, an automatic weapon opened up from a place behind the crowds, joined a moment later by a second one.

None of the bullets struck anyone, but the armed police squad immediately raised their weapons. A second burst rattled and this time, bullets struck the police vehicle and blew out two windows in the church behind.

From where the bullets had been fired, four men leaped out into the road, all carrying automatic rifles and began charging straight at the police cordon, firing as they went. One police officer went down with a gasp of pain.

Without options, the armed police returned a short burst of fire. All four of the attackers went down. One squad raced to them, holding their guns ready for further action, but the four men were dead.

Back in the police van, the Inspector reported to base.

"Armed attack is now subdued, four dead. We have one man down. Need ambulance."

"On its way," replied a voice from the loudspeaker.

The protest had obviously died and the crowd dispersed within minutes. The police line stayed for another twenty minutes then climbed back into the trucks and drove away.

"I hope to God we never need to see that that again," said the Police Superintendent, watching the scene on her television module.

"I hate to think we needed it at all," said the Inspector with her. "This is not very British at all. What the hell has happened to this country?"

"And how the hell did they get those guns?" said the Superintendent. Her face reflected the shock of the sudden multiple, violent deaths in a small town. "I know we've had a number of protests like this around the country, but so far, none of them twice in the same place. This is not supposed to happen in England."

"I never realised that some people here took their religion so seriously," said the younger officer. "I'm a member of that church and I like the new way of doing things. I don't want to see religious warfare in my country."

"It's going to be a while before things settle," said the Superintendent. "We'd better go and debrief the armed squads."

Chapter 11 – May, 2024

"Avram, do you think I could get a few people to work on my problem?"

Avram looked up, startled. He had never before been asked by Bill for assistance and although he had seen Bill come in to the main research area, he hadn't thought about it and had continued working on his own research. He was delving into deep history, following his own ancestry back through ever older generations and had so far found a soldier in the army of Philip of Macedon, the father of Alexander the Great. It was the year 336BC and the soldier was one of the crowds in the theatre at Aegae, the ancient capital of the kingdom of Macedon. The court had gathered there for the celebration of the marriage between Alexander and Cleopatra of Macedon, who was Philip's daughter by his fourth wife Olympias. While the king was entering unprotected into the town's theatre he was killed by one of his seven bodyguards, which was how Avram knew the date and the location and what the event was all about. The soldier watched the assassin try and run, but was tripped by a vine and killed by three of the remaining bodyguards who had pursued him.

"Sure Bill, how can I help?" Avram hid his astonishment, wondering what major problem could have caused the notoriously isolationist worker to ask for assistance.

Bill pulled up a chair and sat down. His face showed tension which Avram put down to his having to ask anyone at all for help.

"It's this identification of time," he said. "I've been battling this for months, as you know, trying to find some indicator of when the events we see are taking place."

"Probably the hardest job any of us have had," said Avram diplomatically. "Any signs of progress?"

"Possibly," said Bill. "This morning I found something, but I'm having trouble working out what it could be. Maybe I'm tired or something, but I really would like a bit of a brain-storming session."

"I'd be delighted," said Avram, curious to know what could possibly stretch the mind of the astonishing genius. "Who would you like to help?"

"Let's just ask Penny. She really is bright and I've seen her solve some tricky ones in the past."

Avram nodded and called out softly to Penny who was in a space quite near to him.

"Free to help Bill with a problem?" he asked.

She displayed the same surprise that Avram had experienced, but nodded and stood up and walked over to where Bill was sitting.

"What's the problem, Bill?"

Bill stood up. "Let's go to my place," he said and set off in the direction of his own workshop, the other two following him with curious expressions.

Settled before his two large computer monitors, with the other two seated on either side of him, Bill brought up a scene on one of the monitors. It showed a middle-aged man wearing a pyjama top looking at his image in the mirror. He looked as if he had just got out of bed and hadn't fully woken up. He was just about to start brushing his teeth when Bill stopped the image.

"See that bottom right-hand corner?" he said. "There's a tiny dot right on the edge. I've noticed it before and it only appears for a few seconds."

"Have you enlarged it?" asked Penny.

Bill said nothing but touched a key and the image exploded to fill the second monitor. All three of them stared. Two roughly equal lines met a point at the bottom of the image at approximately a forty degree angle. A curving line went from the top of the right-hand line, out left, across the second line and curved back to cross both lines again a little above the meeting point and then further for a short distance. Just to the right of the right hand line, near the top of it, was a dot.

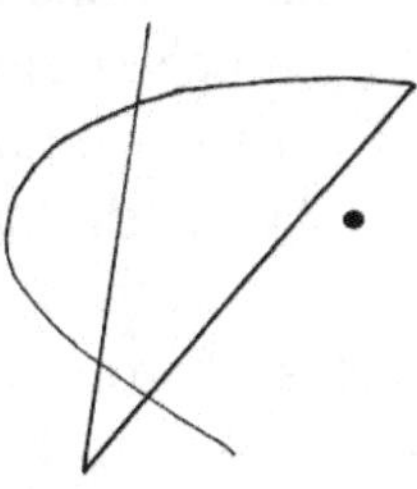

"What the hell is that?" muttered Avram.

"Exactly my question," said Bill, looking annoyed. "I've been staring at that thing for an hour and I can't for the life of me see anything meaningful."

"Does it appear again?" asked Penny.

"It does." Bill touched a key and the image resumed motion and then became a blur as Bill set it into fast rewind. It stopped suddenly. "I set up a search function to look for that image," he said with a shy smile. "And what it looks like is that the image appears at the start of each day just for a few moments."

"And it's the same image every time?" asked Avram.

"Seems to be," said Bill. "I've looked at a few and they all look the same."

"All from this one guy?" asked Penny.

Bill nodded. "I only found this thing a few hours ago and I've been wrestling with it ever since."

"Can I suggest something?" said Penny. "Can you wind back for say, a few months and take a copy of each image as you find it?"

Bill looked shaken. "You think this might be some sort of film image? Play it forward at speed and we might see some changes over time?"

"Exactly what I was thinking," said Penny.

Bill leaned over the keyboard and began typing instructions. Avram tried to see what he was doing, but the instructions were quite meaningless to him.

"A new coding system?' he asked.

"Yup," said Bill and continued working.

Avram sat back and grinned at Penny who returned it. They both knew Bill's genius had created whole new forms of working methods. After fifteen minutes, Bill sat back and the images of the elderly man became a whirl of colour.

"It's going back for six months, recording each image and setting up a stream," said Bill. "It'll only take a minute."

The minute passed in silence and then the screen became an image again, much like before, the man looking around his bedroom, obviously having just got up. On the other monitor, there was movement as the image of the diagram appeared but it looked to be sitting stationary on the screen.

"It's fast forwarding," said Bill. "It will only be a few seconds to play the image for each day over six months."

After just a few moments, Bill spoke again.

"That was it," he said. "I didn't see anything change at all." He sounded depressed.

"Nor did I," agreed Avram. "But try this. Take the first and last images and superimpose one on top of the other."

Bill returned to the keyboard, tapped a few keys and sat back.

"Okay, first day and last day," he said. "Looks like the same image. This is getting nowhere."

"Just hold on," said Penny and leaned forward to peer at the screen. "Have a look, guys. Does that dot look a little less like a circle? Hasn't it grown a fraction?"

For a few moments, the two men examined the image.

"Remove one," said Avram.

Bill touched a key. Nothing seemed to happen, but Penny said loudly, "Now it's a circle again."

"Bring it back," said Avram and this time they saw that the double dot was indeed fractionally different.

"The dot moved," said Bill. "Holy shit, the dot moved!"

"That was six months?" asked Avram.

Bill nodded.

"You'd better take a look at the entire life history," said Avram. "Let's see if anything changes over this man's whole life. Who is it?"

"Just some bloke I've been using as a test platform," said Bill. "He's a volunteer from the local hospital. He was fifty when we got his DNA."

"Good, we may see more obvious changes over fifty years," said Penny. "When do you thing you'll be ready?"

"Give me an hour," said Bill.

"Let's go and get a coffee," said Penny and she and Avram walked out.

Bill was still tapping at his keyboard when Penny and Avram returned but he sat back a moment later.

"That's something over fifty years of daily images there," he said. "Maybe 18,000 or more images. Let's set it running and see what happens. I'll run it in reverse so we start with the image we saw first." He touched a key and the three of them stared at the monitor.

All of them saw it at the same moment. Penny drew her breath in a gasp of surprise, Bill said, "Whoa!" and Avram was more precise.

"It's moving!" he shouted. "The bloody dot's moving!"

They went silent as they watched the dot move down in a track parallel with the right hand line and stopped a distance about three times its width from the starting point.

"It's a counting system," said Bill. "Some sort of counting system and it's counting the days as they pass."

"And it's no human system," said Penny softly. "Nobody can read that tiny difference in position without instrumentation."

"I wonder if the moving dot is the only thing," muttered Bill. "Let's do what we did before, compare first and last images."

A moment later, a new image appeared and this time, something was obvious.

"The angle has changed," said Penny.

"And that little tail at the end is a bit shorter," added Avram. "This is a representation of a number, just like the Arabic numbers we use or the old Roman numerals."

"And a bloody good one," said Bill. "Maybe one of the lines represents millions, the other one thousands, the angle represents hundreds and the dot moves are units. Or something like that."

"Of course, if this is really an alien system, we have no way of knowing what units they would be using," said Penny. "Probably nothing we have ever thought of before."

"But just look how many variables this thing has that could represent values," said Bill. "The line lengths, the tail size, the angle, they could just be a start. What if the line thickness is a variable, we haven't seen a change in that yet."

"And there are three areas within the diagram," added Avram. "Each of those could represent some size or volume or something."

"I think I can get something," muttered Bill, seemingly lost in thought. He was silent for a few moments then spoke again. "I have a device that measures size and dimensions. It's something I modified from the cable-making industry, it can measure the precise thickness of a wire, I rebuilt it to measure just micron diameters. And I have an idea of how we can test this further. Bugger off, you two, come back in an hour and I'll show you."

Penny laughed. "Okay genius, we'll be back!"

She and Avram walked out again.

"We could be on the edge of another massive breakthrough," said Avram. "If this thing identifies the specific day of the scene, it will be enormous."

"It could just be counting the days of the individual's life span," replied Penny. "But the most exciting and rather nerve-wracking thing for me is that it just has to be alien in origin. There's no human system even remotely like that."

"But if you have the ability to read those variables, it looks like a damned efficient system."

"I'm trying to imagine what sort of creature could look at that symbol and read a number without a machine," said Penny. "Something incredibly advanced, I'm sure."

"But then, if that creature is the species that put this whole thing into the human race, it certainly will be something incomprehensible to us," replied Avram.

They returned to their desks in deep thought.

"Okay, here's what I've done," said Bill. "I've set this device to measure the sizes of the bits of the symbol, using the images we have on the monitor. I can't use the originals, those are just too tiny of course. But this will allow us to compare sizes of the variables that we've identified so far."

"Clever," said Avram.

"Simple," said Bill and ignored the snort of laughter from Penny.

"Then I took the samples of DNA that were taken last week from volunteers, there were sixty-seven of them all on the same day, extracted the symbols on that day and now we can have a look at them."

Images began to appear on the monitor. They looked identical, though the dot appeared to be a little lower than they had seen on the first symbol they had seen.

"Now I'll start scanning them," continued Bill. "I've set the reader to measure the length of the two lines, the length of the tail and the position of the dot relative to the nearest line and the distance from where the tail meets that line. Those readings for each image will show on the other monitor. Ready?"

The other two nodded and watched the two screens. The only way they could see that a new symbol had appeared was just a tiny flicker and this occurred every few seconds. On the second monitor, a line of numbers appeared with each new image. Each new line appeared identical to the previous one. When it stopped, Bill sighed.

"All the symbols are identical. It's the same number on each DNA sample for that day. It's showing us the number of that day, starting from some base day."

"What the hell is that base day? What is Day One?" asked Avram, his voice hoarse with the shock of what they had discovered.

"When we know that, we'll know when this system was implanted in the human race," said Bill. "We'd better start looking."

"But we can make a start on building a translation table, a sort of Rosetta Stone," said Penny. "We can start by placing that symbol for today with today's date. Then perhaps we could take somebody's birthday, extract the symbol for that date and put those together. Then take the symbol for each day after in that person's DNA record, place the date next to it. It will be laborious, but we could get a few decades that way."

"Good thinking," said Avram. "We could do that with lots of historical dates, too. If, say, we know the date of birth of somebody born a few hundred years ago, we could do the same thing for each day of their life. Hey, I've just realised! When you came to talk to me, I had just found an ancestor, way, way back in 336 BCE watching the assassination of Philip of Macedon. We have that precise date. I'd gone through hundreds of my direct ancestors, so I could find a translation table from that date at least."

"I'll set up a computer routine to do that," said Bill, looking excited. "It would take months to do manually."

"There'll be a couple of problems," said Penny.

The two men looked at her.

"There have been some calendar changes in the past," she said. "We'll need to find out exactly what happened and when to make sure we have the correct dates."

"I'll do the research," said Bill. "I think I need to get started."

"And we'd better talk to Garry," said Avram.

Chapter 12 – June, 2024

The voice in the President's ear was calm and dispassionate.

"As our people had forecast, Mr President, General Mahmoud is flexing his muscles. Libyan forces invaded Chad fifteen minutes ago. And our Embassy in Benghazi has been sealed off."

"Thank you, John," said the president. "Get the response team to the situation room immediately."

He replaced the phone and stood up.

"Looks like fun and games in Libya again, Wendy," he said cheerfully to his secretary. "Organise coffee and the usual stuff for the situation room, will you? And of course, shift all my appointments. This could take a while."

The elegant, model-like woman who had been his personal assistant since the president had been the senator from Vermont nodded and left the Oval Office. The president put on his jacket, thought carefully for a few moments, picked up his notebook and followed her out. Two security men took him down to the long Situation Room where there were already three other people, one of them the National Security Adviser, the short rotund William Bassinger, the tall, quiet, grey-haired Admiral Laslo of the Joint Chiefs of Staff and Mary Druitt, Middle East expert, a woman in her seventies but fit, trim and with a mind like a supercomputer, as President Carmichael had known for many years.

They all greeted each other with the ease and friendliness of several years of mutual respect.

"You called this one right, Mary," said the president, taking his seat at the conference table.

"It was always glaringly obvious," replied Mary. "Typical behaviour of Middle-East despots. He took over the government by a coup a month ago and we've been watching every move. He could have been following our own checklists, the one called *'What despotic nasties do when they seize power'* he's been so predictable."

The president grinned then turned to the door as more of the team entered. The Army and Air Force representatives of the Joint Chiefs of Staff, the head of the CIA , the Secretary of State, the Vice-President and a few extra aides and assistants. All gave courteous greetings to the president, took their seats and several gave quiet orders to their assistants to get drinks from the side table.

The room was quiet with the atmosphere that comes of the most important decisions in the world being made on almost a daily basis. Walnut panels round the walls hid the numerous video screens that were linked to computer and communications centres in the world's seats of power.

"All right, everybody," said President Carmichael. "As you now know, General Mahmoud has followed Mary Druitt's script to the letter since he took power and he has now invaded Chad in the last thirty minutes as well as sealing off our embassy in Benghazi."

"How many people in the embassy?" asked the Vice President.

"Ninety three," replied the Secretary of State. "We have no communication at the moment, so we have no ideas of any casualties."

"And what forces has he mobilised? Chairman, do you have that information?" asked the president.

"Almost any moment," replied Air Force General, Declan Peterson. "The satellites are about to pass overhead and..." His mobile phone buzzed at that moment. The president nodded and Peterson picked up his phone, studied the screen and read the details.

"Two thousand troops, twenty tanks and mobile artillery, all heading south. Their air force is fully mobilised."

"Thanks, Declan," said the president. "So, is this an opportunity for Operation Revelation?"

A laugh ran round the room and a chorus of agreement rumbled round the table like a distant thunderstorm.

"Do we have everything in place?" asked the president. "Juanita, the CIA has been able to get everything?"

"Yes, Mister President, we have samples of DNA of the General, each of his cronies, his household staff and his two sons." Juanita Alvarez was a stocky woman from Dallas who had been an operational agent in her youth but had demonstrated fine management abilities and risen to become the first female head of the CIA. Carmichael knew that she spoke excellent Russian, German and Arabic.

"And you've gone through them?"

"Indeed we have, sir," she replied, a smile glowing enough to light up the room. "My people have prepared the essentials, expecting this day to come quite soon, just as Mary had told us."

"Then we'd better see all this before we unleash great big clouds of shit all over Mahmoud's head," said the president and sat back. A large screen appeared from behind the walnut covering on the wall at one end of the room. It flickered briefly as Juanita Alvarez manipulated her hand controller and then a scene appeared. The group watched in silence for the few minutes it lasted.

"That will go down like a train smash," said Carmichael. "You have more like this?"

"Lots," said Alvarez and pressed a few buttons.

For the next thirty minutes the room watched, sometimes laughing, sometimes horrified, sometimes disgusted until Carmichael waved his hand and the presentation stopped.

"That should do it," said the president. "Mary, you are sure that seeing those scenes will hit Mahmoud in the most painful way possible?"

"No doubt at all, Mr President. He is committing the worst crimes against Islam, crimes for which he has personally increased penalties in his country. Not only will his own people be disgusted, so will all the other Islamic countries in the region. And the final kicker we've prepared will destroy him."

"Thank you Mary," said the President. "Get me Mahmoud on the network."

A few minutes passed while connections were made and then the face of the Libyan ruler appeared on the large central screen.

"Ah, Mr President!" he said, a wide smile adorning his face. "How nice of you to call! Do you approve of what I am doing?"

"General, let me give you fair warning," said the president without any opening amenities. "You will withdraw your troops back inside your borders immediately and you will release all the hostages in the American Embassy."

The Libyan laughed loudly and more laughter could be heard from others in the same room.

"Mr President, let *ME* give *YOU* full warning," he replied. "If you even *begin* to move your war fleets into the Mediterranean, I will begin killing each of the hostages, one in the morning and one in the afternoon. I will take them out into the road in front of the embassy and I will slice their heads off. The film will be broadcast all over the world. So I suggest that you go away and play at being a world leader without power and I will continue expanding the borders of my country."

"You might like to see this, General," said Carmichael. He nodded at Juanita and the screen filled with the first scene the room had watched earlier. It was also being transmitted to the Libyan's location.

The immensely tall, thin shape of General Mahmoud was in the centre. He was dressed in simple jeans and a tee-shirt, sitting at a table that was loaded with food items. On either side of him was a younger man with a similar body shape to the General. All were tucking into what looked like hamburgers, hot dogs and fries, accompanied by mugs of beer.

"We know that those are your sons, Omar and Fazi," said the president. "The DNA sample came from Colonel Assam al-Yaafi, your personal body-guard who was obviously part of this business lunch. The next thing we hear is the statement that will destroy you."

On the screen, the General laughed, took a deep swig of beer and spoke in Arabic.

"This is a great way to spend Ramadan, eh Omar?" said Juliana in translation when the General stopped and took a bite of his hamburger.

"And as you said yourself," said Carmichael as the scene ended, "this was during Ramadan when all observant Muslims are fasting during the day, apart from which you were also drinking alcohol. I believe your country has begun imposing a penalty of a hundred lashes for that particular crime. How do you think your citizens will react when they see that?"

"Where did you get that?" shouted the Libyan. "You made that up! Your Jewish cronies in Hollywood, they made that. Nobody will believe it."

"Well, how about this?" asked Carmichael. A new scene flickered into life. It showed a woman of great beauty, wearing little but a bikini bottom, her long blonde hair indicating she was a western woman. She stood, her shoulders back to give full views of her generous breasts as a man approached her, quickly recognisable as Omar, the General's son who was quite naked. As the scene moved, it was clear that the observer was another woman as all three appeared in a large mirror on the wall. Then the trio collapsed onto the massive bed.

"Stop that!" shouted the General furiously. "How do you get such scenes? This is the work of the devil."

"General, surely you know about the technology that allows your DNA to be scanned for the images of your life? It's been around for years. We have samples from you, your sons, many of your cronies and your household staff. Let me show you another scene."

This time, it was the General, lying naked on the bed with two more naked women. He had a glass in his hand and the bottle that could be seen on the bedside table was obviously scotch. The General's other hand was cupping the woman's crotch and all were laughing as she spread her legs and moaned in apparent ecstasy.

"Western women again, General," said Carmichael. "Neither of them appears to be your wife. And you're drinking expensive scotch, looks like Talisker from what I can see. That scene came from the DNA of one of your sons. So I ask you again, what do you think your subjects will think when we broadcast these scenes all over the world?"

The General was silent, but his rage was obvious.

"One more for your entertainment," said Carmichael.

It was a featureless patch of ground, surrounded by high walls. Three men and two women stood against one of the walls, all were naked. Into the scene strode the General, carrying a handgun. He walked up to the line of prisoners and proceeded to shoot each one of them in the head. When all five were lying on the ground, he waved his arms in an expression of great triumph, laughing loudly in the direction of the camera.

"This time, it was your bodyguard, Colonel Assam al-Yaffi who provided the DNA, though he has no idea that he did so," said the president. "So, General, what is it to be? You may kill some of my people before we get there, but if you do not follow my request, the Seventh Fleet will be in Libyan waters within hours, your palace will be bombed into rubble and some of the best combat troops in the world will arrive from various American bases in the region and take over your country. And of course, all these scenes, and we have plenty more, will be broadcast all over the world on television and the internet. Your people will turn on you, as will every other Muslim country for your offences against Allah."

The silence was almost a bellow and lasted for a

couple of minutes before the General spoke again, his voice loud, angry and aggressive.

"You will die, Carmichael! My agents will hunt you down and kill you anywhere in the world we find you. My people will never turn against me."

Carmichael was unmoved. "I have another surprise for you, General," he said. "You're broke."

"What does that mean, enemy of Allah?"

"It means we've also seen through the DNA when you and your sons created your bank accounts in the Caymans, Panama and other locations, so we had those secret numbers. It was dead easy therefore to take every cent out of all the accounts! That's eight billion dollars we released just a few minutes ago and we deposited that money into the accounts of Doctors Without Borders. They're doing rather more good with it than you could have done. You're flat busted, General, all of you."

Carmichael watched the General as his rage was gradually replaced by a defeated expression.

"I will withdraw my troops, Mr President and your people are free to leave."

"A good choice," replied Carmichael. "We will be watching closely to make sure you behave. For now, you may remain in power, but I strongly urge you to be a good little boy and behave yourself or we may have to reconsider."

A small signal and the communication was cut off. A sigh ran round the situation room as all the people released their pent-up breath. Carmichael realised his back was damp with sweat but he managed to remain looking calm and in control.

"A hell of a lot quicker and cheaper than an invading force, Mr President," said the Chairman of the Joint Chiefs of Staff, his smile wide and sincere.

The room suddenly exploded in roars of applause and approval.

Carmichael waved his hand and it subsided.

"I know that this technology has been banned in much of the country because of the pressures from the religious fraternity," he said. "But I think we have just proved how valuable it can be. Maybe by the time I leave this job, we can convince the country to rethink its position and join the rest of the world."

He turned to the head of the CIA.

"Juanita, your people did a wonderful job gathering DNA samples from those thugs. I assume you have done the same with lots of others?"

Alvarez smiled. "Indeed sir. But obviously, we have to maintain current samples in order to know what these people are planning. I wish we could have got later samples showing what he was planning in Chad, that way we could have avoided the disaster completely. I've no doubt every world leader will be frantically working on how to maintain security against DNA theft from now on."

The President nodded. "As do we all," he said. "That includes us. We may have averted a crisis here, but some things we would not want seen by the world. And that raises another point."

He paused a moment as if gathering his thoughts.

"We had no trouble seeing images that showed a great crime being committed. The problem now is that any privacy or any secrecy is now just as easy to break down as that. There is no way that we can prevent somebody getting hold of the DNA of one of us and just as easily seeing images we would not wish revealed and then used against us."

He looked round the room and saw some intense worries on all the faces.

"In many ways, we are in the same situation as we have been with nuclear weapons. If one country tried to use a nuke, it's guaranteed that a similar weapon would be used against it. We called it 'Mutually Assured Destruction' and it was the strongest protection for everybody. Now we have 'Mutually Assured Revelation' and I hope it provides the same protection against malicious use of images to embarrass or blackmail people. It's no longer enough to be careful about what we say or do because we simply cannot hide everything from prying eyes any more."

He stood up, followed by everybody else.

"All right, everybody, don't you have jobs to go to?"

In the laughter, he strode out of the room, up the stairs and back to the Oval Office.

"Okay, Wendy, what's next?" he said cheerfully as he walked in.

Chapter 13 – December, 2024

The phone call broke into Garry's deep thoughts as he sat in the armchair in his office trying to get his head round the profusion of world events that had been precipitated by his organisation in recent years.

"Garry, it's Eamon Jackson."

The voice with the slight Manchester accent triggered the memory of the tall, well-dressed man in his sixties who had visited Garry in the old Reading office with two younger men who spoke not a word during the entire demonstration of the DNA visual records.

"Your Eminence, this is a surprise!"

"Garry, I told you before, the name is Eamon," said the Cardinal of the Holy Roman Church. "And I need to come and talk to you."

"You're in Australia?" Garry was feeling unbalanced at this call from one of the most senior men in the Vatican.

"Flew into Sydney yesterday," said the Cardinal. "I'll be doing all the appropriate diplomatic and social stuff during the week, but I really came to see you."

"Good grief, Eamon, why me?"

The Cardinal's voice revealed some amusement.

"Because you're the bloke that's caused all this."

Garry took a deep breath. "When can I expect you?" he asked.

"In about twenty minutes," the Cardinal said. "I drove up from Sydney this morning. You still have that excellent coffee in your office?"

"I do," said Garry, finally feeling relaxed in the obvious friendliness of the Cardinal.

"Good," said Jackson. "Get a second cup ready."

"Yes, boss," said Garry and heard a small echo of a laugh before the Cardinal ended the call.

"Good coffee," said Cardinal Eamon Jackson. He sat in the second armchair across from Garry on the other side of the coffee table. He was dressed in casual grey slacks, a black golf shirt with the logo of the Bondi Beach Golf Club over the left breast, white socks and white shoes. He had a small black document carrier with him. He looked like a prosperous retiree about to head to the golf course. Garry couldn't stop a smile.

"You look amazingly healthy," he said. "Life in Rome must suit you."

"Not always," said Jackson. "The last couple of years have been a series of crises after the Pope realised he had no choice but to accept what your people had found."

"I was astounded that he did and so quickly," said Garry. "But I know it caused some problems."

"Yes, you'll of course know that the Americans went off on their own right away. What you won't know yet is that Cardinal Joseph Maguire of Dallas will soon announce a new American Papacy based in Dallas."

"With himself as Pope, I assume?"

"With himself as Pope," agreed Jackson. "We have no idea just what following he will attract. And you probably know that the Eastern Orthodox Churches have ended all discussions concerning reunification."

"I'd heard that," said Garry. "How is all this going to work out?"

"We're praying for a peaceful transition," said the Cardinal. "Frankly, it's the Americans we worry about most. The Eastern Churches are unlikely to cause problems, we don't expect attacks on heretics or anything like that."

"But you do with the Americans?"

Jackson shrugged his shoulders. "It's possible," he said. "Maguire is not a stable personality."

Garry studied his visitor carefully. He began to see the signs that the Cardinal was not as relaxed and affable as he had first appeared. There was some tension in the deliberately posed air of relaxation and Garry saw some lines in the face that he did not remember from the previous visit.

"Eamon, you said you specifically came to see me," said Garry. "Is there some special purpose?"

"To give you a preview," said the Cardinal.

"Of?"

"Vatican III."

"Vatican III?"

"Vatican III. You've heard of Vatican II?"

"Heavens, that's at least sixty years ago, before I was born," said Garry. "But yes, I'd heard of it. It was pretty dramatic in the changes it indicated in the Catholic Church. But I'm not a Catholic, more of a devoutly committed Agnostic, to be honest, so I never thought much about it."

"It's sort of faded into the past," acknowledged Jackson. "But the recent changes have made a new revision of the Church even more critical than it was in the early sixties and that's what I've been working on the last few months."

"And this is what you have come to tell me about? Good grief, Eamon, this will be world-shaking, I imagine. And I'm getting a preview?"

Jackson slid open the document back and extracted a single sheet. As he did, he seemed to pull it out with more than enough strength and caught one edge on the zip, tearing it slightly. The Cardinal stared down at the sheet.

"I suspect you are seeing that I'm not as relaxed and at ease as I'm trying to appear, Garry."

"I think so. I'm trying to imagine how I would react if my whole world had been torn apart by new knowledge, new realities and turmoil within an organisation to which I had devoted my whole life."

"You're a perceptive man, my friend. And you're right. Do you know I even contemplated ending my life a couple of times? It's totally against all the teachings of my church, it's considered a great evil, but for a while it looked to me to be a better alternative than facing what I had to face."

"Eamon, that terrifies me. I cannot imagine how stressful this has been. I've been somewhat torn apart myself in recent years, ever since Karen was murdered, about the part I have played in this disruption, but for you, it must have been dreadful."

"It was not good, I have to admit. And then the Pope assigned me to developing Vatican III, so I have lived with the situation every day for a long time."

Jackson took a deep breath, laid the sheet on his lap and looked at Garry.

"Anyway..." he said. "Let's press on." He looked down at the paper.

"The amazing thing is that we found that much of

the documentation, especially the summaries is still as valid today as it was in the sixties. In fact, I deliberately used much of the summary for this. So I'm only going to read that summary, not the whole batch of documents that follow, they just amplify the summaries and provide the logical developments."

Garry sat back with a feeling of excitement, though still with some shock at the thought of this extraordinary man contemplating taking his own life. He knew he was about to hear something that would affect the whole world and would be stored in the history books as one of the pivotal moments in human events. To realise that he had played a critical part in this story was both exciting and frightening.

"Forget the preambles," said Jackson. Here's the nugget." He began reading.

"The truths that the Church encountered when the Vatican II Council began its task in 1962 were considered immutable and like the Council of that time, we believe that the church should never depart from the sacred treasure of truth inherited from the Fathers. But at the same time, she should ever look to the present, to the new conditions, to the new forms of life introduced into the modern world.

"In the last two years, the Church has been faced with extraordinary changes and one of these has been the ability to look back into our history and see as absolute truth, events that we had only previously seen from the distance of millennia. The reporting of these events was coloured by personal preferences, modified by time and historical upheavals and could not

always have been as accurate as we had wished."

Jackson put one hand on the sheet on his lap and looked at Garry.

"You can see where this is going?" he said.

"It's pretty clear, but the implications are incredible," Garry replied.

"Indeed," replied the Cardinal and picked the sheet up again.

"Above all else, the Church must accept truth and we cannot ignore the truth that has faced us with absolute certainty. While the teachings of Jesus Christ remain valid, the source of these teachings is no longer what we have believed. There was no divine figure of Jesus, no Son of God, no crucifixion and no resurrection.

"So the work we do need not change. Our role will forever be to serve humanity, to help the poor, help heal the sick, feed and shelter the hungry and the homeless. This is what those young rabbis taught as they went around Palestine and those teachings are as valid now as they were then.

"What will change is the form of the services we perform in the churches and cathedrals around the world. Those details will be presented in later documents."

Jackson replaced the sheet of paper on his lap and smiled at Garry.

"So what do think so far?"

"I like it," said Garry. "What are you going to say about those who won't follow your lead?"

"Coming up," said the Cardinal. "This part is a direct copy from Vatican II because it remains a keystone matter."

> *"Whatever were our opinions about the Council's various doctrines before its conclusions were promulgated, today our decisions about adherence to the Council must be whole-hearted and without reserve; it must be willing and prepared to give them the service of our thought, action and conduct. The Council was something very new; not all were prepared to understand and accept it. But now the conciliar doctrine must be seen as belonging to the magisterium of the Church and indeed be attributed to the breath of the Holy Spirit.*
>
> *"We are saddened by the decisions made by our brothers in the Churches of the East to depart from our family, but we have faith that they will continue the work of the Church, even if they have decided to remain with the old doctrines.*
>
> *"We are just as saddened by the decision of our brothers in America to leave us and we pray that the impending schism does not cause the social and economic problems that previous schisms have caused."*

The Cardinal sat back and put the sheet back in the document carrier. Then he stood up and went to the coffee urn and poured another cup, his back to Garry. He stood motionless for a few seconds before returning to his seat and Garry saw the few small tears on the Cardinal's cheek.

"This has been traumatic for you, hasn't it?" said Garry.

Jackson nodded, took a deep breath and regained control of himself.

"I was a latecomer to the church, as you know," he said. "I had graduated, finished my doctorate and was about to embark on a career in the academic world before I got the call. I never really understood that, but I followed it, regardless and moved up the ranks of the Catholic world rapidly. And now I have been part of the biggest changes ever to hit it. I could have ignored what you showed me back in Reading, rejected the findings of the Israeli project, reported back to the Pope that it was all fantasy and nothing would have changed. Not for some time, anyway."

"But you're a man of scientific rigour and you knew it was the truth," said Garry. "Could you have lived with yourself if you had done that?"

Jackson shook his head. "Of course not. I would have been living a lie. It would have been even worse than creating the mechanisms of massive change, as I have had to do."

"And so what next?"

"Vatican III will be edited, improved, updated and reviewed by numerous people and will become public in a few weeks."

"And what do you expect will happen?"

"Not much more than has happened already, I hope," said the Cardinal. "But we pray that the fact that the Pope has issued these statements will give final approval to all those who have been swaying and doubting their beliefs."

"And the other religions?"

Jackson shook his head. "The Anglicans are saying the same and most will follow Canterbury's lead, though as we have seen, some of the same schisms have occurred as with our Eastern Orthodox Churches. Israel is being a trifle smug about the whole thing, doing that whole, "We told you so" thing, Islam is being quiet. Buddhism seems to be ignoring the entire event as being nothing more than a mildly interesting but irrelevant story."

"And what will you do now, Eamon?"

"I'll go back home next week. The Vatican is still a massive, complex organisation that needs management, little different from any other charitable organisation. There are people revising the services, the whole sacrament has gone. And while we have removed all those dreadful crucifixions which I always found appalling, the simple cross remains as a potent symbol of faith."

"I think your Church is in good hands, Eamon."

"Thank you, Garry. I'll do my best."

Both men stood up and shook hands. Garry watched from his window as the Cardinal climbed into his mid-size rental car and drove out of the parking area, through the manned gate of the high security fence and onto the road back into Newcastle. He couldn't think but believe he had just had coffee with a future Pope.

Chapter 14 – January, 2025

"We don't meet very often," said Garry, "so I thought it was time for another get-together. My researchers are still busy looking at ancient and not-so-ancient history, languages and societies, so we don't hear much of what this group is doing."

"It's been suggested that we should call ourselves The Second Foundation in honour of Isaac Asimov," said Mary Hennessy with a smile.

Garry returned the smile. "I like it," he said. "I move that we are definitely known as The Second Foundation!"

Sounds of approval round the table were accompanied by raised hands.

"The Second Foundation it is," said Garry.

"Perhaps just 2F for short," suggested Robert Swann.

That also received approval.

"We've been thinking," said Mary.

"That's what we pay you to do," broke in Garry.

Mary smiled briefly. "We've been thinking about just what our role really is and what impact we might have on the world as our developments become universally accepted. And all of us keep coming round to seeing parallels with the Renaissance period of the Middle Ages."

"Can you clarify?" asked Garry, his interest rising.

"Yours I think, Annabelle," said Mary, looking at Annabelle Calvert, midway down the table on Garry's right.

"I agree, seeing as I'm the historian," said the middle-aged woman dressed in a smart skirt and white blouse. She looked extremely fit. "My speciality is 20th Century Europe, but I did a lot of work on the Renaissance when I was at University. And I'm a huge fan of Asimov, so when all this developed, Mary invited me into the group."

"I know I read your resume, but can you refresh me on it?"

She nodded. "Undergraduate, Master's and Doctorate from Cambridge, where I first heard about Karen Petrova. I was teaching there when Mary called me. I have two sons, both are pilots with the Australian Air Force. I play golf and squash, so I'm keen to develop that telekinetic talent that Ben has demonstrated."

There was a muted laugh round the table. Garry smiled.

"Then welcome to the 2F, Annabelle. Now, this Renaissance thing?"

"Just bare essentials to make the point," began the historian. "The world changed to an incredible degree in many areas during the century or so that it all happened. We have heard most about the Arts, when painting, drawing, sculpture all changed and developed whole new dimensions. But one of the most significant changes was in religion, as massive upheavals occurred, much like we are seeing today. The almost absolute power of the Catholic Church was broken up, largely by the break away by Henry VIII, the growth of splinter groups like those led by Martin Luther and the huge growth in production of Bibles in different languages, aided by Gutenberg's invention of the printing press."

"That last one is certainly showing itself," agreed Garry. "I haven't seen any changes in the art world so far."

Annabelle nodded. "Yet to occur and I have no idea how it will show. I imagine it will result from something your researchers may find in the coming days. But the other big development that is causing upheavals is in politics, international relationships and diplomacy, as we have already seen."

"Indeed yes," said Garry. "When it becomes possible to see everything somebody has said and done, it's impossible to hide secrets. So the old art of politics has changed dramatically."

"And as we saw in that confrontation between the USA and the Libyan strongman when he invaded Chad, the old games become impossible," added Mary.

"But this is fascinating," said Garry. "Annabelle, what else are you seeing?"

"Social changes we are seeing in great numbers," continued Annabelle. "The massive one occurred with the changes in the justice system, first in Britain and then around the world. Most trials became just routine hearings lasting less than hour. Many convicted criminals were released as their DNA history proved their innocence and crime rates dropped dramatically as the certainty of conviction grew to almost a hundred percent in all cases."

"One of the most productive developments of them all," said Garry. "We were all so proud of that."

"Unfortunately, some countries are using it as a form of repression," said Mary with a frown. "They take random samples from their citizens and look for any evidence of anti-government activities or speech."

"We may be able to use the technology against the leaders," said Garry, thoughtfully.

"Under development," said Mary, more cheerfully.

"Good," replied Garry. "Any more on the parallels with the Renaissance?"

"Not as yet, I imagine we're waiting on more discoveries by your people," said Mary. "But we're all pretty sure that we are seeing a Second Renaissance developing."

Garry was lost in thought for a few seconds, his eyes fixed on his hands on the table then he spoke.

"There's something that has played in my mind ever since our electronics genius, Bill mentioned it and it's become more nagging since he, Penny and Avram decoded the numbering system."

The group looked at him.

"Soon after we found out just what we had, Bill asked the question of just why does Humanity have this feature? Why do we have a record of all our ancestors? It didn't seem to be a necessary requirement for Darwinian survival."

"We might ask the same question about all the higher talents," broke in Jennifer Chang. "Homo Sapiens would have become the dominant species without music, higher maths, all the arts and so on. We didn't need to be able to build space-ships or nuclear weapons or computers, we would have dominated the animal world regardless."

"And that's where Bill's second point comes in," said Garry. "It would be very hard to doubt that the numbering system he found is anything but non-human."

There was silence round the table. Finally, Jennifer Chang broke it.

"If we solve that one, then everything that changed in the first Renaissance and now our growing Second Renaissance will be trivial compared to the effects of the new information."

"And it looks like we've already caused a major split in the major churches," said Mary.

* * *

"So can I count on all of you?"

Cardinal Joseph Maguire looked at the other three seated round the table in his office in Dallas. His stare was piercing and intimidating.

Cardinal Andrew Colmes was the first to break the intense silence. He was a short, heavily-built man of 57 with no signs of grey in his full head of black hair. His face lacked any memorable features except for round eyes that indicated possibly some Asian ancestry.

"I'm with you all the way, Eminence," he said. "We all left with you when you expressed your opposition to the heretical new trends in the Catholic Church and I for one see no reason to change my views."

"Good," said Maguire. "How about the rest of you?"

"What he said," said Cardinal Howard Heinz. He was a large, overweight man, reflecting his earlier years at the University of Notre Dame as a football player, with heavy jowls, receding hair, a loud voice and an intimidating attitude that had left him with few friends in the hierarchies of the American Catholic Church. "What that wimp in the Vatican said was pure heresy as far as I'm concerned. Anyway, I think it's way beyond time that the leadership should be here in America. So yeah, you can count on me."

Maguire nodded but said nothing as he switched his stare to the last man at the table, Cardinal Frank Kozik. Kozic was sixty-seven, a tall man of solid build, balding grey hair and stuck-out ears that had caused him endless misery as a child. He had small hands with thick fingers. He was known to have a drinking problem and had a reputation as a child molester for many years, covered up by the church which had sent him to many different parishes to try and hide his crimes.

"Of course, Eminence," he said, not meeting Maguire's eyes.

"Excellent," said Maguire. "Now, you know what I want. Each of you nominate, say, eight or nine men that can be promoted to Cardinal. These men had better share our views and you must ensure that they'll elect me as the Pope in Dallas. I'll pick fifteen for promotion and when that's sorted, we'll have the meeting to elect me."

"When are you going to announce this to the world?" asked Heinz. His voice was harsh, indicating some tension in him.

"As soon as I'm elected Pope. Then we'll release it to the media and call for a Council of Churches here. We'll invite the heads of the Southern Baptists, the Traditional Anglican Community, the Anglican Province of America and those lunatic Mormons."

"The Mormons?" asked Heinz. "Why ask them? They're all crazy and there's no way they'll agree to this new order."

"We have to invite them," replied Maguire with some irritation. "There's about eight million of them here in America and as far as I can tell, they're pretty well committed to the standard Christian teachings."

"Except for Angels and golden sheet books and all that magic underwear nonsense," said Colmes.

"They can keep all that," snapped Maguire. "Just so long as they stick to the traditional teachings and none of this crap about Jesus never having existed or just being one of a group of rabbis. We need those numbers."

"I suppose so," muttered Colmes.

"And what about the Southern Baptists?" broke in Kozic. "Do you think they'll join us?"

"There's about sixteen million of them, so I hope so," replied Maguire. "But they're declining in numbers, they're losing tens of thousands every year, hell, almost every one of their congregations is shrinking, so they'll need our backing."

"I doubt all them would agree," said Kozic. "Their demographics are changing. Overall, about twenty percent are Africans, Latinos and Asians, here in Texas that's about sixty percent. I think the Latinos will come over, can't be sure about the others."

"They can go," said Maguire. "I'll take the Latinos, we can do without Blacks and Asians."

Kozic shrugged but said no more.

"So, with our eighty million members, if we can get the support of the Mormons, the Southern Baptists and the remaining Anglicans, we could have over a hundred million," continued Maguire. "That's over a quarter of the population. We could have major influence over Congress that way. Enough to get this terrible technology banned, for a start."

"That won't be easy," said Colmes. "A lot of universities already have these things and they're using them heavily."

"Then they'll have to stop," snapped Maguire. "We're not going to have a bunch of liberals and academics try and rewrite history. Those fools in Rome and Canterbury have already done enough damage and I don't want the same nonsense happening here."

"We may face constitutional challenges," said Colmes. "How are you going to stop academics researching history and languages?"

"Remember what happened in Chicago?" said Maguire. "It didn't take much to stir up a riot when that Britisher worked at North Western University for a few days. We didn't have to do much once he'd shot his mouth off on television. Some of our people there made that happen easily."

"It didn't stop them using the gear," said Heinz. "And what happens if they start to see images of the sort of thing Kozic here got up to with the kids? And not just him, we all know a few of our brethren who have got up to the same thing."

For a moment the room was cold and silent as the others stared at Cardinal Kozic who seemed to shrink a little and hot spots burned in his cheeks.

"Then we'll just have to fight harder," replied Maguire. "We'll get a majority of republicans on our side and we can threaten anybody who objects with nasty stuff happening to them and their families. Same with the Supreme Court."

Heinz stared, open-eyed.

"You'd hurt congressmen and senators? Supreme Court justices?"

Maguire smiled without warmth. "This is a fight for God and Jesus Christ. How can anything we do in such a war be wrong?"

Heinz stared at his hands folded on the table.

"Do I have anything to doubt about you, *Eminence?*" said Maguire. His tone was dangerous and he stressed the last word. It was an obvious warning.

"No, Eminence," replied Heinz in a low tone.

"Good, I hope not," said Maguire and looked around the table. "Now, go off and find me suitable candidates for our Curia to elect the new pope."

The other three stood up and walked out without a word.

* * *

A month later, all the major news channels broadcast the same advance notice at the same hour on the same night.

"CNN has been asked by the Catholic Church of America to broadcast a special announcement to be made at 8pm tomorrow evening," said the voice over a full screen advertisement saying simply, "Major address to the nation by Cardinal Joseph Maguire at 8pm on Tuesday, July 14th."

The voice continued, "This notice will be broadcast at intervals for the remainder of the evening and at certain times tomorrow. No further information is available at this time."

The message and announcement appeared again on all channels at 8pm, 10pm and then at noon, 4pm and 6pm the following day.

The announcement seemed to cause no interest in the main stream media. No current affairs or news programs mentioned it beyond noting that it had been made and the major news programs at 6pm on the day of the Cardinal's address who repeated the time for the event that evening.

The only commentary and discussion took place on al Jazeera and the BBC in America. The latter had a talking heads session at 10pm of the day the announcement first appeared and this was repeated at six pm the next day.

"The most astonishing thing about this is that there's been no discussion in America," said Deborah James, senior correspondent for the BBC. Her beautiful speaking voice and clear diction had earned her thousands of adoring followers in the USA.

"Not so astonishing," said Brad Hollingsworth, the political commentator. "There's a lot of evidence that Congress people have been pressuring the networks to downplay the whole discussion of what happened when the Vatican and the Anglican Church in England announced their changes."

"And there hasn't been the furore I would have expected from that anywhere in the world," added Peter Cahill, the BBC's religious commentator.

"Many people have suggested that this period has been the proverbial calm before the storm," said Deborah. "Is it possible that Cardinal Maguire is about to unleash the tempest?"

"It could be," said Hollingsworth. "Though I can't think of what sort of tempest it might be."

"There's some heavy-duty precedent," said Cahill. "We've had schisms in the church before."

"Henry VIII?" said Deborah.

"Henry wasn't quite the example I was thinking of," replied Cahill. "He just broke away from the Vatican for his own selfish reasons and established a whole new church so that he could get a divorce from his first wife. I was thinking of the Avignon Popes."

"Can you refresh the minds of our viewers what that was about?" asked Hollingsworth.

"Sure," said Cahill. "This was time when the French Crown had major conflicts over power and taxes with the Papacy in Rome. There was deadlock in the Curia and they finally elected a French Pope in 1309 and he refused to move to Rome and he set up his own court in

France. It stayed there under seven Popes for sixty-seven years before the next Pope moved back to Rome."

"And that ended it?" asked Hollingsworth.

Cahill grinned. "Not a chance!" he said. "There were two more Avignon Popes and this "Western Schism" as it was known lasted until 1417 before it all got resolved with the Papacy back in Rome."

"I never knew any of that!" said Deborah with a laugh. "You do know your stuff, Peter. But are we seriously thinking Cardinal Maguire may be declaring a new Schism and setting up a Dallas Vatican?"

"I honestly don't know," replied Cahill. "Maguire is known for his bedrock fundamentalism and it seems he walked out of the last meeting of Cardinals in Rome, just about frothing with rage. But if he is, it's a choice fraught with danger."

"How so?" asked Hollingsworth. He had listened to Cahill intently.

"He could lose millions of members," said Cahill. "The Catholics have about eighty million members, the biggest grouping in the USA. Not all will be as devoutly fundamentalist as he is and many could turn against him and remain loyal to Rome."

"What about the other groups?" asked Hollingsworth. "How will they react?"

"Well, there's no doubt, many of the Anglican groups like the Traditional Anglican Community have been moving closer to the Catholics in philosophy and practices," said Cahill. "Some have even adopted a Vatican-created creed that moves their church activities more in line with those of the Vatican, such as High Mass, confessions and so on. But there have been breakaway groups from them, like the Anglican Province of America which is conservative but not fundamentalist."

"It all sounds like a bit of a dog's breakfast," said Deborah. "What about the Southern Baptists?"

Cahill looked thoughtful. "Tricky," he said. "Their reputation is fairly conservative and there are some lunatic fringe groups like that mob that used to protest military funerals because of America's tolerance of homosexuality and abortion and suchlike. But their numbers have been declining rapidly and the demographics changing, far more African-Americans, Latinos and Asians. Hard to say which way they'll jump."

"And the Church of Latter Day Saints?" asked Deborah. "How do think they'll react?"

Cahill smiled. "We can never anticipate what the Mormons will do. While they have some whacky beliefs about gold plates and angels and wotnot, they are certainly heavily biased towards real family concerns, loving the children, reading to them and stuff that frankly, I have always liked. I can't see them tolerating Maguire's style of Christianity."

"Well, we will know after Tuesday evening," said Deborah James. "This might all be a storm in a teacup or the biggest social change in America since World War II. Let us hope that the country will still be at peace over the coming few weeks."

* * *

At that moment, the door opened and the young man who served coffee poked his head in.

"Telephone, Miss Hennessy," he said.

Mary looked annoyed. "Could you tell them I'm in a meeting?"

The man smiled. "I think you should take it," he said.

Annoyance changed to puzzlement. "Switch it

through." The man closed the door and Mary reached under the table and brought out a conference phone, placing it in the middle of the table. It buzzed and Mary pressed a button.

"Mary Hennessy."

"Miss Hennessy, this is Greg Bartlett of the Prime Minister's Department in Canberra."

Mary stared across at Garry and then round the room. Everybody was staring at the phone.

"Yes, Mr Bartlett, what can I do for you?"

"Miss Hennessy, I am calling from the Prime Minister's office. He is sitting with the German Chancellor, Herr Franz Pankow and he would like to talk to you. Are you alone?"

"No, I am not. I am in my conference room with Garry Lawson, the President of Blueprints and the advisory council members."

"Excellent!" said the voice in Canberra. "This concerns all of you. I am putting Herr Pankow on now."

Mary looked at Garry again. He mouthed silently, "What on *EARTH*?" She shook her head as a new voice sounded from the speakers on the table.

"Miss Hennessy, Mr Lawson, it is a great pleasure to talk to you and your extraordinary team."

Mary made gestures at Garry that he should answer. Struggling for composure, Garry spoke.

"Herr Pankow, the pleasure is ours, but we are unsure why you wish to speak with us."

"Because you may be the group best qualified to advise my country and perhaps the world of how to deal with the extraordinary things you have already caused. I have heard of your advisory group, I believe you have modelled it after Isaac Asimov's Second Foundation..." a ghost of a laugh echoed in the voice "... and I would like a representative to come to Germany and talk to my people about how we might plan for the Brave New World you are bringing about."

Garry looked round the room and saw expressions of astonishment and satisfaction. Several of them nodded enthusiastically at him, Mary did the same and Garry made a decision.

"It would be a privilege, Chancellor."

"Then we shall arrange it, Mr Lawson." The laugh rang out more obviously. "I'll have my people call your people!"

Garry couldn't help laughing in response. "I'll look forward to it, Herr Pankow."

The call was disconnected.

"Phew!" said Garry, helplessly.

Mary cleared her throat. "I think the Second Foundation has just acquired a new purpose," she said. "We've become advisors to the world."

Chapter 15 – February, 2025

"I'm preggers," announced Penny. She and Avram sat across from Garry's coffee table holding hands. She had a warm, soft glow in her face.

"You look very happy about it," said Garry. "So sincere congratulations are in order. Frankly, we've all been wondering when you two would make it official."

Avram laughed and looked sideways at Penny.

"We've worked together so closely the last few years, she sort of got used to having me around and taking care of me."

"Something like that," said Penny and smiled back at him. "Anyway, Garry, we're going to get married soon. We're meeting a marriage celebrant this afternoon to get all the paperwork sorted out, that means a wedding in early March, so still lovely weather and we're going to have it on the beach at a hotel in Swansea."

"I think I know the one," said Garry. "Gorgeous place."

"And we'd like you to be Best Man," said Avram.

Garry grinned in great delight. "I'd be truly honoured. "Does this mean I have to hire a morning suit and a top hat?"

"Something a little less formal," said Avram. "Not quite board-shorts and bare feet, but almost."

"Does anyone else know?"

"We're going to announce it after this," said Penny. "We just wanted you to know first."

"Then I'm even more honoured," said Garry. "Now, some organisational stuff. I assume you'll want some months off before and after the birth?"

"Not much," said Penny. "This job is just too much fun and I don't want to miss a minute of what we're doing. And you've built this wonderful crèche and day care centre here, so we can pop in on the sprog at any time and know it's getting the best of care. So maybe a couple of weeks for our honeymoon and a couple of weeks either side of the birth date, that should be enough."

"I'm delighted to hear it," said Garry.

The bride looked quite beautiful as Bill led her down the aisle. The wedding was on a sizeable platform built on the beach and the sea, just a few metres away sparkled with energy and radiance to reflect the happiness everybody was feeling. The weather was perfect. Everybody from the company was there and a few people stood on the deck by the hotel, watching the proceedings.

Garry stood to one side with Avram, both dressed in slacks and golf shirts with blazers over the top of the shirts. The marriage celebrant, a young woman in her mid-thirties wore a long blue dress and a yellow, wide-brimmed hat, holding her documents at her waist in a black, leather case.

The ceremony went without a hitch and when the celebrant said, "And I can now pronounce you Husband and Wife! Penny, Avram, you may now kiss your new spouse," a loud cheer rang out from the congregation.

Laughing, the celebrant touched Avram on his shoulder. "Oye!" she said. "Enough! You can catch up with that later."

Signing the various documents by the couple and by Garry and other witnesses took twenty minutes and then the whole crowd went to the hotel for the party.

* * *

Garry drove home to the small cottage he had bought on five acres of land a little way out of Newcastle, his MGB sports car purring along happily and the top down, still one of the greatest pleasures he had ever had. He parked it under the roof of the extension and went in, poured himself a glass of scotch and took it with him as he did a small tour of the garden at the front of the house. The rose bushes were blooming nicely and there was a colourful mix of flowers along the front of the house.

He planned on having a quiet weekend. He was aware of some growing distress in his mind and understood what it was.

Loneliness.

His thoughts ran back to the difficult marriage he had experienced in his early professional working days and how relieved he had been to complete the separation and divorce and regain his freedom.

There had been a few temporary relationships after that, some had been fun, some had been difficult, the sex had varied between exhilarating and unsatisfying, but had been enough to keep him emotionally stable.

Then there had been Hannah. Initially, it had been wonderful, close, warm and with some exciting, athletic and inventive sex. But the discovery of her betrayal had been shocking, frightening and had left him with a deep distrust of any similar involvement.

He had met some delightful women in Australia, but as before, nobody had really stirred his senses. He wondered if he would ever meet anyone again who could lift him out of the pattern he was following. The work was extraordinary and absorbed him fully, knowing that he was playing a leading role in fulfilling Karen Petrova's dream of changing the world.

Today's wonderful wedding for Avram and Penny had delighted him but it had also increased the slight loneliness he was feeling.

The job still enthralled him and the sense of awe he experienced by being part of the earth-shaking developments resulting from Blueprints' discoveries gave him huge satisfaction. His "management by walking around" revealed no shocks and the discussions with Bill, Penny and Avram about developing a Rosetta Stone Calender which would allow them to fix the date of the events they saw in the past showed only that they were continuing to fill in the equivalent dates corresponding to the symbol found in the daily images of the DNA histories. There was as yet no sign of where they would find "Day 1" of the human race.

He tried to stop thinking and turned his mind to the pruning of some rose bushes and removing the dead blooms.

He stopped and stood straight as a car turned into his driveway. He didn't recognise it and in the glare of the later afternoon sun, couldn't see the occupant. But then the driver opened the door and stood up.

"So where is your protective band of Mossad agents?" said Garry with a delighted laugh.

"Probably hiding among those rose bushes," said Alana Shimova, once Israeli Military Attaché to the British Government.

"Alana, what a pleasure! What brings you here? Have you been appointed Ambassador to Australia?"

She walked up to him, placed her hands on his shoulders and kissed his cheek.

"Just by chance, I heard you were here and I dropped by." She stayed standing close to him and her hands remained on his shoulders.

"Just by chance? Somehow, Alana, somebody who has been a Military Attaché to Britain, a fighter pilot and I suspect a top Mossad agent has never done anything by chance."

She kissed him again. "Garry, how about you get the barbeque going and start on dinner? I've brought a couple of very nice bottles of wine, we can relax for the evening and then I'll tell you all about it."

"Ah!" he said, recalling the first time they had met in the Prime Minister's office in Downing Street. "You want the records of the Kennedy killings, don't you?"

She leaned back against the grip she had on his shoulders and looked at him seriously.

"I always knew you were a very clever man, Garry. Can we talk about it after dinner?"

He took the opportunity of their closeness to study her face. Her complexion was perfect, a straight, slender nose atop a wide, generous mouth, hazel eyes, it could have been the face of a teenager, but he doubted she could be under forty.

"I think so," he replied and regretfully felt her hands move off his shoulders and she moved away.

"I'll get the wine," she said and moved back to the car, returning with a shopping bag and a small suitcase. "Can we get the barbeque fired up?"

"Indeed," he replied. "That's on the back deck."

He led her through the house and she dropped the bag in the corridor, leaving the shopping bag on the kitchen counter top. They continued through to the back deck where he had a large lawn. He opened up the barbeque and set the burners alight.

"We should start on the wine," she said. "I'll make a salad and you can open the bottle."

The evening became a wonderfully relaxed time of sipping wine, sitting on the deck as the sun gradually set in the distance then standing together as he cooked the two steaks before they took seats at the table and ate the meal.

The table cleared, dishes in the dishwasher, Garry put a recording of Vivaldi's choral music on the CD player.

"If I remember Karen properly," said Alana, "she was a real fan of top quality scotch. I imagine you have some here."

"Best Islay," said Garry smiling.

"Pour some while I change," said Alana, picking up her bag. "Which is your room?"

Suddenly sensing huge excitement, Garry pointed to his doorway. She smiled and went in. Garry found the bottle of the best scotch he had and poured two small glasses, sitting down on the settee. A moment later, Alana appeared and Garry couldn't prevent a gasp. She had found one of his business shirts and put that on with nothing else. Long, exceptionally beautiful legs were revealed before him and as he looked further up, the shirt was open for several buttons, showing a generous cleavage. She picked up one of the glasses and sat down close beside him, her perfume reaching his nostrils. Her left arm went round his shoulders.

Garry felt a twinge of irritation, despite the erotic surge.

"Is this my reward for giving you the Kennedy recordings?"

She smiled, almost sadly. "No, Garry. It's my reward for getting them."

He didn't know what to say to that.

He touched her glass with his.

"Slainte Mhath," he whispered.

"Slainte Mhath," she echoed and they took a sip.

"Oh my!" she gasped, put the glass down, took his and did the same and then kissed him.

Garry felt his blood thundering in his head and his heart beating like thunder.

When he pulled away, he had difficulty breathing. He sensed the same reaction in her.

"We'll go to the bank tomorrow and get the records," he said, struggling to get the words out.

"That's tomorrow," she whispered. "This is now."

* * *

In the peace of the following morning as Alana snuggled up against his right side, his arm round her shoulder, he felt able to ask her.

"What does Israel want with those recordings?"

"Blackmail."

"Blackmail?"

"Congress is trying to cut back the defence budget for Israel. We need additional material because we know that Saudi Arabia is funding some more terrorist attacks on us."

"And you'll tell all unless you get what you need?"

"That's about it. When can we go and get them?"

"When the bank opens. One more question. Why did you come to get them? Couldn't they have sent somebody a bit lower on the totem pole?"

She kissed his shoulder. "They could. But I wanted the job. I wanted to see you again."

"That's nice. Meanwhile, what about breakfast?"

She kissed his neck.

"I'm here. You're here. Who needs anything else?"

It was a while before they got up, just in time to get to the bank as it opened.

On handing over the packets to Alana, Garry realised why she had brought her bag along. On returning to his house, she didn't go inside with him but placed her bag in her rented car.

"You have to go, don't you?" Garry said.

She nodded. Garry felt his stomach sink.

"New ambassador position somewhere?"

"Germany," she said.

"I'll never forget your visit," he said.

"Nor will I, Garry. It was beautiful and I'll treasure the memory."

"I wish you could stay."

She shook her head. "I'm not good at relationships," she said. "This is the better way."

She opened the driver's side door and climbed behind the wheel. She drove out of his driveway without looking back.

Garry was certain he had seen a small tear in each eye and he was sure that would be his last memory of her.

Chapter 16 – May, 2025

Garry was at his desk, writing up a summary of the week's work. It was the most routine part of his job and he had become almost bored by it, were it not for some of the astounding things that were still being discovered by his researchers. Increasingly, the young men and women were either following their own family histories or tracking back as far as they could go, often both. Many of them were working with historians, particularly archaeologists as they looked back to pre-historic times and the history of much of humanity was being rapidly rewritten.

The interruption gave him a break.

"Garry, you must really come and see this."

Penny had appeared at his door. She looked excited.

Garry stood up. "What have you got?"

"Something indescribable," she said and began to walk to the main area. At her desk, several of the researchers had gathered, all wearing expressions of excitement and astonishment.

"Put it on the main screen," said Penny and a few seconds later an image appeared on the enormous monitor at the back of the room.

"Stonehenge?" said Garry. "Have you been looking into how it was built?"

"That was the original idea and we've been following generations backward hoping to see that, but then this appeared and it's absolutely gob-smacked us."

Garry stared at the scene. He had visited the ancient and mysterious site in his youth and been affected by the immensity and history as most people were. But the difference now was astonishing. The tall stones were smooth, polished, the horizontal stones on the tops fitted exactly, almost like a modern construction.

"Five thousand years ago," said Penny to Garry's unspoken question. ""We believe this was soon after its completion."

On the monitor, people began to appear. There were men and women and they looked to Garry to be modern humans. They started to form into groups, lined up and all looking towards a central point. It looked like the scene was the viewpoint of one person standing in front of the group. To Garry, it reminded him of a choir lining up to sing in a chorale like *"The Messiah."* Indeed, they looked just like that, two groups of women on one side, two groups of men on the other, three lines of about ten people per line.

And then they began to sing. The sound was completely alien to Garry. It seemed discordant, no obvious melody, and yet... there was something hypnotic.

"We've never had any idea of what forms music took in these times, probably about 3000 BCE."

The speaker was Lorrie, he remembered her as the researcher who had found images of the Italian luthier, Nicolo Amati, one of the greatest makers of stringed instruments and possibly the teacher of Stradivari. Lorrie had played in the symphony orchestra in Reading in the days before the move to Australia and was one of the very first researchers hired in the company.

"So what am I hearing?" Garry asked, still hypnotically gripped by the sounds.

"First, it's a pentatonic scale, that's five tones, not the normal eight tone octave that we're mostly accustomed to," said Lorrie. "And that's astounding, given the fact that the five tone scale is a recent development in western music."

She looked at Garry. "But maybe not so astounding, as several experts, such as Orff think it's the natural scale for children. It's more common in Chinese music, however. It's a shock to hear it being sung five thousand years ago. But that's not the most astonishing thing we're hearing."

She paused and took a deep breath.

"There are thirty people in that choir." She paused again.

Curious, Garry prompted her. "And?"

"We're hearing sixty voices."

"What?"

Lorrie smiled. "Those people are each singing with two voices."

"What?

"There have been examples of something similar, even today. Mongolian throat singing is one and Canadian Inuit have something similar. It can sound almost like the drone of a bagpipe together with the melody of the pipe. But this is quite different. Each singer is actually singing two different melodies."

Feeling overwhelmed, Garry concentrated on the image. Slowly, he began to feel more at home with the music that had at first sounded discordant and he started to hear real beauty. But it was the fact of two voices singing in a single throat that was so startling.

After twenty minutes, the singing stopped. Garry took a deep breath.

"We need to get the experts here to see this," he said.

"I've already called the Australian Opera people in Sydney," said Lorrie. "They're sending up a few people tomorrow."

"Can I see that again?" asked Garry.

"I'm Jacqueline Harvey," said the youthful woman standing in the lobby where Garry had met the arrivals. She was perhaps in the thirties, dressed neatly in a black skirt and yellow blouse and her face was of a style that Garry had always found attractive, displaying a calm serenity and a mouth that settled in repose into a slight smile.

"I'm the Head of Music. This is Gerry Watson, our Chorus Master."

Garry shook hands with the tall, balding man in his fifties, wearing a conservative blue suit.

"And perhaps you know Olivia Baird," continued Jacqueline. "Our wonderful prima soprano."

Garry grinned in delight. "I saw you singing Turandot just a few weeks ago," he said. "I'm not sure I've got over the experience!"

The slender, beautiful woman smiled back. "That's nice to hear," she said. "But I understand that you have something astonishing to show us?"

"I think that barely describes it," said Garry. "Come with me. The staff are on tenterhooks waiting to show you this."

He led the way to the research area where all the staff were sitting on chairs they had moved to the back of the room. Quickly, Garry introduced the visitors, hearing the buzz of excitement when Olivia Baird's name was spoken and she waved and gave a brilliant smile to the group. Garry waved them to seats laid out before the main monitor and turned back to his researchers.

"Lorrie?" he said and stood back. Lorrie came to the middle of the room and stood by her desk.

"As you all know, we can look back in time through visual and aural records in our DNA," she began. "Last week, two of us decided to try and see if we could find the beginnings of Stonehenge. We haven't got there yet because we got distracted by this. It's a scene from 5,000 years ago."

She pressed a button on her keyboard and the huge monitor came alive. Garry decided to watch the visitors rather than the monitor and was not disappointed.

There was a stir of fascination as the first images of Stonehenge appeared.

"Archaeologists estimate that Stonehenge was completed about 3,000 BCE," said Penny. "You can see how new the stones look compared to the present day."

The choir appeared, took their positions and began to sing. The shock on all three of the visitors' faces was striking.

"Good God!" exploded Gerry Watson. The soprano let out a loud gasp, her jaw dropped and she gripped the arms of her chair as if clinging to a life saving support. Jacqueline sat back in her chair, her hands over her mouth, her eyes wide. None of them changed their position until the scene on the monitor ended, but Garry saw tears rolling down the cheeks of Olivia.

There was silence for over a minute. Garry tried to imagine just what a massive shock this was to people whose whole lives were taken up by singing and now had heard and seen a completely new form of their skills.

"I've heard Mongolian throat music," whispered Olivia. "I thought it was amazing. But this is… it's not anything I would have thought was possible."

The other two still seemed overwhelmed by the experience but after a few moments, Jacqueline took a deep breath.

"That was truly earth-shaking," she said. "I wonder if there's any medical knowledge that could indicate different vocal structures in humans of that era. If there was no physical difference, I imagine there will be a huge effort over the coming years to duplicate that skill. And if we succeed, imagine what composers are going to create to utilise it."

Gerry Watson tried to smile, but the shock was in his face still.

"We could save a bundle with only half the singers in the chorus," he said. "But I think you're right, Jacquie, if we find out how to do that, there are going to be astounding changes in music in the coming years."

Olivia wiped her eyes and turned to Lorrie.

"Will you play that again, Lorrie?"

Chapter 17 – February, 2026

Estimates were that over two hundred million people in America watched the broadcast by Cardinal Joseph Maguire.

"Good evening," said the Cardinal. He sat alone at a desk, dressed in his standard regalia of a black robe with a crimson sash and a red skull cap. A large golden crucifix hung on a chain round his neck.

"As all of you know, two years ago, British scientists made astonishing and unverified claims that they could look back through the past using technology that could read human DNA. Somehow, they were able to persuade the leaders of the Holy Roman Catholic Church and those of the Church of England that the eternal stories of our Lord Jesus Christ were nothing but myths and legends. As a result, both organisations abandoned our Lord, removing Him from the structure of our worship of God and amending the services of worship that have been with us for two thousand years.

"Some of the eastern orthodox Churches refused to accept this heresy and have declared their separation from the Vatican.

"I must tell you now that we of the American Catholic Church have also refused to accept this appalling heresy and we have therefore separated from everything the Vatican now stands for. We are telling you now that we have established an American Vatican, here in Dallas, we are completely devoid of any contact with the heretics in Rome, we accept no authority from them and we expect that all good Catholics in America will join us in maintaining the real truth.

"We have created fifteen new American cardinals and we will shortly convene this new curia to elect an American Pope. When that is done, we will be in contact with the leaders of the other churches in America to discuss the relationship they will have with us. May God bless America, may God bless all of you in Christ and we can look forward to a new era in which America truly leads the world in the name of Jesus Christ our Lord."

Maguire gave the sign of cross and the screen went blank.

* * *

"Archbishop Randle Patterson, Your Holiness," announced the young priest at the door to Joseph Maguire's office.

The man who walked in was immensely tall, close to two metres. His full head of red hair belied his sixty years and suggested possible Irish ancestry. He walked up to the heavy, satin-covered chair on which Maguire was seated and just a slight limp indicated the hip replacement of five years ago.

Maguire was dressed in the full white robes of a Pope, a red, gold-encrusted cape over his shoulders and a white skull cap. He held out his hand, palm down to show the ruby stone on the gold ring he wore. Rather than bend down and kiss the ring, Patterson took the hand, shook it and sat down in a less ornate chair across from Maguire.

"It's good to see you, Eminence," said Patterson. His voice was strong, an orator's voice accustomed to projecting over large congregations.

Maguire stared at him, his expression showing some anger.

"The correct address is 'Your Holiness' when addressing the Pope," he said.

"I know that," replied Patterson. "But the only Pope I know is the one in Rome. You may have declared yourself as the new Pope a few weeks ago, but not everybody is buying that."

"Does that mean you are another heretic who has chosen to abandon our Lord and his teachings?" The anger in Maguire's voice became stronger.

Patterson shrugged his shoulders. "Not necessarily," he replied. "I haven't had the experience of having my DNA scanned by this technology and seeing episodes in my life or those of various ancestors and I won't fully believe this until I do. But those guys in the Vatican, they're not fools and many of them have advanced degrees in various subjects, including science."

"And do all of your people in the Anglican Community share this evil?" demanded Maguire. This meeting was not going as he had expected.

"I don't believe so," said Patterson. "But we are faced with an unenviable situation. If I declare that we will follow the leads of Rome and Canterbury in adopting the so-called "New Christianity" then we will lose many thousands of my members who wish to remain in the traditional structures. But equally, if I declare that we will remain in those traditions, then I will also lose many thousands of my members who find the new concepts attractive. Either way, a major split is certain."

"And which way do you believe this split will occur?" asked Maguire.

"Our rather inexpert and non-scientific polling among the Anglican Community suggested that about seventy percent will remain true to the old beliefs," replied Patterson. "The remainder we expect will move to the Anglican Province of America."

Maguire eye's screwed up for a second as if in pain.

"That bastard Rees has declined our invitation to talk to me," he said, more of a mumble than clear speech. "So it's obvious he's joined the heretics. I never did trust that man when he took over from Bishop Grundorf when he died some years ago."

"I talked to *Bishop* Rees a few days ago," replied Patterson, emphasising the title as a light reprimand to Maguire. "And yes, almost all the congregation of the Anglican Province of America has declared their acceptance of the new order."

"And so what are you and your congregation going to do?" asked Maguire. "It is clear you will not join this true Catholic Church."

"You are correct," said Patterson. "We will not unite with you, our members have no appetite for many of your rituals. However, it seems likely that the major portion of us will continue in the traditional ways and then it is probable that we will agree to endorse your new Church and consider you to be the valid Pope."

"And your own personal views, your Grace?" asked Maguire.

"Not fully formulated. I have requested a meeting with one of the Canadian universities that have the equipment and to have a DNA reading done. I will finalise my position after that."

"And if you are lead by that machine of Satan to support the heresy, will you leave your own church?" Maguire looked shocked and angry.

"It's possible. I've already talked to Dai Rees about moving over to his people if that happens."

"Then you will be damned to eternal Hell!" shouted Maguire, losing control of the anger that had been simmering throughout the meeting.

"Unlikely," said Patterson and rose to his feet. He did not move to Maguire's chair but went directly to the door. "I'll keep you informed," he said, opened the door and left.

Chapter 18 – March, 2026

"Okay, everybody, all got your coffee?"

Garry looked round the table. The attendees looked comfortable and eager for discussion.

"I think," Garry began, "we can safely say that we have, as Karen would have put it, changed world."

There was muted laughter round the table.

"The thing I am sad about is that Karen didn't get to see most of what she has brought about," continued Garry. "The huge changes in the legal system were a great cause for satisfaction, she told me, but everything else has happened since her death."

"Those changes have now taken root almost everywhere except for the USA," said Mary Hennessey. "The religious right still has control of Congress and they firmly reject the use of the technology for any research."

"But it's a good sign that the President has refused to go along with that nonsense in international dealings," said Ben Fuller. "The way he blocked that invasion of Chad by the Libyan whacko a couple of years ago must remain one of the greatest examples of gentle persuasion in diplomacy!"

"Which explains why the religious nutcases have

been unable to remove him from office, despite having impeached him twice in Congress," said Garry with an expression of distaste.

"Fortunately there remain some intelligent people in the Senate," agreed Annabelle Calvert. "But I get rumours that the President is planning a nuclear option against those loonies in Congress. The next few weeks are going to be interesting."

"I'll wait with interest to see what happens," said Garry. "Meanwhile, I'm delighted to see that the total lack of privacy has resulted in extraordinary changes in international diplomacy."

* * *

"This is all a bit weird," said the British Prime Minister.

"I agree, Sir," said his personal assistant. "But it certainly guarantees there will be no surprises."

The PM stood in the small conference room next to the major meeting room that would be the scene of the Summit Conference between the United Kingdom and China. He had been briefed on all the topics scheduled for discussion, he had been similarly briefed on the Chinese Premier's life and personal details, what was safe for discussion, what was not. In earlier days, he had viewed scenes of the Premier's life taken from DNA samples in the hair clippings from his last haircut and he knew that Premier Ng Wah Lee would have done the same with the Englishman's life.

But this was still a little strange.

"It's time," said the PA. He was a man in his early thirties, recently retired from the Royal Air Force as a Squadron Leader, a pilot in the Transport group. He stood straight, as if on the parade square and his hazel eyes seemed to miss nothing. "Remember, Sir, it's

Premier Ng, pronounced Ung." He opened the door and the Prime Minister walked out into the brightly lit arena, already lit for the television cameras.

At the same moment, a door opened on the other side of the stage and the leader of the Chinese nation walked out. He was unusually tall, a good six feet despite a slight stoop. Jet black hair, horn-rimmed glasses framed a severe, thin face.

The two men advanced to the middle of the stage and shook hands.

"Premier Ng, a great pleasure," said the PM.

"Prime Minister Campbell, for me, also." The Chinese Premier had no accent that Campbell could identify, it could have easily been that of an educated Englishman but for the almost too-perfect intonation, so often encountered in Chinese with a sound British education. Campbell knew that Ng had been sent to Britain when he was twelve and had been schooled in Oxfordshire and then at London University with a First Class Honours degree in International Economics. Despite that, they would have interpreters behind them when they finally started the meeting.

"Shall we get this rather strange ritual over?" said Campbell.

A minute smile twitched the Premier's lips. "Let us," he responded.

Each man took his seat on either side of a small side table. They were immediately approached by their assistants who had now donned surgical gloves and carried a sample tube. Campbell opened his mouth, his assistant took a swab from inside his cheek and sealed the stick and sponge inside the tube. At the other seat, the same was happening with the Chinese Premier.

Both men rose, took the tubes from their assistants and turned to each other. Simultaneously, they handed the tubes to the other man.

"You now have a record of every second of my life until this moment," said Campbell. "I can deceive you about nothing."

The Premier nodded. "And I have given you a record of every second of my life until this moment," he said. "I can deceive you about nothing."

The words were specified and were the standard for every top level international meeting between heads of state.

"Then let us get down to business," said Campbell and took his seat.

"Indeed," said the Premier and did the same.

* * *

It's been a huge improvement," said Mary Hennessey. "One might call it The Day Bullshit Died!"

This time, the laughter round the table was loud and uninhibited.

Brad Robertson, the Canadian Futurist was the first to recover.

"This is truly an earth-shaking development," he said. "All the game-playing, the posturing, the sabre-rattling, it's all gone down the gurgler. Nobody can hide anything from anybody. It's bloody uncomfortable, but if it makes the world safer, I'm all for it."

"Damn right," said Garry. "Meanwhile, who has volunteered to go to Germany and talk to the Chancellor about implementing this new world?"

"I have," said Mark Craymer. "The easiest new implementation is in the justice system, as the Pommies have already done. So I'm heading up there next week and it's timely, because the Brits have expanded the system beyond the relatively simple and obvious case of murder and physical assault and we are doing the same here…"

*   *   *

The Judge looked curiously at the woman in the dock. She sat immobile, her jaw clenched and rigid anger showing in every atom of her body. She wore an expensive blue suit with a white shirt open at the neck. Diamond earrings hung from her earlobes and a large emerald ring was visible on her right hand.

The Judge nodded at the man sitting at a desk before him and he rose to his feet, addressing the woman.

"Gabrielle Helen Miller, you are charged with fraud in that you deliberately manipulated the stock price of your company to drive it very low, allowing you to buy large quantities, knowing that the company was about to acquire the rights to a new product that would return the stock to higher than previous levels. Do you plead guilty or not guilty?"

The woman remained silent. A woman at a desk to her left rose. Like her opposite at the Prosecution desk, she wore neither a wig nor a gown.

"Regina Simmons, Kings Counsel for the Defence, Your Honour. My client declines to enter a plea."

"Very well, Ms Simmons," said the Judge. "We will assume a plea of not guilty. Prosecution, are you ready to begin?"

"We are, Your Honour," replied the man at the table to the left of the centre of the court before the Judge. "Declan Reynolds, KC for the Crown." He continued to address the Judge.

"Your Honour, Ms Miller is the President of Cartwright Pharmaceuticals, a company in Bedford that manufactures numerous pharmaceutical products, both prescription and non-prescription. The company's records showed earnings of over a hundred million pounds for the last financial year and after accounting for depreciation and taxes, profits were over thirty million pounds. The company had recently been negotiating with the well-known scientific research company, Life Technology in Reading to manufacture a new product, a capsule that had displayed extraordinary results in curing eczema of the skin. It had been fully approved by the British Health authorities and was ready for commercial release. All the marketing research indicated the product would be a huge success, like all the products from this famous organisation created by the renowned Doctor Karen Petrova some years ago."

He paused and took a drink of water from a glass on his desk.

"Your Honour, we will show conclusively, that Cartwright had been notified of the success of their negotiations to win a licence and that all arrangements had been made to begin manufacture, once testing of the machinery had been completed and detailed auditing by Life Source of the chemical formula and manufacturing process had been completed. That would require approximately six weeks."

"And how will you demonstrate this, Mr Reynolds?" asked the Judge.

The barrister smiled.

"In accordance with all the laws established by law several years ago, Your Honour. Details of the group and personnel who conducted the extraction of Ms Miller's DNA and read the data are included in your bundle on page three."

"Very well, Mr Reynolds, let's see it."

A large screen dropped down from the ceiling against the wall on the Judge's left. The screen flickered then an image appeared. It was a single sheet of paper with the heading of Life Source Technologies clearly at the top.

"Your Honour will see that the letter formally informs Ms Simmons of the success of the application to manufacture the new product under licence."

"And this is the viewpoint through Ms Miller's eyes recorded on her DNA?"

"It is, Your Honour," replied the Barrister. "You will also see that the letter lays out the final details and timetable for manufacture and sales of the product."

"All right, Mr Reynolds, that point appears to be shown. Your next step?"

"This, Your Honour."

The screen showed a new image. A young man appeared to be listening intently as Gabrielle Miller's voice was heard.

"John, I hate to say it," said the voice of Miller, "but our profit levels will be down sharply in the coming quarter."

"How come?" asked the young man.

"The machines for making the packets of cold and 'flu medication are causing trouble," said Miller. "They're just not sealing properly. And the other production line for antacid caplets are also playing up. We've having to shut down both lines for at least a week and these are a couple of our biggest products."

"I can see that will hit you," replied the man. "Is this off the record?"

"Off it, of course," replied Miller. "So be discrete."

"As always," replied the man and strolled off.

"We have identified the man as John Carling, a reporter with the *"Financial Post"* said the Barrister.

"We have three more similar conversations with other people in the financial world and I can play those if Your Honour wishes."

The judge looked across at the Defence Barrister. She rose to her feet and shook her head.

"Defence concedes the accuracy of the recordings, Your Honour."

"What followed, Mr Reynolds?" asked the Judge.

"Shares in Cartwright plummeted by over forty percent," replied the Barrister. "Approximately eight pounds a share. We have the official data from the Stock Exchange to show that and that document is in your bundle, page five."

"And what happened?"

"Miss Miller bought one hundred thousand shares in the Cartwright company," replied the Barrister. "She accomplished that through a shell company that had been created two years ago. Three weeks later, the official word was released about the new deal with Life Source. Given the fame of that company and its products, it was no surprise that Cartwright's stock rose by over twenty-five pounds, seventeen pounds above its pre-fall level. Ms Miller then sold her shares and made a profit of one point seven million pounds, hidden away in her shell company."

"And what about those machine failures that Ms Miller had mentioned?" asked the Judge.

"No such failures had occurred," said the Barrister. "There was no loss of production and no drop in earnings for the quarter."

The Judge looked at the Defence Counsel.

"Anything to add, Ms Simmons?"

The woman rose to her feet.

"We cannot dispute the recordings shown, Your Honour. We have seen them and had them verified by own technical staff as recorded in your bundle, page four. We would now like time to prepare our statement of mitigation."

"Very well," said the Judge. "A week today?"

He rose to his feet and the court adjourned.

*   *   *

"Ah yes, I read about that case," said Mary. "It horrified me. That woman, Gabrielle Miller was worth about forty million pounds, I heard. What the hell did she need with another couple of million?"

"That's the super rich," said Jennifer Soo Ling Chang. "They never have enough. It's not what they can do with it, it's just numbers on the board."

"What happened?" asked Garry.

"Fined double the ill-gotten gains, ten years in prison, career destroyed," replied Mary. "But she'll be out in six, still have about twenty million and she'll still live the life of the very rich. Seems all wrong to me."

"Hey!" Mark Craymer let out a shout of surprise. He was staring at his mobile phone. "I just checked the ABC news. You'll never guess what's happened in the USA!"

Chapter 19 – April, 2026

"I bet you never thought you'd see the Situation Room," the president said. He stood at the head of the table as the five men and two women walked into the room. "I suppose I could say that you should be honoured, very few people see this room, but frankly, honour is not what this visit is all about."

He took his seat and waved at the others to do the same. They did, cautiously as if expecting the seats to collapse or blow up under them.

"I asked you here, because this room is more suited to our purposes and anyway, I didn't want you fouling the Oval Office. I have to work there."

The faces round the table looked shocked.

"What?" asked one of the men.

The President smiled a cold, chilling smile.

"Ah, Mr Harper, how appropriate that the Speaker of the House should be the first to speak! How about you, Mrs Druitt, does the Leader of the Senate want to add to your colleague's fine words?"

The older of the two women replied. She was in her mid-sixties, dressed in a conservative black dress with a string of pearls round her neck.

"Just why have you asked us here today, Mr President? It sounded threatening and I find that offensive."

"Well, you're quite right, Mrs Druitt. It was certainly threatening and as you will find, highly offensive. We are going to put a stop to your insanity of the last two years."

"And just what does that mean?" said Harper, the Speaker of the House. "What insanity are you talking about?"

"Let's start with your ban on the technology of reading DNA," said the president. "It's now in wide use around the world and proving invaluable. Tomorrow, you and your party are going to repeal that ban."

"Like hell we will," shouted Harper. "That's the work of the Devil! They used it to try and prove Jesus Christ never existed."

"Indeed they did. And proved it very well, judging by the acceptance of the fact by the Catholic and Anglican Churches. And instead of rational behaviour as they showed, you silly bastards banned the whole thing and broke away to start your own all-American Vatican."

"His Holiness is a true man of God," snapped Senator Druitt. "He was right to break away from that gang of heretics."

"And in the process, you have stifled vast schools of research at America's universities," continued the president, ignoring the interruption.

"We don't need research and we don't need universities," broke in another of the men. He was tall, thin, with an enormous forehead under a bald head.

"I'm sure you believe that Senator Barrow," said the president. "Educated people are dangerous, aren't they? They tend to see through your mob all too easily."

The Speaker looked furious but said nothing.

"Now I know that one of the things for which you have twice now had me impeached is that I refused to go along with that ban because it was vital for American security that I use it. Without it, I would have been at a serious disadvantage dealing with the rest of the world. There have been explosive issues of which you know nothing and I have been able to defuse them with this technology."

"And you will be damned to Hell for that crime," shouted another of the men at the table.

The president looked briefly at him.

"Somehow I doubt it," he replied.

"Is there something you want to say, Mr President?" said Senator Druitt. "If you have nothing useful to say but insulting us, we will leave."

"Oh, there's plenty more to say and even more for you to see," replied the President. "The second bit of insanity that will be removed today is your current plan to impeach me once more. You've done it twice and failed to have me removed."

"And we'll keep impeaching you until we succeed," said the woman harshly. "Godless devils like you should never be allowed in the White House."

"And you are all men and women of God, eh?" said the president with a smile.

"Certainly more than you," the senator replied.

"Well, let's see, shall we? Over the last two weeks, we have been able to acquire samples of DNA of all of you here. It's very easy to do. Actually, we have samples of many more members of your party, but you will do for now."

There was a shocked silence in the room.

"And you know what's coming now, don't you," said the president. "Shall we start with you, Senator Druitt?"

On one side wall, a panel slid aside to show a large television monitor. A woman appeared on the screen, fully displayed in a mirror. It was the senator, looking at herself. She wore silk pyjamas and gave herself a satisfied smile.

The view changed as the woman walked to a chair by a coffee table on which was a bowl of something black, a plate of smoked salmon and a bottle in a cooler.

"That's Beluga Caviar, senator, smoked salmon and a bottle of the finest French Champagne, *Bollinger Les Vieilles Vignes Francaises* in fact," said the president. "Retails at about $275 a bottle. We know that because we watched through your DNA as you bought these a few days ago."

All the faces were riveted to the screen. The senator seemed to be breathing heavily, the breath rasping in her throat. The image showed the woman helping herself to a glass of champagne and then reaching for a television controller, switching on a huge television in front her.

A scene appeared on the television. It showed a young man, stripped to just his underpants tied to a wooden chair. It appeared to be in a garage or workshop, the floor was concrete and no fixtures could be seen on the walls, nor any window.

The senator suddenly screamed.

"Stop this! For God's sake, stop this!"

"I think not, Senator Druitt," replied the president. "We need to see your taste in entertainment."

The scene on the television now showed two large, muscular men dressed only in loin cloths. One of them slammed a fist into the young man's face while the other held a knife which he used to slash a deep cut across the victim's chest. The young man screamed.

"Oh please, I beg of you," whispered the senator. "For the love of God, stop this."

"God, senator? You have accused me of being a Godless devil. What has the love of God got to do with this? Let's see how this ends, eh?"

The man with the knife plunged the weapon into the victim's chest, withdrew it and then sliced the young man's throat. Blood poured in hideous gushes over the concrete floor.

The men and women round the table were horrified. One of them got up and was sick in a corner. All of them were white-faced, breathing heavily.

"I think they're called snuff films," said the president calmly. "Very hard to obtain and seriously expensive. You've bought a few of them, we have found. Of course, now we know where you get them, who makes them and especially who those two killers were. Police officers are arresting all of them about now. The young man was an eighteen-year old student at Princeton, studying mechanical engineering. He leaves behind his parents and a young sister who adored him."

The senator was weeping into her hands and didn't respond. The monitor went blank.

"Do you ever wonder what your extraordinary taste in entertainment costs the people who lose loved ones, Senator, never mind the gratuitous waste of young lives that you enjoy watching?"

The woman didn't respond.

"Okay, who's next?" said the president. "How about you, Speaker Harper?"

The Speaker seemed to be catatonic, staring into the distance.

"This happened in your apartment three nights ago," said the president.

The screen came alive again as the watcher advanced to the door at the sound of a knock. The door opened to reveal two young girls wearing school uniforms. They looked barely in their teens.

"No! No! No!" screamed Harper. "You can't do this!"

"Oh, but I can," replied the president, but stopped the display. "And what's more, I have similar very ugly stuff on all of you. Congresswoman Laslo, you have young male escorts come to your house and give you some rather violent sexual experiences."

The second women remained silent.

"I'm sure your husband wouldn't approve," continued the president. "And you, Congressman Walters, you have a whole series of prostitutes visiting and it seems you like them to hit you with a cane across the buttocks and give you golden showers. Not very nice, is it?"

He smiled round the table.

"Now, I have no stomach for watching any more of the depraved madness you get up to, but obviously, it's not difficult to find anything at all. That's the upside and downside of our brave new world where there's no privacy any more. So here's what is going to happen."

He pointed at Senator Druitt and Congressman Harper.

"You will announce your resignations on medical grounds tomorrow. You will also advise your party that you will repeal the ban on the DNA technology immediately. Both of you will be allowed the time to arrange this before your arrest. And unless you can find some actual High Crimes and Misdemeanours for a genuine impeachment process, you will abandon your current attempt. The country is sick of your behaviour. Have I made myself understood?"

He looked around the table and saw nothing but white, frightened faces.

"Good," said the president. "Now get the hell out of this house."

* * *

"That's amazing," said Garry. "The ban on the technology has been lifted?"

"They announced that a few hours ago," said Mark. "And it seems that both the Speaker of the House and the Senate Leader are retiring on medical grounds."

"You know what," said Mary. "Having heard how that president dealt with the Libyan thing, I wonder if he showed some nasty secrets to those people and somewhat forced the issue?"

"Probably," said Mark. "That's a massive breakthrough."

"Okay, back to business," said Garry. "What's next?"

"I got a letter from the Australian Psychological Society," said Ben Fuller. "I've been talking to them because my brother-in-law is a shrink and he suggested that our technology could be a great help in their work. They said they've been trialling the systems with a few of their best professionals and they see great value."

* * *

"Come in, Alexis," said the therapist as the tall, fit-looking young woman appeared in the doorway.

"Thanks, doc." Alexis moved into the small consulting room and took the comfortable seat across from the therapist. "You said you had something special for me today," she said and wriggled herself into a more settled position.

"Indeed I do," replied the middle-aged woman in the other seat. She wore a plain blue sweater over a grey skirt and she looked relaxed. Her mouth seemed to smile as a habit.

"Alexis, a few days ago, we came across the traumas from your childhood with a bullying, abusive mother. I believe we can do something significant today."

The woman grimaced in embarrassment, looked down at her lap and scratched her cheek. "I don't think I have collapsed in tears like that since I was a sprog," she said. "I had no idea how hard those memories hit me."

"It's not uncommon. You'd be surprised how many of my patients have had similar experiences and share the same sort of emotional scars as you have."

Alexis coughed nervously. "Sometimes I think people should have to get a licence to have kids," she said. "And then only after passing a series of psychology tests. Maybe you could develop some?"

The therapist smiled. "We may have better ways of helping now," she said. "Alexis, I told you I'd acquired some new technology a few weeks ago and with your consent, I took a DNA sample from you. You said I could review the data and as you know, this is how the courts work now. We can look back at your life and also the early life of both your parents and even further back."

The young woman looked interested and leaned forward, her elbows on her knees.

"Is this what you're going to show me?"

"It is. But I must warn you, the first part of this is going to be very painful, but by the time we have finished, I believe you will have realised the truth of what happened to you and understand it."

"That sounds good. What are you going to do?"

The psychologist took a plastic slide and inserted it into a reading device on the small computer on her desk. "Over the last couple of days, I've gone through your childhood and found the episodes that caused the main damage. I'm going to show one of those now. Ready? Watch the screen."

Alexis moved her seat round a little and faced the large monitor on the wall. It came alive with a woman's face, displaying huge anger, her eyes wide open, staring straight at the viewers. Alexis shrank back in her chair.

"Oh my God! That's my mother!" she whispered.

"You're a rude, stupid little girl!" shouted the woman on the screen. "You're a pest! I wish I'd never had you!"

The image was rocked as the woman swung her hand hard against the little girl's face.

"Oh, Jesus," groaned Alexis. "This is horrible."

"Stay with it," the therapist said. "Just a little longer."

The image shook again as another blow landed on the child's face.

"You're stupid!" screamed the woman in the screen, "utterly stupid! You're a complete failure!"

Yet another blow landed and the girl obviously fell off her chair. All the screen showed was the dull carpet and the image was corrupted by the tears in the child's eyes.

"Now get up to your room and stay there," said the mother's voice. The young Alexis climbed to her feet, weeping and ran out of the room, up the stairs and the image went dark as she fell onto her bed, face against the pillow. The sound of her sobbing was the only feature to be heard.

The therapist stopped the scene.

Alexis was breathing hard, tears rolling down her cheeks. "That was bloody awful," she muttered. "I think I might have been about six or seven. What good did it do to show me that? I thought I was getting over it."

"You'll understand soon," the therapist said. "Now, to explain a bit. As you probably know, the record of your mother's life is passed to you at the moment of procreation. So that means, the images we could get of her life from the images in your DNA would be up to that moment only. But luckily, you have a sister who is a few years younger than you. I called her a couple of days ago."

Alexis sat up. "You called Evie? How did she react?"

"When I told her what I wanted, she was fascinated, because you've both had the rotten experience with your mother. So she was happy to come in and give me a DNA sample and I was then able to see your mother's life for a few more years after she'd had you and this is what I got. This is from your mother's memory moments after that beating we just saw."

The screen came alive again. The viewer was focused on the seat in front, obviously the seat just vacated by the weeping young Alexis.

"Oh Jesus Christ! Why do I do it?" came a voice.

"That's my mother speaking!" said Alexis in astonishment.

On the monitor, the image became blurred as tears rolled out of the woman's eyes. The view changed as her head turned to see the door open and a man came in.

"That's my father!" exclaimed Alexis. "Jeez, he looks young!"

"So you've been hitting her again, have you, you rotten bully?" said the man, Alexis' father. "Amazing how you always manage to do it when I'm out."

His face was furious, spoiling what would otherwise be handsome features. "So what the hell brought this latest ugliness?"

The mother shook her head and more tears filled her eyes. She wiped them away with one hand.

"She was insolent. And I lost my temper."

"You mean she tried to tell you she hadn't done whatever it was you were yelling about? Can't you ever control yourself enough to think about what you're doing?"

The woman said nothing, but the watchers in the room heard a loud sniff and a deep breath being taken.

"You're just a bully," continued the father, his anger growing. "And I bet like all bullies, you're a bloody coward. What do think will happen when she gets a bit older? She's a big girl for her age now, she'll be bigger than you when she gets to be about sixteen and what do you think will happen when you try this stupidity on her?"

"Maybe that's what I deserve," the woman muttered. "I wish to God I knew how to stop myself."

The man's face softened as did his tone.

"You need help, Jennifer. And if you don't see a doctor about this and get some treatment, I'll leave you and take the kids. I'm not going to live with a child-beating sociopath and nor are they."

He turned and walked out of the room. The woman collapsed in her seat and began to weep uncontrollably.

The scene ended.

Alexis let out a long sigh.

"Holy crap!" she said. "I had no idea. It looks like she had some pretty severe mental issues herself."

"And possibly not surprising, she took your father's ultimatum and sought help," continued the doctor. "This is what I found about a week after the episode we just saw."

She turned back to the keyboard and a moment later, another scene appeared. The eyes of the watcher looked at an elderly man sitting in an armchair across from the watcher, perhaps two metres away. He wore a dark suit, a white shirt and a blue tie. Gold cufflinks showed on his sleeves. He looked like a successful business executive or banker.

"I just can't stop myself," said a woman's voice, the same voice of Alexis's mother from the earlier episode.

"What happens?" asked the man across from her.

"The kid does something and I feel my temper rising."

"Is what your daughter does something wrong?"

The scene went dark for a few seconds as the mother closed her eyes.

"Not usually. Sometimes she answers back, denies having done what I said she'd done..."

"And is she right?" asked the therapist.

The scene blurred as tears appeared in the mother's eyes.

"Usually," she replied.

"And yet you carry on with your temper and start shouting at her and hitting her?"

The tears got worse.

"Yes."

"And why do think you do that?" The therapist leaned forward in his seat.

"I don't know." The mother's voice was thick with tears now. "I just lose it."

"Is that how your mother treated you?"

"Very often."

"Then I think, Jennifer, we have something to work on. You've done what so many people do, carried on with learned habits from childhood."

The screen went blank and the therapist sat back in her seat.

"So you see, your mother really regretted her bullying but was driven by other factors. And now you'll see where they came from." The therapist tapped a few keys. "I spent a few hours yesterday seeking out these moments and now I'll show you something else. I went back through your mother's life to her early years and this is what I found from when she was about the same age you were when that first episode was shown."

The scene was much worse than the first one Alexis had seen from her own childhood. From the eyes of her mother as a young girl, Alexis saw an enraged woman swing a full fist into her cheeks and she collapsed onto the floor, Briefly, Alexis could see a dingy room, dirty curtains and badly worn armchairs. Then the furious woman that Alexis now realised was her grandmother hauled up the little girl by her blouse and swung a fist into her face again.

"You little bitch, I'll beat the crap out of you if you ever do that again! Do you understand? Eh? I said, do you understand?"

Another blow landed and the girl fell down onto the carpet again. She wriggled away and found the door, opened it and ran for the outside.

The therapist stopped the scene and sat back in her seat.

"Now do you understand?" she asked softly.

Alexis sat silent for several minutes, staring at the floor.

"God God!" she finally said. "I had no idea what she had gone through."

"I'm pretty sure that if we went back through your grandmother's life, we'd see similar scenes," said the therapist. "These habits are learned and it becomes very difficulty to avoid repeating them."

"Paul and I are planning to have a kid in the next couple of years," murmured Alexis. "I realise now I've always been a bit worried about how I'd handle that."

"People either follow the habits they learned in their youth or they realise the problem and break as far away as they can. I think that having seen these episodes, you will understand how they happened and be able to avoid the problems. With understanding comes forgiveness and maybe now you can forgive your mother for what she did to you."

Alexis was leaning forward, her elbows on her knees again. Tears were running down her face.

"I wish I'd know all this before," she said, having difficulty speaking through the tears in her throat. "I wouldn't have hated the woman so much. But you're right, there's no way I'll be able to treat my own kids that way now."

She paused for a few moments. "Will you show my sister these things as well? I'm sure she'd understand a lot better."

"She's coming in this afternoon," replied the therapist. "And I'm sure you're right. I bet you two will have some interesting talks after!"

Alexis waved at the computer and the monitor.

"I'd heard about this stuff, of course and I knew how the police and courts were using it, but I never really understood. Now I do. Thank God for it, doctor! I think I can handle things a lot better now."

"I'm sure of it," said the therapist with a smile.

"Now go home and start living your life as a much healthier person. I don't think I need to see you again."

Alexis stood up. "I think I need to wash my face and freshen up," she said with a smile. "Thank you doc, I think you've saved my marriage, maybe my life."

She walked out and the therapist stayed on her feet, smiling at the closed door.

"Thank you, Karen Petrova," she said softly. "You've made my job a lot easier."

* * *

"I'm sure Karen would be delighted with that development," said Garry with a smile. "How much is that in use so far?"

"Just trials with five psychologists," said Ben. "My brother-in-law says all of them are delighted with the results. He reckons it will be nation-wide within a year."

"I can hardly begin to imagine the value of that development," said Brad Robertson. "Just think of how much mental trauma it might relieve."

"I do wish Karen could be here," said Garry. "I doubt she ever truly envisaged just how much she would change this world, mostly for the better. She and Hector must go down as the most incredible people in history, right up there with Pasteur, Madame Curie and the rest of them."

"What's happening in the medical world?" asked Robert Swann. "Ever since young Avram started growing back his finger, I imagine even more upheavals among the surgeons."

"It's being quietly used," said Mary. "We've found out where the stimulus happens in the brain and there are trials happening in that field also…

* * *

The surgeon pushed back the X-ray machine from the chest of the man lying in the table.

"It's a very good job you came in when you did," she said. "Michael, you could have died within a few days."

"Good god!" explained the patient. "I thought I was just getting chest pains. What's wrong?"

"Two of your heart valves are nearly gone," said the surgeon. "The mitral valve that helps pump blood into the heart is leaking badly, and the aortic valve that pumps blood out from the heart is a bit worse, some decay setting in."

"So it's surgery?" Michael said, struggling to keep his voice calm. "Two valve replacements? I think I've read somewhere that it's pretty standard surgery. What do you think, doc, a mechanical valve or a donor from a pig or cow?"

The surgeon was taking off her gown. "That used to be the choice," she said. "We began some major developments with stem cells some years ago and that showed a lot of promise, but the new discoveries gave us a much better path."

"What's that?" The patient seemed more interested than fearful.

"You'll regrow new valves yourself," said the surgeon. She returned to the table from disposing of her gown. Without her face mask, she seemed surprisingly young, perhaps in her thirties and without any trace of make-up, looked almost like a school girl.

"Can you tell me?" the man asked.

"Let's get you safely back into the ward first," the surgeon said and waved the two attendants in. Very gently, they lifted the man onto a trolley.

"As of right now, you must stay very still to prevent any undue stress on those valves. You're not getting out of your bed, you're not going to sit up, you're not going to apply any effort anywhere at all."

"Oh god, that sound dreadful," said Michael, some stress showing at last. "How long is this going to last?"

"Two months."

"Two months? My god, I can't lie here for two months! I'll go mad."

"We'll actually keep you unconscious most of the time," said the surgeon. "We'll put in drains to eliminate all surplus materials, feed you through tubes and then just wake you for a couple of hours a day so that you can see visitors, retain a sense of time passing and just let us know how you're feeling. We'll remove the faulty valves, put in temporary valves that still allow the new ones to grow and we've learned which part of the brain to stimulate to start the regrowth."

"But won't my arm and leg muscles atrophy if they don't move for a month?"

"Good question, but don't worry. We'll apply electrical stimulation frequently. "You'll certainly be very weak when you finally are ready, but a few days of exercise will clear that."

"And you're sure this will work?"

"Michael, we've done this several times. It works. Do you know that people have been able to grow new livers, new kidneys, even fingers and toes after accidents?"

"I had no idea. Okay, Doctor, let's get this started."

The surgeon smiled and waved at the orderlies to take the man back to his ward.

* * *

"There's no doubt, the world is changing," said

Mary. "This is truly a Second Renaissance happening here. Garry, what are your people working on? Anything as astounding as the vocal abilities of pre-historic Man or equally mind-blowing discoveries?"

"Aren't those enough?" retorted Garry with a laugh. "But yes, they keep looking for stuff like that. But maybe the critical one is working out how the numbering system works and how it relates to historical events."

"Can you clarify that a little?" asked Annabelle, the historian. "I haven't heard much about this."

"I suspect it may be the most earth-shattering development of all of them, once we get to the bottom of it," said Garry. "Let me refresh your minds. Our resident genius, Bill, found a small symbol at the start of each day of a person's DNA record. It baffled him and if something baffles Bill, be sure it's bloody important. So he actually called in help, something he has never done before, in the shape of Avram and Penny.

"They turned their almost immeasurable combined IQ points to the problem and eventually realised the symbol was actually a representation of a number."

"What sort of number?" asked Salmaan Basrai, the statistician.

Garry shrugged. "So far, we have very little idea. But what they did find was that the symbol changed one of its variables by incredibly tiny increments when they went back a few years in the DNA record. And when they checked a number of records from different people, the symbol was identical on the same day of each of those records."

"So it's a numbering system!" exclaimed Basrai. "Does that mean we'll be able to pin-point the date of an event or any day at all?" Excitement shone in his face.

"That's what we hope," said Garry. "So they've taken on a huge, laborious task to find dates which are known and they can relate the DNA record to it. Then they copy the symbol and display the number of days that have passed since our base record."

"So how far back will this go?" asked Annabelle, also displaying huge interest.

Garry shrugged. "That's what the three are looking for," he said.

"Can you show us this thing?" asked Mark Craymer.

Garry turned to the white board behind him and drew a rough representation of the symbol.

"Let's see if I can describe this," he said. "That dot moves along the line a specific distance each day. Now, the symbol is tiny, only readable with a scanner that sees down to the atomic level. So when the team look at the images, they expand them to about twenty-five by twenty-five centimetres. Even then, without powerful instrumentation, we can't see a single day's movement, but Bill found that one millimetre represents 472 days. That doesn't relate to any numeric system that we know of.

"Other variables probably include the angle of the two straight lines where they meet at the bottom, the length of the short tail of the curve at the bottom, right-hand end, the length of the tail of the straight line at the top left-hand corner and the size of the three enclosed areas. But we haven't yet been able to check out this theory."

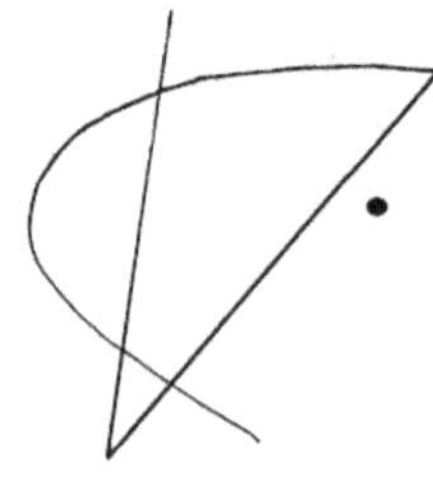

"Have they worked out what the variables are worth, what they represent?" asked Basrai, staring at the symbol.

"Nowhere near," said Garry. "But they also think that additional variables are in the thickness of each line. So far, they haven't gone back far enough to see any changes in those."

"This is quite stunning," said Brad Robertson. "It certainly seems to point to one of our more way-out concepts."

Garry nodded. "It's nothing human, that's a fact," he said. "Meanwhile, we're still getting reports that the American Catholic breakaway Church is having problems."

Chapter 20 – June, 2026

Newly elected Pontiff by the Dallas-based break-away Catholic Church of America, Joseph Maguire now proclaimed as Pope Clement 15th was furious.

"What do you mean, he won't come and see me?" he shouted.

The young priest who acted as the new pope's personal secretary flinched visibly but stood his ground.

"When I received no answer to my letter to President Sanders in Utah inviting him to Dallas, Holiness, I called him. He took my call personally and was very courteous but he said he saw no value in a meeting."

"Did he explain why?" Maguire was visibly angry, red spots appearing on his cheeks and his lips pressed in a thin line before he spoke.

"He did, Holiness. He said that the Church of Latter Day Saints could not accept a schism in the Catholic Church and so could not recognise an American Vatican. He said he would be quite happy to discuss this with you by phone or preferably by Skype but he would not travel to Dallas."

"Skype? What the hell is Skype?"

The priest was unmoved.

"It's a technology, Holiness, by which we can use the Internet for a telephone call and also permits visual contact at a computer screen so you can talk face to face."

"And do we have this thing here?"

"We do, Holiness and I can set it up in your office within an hour if you wish it."

Maguire looked worried and tapped the top of his desk for a few moments.

"Okay, do that and arrange a time when we can have this discussion," he said finally.

The priest bowed. "Of course, Holiness," he said and left the room.

It was the following morning before a suitable time for both parties could be found. Meanwhile, a computer had been set up in Maguire's office with a large monitor and sound speakers. A second monitor was set up to one side for the Pope's personal assistant to manage the system.

"Where do I speak?" asked Maguire, looking uncomfortable.

"The Skype camera has its own inbuilt microphone," replied the priest.

"What camera?" asked Maguire in bewilderment.

The priest pointed at the tiny camera perched on top of the monitor.

"That's a camera?"

"It is, Holiness. No need to look directly at it when you speak, President Sanders' face will almost fill the monitor, so just look at him as if you were in the same room."

"Quite extraordinary," muttered Maguire. "Let's get on with it."

A few moments later, the blank screen was filled with the lean, distinguished face of the president of the Church of Latter Day Saints, Jeremy Sanders.

"Good morning, Cardinal," said Sanders.

"I am no longer a Cardinal," said Maguire. "You must address me as "Holiness" or Holy Father."

"Sorry, no," replied Sanders. "As I explained to that pleasant young man who called me, the Church of Latter Day Saints does not recognise this new Western Schism as valid, so I will not apply such an invalid title to you."

Maguire struggled to control his anger.

"Does that mean you accept this appalling heresy that is afflicting the world that Jesus Christ did not exist?"

"My people are in two minds, Cardinal," replied Sanders. "Most do, many do not, but honestly, it makes no difference."

"That's terrible!" said Maguire. "How can you accept a bunch of scientists denying the Biblical truth? And how can it make no difference?"

Sanders shrugged and smiled.

"Cardinal, I have a master's degree in physics. Many of my people are educated scientists and we have seen demonstrations of this technology. I myself went to Chicago a few weeks ago, to Northwestern University and the people there were happy to show me. Do you know, I saw scenes from when I just five years old? And then I saw my grandfather as a teenager and then *his* father as a middle-aged preacher in Wisconsin? It convinced me that we can look back through time and if the Pope, the *real* Pope, that is," he smiled slightly at the gasp of rage that Maguire emitted, "can change the entire Catholic Church on the basis of what he and his people have seen, that's good enough for me."

Maguire took a deep breath.

"You said your own people are split on this. Does that mean that the Mormons might break apart?"

"I have no doubt many might leave the church," replied Sanders. "But so far, nobody has, to my knowledge. As I said, belief or otherwise in the divinity of Jesus makes no difference to us. We will do as the Roman Vatican and Canterbury have done, continue to believe in and support the teachings of the young Rabbi, Jesus of Nazareth and his colleagues. Our main focus is on strong families, loving our kids and helping the poor and the sick, it has always been that and nothing will change it."

Maguire sensed that he had lost control of the discussion. The tall, impressive Mormon in the computer monitor was showing no signs of reverence to him and had quite plainly refused to acknowledge Maguire's new American Church.

"Then I cannot count on you to support my church?" he said.

Sanders shrugged. "Our support is irrelevant. We certainly cannot endorse your claim to be the new Catholic Church that has replaced the Roman Vatican, but we see no reason to oppose you actively in any way."

"Your missionary work in Thailand obviously corrupted you," said Maguire, contempt in his voice. "I'm surprised you didn't become a Buddhist."

Sanders laughed. "It presented its attractions," he said. "I met many Buddhist monks and delightful people they were, all of them. We discussed our faiths and found many common elements, far more than I do with your brand of Christianity, Cardinal."

Maguire became enraged.

"Then may all of you, Mormons, Buddhists,

heretics, all of you will rot in Hell!" he shouted. "Turn this thing off," he snapped at his assistant and walked out of his office.

Maguire watched in satisfaction as Allan Denton bowed at the door before advancing and bending over, kissed the ring on the hand proffered to him.

"A great honour, Holiness," said the President of the Southern Baptist Congregation. His voice was a pleasant tenor with just a slight edge of tension in the tones.

"We are glad that you accepted our invitation, Reverend Denton," said Maguire with a smile of welcome. "Please take a seat."

Denton did as instructed, moving easily, no sign of any physical infirmity, looking very much younger than his 61 years, aided by a full head of light brown hair.

"I understand that the Southern Baptists have rejected the heresy of the Roman Vatican," said Maguire.

Denton inclined his head.

"Indeed we have, Holy Father," he replied. "We were shocked and horrified when the pretender in Rome used the power of his office to embrace such an appalling wickedness and deny the divinity of our Lord Jesus Christ."

"And do you then support the moves we true believers in America have made?"

Denton nodded. "Of course, Holy Father, what other options could there be? Going with those Eastern Orthodox churches who have also stayed with the truth was not a viable course for us apart from the simple fact is that we truly believe that the leadership of the Mother of Churches should come to America."

"God bless you," said Maguire and made the sign of the cross. "Reverend Denton, I believe we can achieve more together than as two entities. Could your people look with interest on merging our two churches?"

Denton showed no surprise at the question.

"I believe most would," he replied. "You must know that we have been losing numbers heavily in recent years, largely because of the influx of perhaps less desirable elements, especially here in Texas."

Maguire gave a sympathetic smile. "The numbers of Hispanics, Blacks and Asians has been a worrying factor for us also."

"I believe that we would lose the Blacks and the Asians," said Denton. "The Hispanics tend to a more conservative form of Christianity and would probably be most enthusiastic about joining you. Frankly, I would consider it no loss if those other two groups left us."

"We appear to be of the same mind," said Maguire. "I suggest that we set up a working party of people from both our churches and have them develop the action plan for you to show your true Christian beliefs by merging with us."

"I will propose that to my ruling council as soon as I get back," said Denton.

"Wonderful," said Maguire and extended hand, palm down. Recognising the dismissal, Denton stood up, walked over and again kissed the ring.

"Holy Father, my people will rejoice," he said and walked out quietly.

*   *   *

"So some sects have aligned with the new American church, some have refused?" said Mark.

"That's about it," said Garry. "There are deep concerns within the old Catholic Church that the split will lead to violence, given the American propensity for solving problems with guns."

"And now that the President has forced Congress into accepting the technology, it may get worse," said Ben Fuller, the sociologist. "Many millions of people in strong, deeply religious opposition to the government is a recipe for disaster."

"You're thinking another civil war?" asked Mary in horror.

"Not out of the question," replied Ben. "It's probably an even more divisive issue than slavery was."

The rest of the meeting was subdued.

Chapter 21 – August, 2026
Tracking the Date

Penny sat back and stretched. Then she leaned back to the monitor and continued following the timeline of a woman who apparently lived in Victorian times, judging by dress. Penny had already seen the woman look at a newspaper and read of a robbery in Manchester, but the date had not been clear. Penny was hoping to find a specific date that could be clearly identified. She went forward another day, then a third and suddenly heard a voice coming from somewhere in the room.

"Margaret! It's all over the town!" said a deep male voice and a man appeared in the subject's vision. He was rather stout, though tall and clean-shaven. He looked quite prosperous. "The Queen is dead!"

"Oh my God!" exclaimed the woman. "How awful!"

"Aha!" said Penny. "It's the twenty-second of January, 1901." She looked for the minute symbol that indicated the day's number and copied it to the file she was building. "Good! Another one found."

She checked her watch and realised she had been sitting at her computer for four hours straight without a break.

"Time for lunch," she muttered to herself and got to her feet.

The canteen was busy when she got there. Filling a plate with cold cuts and salad, she saw Bill sitting alone in one corner, though Avram was approaching him with his own tray of food. She walked up, greeted them and sat down. She knew that she and Avram were probably the only people in the whole organisation who could do that, most everybody else left their resident genius strictly alone. But a barrier had been dropped when the three of them had identified the numbering system involved in the strange symbol of the DNA records.

"Hey!" she said as she sat down.

"Hey," echoed Avram.

Bill raised one finger in a tiny salute. Penny and Avram grinned at each other. They knew that for Bill, that was an ecstatic welcome.

"How's it going?" Bill looked up from his beef stew and rice.

"This is a long, hard project," Penny replied.

"We knew it would be," said Avram. "What have you done this morning?"

"Recent history is far easier than older stuff," said Penny. "But I got lucky, I tracked back somebody who gave us their DNA a few days ago and she had told us that her great grandparents had lived during Victoria's reign. So I worked back and found the day when Victoria died. She and her husband were both terribly upset. So that was easy, I copied over the symbol with the day's date."

"I was doing something similar," said Avram. "I followed my own DNA back through my grandfather and then my great grandfather who I knew served in World War One. So I saw a newspaper he was reading when the War was declared and that gave me one day's symbol and I was also able to find the day the War ended, so that gave me a second symbol."

"It's going to get harder and harder as we go back," said Bill. "Nothing for it but to work our way through hundreds of life records and hope we stumble on historic moments that we can identify with an actual date."

"Eventually, we'll have enough key dates and we can count the number of days between each one." Penny took a bite of her cold ham with a slice of tomato and chewed thoughtfully. "If those dates stretch over a few thousand years, we should be able to work out how the symbol changes each day and start filling in each day's number.

"How are you doing with measuring those changes, Bill?" asked Avram.

"Like Penny said, once we have enough key points in time, I reckon I'll be able to count accurately enough to complete just about every day back to the beginning," said Bill. "But there's no doubt, the scale is incredibly tiny."

"But you think you'll be able to read it accurately?" Penny cut another slice of ham and added cucumber.

"Yes. At some stage, we'll be able to look at that symbol and see how many days ago it was and so tell the date."

"That will open up the whole of human history," said Avram. "Just imagine how that will change things."

"The biggest problem is going to identifying just what we're seeing," said Penny.

"And mostly, it's going to be battles," said Bill. "By the time we're before the Common Era, battles will be the only thing that we'll be able to see where we know something critical is happening."

"Unless we see something that the history buffs could recognise and place it to a firm date," added Penny.

Avram thought about it. "We'll have to get the history geniuses back," he said finally. "Remember how that Cambridge guy identified the Battle of Bosworth? We're going to need the same sort of help. Maybe Garry can set up some sort of arrangement with Cambridge University so that we can request assistance now and again?"

Bill was staring at the wall, a fork full of rice and beef sitting ignored on his plate. After a minute of silence, he got up without a word and left.

Not at all offended, Avram and Penny laughed.

"He'll tell us eventually what lightning strike just hit him," said Penny.

"And it will be a big one," replied Avram. "Do you want a coffee?"

"And some of that apple crumble. Then we can go and talk to Garry about getting the Cambridge people to help us."

* * *

Avram stopped the recording and stared at the scene. The viewpoint seemed to be from a sailing ship and as the watcher moved his head, there were signs of a township nearby.

The startling sight was the surrounding. There were endless numbers of sailing ships, ancient galleons, Avram thought. The fleet was enormous, at least a hundred ships and on those that were nearest, Avram could see that there were large numbers of men aboard. As the watcher moved away from the side of the vessel,

Avram saw numerous soldiers on the deck, all crammed around. The metal breastplates, the pikes and swords triggered some memory in Avram but he couldn't place it. As he had tracked through the life memories of the ancestors of the DNA donor, he knew that he was somewhere around the year 1600 but he was no more sure than that.

He checked the list on his desk, identified the name he wanted and looked at the time. It was just before six o'clock.

"They're on Summer Time, we're not, so coming up to nine in the morning in England," he muttered. "Let's hope he's at his desk."

He started up Skype, entered the address of the history professor at Cambridge and waited a few moments as the noise of the call rang out. A face appeared on the computer monitor.

"Good morning," said the youthful, round face of a man with shaggy, overgrown hair. "Who's calling?"

"Professor John Sheppard?" said Avram. "This is Avram Fischer from Blueprints in Australia. I hope this is a good time to call."

"Blueprints!" said the professor. "How delightful! I've heard all about you people and the work you did with this department! Between us, we've really put the cat among the pigeons."

"It's been an amazing adventure," said Avram. "I'm hoping you could help me with this latest bit of history. Your specialty is European History, I believe?"

"Right. You have something in that area?"

"I do. Would you have a look?"

"Not a problem," replied Sheppard. "We've been asked to assist and obviously, we're all delighted to keep playing a role here. Karen Petrova is an icon to Cambridge University. So what have you got?"

"Have a look at this scene." Avram directed the image of the ancient sailing ships to the other man. He watched in silence for a few minutes and then cut back to Avram.

"I know exactly what that is," he said. "You're looking at the Spanish Armada preparing to sail to invade England. The date is probably the twenty-fifth of May, 1588, though it could be a week or two later. It's never been fixed exactly. The location is Lisbon and there are 130 ships in that fleet and about 30,000 troops."

"Aha!" exclaimed Avram. "Somehow I just knew those uniforms were familiar."

"Where did this DNA sample come from?" asked Sheppard.

"An unlikely source," said Avram. "It's a farmer from the Shetland Isles."

Sheppard laughed. "Not as unlikely as all that! You'll find that the Armada was absolutely mauled by a combination of British Navy tactics under Francis Drake and some severe storms. Eventually the fleet could only escape by sailing north round Scotland and quite a few ships were wrecked up there. Your Shetlander is a descendent of one of those unfortunate soldiers or sailors who survived the wreck and stayed in Scotland."

"Amazing!" said Avram. "This has been the best part of this job, seeing history as it happened."

"Indeed it is, for all of us here, too," said Sheppard. "We've got a few of the machines here and we all spend a lot of time doing just that. I can tell you, every one of us is busy re-writing some of our textbooks. It can get quite embarrassing sometimes!"

Avram laughed. "I can imagine! I'll send you a copy of the entire DNA sample, you can probably find a lot more embarrassing stuff."

Sheppard grinned. "That'll be great! It will be of interest to a lot of naval historians here. Good luck with the ongoing research."

In great satisfaction, Avram cut the connection. Then as Penny had done, he updated the file of dates and the alien symbol that indicated another point in time.

* * *

Penny had found another one.

She had taken a severely deep dive into history, racing through generation after generation of a sample taken from a Turkish professor of languages at Istanbul University. She wanted to reach pre-Christian ages to get a very early fixed date for the time scale they were developing. When she felt she was far back enough, she started looking rapidly through lifelines and stopped when she saw an appalling scene of carnage as thousands of armed men hacked and cut at each other.

"Good grief," she muttered. "Why do we see so much of this sort of thing?"

The scene was utter confusion and the observer appeared to be a foot soldier right in the thick of it. Penny could make out very little of the style of clothing the men wore. She flinched as the observer struck with his sword at a man opposite and the head separated from the man's shoulders with an enormous gush of blood. Despite her experience and trained academic self-discipline, Penny shuddered. She looked up the list of Cambridge history professors, selected one that looked most appropriate and went to Skype.

A few moments later, she was talking to an old

women, grey hair framed a tiny face, heavily lined. Penny saw from her bent over position that she was sitting in a wheelchair.

"Good morning," said the old woman. "Who is Penny Barstow?"

"Good morning, Professor Dalrymple I believe?"

"You are correct, young lady. Do I presume that you are one of the researchers at Blueprints in Australia?"

"That is correct, Professor."

The tight face suddenly broke into a smile and the old eyes sparkled.

"Then I'm delighted to talk to you, Penny. Call me Amanda. I met Karen Petrova a few times when she was a student here and I've heard so much about the work your people have done with this department. How can I help you?"

"Amanda, I've found this appalling scene as I've been going as far back in time as I have been able. I'm sure it's pre-Christian era but I can't work out any details."

She switched it through to the English academic and waited for nearly five minutes before anything was said. Finally, the old face reappeared on the monitor.

"Horrible, wasn't it?" said Amanda. "And you are certainly way back before the Common Era. There's no doubt, this is a battle between Macedonian troops of the army of Alexander the Great and Persian armies of Darius. The uniforms tell me that much. Now, can you go back a few hours and see how this business started?"

"Stand by, Amanda," replied Penny and began slowly moving back in time, watching the two armies separate. After another hour, she saw that one side was crossing a wide river.

"Ah! Stop there!" said Amanda. "Now I think I have it. This is the Battle of Granicus, it's 334 BCE."

"Wow," said Penny. "What happened?"

"It was a massive show-down," said the English professor. "Alexander took an army of about 35,000 men into battle against the Persian Army led by Darius III who had an army of 40,000. But first, Alexander had to cross the river of Granicus and he was able to do that. Then it was a major battle as you have already seen until Alexander's army was able to get the advantage. They killed or captured half of Darius' army which was forced to retreat."

"That was so ugly," said Penny. "You don't have a more accurate date for that?"

"Yes, I do! You can place it fairly well in early May of that year, probably the third," said Amanda. "There are some conflicting accounts of that battle from different witnesses, so being able to follow it accurately will clear a lot of questions.

"I'm hoping we can help you get more accurate timings for more events in the near future," said Penny. Quickly, she summarised the work she, Avram and Bill were doing to develop a calendar from the alien symbol.

"That would be amazing!" responded the professor. "It's one problem we have, being unable to fix dates accurately back in those early days. Please let me know if I can help you further. And will you send me a copy of that lifetime? I have several colleagues who will be fascinated by seeing the battle in such detail. There are many areas of dispute about it."

"Of course," said Penny and with a few more words of pleasant conversation, disconnected the call and updated her calendar with the new date and symbol.

* * *

"Looks like we're building up a decent calendar," said Avram. As had become a small routine for them, they had claimed the corner table in the canteen and this time, Garry had joined them.

"Give me some details," said Garry.

"As we obviously saw, finding recent history dates has been easy," said Avram. "So we have almost a daily record of events such as the births and deaths of royalty, major political figures, movie stars and suchlike, plus the wars of this time, like both World Wars, the Boer War, the Crimea, minor wars like the Falklands and so on."

"Any obvious changes in the symbol?"

Bill took up the tale. "Tiny, tiny, tiny! So far, only the dot has moved and then not a lot. It hasn't reached the bottom of the track down the line and that's been a bit over a hundred and fifty years, about 55,000 days."

"But we've been reaching out to much older times to see if we can find a significant movement," said Penny.

"Such as?" Garry took a bite of his ham sandwich.

"Well, as you know, Avram found the Battle of Bosworth a long time ago when we were still in Reading and that was in August, 1485, so that gave us a major shift, about 200,000 days."

"What did you see?" asked Garry, fascinated.

"The dot had moved to a second track parallel with the first," said Bill. "Nothing else had changed."

"But you must remember, we're working with a symbol that is itself, microscopic," said Avram. "What we have done is expand it to a standard size that we can work with which is a square, twenty five centimetres on each side and it was on that scale that we found one millimetre equates to 472 days."

"And the line we're referring to, the one the dot moves down is twenty centimetres long, so that represents about 95,000 days or about 260 years. We think the dot had already moved a bit down the line when we first saw it, so we don't know how many times it travels up and down on parallel lines and when any other changes occur."

"Incredible," said Garry. "Please carry on."

"We keep finding events that can be placed in time," said Penny. "Avram saw the sailing of the Armada Fleet to attack England in 1588 and I got a nicely early one, the Battle of Hastings in 1066."

"And did that show anything changing?" asked Garry. He took out his calculator, punched a few numbers. "That's about 715,000 days."

"And this time, I found something else," said Bill with a wide grin. "The dot had returned to a track next to the line, but the tail at the bottom of the chart had increased by just over half a millimetre."

"Oh my!" exclaimed Garry. "This is incredible."

"Ah but it gets better," said Penny, keeping a straight face. "I went to 334BCE!"

"And what did you find?"

"As we had thought, finding battles would be the most likely result for us, they tend to get recorded in history."

"And the people in Cambridge have been helpful?"

"Couldn't have done it without them," said Penny. "The battle I found was identified as the Battle of Granicus, when Alexander the Great of Macedonia defeated Darius III of Persia. The lovely old lady in Cambridge, Amanda said it was probably May the third, but some historians were less sure. I sent her the recording and her department will research it further."

"Bill?" asked Garry.

"That was about 865,000 days ago," said Bill. "The dot had moved down the track a bit and the tail of the line was a further tenth of a millimetre longer."

Garry took a deep breath.

"You guys are really pinning this thing down," he said. "No doubt you've seen some amazing events?"

"Well, remember we've seen the oldest event yet," said Penny. "3000BCE estimated, the multi-voiced choir at Stonehenge. I know we recorded the symbol there, but I didn't enter it to the Calendar yet."

"The trouble with that one is that we have no accurate measure of a date," said Avram. "It's about one million, eight hundred thousand days ago, but the actual year is impossible to fix for now."

"Still, let's have a look at it and see if the symbol has changed in more obvious ways," said Penny.

Bill nodded. "I'll do that. It won't be too accurate yet. But we'll fix it when the Calendar gets more firm dates to it," he said. "Anyway, I saw the death of Henry VIII," he continued. "And then I decided I couldn't let these two find the really historic stuff on their own, I had a deep dive session also. I found the death of Buddha. That was 483BC."

"How on earth did you identify that one?" asked Garry, astonished.

"I caught a few men speaking a language I just could not identify, but they were wearing saffron robes, much like Buddhist monks wear today. I played a hunch, called the ancient languages people in Cambridge. It took them a while, but they identified the language as a relative of Sanskrit, called Magadi Prakrit. They said the Buddha spoke both, but Sanskrit was the language of the upper castes, and Buddha was a prince, but he preferred to preach in the Magadi tongue, the language of the lower castes. Eventually, the Cambridge people were able to translate what these monks were saying and it was telling of the death of the Buddha just days before."

Garry was staring at him, transfixed by what he was hearing.

"So I slowly worked back a few days," continued Bill, "and then I found the moment when the Buddha died, surrounded by just a small group of followers."

"I would love to see that scene," said Garry, letting out a slow breath.

"Get in line!" retorted Bill. "But I think you should contact the Dalai Lama through our Foreign Office and arrange for him to have first pick."

"Absolutely," agreed Garry. "That is quite earth-shaking."

"And there's more!" continued Bill. "I found scenes of the Buddha preaching to his followers. Imagine how the world's Buddhists will want those."

"Even more earth-shaking," said Garry. "I'll contact the Department of Foreign Affairs. This will give them something new!"

Chapter 22 – September, 2026

"Hey! Wow! You have to see this!"

Garry was sitting with Penny at her desk discussing the advances in developing a calendar to identify dates with the alien numerical symbol. She had decided to call it the "Rosetta Calendar" and it was a topic of interest to all the researchers.

But the shout of delight from Lorrie, the musician caused everybody to look up from their work. She had stood up and looked highly excited.

"What have you found, Lorrie?" asked one of the other researchers?

"Biblical stuff," she replied. "This is going to cause some problems for the cynics and unbelievers."

"How about you put it up on the main board?" said Garry, intrigued by Lorrie's obvious delight with her find.

Everybody turned to face the massive monitor on the far wall and an entrancing scene appeared. It was the rear view of a naked woman standing before a large bush. She had long blonde hair that fell down her back to her waist and her body appeared to be about perfect, long, slender legs and the sides of her generous breasts were just visible as she moved.

But what was more astonishing was the sight of a massive python coiled around the bush. Garry thought it was a diamond-back, a common variety in Australia and he estimated it was unusually large, possibly five metres and at the thickest part he could see, as wide as a man's waist.

There was no sound or movement on the monitor, though some small air currents moved the woman's long, beautiful hair in small waves. The python's head moved in small circular directions and its cold eyes seemed focused on the woman.

"What the hell...?" exclaimed somebody in the room.

"Who's the watcher?" whispered Penny to Garry, but he just shook his head, fascinated by the scene unfolding. Something was bothering him, he knew, but he couldn't identify what. Surely this couldn't be an ancient view of a biblical story he had long discounted as mere fable?

Then a sound was heard. The python let out a long hiss. It lasted several seconds. But there was more to the sound, there was a fluctuation in tone, there were a couple of breaks in continuity. Garry felt coldness in his chest, this was not possible, surely, everything they had learned in recent years denied it...

"Did I hear that thing say something?" asked another of the staff.

"I think it said, 'eat' or something like that," said somebody else.

"No, this can't be happening," said another voice. "It's surely something different, it just can't be that silly old biblical story."

"You're scaring me," said the first voice. "Because if it is, it'll cause more hysteria than finding Christianity was just a myth."

"But we're sure as hell seeing something." This voice was raw with tension.

"Then who the hell is the observer? Are you trying to tell me it's actually *Adam?* This is insane."

But then the scene changed. The beautiful blonde woman turned, holding a red apple in one hand, displaying a magnificent pair of breasts, bright red lips and perfect white teeth and appeared to address the watchers.

"Well, fuck me!" she said. "A talking snake!"

There was a moment of dead silence in the room. Garry looked over at Lorrie who seemed like she was bursting. But she managed to say something with a straight face.

"Ain't computer graphics great?" she said.

Then she collapsed into her chair, laughing helplessly, just a second before everybody else in the room followed suit.

It was some minutes before normality returned.

Chapter 23 – May, 2027

"The board asked me to look into this problem," said Bill.

He was sitting at his workbench, his back to the pile of assorted electronics, wires and tools while Garry sat in an armchair across from him.

"The telekinesis issue?" Garry was intrigued. It was unusual for Bill to ask him into his work area. In fact, Garry could only recall two such occasions over the years.

"Exactly. They're worried about the impact it could have on sports if it becomes widespread and stronger."

"I'm worried, that's a fact," said Garry. "I've been thinking about what happens with golf especially, if some players can direct the ball into the hole the way Mark can do."

"It'll be buggered," said Bill. "Same with darts, billiards and any number of sports. If somebody develops real power at greater distances and can direct a football into the goal or between the posts, then everything is messed up. Or imagine a tennis player being able to change the path of his ball so that he never misses a line. It would destroy the game."

"And Ben asked you if there was anything you could think of that might counter it?"

"He did. So for the last few weeks, I've been trying to get the first bit worked out, just what is the telekinetic force that occurs."

Garry said nothing. He knew that Bill would take his own time on this.

"I've had Ben in here for days, lifting things with his mind while I've tried to find just what is going on. Finally, I was able to detect a very small wave coming from his head while he does this."

Garry tried to hide the shock he felt on hearing this. He was sure that Bill had found a side of physics that had not been seriously dreamed of outside the realms of science fiction. But Bill saw it and grinned.

"Bloody mind-boggling, eh?" he said.

"Now there's an understatement," said Garry.

"I did find one thing, though," continued Bill. "Whatever this force is, it's still ruled by the Inverse Square Law."

Garry was sure he understood that, but decided to let Bill run the discussion. "Explain," he said.

"Let's say the force is at its maximum at the source, in this case Mark's head," said Bill. "But move two metres away and the force is only one-fourth, a quarter of what it was. Move another metre away, and it's one ninth of what it was. It means that the force reduces very sharply for every increase in distance away."

"So somebody would have to be a real superman to be able to control a fast-moving tennis ball nearly twenty-four metres away from one base line to the other?" Garry thought for a moment. "But a lot easier for a player to steer his opponent's ball out if it's at his own base line."

"That's true, but it gets better," continued Bill. "Or

worse, depending on your view. What Ben wanted was some form of suppressor that could be placed by a putting green or darts board so nobody could use this unfair advantage."

"And no doubt that's exactly what you've developed," said Garry.

"Er... well... actually, no," said Bill with a slightly embarrassed look. "Everything I tried, shielding, generating counter waves, nothing worked."

Garry said nothing. He knew that Bill so rarely failed to solve a problem that this lack of success probably hurt him badly.

"But I found a couple of things," said Bill. "First, I can track the signal to its source. So if somebody is trying to move something, I can identify who it is."

"That could be useful."

Bill nodded. "And then Ben suggested I go the other way. And he was right! I worked on the opposite idea and I found that while I can't block it or suppress it, what I *can* do is amplify it."

"Amplify it? By how much?" Garry was startled. This was unexpected.

"Up to three hundred percent," said Bill, looking smug.

"So the problem with sport remains," said Garry.

"But solvable," said Bill. "It would mean having a detector anywhere it would be needed, identifying the source and removing it. If it was, say, a golf player, the rules would have to call for immediate disqualification and possibly banning from the game, but that would be up to the authorities."

"How big are these things?" asked Garry, feeling somewhat overwhelmed by the implications of what he was hearing.

"I reckon I can get the amplifier down to suitcase size and the detector about the size of a mobile phone."

"I think this scares me," said Garry. "I'm having trouble trying to think of just what use the amplifier could be. The detector, yes, almost all sports are going to have to use them, but the amplifier just makes Mark's concerns more valid."

"Maybe," said Bill. "But I have a funny suspicion that most new inventions find some unusual applications. We just haven't thought about one so far."

Garry stood up. "Fantastic work, Bill. I suggest you keep on developing both devices, get them down to workable size and let's see how they find their applications. Meanwhile, how are you three doing with finding the Rosetta Calendar?"

"Getting there," said Bill.

"I had a brilliant idea," said Avram. The three of them were sitting at a table in the canteen.

"What an extraordinary concept!" replied Penny with a wide grin. "Avram? Brilliant idea? That doesn't compute!"

"Careful, young lady," said Avram. "That's fighting talk!"

"All right, what's the brilliant idea?" she said, rubbing his arm in a friendly fashion.

"So here we are, searching for dates we can pinpoint and find an equivalent image in somebody's DNA record to give us the symbol," said Avram.

"Right," agreed Bill. "And we've recruited all the rest of the staff to finding such dates and giving them to us."

"And there have been some beauties," said Avram. "But we've missed a perfect one, a regular event at relatively small intervals of time that we can pinpoint back for some thousands of years and so many people will have seen it that we can almost certainly find DNA records of it."

"Ah!" exclaimed Penny. "Yes, that's brilliant!"

"Halley's Comet," said Bill with a smile. "Perfect! Every seventy-six years, bang on the nose, thousands of people have seen every occurrence way back for at least two thousand years."

Penny took out her mobile phone and tapped a few keys.

"First identified by Chinese astronomers in 240BCE," she said. "And the orbit isn't as tight as we thought, more like every seventy-six through seventy-nine years. But it has probably been in this orbit for as long as 200,000 years, so it could certainly give us a long projection to the calendar."

"Sounds good," said Avram. "I'll send an email round the team asking for them to see if they can recognise any sightings and date them as near as possible from other events going on."

"I've got you a beauty," said the young man. His name was Richard Devlin, a doctorate holder in Genetics from Sydney University and a recent addition to the team at Blueprints. He was slender, blond hair already going thin and an ardent cricket follower.

"Show me," said Avram. He signalled over to Penny and she joined the other two at Richard's monitor which came alive with another scene of violent battle.

"Somebody is attacking a city," said Richard. "It looks like a major city, I estimate this is about three thousand years ago, based on the timelines I've been tracking. I'm certain it's a critical date but we'll need a specialist to confirm it."

"Where did you get the original DNA?" asked Penny.

"From the batches that the team got in Israel when they found that the Christian thing was all legends."

"I have a funny feeling about this," said Avram. "Let's call in the historians."

"Interesting," said Professor Janet Blackstone. The Cambridge academic had spent an hour looking at the images sent to her over the internet before calling back the three members of the research team.

"That's British understatement, is it?" said Avram.

"Possibly," replied Professor Blackstone. There was just the ghost of a smile on her lips. Avram estimated she was about forty, very slender and with a face that bordered on beautiful without any make-up at all. He decided she would be a raving knock-out if she scrubbed up, to use an Australian expression, then he concentrated on what she was saying.

"What gives it away is the geography," continued Janet. "It's a city that has natural protective qualities. It's built on a hill for a start then it has deep valleys to the east and west with lowlands to the south. Only the north is unprotected and there are some Biblical references to this fact."

"Biblical?" broke in Penny. "You know where this is, don't you?"

"Oh yes," said the woman in England. "And it's confirmed by seeing the huge vertical tunnel up from the springs at the bottom. Some historians thought that the invaders climbed up that tunnel, thought to be a well, but that theory has been abandoned as more research has taken place. However, it's a physical characteristic that pins down the geography."

She smiled at the looks of anticipation on the researchers.

"You are looking at an event taking place between 1004BCE and 999BCE," she said. "The valley to the east is known as the Kidron Valley, the one to the west is called "HaGai" or the Tyropoeon valley. It's Jerusalem. This is the capture of an ancient Canaanite city from the Jebusites by King David."

There was silence in the room. All the other researchers had gone silent and were listening in to the conversation, aware of the importance of what they were seeing. After a few moments, a deep sigh could be heard around the room as everyone released pent-up breaths at the same moment.

Avram had tears rolling down his cheeks, unable to speak. Even though he had never practiced any religion, he could see that he had just witnessed the start of the nation of Israel. He had been born not far from the site of the battle he had witnessed.

"Keep looking at that scene and you will probably see King David himself," continued Janet. "Would you please send me these images? Many of us here, both historians and Biblical scholars will be completely stunned by seeing them."

"Of course," said Penny. "Richard, put that up on the main screen so everybody can see it. I think I have to take Avram away for a while."

Chapter 24 – July, 2027
A New Crime Wave

"Life has sure changed in the last ten years," said Detective Inspector Ralph Clyman. He was sitting in the canteen at the Waverly Police Station in Sydney's Eastern Suburbs. He didn't look happy.

"For better or worse?" asked Detective Sergeant Sue Wallis, sitting across from him. Her slender, dark face with minimal make-up looked concerned.

"Both," relied Clyman. "There's no doubt, the numbers of crimes have dropped sharply. Even stupid crims have realised they'll get caught, almost a hundred percent guarantee. If it's murder or any violence, we just take a DNA sample from the victim and that'll almost certainly show the perp's face. Fraud is just the same. Once we have suspects, and they're easy to determine, same thing. DNA shows them doing the crime. And conviction is guaranteed, we don't lose cases on technicalities any more."

"So what's the down side?" asked Sue Wallis.

"It's all got too bloody easy," said Clyman. "We haven't had to do any real police work for some years now. And that means we're in trouble with our careers."

"That's true," said the sergeant. "Numbers are dropping and promotions are limited. I passed my Inspector's exams a year ago, but there's no vacancy for me anywhere in the Sydney region. The only spot that opened up in the last twelve months was in Broken Hill and four sergeants applied for that one. I didn't even get an interview."

"Exactly right," said Clyman. "Oh! Look out! Chief Super on the prowl!"

Both of them began to get to their feet as the tall, thin shape of Chief Superintendent Andrew Blake approached.

"Sit down, please," said Blake and joined them at the table, sitting at the head, with Clyman to his left and Sue to his right. Automatically, a waitress poured a mug of coffee and brought it to him. He smiled and she retreated. The boss was well regarded at the station for his simple courtesy to all the staff.

"Something I want to talk to you both about," continued Blake. "It's a common debating point these days that crime is dropping and our clean-up rate is getting higher as this new DNA technology becomes widespread."

"We were just talking about that," said Sue Wallis.

"Almost the entire detective population is doing just that as well," replied Blake with a sympathetic smile. "Our jobs are getting easier but rather boring and we've seen how the numbers are dropping."

"Exactly," said Sue.

"But there are a couple of areas that remain problematic," said Blake. "While prostitution became legal some years ago, child prostitution has not, but it's all gone indoors and hidden. We can't see who's organising it, we can't find any of the children because they're not out on the street anymore, so the usual methods no longer work."

"What are you suggesting, Sir?" asked Clyman, his interest piqued by the senior officer's words.

"Feel like going undercover a bit?" asked Blake.

"You want me to be a customer at one of these places?" said Clyman.

"Exactly. They keep a very low profile, but it's clear they advertise in the local papers."

"It's hard to identify these adverts," said Clyman. "They seem to be coded in special ways."

"You've been looking, eh?" said Sue with a grin.

"Doing my job," replied Clyman. "I think I can spot a couple of them, but I've never followed up."

"Now I'd like you to do so," said Blake. "We need to get a DNA sample from one of these kids because try as we might, we just cannot identify the people behind this business."

"I'll need a few days," said Clyman.

"Not a problem," replied Blake. "And it's a lot bigger than just child prostitution. We think whoever is behind it is probably also behind the drug influx and people smuggling. They're very clever at hiding their tracks, obviously well aware of the DNA procedures. We occasionally film the drug transactions but the sellers are always masked and they wear gloves. Similarly, when we nab an illegal immigrant, they have always dealt with anonymous people the same way, fully masked identities. So, both of you, work out a way of handling this, come and see me when you have a plan and let's tackle this nastiness."

* * *

"I'm pretty sure this is the sort of advert we're looking for," said Clyman. He passed a copy of an advertisements page from a local newspaper over the desk to Blake who studied it.

"It's a gardening advert," said Blake, puzzled.

"Well, it was in the gardening section, that's for sure," agreed Clyman. "But look at that reference to "fresh young plants." I think that's the give-way, it's referring to underage girls. It just isn't a natural phrase in any gardening magazine I've ever seen."

"You plan to call?"

"Yes, Sir. I'll use a pay as you go mobile phone, they won't easily identify the caller. If I get a go-ahead, I'll want some cash in hand and somebody following me with a camera, because they'll probably ask for a meeting somewhere near the establishment. You might be able to see who it is."

"Okay, Ralph, I'll see to it. Let me know when you've made contact. I'll have Sue Wallis be your follower."

* * *

A few days later, Clyman stood on a corner in Kings Cross as instructed after a phone call to the seller of "fresh young plants." After ten minutes, a middle-aged man in jeans and t-shirt approached him.

"Charlie?" he asked.

Clyman nodded. "That's me," he said.

"Doing some gardening, eh?"

"Indeed. And I need some fresh young plants."

"Okay. That building there." The man pointed at a block of apartments. "Apartment 9A."

Without another word, the man walked away. Clyman was sure that Sue Wallis had been able to get a clear shot of him and it had already been transmitted to the police station. He walked slowly up to the building that had been pointed out to him and opened the front door. There was a reception area staffed by another middle-aged man.

"Which apartment?" he said.

"9A," replied Clyman.

The man nodded and a door to his right buzzed open. Feeling nervous, Clyman entered, saw the elevators and pressed the button. A few moments later he exited on the ninth floor. There was a woman standing by one door and she waved at him. He walked up, entered the room and she closed the door behind her.

"That will be one thousand," she said. Her voice was a pleasant contralto and she was dressed well, in a figure-hugging woollen dress, her light brown hair in a pony-tail and immaculate make-up. Clyman extracted his wallet, counted out the money in $100 bills and she took it, stepped to a counter where her handbag was lying and put it away.

"I'll leave you to it," she said with a pleasant smile, opened the door and walked out. A second later, the door to the bathroom opened and a girl walked out.

At first sight, Clyman thought she was perhaps eighteen. But looking more carefully with a detective's trained observation skills, he realised she was no more than twelve or thirteen, despite the curves of her hips and breasts. She looked nervous. She wore a very short blue skirt and a white blouse with a deep neckline, revealing a significant cleavage.

"Hello," she said. "I'm Gerda."

"Where are you from, Gerda?"

"Lithuania."

"And how did you get here?"

She looked frightened. "I can't tell you. They'll hurt me."

He nodded in understanding and sat down on the

couch by the window. "Did your family come here with you?"

"Yes. My parents and my little sister."

"And the people who brought you, did you ever see their faces?"

"No. You're frightening me."

"Okay, let's do it differently. I'm not going to touch you, we'll just sit here long enough to think you've earned your money, but I do want one thing. I'm sure you have a pair of scissors in the bathroom, right?"

She nodded, looking puzzled.

"Go and get them, will you?"

She walked into the bathroom, re-appearing a few seconds later holding a pair of nail scissors. Clyman took them gently from her and cut a tiny lock of hair from the back of her head, making sure it was not noticeable. He took a small plastic bag from his pocket, folded the small lock of hair inside it and put it away.

"Now," he said and smiled at her. "We'll just sit quietly for half an hour until it's time for me to go."

"What's going to happen then?"

"Later this evening, police will come here, arrest the people who run this place and rescue you and the other girls here. I have been promised that no action will be taken against any of you, you will be allowed to stay in Australia, you and your sister can go to school and your parents will be helped to settle properly."

She stared at him, wide-eyed. Then she smiled.

"I'd better make the bed look like it's been used," she said.

Her words horrified Clyman. This twelve year old girl knew about sex, about prostitution, she had probably been subjected to abuse. He watched her as she stripped the top blanket away and opened up the bedclothes to make them look disturbed.

But then she astonished him even further. She came over to where he was sitting, sat next to him and put her arms round his neck, placing her head on his shoulder.

"Will you be my daddy for a little while until it's time for you to go?"

Her voice had become a little girl's and despite the sensual clothes and woman's body, Clyman held her like any father giving comfort and protection to his daughter.

* * *

"So we have her DNA," said Blake. "And we'll have the DNA of twelve other girls fairly soon. The bloke who met you is known to us, he's James Potter, a small-time thug and we've arrested him. We got the woman too, when we raided the joint. She's Emily Benson, she's got form for theft and fraud. We've taken their DNA as well. They're both in the cells."

"All the girls are under-age?" Clyman asked.

Blake nodded. "That's the charge we're bringing against them. With luck, we'll identify the people that brought them here. You did good work, Ralph."

There was a knock on the door and a young woman entered. Clyman recognised her as a lab technician who specialised in reading the DNA samples taken from suspects and victims. She looked worried.

"Sir, we examined the DNA of both the people you arrested last night."

"A problem, Judy?" asked Blake.

"Major league," said Judy. "We can't read it."

"What?" Blake looked stunned and Clyman sensed an awful foreboding in the air.

"It's been scrambled," said Judy. "I've never seen anything like this. We can't see images, we can't get sound."

"Good grief!" exclaimed Blake. "How the hell did this happen?"

"That's not the worst," said Judy. "The guys took breakfast into their cells this morning."

"And?" asked Blake as she hesitated.

"Both of them are dead."

Chapter 25 – Hunting the Snark Again

"Garry, Inspector Clyman of the State Police to see you."

The receptionist's voice echoed in Garry's speakerphone. It was no surprise, the detective had called Garry the previous day and made the appointment, through Garry remained puzzled by the nature of the call. Clyman had been most reticent about it. He rose to his feet and went to his open door just as a middle-height, slightly over-weight young man appeared. Garry estimated he was in his mid thirties. He was neatly dressed, wore a blue tie in an immaculately-tied Double Windsor knot and his shoes almost sparkled in the black depths of the polish.

"Come in and have a coffee," said Garry, saw the detective to a seat across from the coffee-table and poured two coffees from the urn kept permanently in the room.

"Now, how can I help you?" he asked, returning to the table and placing the two mugs on the table before taking his seat.

"The crims are getting more and more sophisticated," said Clyman. "We've almost wiped out ordinary crime as a result of what your people have done, just the really stupid ones still do the usual stuff, beatings, robberies, murder, but these days we get them within a couple of days, but the numbers are really down."

Garry nodded. He sensed that Clyman was working up to something and would take his own time getting there.

"One of the worst problems these days is child prostitution," the detective continued. "It's gone underground, finding the kids is difficult and even when we do, the pimps have learned how to hide themselves so even reading a kid's DNA gives us nothing. Mind you, we got their clients, so we've cleaned up a lot of shit that way."

He paused and sipped at his coffee and stared at the table for a few moments, gathering his thoughts.

"The other, one of them, actually three of them made stupid errors. We got some DNA of a twelve-year old prostitute, but even before, we were able to identify three of the people facilitating the business. We arrested them, charged them and held them overnight while their DNA was being read."

He smiled slightly at Garry.

"We don't have the technology you have for reading it almost immediately. But here's the problem. Actually two problems. Both the people we had turned up dead the following morning. What's worse, their DNA had been scrambled. We couldn't get either pictures or sound."

Garry sat back in his seat.

"Holy shit!" he said. "Has a pathologist examined the bodies?"

Clyman nodded. "She did that this morning and found nothing to explain the deaths. And we tracked down the third bloke to his house and the same thing. Scrambled DNA, dead as a drowned rat."

Garry tried to hide the deep worry that was threatening to engulf him. He took a sip of coffee and gathered his thoughts.

"Now I know why you drove up here rather than call me," he said.

Clyman nodded.

"I thought it safer." He paused. "Have you encountered anything like this at all before?"

Garry shook his head. "No. And you have me seriously worried. I'm willing to bet this can't happen naturally. After all these years, we've never seen anything like this, not in the present, not in all the past generations we've gone through."

"I came here because you're the only people I can think of who might be able to help us," said Clyman. "What you've said doesn't encourage me. It's not just the child prostitution. It's large-scale people-smuggling, gun-smuggling, just about any crime that crosses national borders."

"Then it needs some heavy activity from us," said Garry. "I agree, this is serious. I think I know where to start, so leave it with me. I'll keep you informed."

"Wonderful!" said Clyman. "Can I request a favour?"

"Sure," said Garry. "What is it?"

"We're severely restricted from using this technology for anything but police matters. But I'd love to see something of my ancestry. Could you do that for me?"

"Not a problem," said Garry. "Let me call one of my team and we'll do that right away."

As Clyman was led away by one of the research team, Garry checked his watch. Soon after 1pm. He'd call England later that evening.

* * *

"Greg, it's Garry Lawson."

"Garry! What a pleasure! This is surely a surprise!"

Garry smiled at the image of Greg Mullaney, the first CEO of Life Technology, retired and cheerful in his large house in the northern suburb of Reading, looking over the Thames.

"How's retirement, Greg? You're certainly looking well."

"As most people seem to find, Garry, I'm busier than I ever was when I had an actual job and commuted to the office every day! I have never-ending commitments to write articles for medical magazines or descriptions of working for Karen Petrova. I've got a book in development and I still do a couple of days a week with the old company working on submissions to the health authorities. We miss having Blueprints here though. You people kept us permanently astonished!"

"And they still keep me in a permanent state of astonishment!" said Garry with a laugh. "Maybe you should take a break and come out here for a time and meet the Second Foundation?"

"The what?"

"Well, officially we're known as the Karen Petrova Foundation, but once we learned how much Isaac Asimov had influenced Karen, that's our unofficial name."

Greg's laugh echoed down the line.

"Highly appropriate, I think! But Garry, you didn't call me to invite me for an Australian holiday. Have you got a problem?"

"A nasty one."

Garry swiftly outlined the details of the conversation with Inspector Clyman.

Greg's face showed no emotion but there was a short silence at the other end and then Greg spoke briefly.

"Oh dear," he said.

"Exactly," said Garry. "Do you have any idea at all of who could do such a thing? Who has that talent and knowledge of genetics?"

"I could think of about four or five people with the ability," said Greg. "But as it happens, I know exactly who created that technique."

"Good grief! Who?"

"Karen Petrova," said Greg.

* * *

"It was something that occurred to her while we were reviewing some new compounds," said Greg. "She remembered something the Prime Minister had said about how horrible it would be if somebody got hold of the Queen's DNA and started selling intimate scenes from her life. She thought about the idea of making DNA unreadable for some people, such as State Leaders or top military men with classified military information."

"I remember the PM saying that," said Garry. "I never thought she'd do anything about it."

"You know Karen," replied Greg. "Anything that might be a problem, she had to solve it. Anyway, I know she went away to her private lab in the office. Then one day, she told me she'd achieved a pill that would scramble the sight and sound records of the DNA. She'd experimented on mice but she told me that the mice had all died within a couple of weeks."

"Interesting," said Garry. "She never said a word about this to me."

"I think she abandoned the whole thing," said Greg. "She decided that nobody, not queens, kings, generals, prime ministers, nobody should have their histories blocked out from researchers, either present-day or in the future."

"But did she continue with the research?" asked Garry. "I can see why some people might want the ability to make themselves unreadable, but not if it kills them!"

"That's what worries me," said Greg. "A few weeks before she died, she gave me four USB flash drives, told me to hide them, lock them away, never disclose them."

"Oops!" said Garry. "Again, knowing Karen, she wouldn't let a line of research go uncompleted. What did you do with them?"

"In the bank vault," replied Greg. "The key to the safety deposit box is locked in my own safe at home and nobody knows that combination. In my will, I have instructed my lawyer how to obtain my key and the data on the flash drives and then to destroy the files."

"But somehow, somebody has got hold of the drug without knowing what it does. Could Karen have been a bit careless at some point?"

"You know Karen. What do you think?" asked Garry.

"Not a chance."

"What about your replacement?"

"James Boulter?" replied Greg. "He was selected after months of reviews, security examinations, our own DNA tests, everything. Not a chance he could be behind this, either."

"Well, I'm a suspicious bastard," said Garry. "Somehow, the drug has found its way into the outside world. Do something for me, Greg. Next time you're in the office, try somehow to get a sample of James Boulter's DNA. From my viewpoint, either Karen was careless or somebody has managed to get a copy of her research. Boulter has to be the prime suspect."

"This is ugly, old friend." Garry could see the doubts in Greg's face and hear it in his voice.

"Very ugly. I don't like either option."

"Okay, I'll see what I can do," replied Greg.

After a few more minutes of conversation between old friends, Garry cut the Skype call and settled down to some very unpleasant thoughts.

Chapter 26 – Death of a Crime Boss

"Garry, I have a Lieutenant Peter Haas of the Leichtenstein National Police on the phone."

Garry turned his attention away from Penny's update on the Rosetta Calendar.

"You have WHO?"

"He says he is Lieutenant Peter Haas of the Leichtenstein National Police."

"This week is already crazy," said Garry. "It can't get any dafter. Put him through."

He waited a second, heard the click on the phone.

"Lieutenant Haas, good morning. How can I help you?"

"I don't imagine this is a regular part of your duties, talking to a cop from Leichtenstein," said an amused baritone voice. Garry heard just a trace of a German accent. He couldn't help but warm to the obvious friendliness.

"I'm pretty sure this is the first time ever," he replied. "I have driven through your beautiful country but I didn't encounter any cops during the trip."

The police officer laughed.

"There aren't many of us," he said. "And we've had an easy time of it since your DNA technology was introduced here. Do you know, we haven't had a homicide since 2004? And we haven't had an unsolved crime since we got your equipment a few years ago."

"So, Lieutenant, just why are you calling me in Australia?"

"Mr Lawson, we've had something weird happen and you are the obvious person to call."

"Please call me Garry. What is this weird thing?"

"Garry, we have a tiny population here and a few of them are well known to us. We have a few millionaires and billionaires, a handful of sports stars, especially tennis stars escaping their own country's tax laws."

"Yes, I think I've read that."

"And for the same reasons, we also have a small number of people we suspect are top level crime figures."

"That I didn't know," said Garry, aware that something critical was happening.

"One of them, an Englishman called Walter Clarke was here. We have long suspected he ran several global crime operations, but we have never been able to find the evidence. Two days ago, he was killed in a motor accident."

Garry shivered. He knew what was coming next.

"It gave us the chance to take his DNA and read it," said Haas. "We hoped we'd find evidence of his operations."

"And you couldn't read it. It was scrambled."

The cop seemed unsurprised. "You've had this before?"

"Just this week," said Garry.

"And were you able to find anything?"

"Three people involved in child prostitution and probably people smuggling died soon after we arrested them. Their DNA was scrambled, we couldn't read it."

The Lieutenant was silent for a moment. "Two of Clarke's closest helpers also died in recent weeks. The pathologist found they also had scrambled DNA."

"And did your people find any cause for their deaths?"

"Nothing," replied the Lieutenant. "They just died. But Clarke definitely was killed by the accident, no doubt of that."

"Lieutenant, we've already begun inquiries into this thing, especially trying to identify just who would have the ability to do this. The thing that worries me is just why would anyone allow this to be done to them if it kills them at some point?"

"I suppose it would be wonderfully useful for somebody like Clarke who needs to hide his criminal activities," said the police officer. "But you're right, not a lot of point if it's going to kill you."

"Lieutenant, will you send me samples of the DNA of all the people connected to Clarke who have died in recent days?"

"Of course, I'll organise that right away. Do you think you can help?"

"Can you leave it with me, Lieutenant?" asked Garry. "I have some inquiries to make and I promise I'll keep you up to date as I find stuff."

"Sounds fine, Garry. Let me give you my contact details."

"Sounds good. We'll talk again later."

* * *

Greg Mullany felt worried as he dressed that morning. He wished he had his wife to discuss the problem with but she had died the year before after a short bout with cancer. He missed her calm, cool-headed advice. And now he had to go to work at the laboratory which he had managed for twenty years and be a spy on the man who had replaced him on his retirement.

His job was not difficult. He had taken over the role of liaison between the company and the drug approval authorities of various countries for the complex but standard procedures of getting of getting approval for new drugs when the company produced them. After years of this relationship, Karen's reputation had made the process almost automatic and his two days a week was enough to handle it.

His relationship with James Boulter had never been warm, nothing like the friendship he had developed with Garry, but he had total respect for the professionalism Boulter had displayed and he had strongly endorsed Boulter's hiring a year ago after the intensive battery of interviews and examination of his history conducted by the consultants.

But now he had to spy on the man and this made him uncomfortable.

He drove out of his garage not far from the house Garry still owned in the suburb of Earley and steered his way through the traffic to the industrial estate near Reading. As always, he gave a fond glance at the boathouse by the river from where had rowed as a schoolboy before parking in the Life Technology parking lot, made his way to the canteen and got a coffee before heading to his office. He sat immobile for nearly fifteen minutes, wondering what to do next then gave up and opened up the file on the latest product to be submitted to the Medicines & Healthcare products Regulatory Agency.

It was almost noon before an opportunity came to see Boulter. His signature was required on several forms for submission and Greg picked up the phone.

"James, you in?"

"Sure Greg. Come on up."

Greg took a deep breath, replaced the phone and left his office, wondering how he might obtain a sample of Boulter's DNA and if he did, what he might find.

Boulter was in his office, papers strewn across his desk. For a scientist, Greg thought, Boulter was a most untidy man. He was not a large man, his age was forty-two, Greg knew, below average height and built on slender lines. But he seemed fit and had a healthy complexion, a full head of black hair and moved with energy.

"Can you sign these?" Greg asked.

As Boulter scrawled his signature, Greg noticed something unusual. The other man was wearing surgical gloves, the sort worn by surgeons while operating. Greg had never seen this before in the months in which Boulter had been the CEO of Life Technology.

Curious, but unwilling to ask Boulter about it, Greg took back the forms and left the office. He replaced the papers in the file on his desk and decided on lunch.

The canteen was about half full and he was greeted in a friendly manner by several of the staff whom he had known during his tenure as CEO. Taking his plate of roast chicken and vegetables, he joined a group which included his one-time personal assistant, Carrie Walters who now served in the same role for Boulter.

"So how is the new world?" he asked the group generally.

"Okay, but not as relaxed as when you ran things," was a comment from a young man in a white laboratory-coat. It received general agreement. Greg changed the subject. He didn't want to start a series of complaints against the new boss. The rest of the meal passed in general discussions about the drugs being developed for release in the next couple of years.

Carrie checked her watch.

"Time for me to go," she said. "James is getting a haircut at one."

There was a soft laughter round the table.

"A haircut? In his office?" Greg echoed.

"A new thing since two months ago," Carrie said. "He has his own barber come in to trim his hair and then he has the man vacuum the floor. And really *seriously*. Even more oddly, the man has to empty the cleaner and take the contents away and burn them. I saw James give him a pile of cash last time, he really wants that hair destroyed."

"That's weird," said Greg.

"It is," agreed Carrie. "He actually bought an industrial-strength vacuum cleaner and he keeps it in his office for just that purpose. Nobody else gets to use it."

She picked up her tray and walked to the counter to leave it. Greg sat thoughtfully for a few moments before doing the same.

* * *

"There's definitely something peculiar about James Boulter," said Greg earlier the following morning. He had called the Australian offices at 7am from his home and got through to Garry in his mid-afternoon.

"It sounds like it," said Garry. "Surgical gloves? Who the hell wears surgical gloves all day?"

"Somebody who doesn't want to leave any fingerprints or skin particles around."

"And the haircuts in the office with the intensive clean-up after. Now that is definitely suspicious."

"I agree. Right now, I don't see any way of getting a sample from him."

"He's certainly being ultra-careful. Don't you find that suspicious, Greg?"

"I sure do. But remember, we read his DNA before we hired him about a year ago. It's standard procedure these days for senior management positions."

"And he was quite clean then?"

"He was."

"I'll leave it with you, Greg. A man of your intelligence will find a way."

"I hope so."

* * *

Greg left the office a little earlier than normal. He'd completed the paperwork for submission to the authorities and his working contract did not specify the hours he would work. He reached his blue Volvo and fumbled for his keys in his briefcase, extracted them and selected the bunch of keys that included his house keys and car key. As he did so, he saw a key he had not used for a long time. He stared at it for a few moments, trying to identify it.

"My old office key," he muttered. "I never did hand that over."

An idea came to him.

Two days later, his second scheduled day in the office, he found the opportunity. Boulter had left at lunchtime to visit a pharmaceutical client in Hereford about renewing the licence for the manufacture of a blood pressure pill, so Carrie had taken the opportunity to leave early to go to the gym.

Greg walked up to Boulter's office, saw nobody around and took out the key. Once inside, he closed the door and looked around. There was nothing to be seen, the desk was empty, but Greg saw the coat cupboard where he had always known it to be and opened it. On the floor was a vacuum cleaner.

He pulled it out, examined the top and saw how it opened. Carefully, he took the cap off and almost immediately saw what he wanted – several strands of black hair were stuck to the top of the removable container.

He took a plastic bag from his pocket, brought along for that purpose, gently eased several of the hairs off the container and dropped them into the bag. Then he replaced the cap, put the vacuum cleaner back in its place, closed the cupboard door and left the office again.

Ten minutes later, he was in his Volvo heading back to Earley. He was nearly home before his heart stopped pounding and his hands stopped shaking.

"I remember a cop in Reading telling me when we saw our first murder, that most crimes are solved because the crim made some simple mistake," said Garry when Greg called him that evening. "You would have thought that a man of Boulter's intelligence would have taken even more extreme measures to stop anyone seeing his DNA."

"I've heard the same," said Greg. "I've sent you the sample by express post, your people can analyse it better than anyone here and anyway, that's more secure."

"It doesn't solve the main problem," said Garry. "How did the people who have scrambled their DNA get hold of the drug? If it has come from Boulter, then we have more problems. How did he get hold of it and did he pass it on to other people? If he did, how come they're still alive?"

"I'm hoping his DNA will reveal these answers," replied Greg. "Call me when you know."

"For sure. Well done, Greg."

"I've never done anything like that before," replied Greg.

"It was necessary," said Garry. "I'll get back to you soon."

A week later, Garry called Greg at his home.

"We have a problem," he said. "Boulter's DNA has been scrambled."

"Bugger," said Greg.

* * *

"Let me escort you to the security area," said the bank manager. "It's been a while since you were here last, Mr Mullaney."

"Not since I deposited some things here the last time," replied Greg as they entered the highly secure area of personal safety deposit boxes.

"That's your box," said the bank manager. "But I do remember, Mr Boulter was here some months ago."

"Mr Boulter?" Greg was seriously shocked. "He had the key to the box?"

"I must assume so. As you know, we leave you alone once we have shown you your deposit box. I'll check the records for the actual date of his visit."

Greg said nothing. The key he had just taken out was the only one and he had stored it in the safe at home. Only he knew the combination of that safe and that number was encoded and stored on his lap top computer that he had brought with him. Something was seriously wrong.

He waited until the bank manager had left the room, opened the computer on the table and then used the key to open the safety deposit box. The USB flash drives were as he had left them some years ago. He took them out and copied the contents of each into a file on his computer. It took a while.

When finished, he returned the drives to the deposit box, locked it up and left the room.

* * *

When he reached home, he headed to his safe, opened it, placed the key back in its slot and then hesitated. There was something else in the safe, something he had not told Garry about. It was an envelope, addressed to him and even though padded, it obviously contained another USB flash drive. Karen had given it to him when she had said she had ceased experimentation into DNA scrambling drugs.

"Keep this separate," she had said.

"What is it?"

"It may solve problems one day."

"When do I open it?"

"You will know," she had replied.

He had said no more, trusting Karen implicitly, but placed the package in his safe.

Now he took out that package and opened it. There was another USB drive and a short note written in Karen's immaculate copperplate script. It took only a few moments to read her letter.

"Karen, you're bloody amazing," he muttered.

* * *

The following day, he was not scheduled to be at the office. He brewed a large pot of coffee, expecting to be intensely busy the entire time.

He opened the safe, took out the flash drive and copied the contents to his computer. He had been a superb administrator for some years but he had not forgotten his own doctorate in Pharmacology.

Carefully, he worked his way through the detailed formulae and instructions.

"Clever," he muttered. "Classic Karen Petrova genius here. This looks like the original research and design."

Four hours later, he sat back, stretched and rose to refill his coffee mug. Returning to his seat, he reviewed the notes he had made and went back to the document.

"So that's how you scramble DNA," he said aloud. "Bloody brilliant!" Another three hours later, he sat back in astonishment. "And that's why it kills the user," he said aloud. "Holy shit! No wonder she abandoned this line of research! So why is that less than half way through the files?"

There was still a huge mass of data to go through. He took a sip of coffee and pressed on.

Two hours later, he realised what had happened.

"You didn't abandon it, did you Karen?" he said aloud. "Why would I ever think that you had? This is now the second instalment."

It took another six hours before Greg sat back in his seat, astonished by what he had seen.

"Holy clucking duckshit, Batman," he said softly. "I always knew you were a genius, Karen, but this beats everything."

He deleted the files from his computer, ensured the flash drive was securely back in the safe, checked his watch and realised it was after nine o'clock in the evening and he hadn't eaten since breakfast.

"Garry, have I got a surprise for you," he said as he waited for the steak he had taken from the fridge to grill. "This will blow your socks off."

* * *

"Well, there's no doubt Boulter is behind all this," said Greg. "Somehow he has accessed the data I had left in a safety deposit vault."

"How the hell did he do that?" Garry showed severe shock in his face.

"Garry, it's too easy for us all to forget the age in which we live. I can only think that somehow Boulter got my DNA, read the combination to my safe and somehow got to it while I was away sometime. It really wouldn't have been difficult and I wasn't taking any precautions against it."

"Have you been away for any period?"

"A couple of times. I took a few days off in the Lake District soon after I retired and more recently, I went to my daughter's wedding in Preston in July. I was away for a week."

"When did you last check the deposit box key?"

"A long time ago. I keep it in a separate drawer in the safe, it's not obvious and I don't open the safe all that often."

"And the bank manager said he went to the box some time ago?"

"Seven months ago, five months after joining Life Technology and it was during the week I was in Preston."

"So it sounds like he organised a break-in to your place while you were away, took the key, went to the bank and copied the files then returned the key to your safe."

"That's about it," said Greg.

"Did the manager remember if Boulter took a computer in with him?"

"No, he doesn't recall."

"I'd say we must assume he did and now he has the formulae for the compounds and he's sold them to some very ugly people. There was no sign of any criminal propensity when he was interviewed, so somebody must have got to him."

"Yes, you're right. But things are not as bad as we might have thought."

"Greg? What do you know that the rest of us don't?"

"Karen left me something else when she gave me the data. And this was something she asked me to keep quite separate from the flash drives and she was very secretive about it."

"Did she tell you what it was?"

Greg shook his head. "She said it might solve problems one day. I'm sure she anticipated difficulties arising from something in the bank vault."

"Where did you keep it?"

"In another drawer in the safe. We've been very lucky. Whoever read my DNA to find the key didn't look any further than that, so they didn't see my conversation with Karen or where I had stored that package. If they had, we'd be in serious shit now."

Garry had to laugh.

"Okay, Greg, you've opened that package and it's somehow related to the formulae for DNA scrambling, right?"

"Indeed it is. First thing, we were right that Karen wouldn't stop the research. So she found a drug that would scramble the DNA but would kill the user in a few weeks. But she kept looking and found the advanced version that didn't kill the user."

"Good grief, that's amazing!" exclaimed Garry. "So what it looks like is that Boulter took the advanced version and sold that to various people, especially crime bosses like Walter Clarke."

"Yes, but even worse, I think that he sold the lower version to these people as well and they fed them to their underlings to convince them they'd be unreadable, but not telling them what they were getting, so they'd die quite soon. Just extra security."

"God, that is really ugly," said Garry.

"Isn't it just? But trust our beloved Karen to anticipate this."

"What did she do?"

"She certainly found a way of scrambling the DNA so that it wouldn't kill the user. But the scrambling was done to a clever mathematical formula."

Garry laughed. "And that can be unscrambled, I bet!"

"And that can be unscrambled, correct," said Greg. "All it needs is the combination, just like a safe."

"And you have that combination, no doubt?"

"Indeed I do. The only problem is that it doesn't work on the lower level drug and it doesn't work on a corpse."

"So now we have to work out some way of getting Boulter's DNA, unscrambling it and we can find out who bought the drugs."

Greg smiled. "You have Boulter's hair sample already. I'll send you the data from the flash drive she left me and you should be able to make the drug in a week or so."

"And then you can talk to the local police," said Garry. "From what you've told me, nobody will mourn the departure of James Boulter."

"Finding a replacement will be a problem," said Greg. "It took us months to find him."

"You may just have to take over his office again, at least for a time," said Garry. "I suspect that would be well received."

Greg laughed. "I'll just sit and wait quietly until you have done the work," he said.

"And I have a cop in Leichtenstein to talk to," said Garry.

Cheerfully, both of them disconnected the call.

Chapter 27 – June, 2026
The Hunt for Day One

"The problem with building this Rosetta Stone Calendar is that beyond a few hundred years in the last, there are fewer and fewer fixed dates we can find."

The same three sat in the dining room, having finished their lunch and starting the regular discussion that had been the pattern for some weeks.

Penny's comments caused the other three to nod thoughtfully.

"It's true," said Avram. "We've gone back over a thousand years now, but even after five or six hundred years, firm dates started becoming difficult to pin down. And we still haven't worked out the logic of that numbering system."

"But we have filled out almost every date for that period," said Bill.

"And bloody laborious that has been," said Avram. "So, okay, we fix a date, say the death of Henry the Eighth, extract the symbol and then we can go back, day by day to Henry's birth, extracting the symbol each time. But that takes hours and hours."

"And we can forward, the same way," continued Penny. "We take a known date like, say, the birth of

Elizabeth the First, extract the symbol for that date and then start counting, one day at a time until her death. So, okay, we've got a symbol for every day over a century of so, but it's seriously hard work and frankly, boring as hell."

"And what are we going to do as we go further back in time?" said Avram. "There will be far fewer dates we can fix and we'll get to a point where there are no defined dates at all."

"Can't we automate it?" asked Penny. "Bill, could we set up a system that automatically reads through every day of a lifetime, records the symbol and later we might be able to work out the logic of the counting symbol?"

Bill was silent for a moment and then he smiled, such a rare event that Penny and Avram sat back in their seats.

"You know what?" he said, excitement showing in his normally placid face. "Whatever else we could do with that idea, we could start a real effort to find Day One."

"Go on," said Avram, though his smile indicated that he was seeing where Bill's idea was leading.

"Day One could be many millions of days in the past," said Penny, also showing some excitement. "Tracking that down could take years if we do it manually and it would drive anybody nuts doing it manually."

"I have an idea," said Bill.

"Of course you do," said Penny.

* * *

"You want to do WHAT?" said Garry.

"Buy the biggest, fastest, bad-ass computer in the world and set it up here," said Bill. On either side of him, Penny and Avram smiled at Garry's reaction.

"And what do you propose to do with this big, fast, bad-ass computer?" asked Garry. Despite the initial reaction he sensed that the group had developed a hugely critical idea.

"Find Day One," said Bill.

Garry looked at each of them in turn and they returned his look without expression.

"How?" he said.

"First thing I do is work with the manufacturers of the beast to install our scanning system onto it. In fact, I'd like to link about fifty or so scanners. Then we add an automatic feeder to each of the scanners so that they will read every sample one after the other, scan to just the start of each day, extract the mathematical symbol and when the entire life has been scanned, draw another sample in."

"I think I see where you're going," said Garry, his excitement rising. "Then the system will automatically scan through every ancestor of each sample, as far back in time as it can. Yes, this is going to take some grunt power."

"We have eighty thousand samples in store," said Penny. "I just checked. Once Bill has designed and installed the readers and feeder mechanism we should have material to look back to the very earliest times of humans."

"How about back to Neanderthal?" asked Garry. "What if Day One is in that time line?"

"There were about thirty thousand years when Neanderthal and Cro-Magon coexisted," said Avram. "And we already know there was some interbreeding. We stand a really good job of finding some tracks back to Neanderthal Man. And anyway, we might be able to get some fossil bones from that era and see if viable

DNA can be extracted and then add that to the system. I'll contact some of the groups that have been working on Neanderthal DNA and see if they can let us have some good samples."

"Okay, so what exactly do you have in mind for the computer that will do this?" asked Garry.

"I did some studying," said Bill. "I think we should get the latest Cray Supercomputer, fully maxed out with memory and storage."

"And that will cost?" asked Garry.

"About fifty million dollars," replied Bill.

"Good grief!" said Garry.

"That's US dollars," said Bill, smiling gently. "Say about seventy-five million Australian."

"Any more?" Garry was finding the situation becoming quite funny. He knew this was easily within the Foundation's capacity.

"A secure computer room," said Bill. "That will be substantial, we'll need a new, custom-built building but there's space here for that. It will need one humungous cooling system according to the manufacturer's specs. Then we'll need some more scanners, some support from Cray, all the usual stuff."

"Give me a detailed cost breakdown," said Garry. "Once I know the exact amount, we'll go ahead."

"Just like that?" asked Penny.

"Just like that," agreed Garry. "This could well turn out to be the most critical thing we have ever done."

* * *

"One of the reasons behind moving to Australia was that we would be less at risk of the sort of madness that happened in England," said Garry. "And so far, this has been the case."

"But you think things may change?" said Mary.

"I think the new computer building may cause the issue."

"The office we're in now was designed by a British security specialist architect," said Mary. "Karen always saw the potential for religious lunacy and got him to build in some amazing features."

"Thankfully, we've never needed to test them out. But as we get deeper and deeper into human history, I can't help but worry that we're going to offend somebody, sometime."

"So you think we need to get a specialist security expert?" asked Ben Fuller.

"I do," said Garry.

"I go along with that," said Mark Craymer. "There's no doubt, we're turning human history and culture on its head, the changes we're bringing about are giving new meaning to what it is to be a human being. Huge change can cause huge opposition."

"And we have already agreed to make the new computer facilities available to government and universities," said Mary. "That means new people coming in. I think this is the right idea."

"Mary, do you still have all your spooky connections with ASIO?" asked Garry.

"Once a spook, always a spook," said Mary, barely hiding a smile. "Of course I do!"

"Then can you put the word out that we need a top class security specialist?"

Mary nodded. "Leave it with me," she said.

Chapter 28 – February, 2028

"Welcome to another meeting of the Second Foundation," said Garry and smiled at the group round the table. Numbers were reduced as four of them had been called for advice by governments around the world.

"Let's get the bad news over with first," he said and described the criminal activities of James Boulter at the original parent company, Life Technology at the base in Reading in England.

Faces round the table expressed varying degrees of shock and dismay.

"What's being done with this drug?" asked Mary. "I would hope it's been destroyed."

Garry shook his head.

"It remains locked away," he said. "Apart from the fact that I can't bring myself to destroy original and brilliant work by Karen, it's simply that one never knows when such a capability might prove useful."

Mary looked doubtful. "Hard to imagine," she said. "It seems more likely somebody will use it again in the same manner."

"If they can get hold of it and have the capability of making the stuff," said Garry. "Anyway, Greg has set up far more secure storage than he had before."

Still unconvinced, Mary acknowledged Garry's authority and indicated her acceptance.

"And so to more cheerful stuff," said Garry. "The Second Renaissance continues well. Some of us here went to the Opera in Sydney last week. It was stunning."

* * *

Garry had always found the walk up to the Sydney Opera House one of the most exciting events. From their hotel by Circular Quay, they strolled past the various wharves where the constant coming and going of the ferries never seemed to stop. Then they turned towards the enormous shape of the Opera House, walked along the quayside while the roar of music and conversation emanated from the restaurants and bars down below them. The huge sculpture of the Harbour Bridge loomed massively in the light evening sky to their left. Garry felt the increasing excitement of the other members of the Second Foundation as they approached the Opera House, entered the doors for the Opera Theatre and climbed the steps up to the main area where drinks were being served, programs handed out and masses of equally excited people prepared to enter the hall.

Fifteen minutes later, seated in the middle of a row looking down on the stage, the sense of occasion had not faded. Garry looked at the program.

"This is the first opera by Australian composer, John Hartford," it said. "It is also the first work composed entirely to make use of the new technique of double-voiced singing discovered during research into the music of pre-historic times, notably the choirs at Stonehenge soon after completion of that edifice.

"Few singers have been able to master this technique as yet, though many are in training around the world. Six accomplished singers are with us tonight, and we are fortunate that renowned Australian Soprano, Olivia Baird is one of them."

Feeling delighted with the memory of being there when Olivia Baird was first shown the double-voiced singing of over three thousand years ago, Garry scanned through the rest of the program, not really concerned with the story but eager to hear what had been done by a modern composer.

There was a short burst of applause as the conductor took his place at his podium below stage level and then the lights faded.

The scenery was beautiful, Garry thought, though didn't seem to represent any specific scene. A single line of singers, male and female were in a crescent shape at the back of the stage, two individuals stood at the front. Garry recognised Olivia Baird but not the man.

Olivia began to sing. At first, there were only the solo, beautiful notes of a world-class soprano singing a simple, slow melody. But then a second voice joined in, perfectly harmonised with the first and Garry felt a shiver run up his spine. Only Olivia was singing. He sensed a small wave run through the audience as they experienced the same shock of a new sound, an impossible sound of great beauty, not at all human in its range and complexity.

The tenor joined and began with a single song that matched Olivia's two voices perfectly but then he too added a second voice and four voices produced a song of incredible beauty coming from only two singers.

Garry felt overwhelmed by what he was hearing. He could never have anticipated the incredible shock of the sounds coming from just two people and he realised he was not breathing. Gasping, he took a deep breath, realising that the people around him were similarly in a state of disbelief.

The chorus joined in and Garry could hear that they were conventional singers, just one voice per person and somehow that made the multiple voices even more astounding.

Not bothering to try and follow any story, Garry just hung on the experience of the multiple voices and the fascination and overwhelming sounds grew to a climax when six singers were on stage producing twelve melodies in a complex, unearthly sound like nothing he had ever heard before.

He had no recollection of time passing, but the opera ended and the curtain came down. There was a long, drawn-out sigh from the packed Opera Hall and when the curtain rose again to reveal the six soloists, the roar of appreciation almost hurt Garry's ears.

Later, as Garry and his colleagues walked back to their hotel, none of them could speak, so shattering had been the experience.

I bet you never anticipated this, Karen, thought Garry as he entered his hotel room.

* * *

"I don't think Karen could have possibly anticipated what we experienced in Sydney," said Garry to the people round the table.

Murmurs of agreement ran round the table.

"I've heard that several hundred singers around the world are working on developing these new abilities," said Brad Robertson, the futurist. "And the abilities vary. Some have picked it up like Olivia Baird, some are struggling but getting there, some just can't get it at all."

"And there's a whole new wave of composers writing music for them," added Annabelle Calvert. "The work you saw by John Hartford was the first in a wave that we can expect over the next few years."

"Talk about a Second Renaissance," said Mary Hennessey. "Karen Petrova sure as hell changed the world all right!"

"That was my thought afterwards," said Garry. "I don't think she anticipated the scope of what she set in motion."

"Not even Karen could have anticipated that," agreed Mary. "Now, can you update us with the appalling story of Life Technology and the criminal use of Karen's last research project?"

"I hate even thinking about it," said Garry with a grimace. "But yes, the worst happened."

* * *

The arrest of James Boulter brought the offices of Life Technology to a complete halt. An unmarked police car arrived at the front door, followed by a regular patrol car, a plain-clothes officer led two uniformed officers inside and walked straight up to Boulter's office, having been given directions by Greg Mullaney.

Carrie Walters stared open-mouthed as the officers walked past her with a polite "Good morning" from the detective. Boulter was at his desk and his face went white as the officers entered.

"James Boulter, I am arresting you for illegal sales of company assets and knowingly facilitating the crimes of other suspects," said the detective and proceeded to recite the standard precautions. Boulter said nothing as an officer placed handcuffs on his wrists and the four men walked out of the office, downstairs and to the police cars.

A crowd of silent employees watched the departure, all of them anxious about what this event might mean for the company and themselves. Then a blue Volvo arrived and parked in the spot near the front door. Greg Mullaney climbed out and walked up to the entrance.

"What are you lot doing standing here?" he said loudly. "Haven't you got jobs to go to?"

As the realisation spread that he had returned to his old position, loud cheers and whistles erupted through the crowd. Grinning widely, he walked into the building and to his office.

"Coffee, I think," he said to Carrie as he walked into his old office. She nodded, smiling as tears rolled down her cheeks.

* * *

"It feels like I was never away," said Greg as the image of Garry appeared on the computer monitor.

"No trouble getting back on the horse?" asked Garry. "It's only been a week."

"Give Boulter his due," said Greg. "He looked untidy, but the operation was perfectly documented. I had no difficulty picking up the strings."

"And what's the story with him?"

"He just folded," said Greg. "He took the pill when asked and that unscrambled his DNA and we read the whole story. He didn't know what I'd put in the safety deposit box, he only learned about it when the bank manager called and accidently dropped the information. That's when he arranged the break-in at my place, copied the files to his laptop and then discovered what he had. He's got a doctorate in pharmacology like I have and he eventually worked out what Karen had done."

"But what drove him down this path of crime?" asked Garry. "There was nothing evident in the DNA scans you did before hiring him."

Greg looked irritated. "We missed something," he said. "It was nothing about his personal life that we could see at the time. But it all started after he'd joined us and so we never saw it."

*　*　*

February, 2025

"Mr Boulter, a Mr Jackson is here to see you."

Carrie's voice from the speaker interrupted Boulter's concentration on the paperwork. He had been in the job for three months and it was taking all his efforts to get his hands round some of the complexities. The increasing tensions at home were a severe problem as well.

A large, muscular man appeared in the open doorway. He was wearing jeans and a golf shirt and displayed a light tan. Boulter was sure he had never met this man before. He stood up and offered his hand.

"Mr Jackson? How can I help you?"

The man's grip was firm and he smiled in a friendly manner before walking back and closing the door then sitting down across from Boulter. The move disconcerted Boulter.

"James, I represent the management at the Oceania Casino in Oxford."

"I haven't heard of the Casino. But why are you calling on me? This is a pharmaceutical manufacturing operation."

"Yes, we know that. It's your wife that concerns us."

"Jennifer? Mr Jackson, I'm totally confused."

"James, do you not know that your wife has been a regular daytime visitor to the casino for the last three months?"

Boulter was shaken. "No, I didn't."

"She seems hooked on the roulette wheel. She's become a bit silly, and I have to tell you, we've stopped her playing. But in the meanwhile, she's run up a tab of over sixty thousand pounds."

"Sixty...?" Boulter found he was having trouble breathing.

"To be precise, sixty-two thousand, five hundred. Now, James, this is a legitimate, legal business and your wife is a responsible adult and please note, we actually stopped her losing any more money. We're not entirely without ethics. But we want the money. Can you pay it?"

Boulter felt frightened. Despite the reasonable tone of Jackson's utterances, he sensed an implacable menace.

"I don't have that sort of money," he stammered. "We've just bought this new house and we spent far more on it than we got for the old one. And Jennifer has been spending money like water..."

"You earn a big salary, James. I'm sure the bank will lend it. Anyway, you have a month. If it's not paid by that time, we will make things unpleasant for you, I promise."

The mask of geniality had gone. Boulter realised he had been threatened by forces outside of his comprehension.

Jackson stood up, didn't offer to shake hands and walked out.

Boulter found he was trembling.

* * *

The evening at home was unpleasant. Confronted with the revelations of her gambling, added to the heavy spending she had indulged in since moving to Reading, Jennifer started screaming in rage, packed a bag and left, saying she would go and live with her sister in London.

Boulter felt relief at her departure then settled down to attempt to find a solution to his problem. He knew that Jackson's suggestion of a bank loan was not viable. As he had said, he had extended himself in buying the house, mostly at Jennifer's urging and the mortgage was painful. The house he had sold in order to move had fetched nothing like the cost of the new one and by the time he had paid legal fees, registration fees and all the rest, he was seriously stretched. His credit card was almost maxed out, mostly as a result of Jennifer's expenditures.

At some point, he recalled the surprise of the call from the bank manager advising him of the safety deposit box account opened by Greg Mullaney a few years ago. He wondered why Greg had never told him about it and what could possibly be in there. Then he remembered the social visit he and Jennifer had made to Greg's house soon after he had started the new position as Greg's replacement and had seen the safe in Greg's study. One thought led to another and soon he recalled how his brother, a barrister had once successfully defended a burglar against charges of break and enter.

He picked up the phone.

* * *

The Present

"And it all went from there," said Greg. "This time, we went through his DNA thoroughly and saw the whole story of the last year which was not in his DNA when we first examined it. He had a crim break into my house and open the safe, because Boulter had been able to get my DNA easily enough and read the combination code, take the key and then he'd been able to access the safety deposit box without a problem."

"Bloody lucky that the guy who broke in didn't see the envelope from Karen addressed to you," said Garry.

"Christ, yes! But I suppose if he'd seen it, he wouldn't have recognised Karen's writing."

"And then Boulter had offered the drug to the casino bloke?" continued Garry.

"Exactly. His brother is a barrister and he knew that the casino was one of several owned by that Walter Clarke thug in Leichtenstein, a major player in the drug smuggling, prostitution business and people smuggling around the world. Boulter realised how valuable a DNA scrambling facility would be useful to a man like that. He asked for a million pounds and cancellation of his wife's debt and got it without question."

"What about the fatal Level Two drug?" asked Garry, feeling rage about the damage done to the company by this act of criminality.

"That's where we found a nasty side to Boulter that we had never suspected," said Greg. "He'd had a dozen pills of each formulation made at the company. That was easy enough, he just said it was a new formula that Karen had left and the laboratory had made it without question, not realising what its real capability was. Then he also offered the level two drug to Clarke as well, explaining what a great security feature it was if he wanted his underlings out of the way at some time and got another half million for it."

"This is really ugly, Greg," said Garry.

"It gets worse. Through his barrister brother, he was able to make contact with a few crime bosses around the world and sell them the same drugs."

"I hope you're hammering both men?"

"Indeed we are. The Crown Prosecutors are charging the brothers with all sorts of crimes, both men are going down for a long time. In a way, I feel sorry for Boulter. He just got hit with things beyond his control."

"What about the international players?"

"The authorities in the USA, France, South Africa and Latvia have been informed and they'll take it from there. Obviously, we got all the names and the details of the sales when we examined his DNA. What the cops there are working on is reading those crooks' DNA to find out who got the fatal drug."

"Will you be able to do anything for them?"

"Doubtful. But at least they'll be in hospital and we can try and find a recovery process. The code Karen gave me doesn't work."

"Maybe you can assign a couple of people to look for a way of cleaning it up?"

"I've already done that. But we're all pharmacologists, not geneticists. Maybe a couple of your people might like to come and help us?"

"I'll ask the team, Greg. I'm sure there'll be a couple of people who might like to work directly on something Karen produced."

"That would be a great help."

Garry sat back, feeling satisfied with the developments.

"Karen was right, Greg. She really did change the world!"

"The Second Renaissance continues, it seems!"

Feeling cheerful, Garry ended the Skype call and went back to work.

* * *

"As you said, Garry, an ugly story," said Mary.

"It really hurts when I think of Karen's legacy being messed up like that," agreed Garry.

There was a short break while the young man who served as office boy and general assistant wheeled in a trolley with tea and coffee and everybody relaxed for a few minutes.

"Something I need to advise you all about," said Garry when they had resumed their seats. "It might be critical and a pointer to how humanity is changing, but I've got no idea how this development occurred."

* * *

"I've got to have an abortion," said the young woman. The panic in her eyes was obvious.

The doctor looked at her curiously and with sadness in his face.

"Irene, this is America, you know abortion has totally banned for some years ever since the Supreme Court somehow reversed its old decision."

"But I've got to! My baby is damaged."

The doctor looked worried.

"Irene, even talking to you about this could get me into trouble. But what makes you so sure there's a problem? You last examination two weeks ago showed everything was healthy."

"I can feel it," she said. "I don't know how, but it's as if I can read the baby's body and there's something awfully wrong. This child will be born deformed or ill or something so bad it will make his life hell."

"But the law is very strict, Irene. No abortions under any circumstances, not even to save your life and every state in America has this law in place."

"Oh God, what am I going to do?" the woman moaned, hiding her face in her hands.

"Let's give you an inspection," the doctor said. "Maybe there's something I can see."

"You won't see it," the woman sobbed. "You can't."

"Now here is where I can really get into trouble," the doctor said softly. "But if you're that certain, your only choice is to go out of America. You could drive up to Canada or maybe fly to Europe, but please don't tell anyone I suggested that. I could lose my license."

"Could I do that?" Suddenly there was hope in the young woman's face.

"You're only four months along. Yes, a hospital in England or Canada can help you and you don't look so obvious that an inspector at the border would see that you're pregnant."

"They have inspectors?"

"They do, for exactly women like you and they can arrest you on suspicion of intending to get an abortion outside the USA. What I suggest is that you drive over to Canada at the busy time of the day at a major crossing, the border guards will be too occupied to study you, make sure you have a guy with you, because a single woman is more likely to get looked at. But please, never tell anyone that I told you. I would lose my licence."

She nodded, tears running down her cheeks and left without another word.

* * *

"The medical people in Toronto wrote to me a week or so ago," said Garry. "Irene was able to cross the border at the Windsor crossing and arranged an abortion. Because of her concerns, the pathologist examined the foetus and with all our new technologies was able to identify an issue with the child's DNA."

There was an expectant pause round the table.

"The DNA showed signs of motor neurone disease," said Garry. "Irene was right. The child would have been born with a dreadful disease."

There was silence for a few moments.

"How the hell did she know?" asked Mary.

Garry looked at his notes.

"Well, it seems she had a little contact, but so short as to make this unlikely. She went to England for a month two years ago. She has a brother who teaches at Nottingham University and she was able to use one of their machine a few times to look at her parents' history."

"No more than that?" asked Mary.

Garry shook his head.

"That appears to be the total."

"She's had no contact with the scanning systems in her work?" asked Annabelle.

"None, as far as we know," said Garry. "She was an accounts clerk with a company in Chicago and as we all know, the technology has been banned in the USA until just recently."

"They have inspectors at borders looking for pregnant women?" said Salmaan Basrai.

"And at airports and train crossings," said Garry. "I fear that we caused this religious fanaticism."

"Good grief!" said Salmaan. "So what will happen to poor Irene?"

"She's applied for refugee status in Canada on the grounds of religious persecution."

"That doesn't solve the issue of how come she was able to see the problem without any technical assistance," said Mary. "She's had almost no exposure to the technology. Can we expect this to become more widespread?"

"Almost certainly," said Garry. "And nobody has any idea of what the implications are."

"How tragic that this religious madness has taken over in the USA," said Salmaan. "I suppose it's what made the new American papacy a reality.

"Probably," said Mary. "But it's always been there. Just look at how many Americans believe in Creationism and Young Earth philosophies. Nearly half of them, I believe."

"Just as well the president has refused to join the madness," said Garry. "He stated publicly that he will use the DNA technology for national security and the Pentagon has endorsed that view. Luckily, as we just found out, the Senate and the House have now lifted their ban on it. Whether that will change attitudes among the majority of people remains to be seen."

Chapter 29 – March, 2028

"Alana, come in," said the Israeli Prime Minister.

Alana walked through the door held open by an aide into the Prime Minister's office.

"Good morning, sir," she said.

The Prime Minister was seated behind a huge polished wooden desk. Four leather padded seats were on the other side, three were occupied. She recognised one immediately.

"Good morning, sir," she said again.

Amir Levi, the new Director of Mossad smiled. "Hi there, Alana," he said in his usual informal manner.

"Alana, this is Sir Peter Charlton," said the Prime Minister. "Sir Peter is the British Ambassador here."

The Englishman was painfully thin with a perfectly bald head. Bright blue eyes illuminated a fair complexion that would not tolerate a Middle East climate well. He did not rise to his feet and merely nodded at Alana from the distance of a couple of metres.

"I've heard a lot about you, Colonel Shimova," he said. "You have an impressive record and you made some good friends during your attachment as Military Attaché to my country."

"Thank you," said Alana. The third man she knew. She had paid a courtesy call on him during her last visit to Australia. Andrew Troutman, the Director General of

Security was the head of the Australian Secret Intelligence Organisation and like her, an ex-fighter pilot, having flown F-18s in the Royal Australian Air Force. They had compared notes and shared some war stories during her visit and become friends.

"G'day Andrew," she said and he stood up and shook her hand.

"Good to see you again, Alana," he said. "Take a seat."

She sat down next to him and looked at the Prime Minister.

"This is a heavy-duty meeting, sir," she said.

The Prime Minister nodded.

"Seriously heavy duty," he said. "I've been meeting with Cabinet all morning until now, talking about you."

Alana said nothing but felt a stir of mixed excitement and worry.

"One recommendation we received was that you take the highest profile international post there is, Ambassador to the United States," said the Prime Minister.

"That would certainly be an honour," said Alana, struggling to keep her composure.

"However, continued the PM, "the presence of these other gentlemen obviously suggests that there may be an alternative task for you."

Alana said nothing.

"You were in the UK during the attacks on the offices of Karen Petrova's scientific research organisation and we know you have established a personal relationship with Garry Lawson. As a result of your influence, Israel was the first nation outside the UK to learn of the immense discoveries about Christianity and we have been able to prepare for the sometimes catastrophic events that resulted."

Alana began to see where this conversation was leading but remained silent. The PM would take his time, she knew, but he would get there.

"We need to have a close source within Blueprints," continued the PM. "We believe that while things have been peaceful there, this may not last. There are many UK nationals in the organisation, which is why Sir Peter is here and we are clearly aware of the potential for the influence that Blueprints will have on the world. That's why Andrew is here."

"So you want me to move to Australia and become involved with Blueprints again," said Alana.

"Exactly," said the PM.

"It means resigning from Mossad and our Diplomatic Corp," she said.

"Alana," said Amir Levi with a wide grin. "Everybody knows that you never resign from Mossad. Once a spook, always a spook."

"But officially, yes, you must become a private citizen again," said the PM.

"Naturally, you'll have ASIO's full support and cooperation," said Andrew Troutman. "We'll establish contact protocols and help in any way we can."

"And Mossad may sort of be around a bit," said Levi with a straight face.

There was a small laugh round the table, though Sir Peter did not join in. The PM turned to him.

"What about you, Sir Peter? Any comments?"

"His Majesty's Government will be completely cooperative," he said. "Naturally, we require to be fully briefed on all events that may concern ours and the world's security."

"We'll go along with that, seeing as you used to own most it, including our nation," said the PM.

Sir Peter did not join in the gentle laughter.

Chapter 30 – The Ballet

"We have an invitation to the ballet," said Mary, opening the envelope that had been hand-delivered. "And what's more, it comes from the management at the Australian Ballet."

"Interesting," said Garry. "I wonder why they've done that? Is it just for you and me or all of us?"

"All of us. And there's a hand-written note with the tickets. It says we should show this note to the people checking tickets and we'll be shown back stage. And this is odd. They've specifically asked that we bring Bill."

"Bill? I don't think Bill is a ballet sort of person."

"Who knows with Bill?" said Mary with a laugh. "It would not surprise me in the least to find he choreographed this ballet!"

"And when?"

"Three days," said Mary. "This sounds like fun."

Once more, the members of the Second Foundation did the exhilarating walk along the side of Circular Quay and entered the Opera House, this time to the Joan Sutherland Opera Theatre. On presenting their tickets and the note, they were shown through a different door and found themselves in the Green

Room where many people were gathered, most with drinks in their hands. The air of excitement was palpable.

They were met by a young woman who carried herself with the unmistakeable poise and grace of a dancer. She wore a short, tartan skirt and a silk blouse and her hair was swept up above her head.

"Hello," she said. "I'm Kelly Ward. I'm glad you could all make it because what happens tonight is all because of your work."

"Can you tell us more?" asked Garry. He was curious because the program he had bought indicated nothing beyond a regular performance of a new ballet called "Flights of Fantasy."

"I'd rather not," said Kelly. "Nobody here apart from the dancers and the orchestra knows about this evening. But I'm going to take you to the side of the stage and then you'll understand."

"Curiouser and curiouser," said Mary.

"Maybe one of the six impossible things the Red Queen could imagine before breakfast," said Bill.

Kelly looked at him with a small smile.

"Of all people, you could imagine this one," she said.

Bill looked baffled.

"Come with me," said Kelly and led the group out of the Green Room and to the side of the stage. The curtain was drawn. Several dancers were doing stretches and occasional jumps on the stage and Garry recognised the dancer who had been the lead in one of the most amazing performances of "Sleeping Beauty" that he had ever seen. None of the female dancers wore any sort of traditional clothing such as a tutu, all wore body stockings of various colours. The men wore black tights and nothing above the waist. Garry found himself envying the remarkable physical condition all the men seemed to possess.

Two men entered the area, both carrying cases about twice the size of a large suitcase and looking very heavy. They placed them just a short distance from the stage, about five metres apart then each of them took a chair and sat down next to one of the cases.

Garry recognised the cases. These were the finished product of Bill's experimental work in enhancing the telekinetic powers that could move objects with the mind. He began to get some idea of what they would see tonight.

"Those are my developments," said Bill, only the second time he had spoken all day. He had driven down in Garry's car earlier that day and had sat in a private world of his own the whole time. Garry knew him well enough not to disturb whatever amazing things were going on behind that bland, farmer's face.

Dancers took their positions, the orchestra struck up and the curtain lifted. Dancers began to move and the absolute beauty immediately grabbed Garry's attention and he watched, utterly charmed and delighted.

Suddenly two coloured streamers flew from the side of the stage. They encircled the four lead dancers and flew in hypnotic patters, seeming to follow the hands of the dancers as if under their command. The result was quite beautiful and a collective sigh rose from the audience. Garry realised that the movements were being controlled by telekinetic forces from the two men sitting in the wings assisted by the enhancement of the cases by their sides.

The scene became even more complex. From the other side of the stage, two clouds of smoke appeared and Garry saw that there were two people sitting there, one man, one woman, each with Bill's creation by their sides. The smoke began to follow the dancers, as if controlled by their hands and the streamers intertwined with the smoke producing a highly hypnotic effect. It went on and on and Garry realised he was standing with his jaw wide open, so involved was he in the incredible shapes being made by smoke, streamers and beautiful bodies.

Despite the effect it was having on him, he stole a look at Bill and saw that he was similarly affected, quite hypnotised by the magical scene before him.

Then the smoke seemed as if released from the control of the dancers, it formed into a huge coloured cloud and filled the stage so the dancers could barely be seen, the music stopped and all the lights went out.

Garry took a deep breath. The audience was silent for a few moments and then broke into applause like thunder moving closer.

"Now do you see what we have done with your discoveries," said Kelly, standing by Garry's side. "Dance has become so much more complex and we are only just exploring the possibilities."

Garry could only nod and saw that the four people who had been controlling the smoke and streamers had joined them.

"We wanted to meet the man who first found he could do this," said one of them and shook Ben's hand, followed by the other three.

"Believe me, it was as much a shock to me," said Ben. "The way you have used Bill's developments is an even greater shock."

"How were you able to do this?" asked Garry. "Do you work with the DNA scanners much?"

"A lot," replied one of the men. "Three of us are historians at the university and Bethany here is an epidemiologist."

"I've been tracking diseases back through generations," said Bethany. "I find out the absolute start of them and that helps us understand how they began. So we've all been exposed to the influence."

"How did you get so good at this?" asked Bill, still showing signs of shock from the performance.

"I doubt we're any better than you," replied the woman. "I found I could move a golf ball, much as you did, but that was the limit. Then we got these machines and that opened up all sorts of possibilities."

"There are many choreographers experimenting with these new forms," said Kelly. "What we're hoping is that eventually one of our telekinetic specialists will be able to lift a human body so we can have a dancer in mid-air and that will open up even more possibilities. This is as explosive as the singing techniques that are developing all over the world."

"More of the Second Renaissance," murmured Mary. "Whatever next, I wonder."

"I'm sure we'll find out," said Garry.

"You all look like you're in shock," said Kelly with a smile. "It's the usual effect of seeing this for the first time. Let's go back to the Green Room. I think you all need a drink."

"Great idea," said Mary.

Chapter 31 – June, 2028
Open Warfare

The crowd began to gather soon after ten that Sunday morning on Willow Lane, a few miles north of downtown Dallas. The beautiful temple of the Mormons had over a thousand worshippers that beautiful morning in early September. The sun reflected off the six spires that marked the temple and created a lovely scene of peace and calm.

The crowd outside the temple was not interested in peace and calm, quite the reverse. Nearly all of them, men and women carried handguns in holsters hung on their belts, many of them carried automatic rifles slung over one shoulder. There were many signs held up among the crowd.

"THOSE WHO ARE NOT WITH US ARE AGAINST US," said one.

"THOSE WHO DO NOT FOLLOW GOD'S TRUE PATH SHALL DIE," said another.

Several others said much the same. A huge voice began to bellow out over the crowd. It came from a man at the front with a portable public address system by his feet.

"The heretics who will not follow the Holy Father in

Dallas deserve death!" he shouted. "Let us now go into this temple of hell and show them we mean what we say."

A massive cheer rang out from the hundreds of armed men and women and they began advancing on the Mormon temple.

Several doors were open and the mob rapidly poured into the hall, unslinging their automatic rifles and taking handguns out of their holsters.

The congregation was startled and the prayer they were reciting stopped. Some of the children began crying as they sensed the fear in the adults.

The automatic rifles began chattering and bodies fell to the floor, screams rang out but the rifles continued their awful song. When all the standing congregation had fallen among the pews the huge voice rang out again.

"Go among the pews! Find anyone still alive and kill them."

The killers began spreading out, men and women marched up and down the pews, pistol shots sounded and the racket lasted for twenty minutes before silence fell and the executioners returned to the sides of the temple. Without another word being spoken, the mob left the temple and walked away from their work.

Within moments, the floor of the temple was a sea of blood.

But the work was not done. Several men carried packages to the six towers and began drilling holes at the bases. They inserted the dynamite sticks, attached the electronic leads and then walked away, unravelling the cables as they went.

From a safe distance, they waited for their final instructions. When they came, the switches were turned, the explosions rang out in the calm morning air and all six towers collapsed in a giant mushroom of dust and the cheers of the watchers.

Then everybody left.

"A very satisfactory result," said Joseph Maguire, now self-titled Pope Clement 15th. "Those bastards will now realise they'd better tuck in behind me or more the same thing will occur."

"Did you arrange that?" Cardinal Andrew Colmes looked shocked and frightened.

Maguire glared at him with contempt.

"They needed the lesson," he said. "Anything that makes people follow the true word of God is fully justified."

"But they did," said Colmes. "They'd rejected the new heresies."

"But they didn't accept me as the new leader of the Christian churches," snapped Maguire. "We of the new Catholic Church are the one true Mother of Churches and anyone who won't accept that gets everything they ask for. Now let's see if any more of those Mormon heretics reject me after that little object lesson."

"Would you do that again?" asked Colmes. His voice was hoarse with tension.

"Maybe," said Maguire. "But maybe some of the spineless fools in Congress need a lesson first. They've gone back on the original orders I gave them and allowed those machines from hell to be used. So here's what I want you to do, Colmes. Prepare an edict from me, to all my followers, they will not use these machines. If they do, they are damned to everlasting Hell and they will be excommunicated from the Church. Got that?"

"Yes, Holiness," muttered Colmes and backed his way out of the office.

* * *

The BBC's American commentary that evening was tense.

"Over a thousand dead," said Deborah James, the senior correspondent for BBC America. "That's the greatest mass shooting ever in America, many times greater than any previous such event in the country's history."

"One thousand and sixty seven," said Brad Hollingsworth, the political reporter. "One hundred and twelve were children, there were fifty three pregnant women among the dead. The church had installed video cameras only a year ago and they show that after the automatic rifle slaughter, men and women with hand guns searched the pews and killed anyone left alive."

"From the signs outside carried by the mob, it appears this appalling act was conducted by people supporting Joseph Maguire's self-proclaimed American Vatican," said Peter Cahill, the religious commentator. His face was white with shock. "They were complaining that the Mormon Church had refused to support the new American Vatican. I never thought that my job talking about religion would ever involve a discussion on an act of mass slaughter in the name of God such as this one."

"So those video cameras," said Deborah. "Does that mean the killers can be identified?"

"It should," replied Brad. "But so far, the Dallas police have refused to release the images or take any action against the killers."

"This might be evidence that the entire tragedy was committed on the initiative of Joseph Maguire's people," said Deborah, her shocked expression fully the centre of the television picture. "Are the police in Maguire's pocket as well?"

"Even on the orders of Maguire himself, possibly," added Hollingsworth.

"What about DNA images?" asked Peter Cahill. "Can anyone access those?"

"Again, doubtful," replied Hollingsworth. "It seems multiple vehicles were summoned immediately by somebody unidentified and all the bodies taken to a temporary morgue kept under National Guard watch. Somebody does not want the killers identified and interrogated."

"The big question now," said Deborah, "is will there be another event of this kind? Will another bunch of religious fanatics decide that they must enforce the authority of this new American Catholic Church by slaughtering any group that has not accepted Maguire's authority or has gone the way of the new theology accepted by most of the rest of the world?"

"That is just too horrible a prospect," said Peter. "If another one like that happens, America could be looking at another Religious War."

"We've been advised that the President will address the nation this evening," said Brad. "I hope to God he can suggest something that might stem this flow of blood and hatred."

"Amen," said the other two.

"The President of the United States," announced a voice. An image of the US flag fluttered for a few seconds while the National Anthem was played and then the President's face appeared on the screen. The sadness in his features was obvious.

"All too often," he began, with no salutations, "my predecessors have appeared as I do now, following massacres of innocents, often children at a school, by some lunatic who has been able to acquire a military weapon of mass slaughter because nobody in Congress has ever had the courage to do anything to avert such a tragedy. The killer has perhaps been executed or died at his own hands or by a police weapon. It has never solved anything. Most of my predecessors have offered nothing but thoughts and prayers, but thoughts and prayers have never been shown to prevent a bullet hitting the body of a child.

"This is the first case of the killers being a large group and their motives are quite clear. It is interesting to see the care that the local authorities have taken to hide their identities, refusing to release the video images from the church and trying to ensure that no DNA samples may be taken from the corpses so that the images of what they saw cannot be examined. Apparently, the plan is to cremate all those bodies, regardless of the religious beliefs they, their families or their church may hold. This again is to hide the images from DNA examination.

"I am pleased to tell you that these efforts have failed. What they did not know is that two of the people in that crowd of killers were FBI agents. Those two left Dallas immediately and arrived here in Washington where their DNA samples were taken. These two courageous people ensured that they saw the faces of all the leaders and every single one of the crowd, a total of thirty-three men and women. We now know the identities of all of them. An hour ago, every one of them was arrested by FBI agents and are being brought to Washington where their DNA will be examined and if it is found that they received their orders from somebody else, those people will also be arrested, regardless of their station in life or organisation to which they belong.

"Let me repeat that. They will be arrested regardless of who they are."

The President paused to let the words sink in, particularly into the minds of a few people in Dallas.

"Now, I am well aware that my actions already contravene some rules. We should have left the arrests to the local Dallas Police but for reasons I will not reveal just yet, that was considered impractical. The same is true of what may be another round of arrests.

"But I see my duty as protecting the citizens of America and going round the regulations that permit mass slaughter. I will deal with any legal repercussions that may arise later.

"I bid you all good night."

The broadcast ended without the usual call for blessings on America, no images of the American flag, nothing about thoughts and prayers for anyone. It reflected the immense anger the President felt for those who committed this appalling crime of mass murder and those who commanded it to happen.

* * *

The interrogation room was large but had little furniture. An oblong table in the centre had four wooden chairs, two on each side, there were more comfortable armchairs against three of the walls and the fourth wall was covered by a large screen that had been unrolled from the ceiling.

A man and a woman sat side by side facing the screen. Two uniformed guard stood, one in each corner furthest from the screen. A tall, lean, dark man sat, legs crossed in one of the armchairs, a notepad on his knee.

The woman spoke.

"Terence Wilberforce Alvaro, do you understand why you are here?"

The man opposite her was sweating badly despite the airconditioning in the room. He was of middle height, about forty years old, a little overweight and his hair was thinning badly.

"No, I don't," he replied. "I ain't done nothing. You people, you come into my house, arrest me and fly me here. I'm gunna sue you for everything I can."

His bluster was cut off by the woman raising her hand. She was about the same age as the man next to her, dressed in a simple blue business suit with a white shirt. She wore very little make-up and wore her hair in a bun at the back of her neck. Despite the unassuming image, she had an air of command about her and it worked on the other man.

"Watch this," she said.

An image appeared on the screen. It showed Alvaro holding a microphone, shouting. His words were clearly audible.

"The heretics who will not follow the Holy Father in Dallas deserve death!" he shouted. "Let us now go into this temple of hell and show them we mean what we say."

"Is that you speaking those words?" asked the woman.

"How the hell did you get that?" shouted Alvaro. "There were no cameras there."

"You obviously haven't kept up with technology," said the woman. "That image comes from the DNA of one of our agents who was in the crowd, deliberately watching you."

"What sort of crap is this?" Alvaro was furious. "That's not legal. You can't use that."

"Mr District Attorney?" said the woman.

The tall man in the armchair didn't stir.

"It's legal," he said. "Congress permitted the use of DNA imaging a few weeks ago. Its use as evidence in criminal trials will be approved any day now."

Alvaro was silent.

"Let's move on a little, shall we?" said the woman.

The screen showed the awful slaughter in the church as the gunmen began firing their automatic rifles and bodies fell to the floor. The screen showed Alvaro taking part in the shooting with the rifle he had carried into the church. The killing stopped for a moment as Alvaro's face appeared in the centre of the screen and his voice rang out again.

"Go among the pews! Find anyone still alive and kill them."

"That does appear to be you shouting that order, does it not?" said the woman.

Alvaro remained silent, looking to be in deep shock.

"So, Mr District Attorney, will the court find Mr Alvaro guilty of premeditated murder, based on this DNA evidence?"

"Absolutely," said the man in the armchair.

"And will you be seeking the death penalty?"

"Most certainly."

Alvaro drew in his breath in horror. "What? You can't! I was just following orders. Hey, I can do a deal! I can tell you who else was involved! Cut me some slack, for God's sake."

The woman was unmoved. "We already know who else was involved. And we can find out who gave you the orders as soon as we take your DNA."

Alvaro put his head on the table, sobbing.

"Don't worry," said the woman. "We've improved the lethal injection process a lot. You'll be in pain for only about five minutes, but you'll certainly be dead then."

Alvaro seemed not to hear. He began wailing like a child deprived of its favourite toy and dropped his head back on his arms on the table.

"So now, I want that DNA sample," the woman said. "Head up, Alvaro."

The man didn't move. The woman nodded at the guards, one of whom advanced on the weeping man and raised his head. The woman reached down to her handbag, extracted a sample tube and took out the swab.

"Open your mouth, Terence."

Alvaro struggled against the tight grip on his head and the second guard advanced, took hold of Alvaro's nose and closed it firmly. Alvaro struggled a few moments more but was unable to stop himself opening his mouth and taking a deep breath. The guard held it open with his gloved hand and the woman quickly and expertly rubbed the swab against the inside of Alvaro's cheek and replaced the swab.

"Thank you, Terence," she said without a trace of irony and the guards released him and returned to their positions.

The woman took a moment to write Alvaro's name on the sample tube then nodded at the officers again.

"Next," she said.

Five minutes later the door opened again. This time, three women entered. Two of them were female armed guards, the third was a tall, beautiful blonde. She looked in her thirties, her blonde hair set in tight curls. She wore a silk dress with a purple jacket.

The officers led her to the chair next to the FBI agent, waited until she had sat down then retreated to the positions their colleagues had taken earlier.

The agent looked at her carefully. The first impression of classic beauty faded on closer examination. The woman's mouth had a downturn at the ends and the face was set, no sign of awareness, almost like a wax model without sign of life.

The agent looked at her papers.

"Gabrielle Malloy?"

The woman didn't answer.

The agent smiled. "No worries," she said. "Watch the screen."

Images appeared on the screen, the same appalling sights as had been shown before, but this time they concentrated on the slaughter of the church congregation, bodies falling or trying to take shelter behind a pew.

"This is what you were seeing, isn't it?" said the agent. "We know that because we've already taken a sample of your DNA and this scene is actually through your eyes."

"Horseshit!" said Malloy. "That's not possible."

"Well, let's see," said the agent.

The scene changed as the woman moved to the pews. Her hand gun was visible in a few shots and then she walked into the first pew. A young woman, obviously pregnant lay on the floor, weeping in terror. The handgun appeared and fired straight into the head of the pregnant woman.

There was a laugh heard and then a woman's voice spoke.

"That's what all you fucking liberals should get. A bullet in the head. Now let's see who else I can find."

"Your voice, I think," said the agent.

Malloy's composure broke.

"Well, I was right. Those treasonous, Christ-hating liberals, they should all die."

"And you certainly did your best," said the agent.

The images on the screen showed the entry to another pew and Malloy shot two children, one about five years old, the other about ten. They screamed in terror as Malloy's gun took aim at them and fired twice.

The agent stopped the images.

"You killed five people with that gun. We took the bullets from the wooden pews that gone through the bodies and checked against the pistol we found in your house when our people arrested you."

She turned to the man in the chair.

"Would that be enough to convict Gabrielle of first degree murder, Mr District Attorney?"

Mallow turned to him in shock.

"It certainly would," said the D.A.

"And the DNA images of her committing the murders?"

"Simply confirming the premeditation."

"And will you be seeking the death penalty."

"Absolutely."

The blonde woman went white.

"No!" she screamed. "You can't do that! We were doing God's work, killing his enemies!"

"I'm sure that's how you see it," aid the agent. "Let me tell you how the justice system is changing with the new technology. What we have seen is absolute proof of your guilt. There will be no appeals, simply a waste of time. You might only have to wait about six weeks before you go to the death chamber. But don't worry, we don't mess up like we used to. The drugs work perfectly, you'll be dead in about five minutes. It'll hurt like hell in that time, but far less than most of your victims had to go through."

The agent watched as all composure vanished from the woman's face, revealing the ugliness that was inside her. She began breathing noisily and slumped in her chair. The agent nodded at the police officers.

*   *   *

"I have a problem," said Maguire.

He sat behind his enormous desk, a huge, gold crucifix on the wall behind him, wearing pure white robes and a white skull cap. The heavily jewelled golden crucifix around his neck almost radiated light.

Several FBI agents watched the scene on the huge monitor on the wall.

"This is from the sample we took from Alvaro at the end of his interview," said the FBI agent to her boss. The man next to her was muscular, apparently very fit, displayed a full head of black hair over deep black eyes. He was not tall, but somehow radiated a personality that made him seem bigger than anyone else in the room.

Behind them six more agents sat in a row.

They continued to study the monitor and the discussion it showed.

"What is your problem, Holiness?" said Alvaro.

"Those damned heretics, the Mormons," said Maguire. "I offered them a place with me, they scoffed at it. Now, I don't care what they believe, though they appear to follow the true path and reject all this modern crap. But they disobeyed me. I want them taught a lesson."

"What sort of lesson, Holiness?" asked Alvaro.

"One that they won't come back from. And wipe out that goddamned ugly church of theirs, too. It offends my eyes every time I go past it. I want it taken out of my sight."

"I shall do as you command, Holiness, with great pleasure and my followers in your church will be delighted to help me."

"And can I rely on your silence?"

"Of course, Holiness. We are doing God's work."

The FBI supervisor laughed softly.

"Too fucking stupid to realise we only needed the DNA of one of them and we'd have them all cold."

He turned to the line of agents behind him.

"Okay, conspiracy to commit mass murder, incitement to mass murder, I don't care if he calls himself the Pope or Jesus Christ himself, bring the bastard in. Take the Gulfstream, take a detail of armed troops in case the cops there give you some grief, but bring the bastard here."

The group broke up.

At 10:00am on a warm, sunny September morning, a Gulf Jet G550 belonging to the FBI landed at Dallas Fort Worth Airport and taxied to a hangar that had been reserved for it. The door swung open and steps were lowered as the female agent who had interrogated Alvaro and Malloy walked down. She was greeted by a National Guard officer who saluted her.

"Good morning, Ma'am," he said. "Captain Patrick Halloran at your service."

"Good to see you, Captain. Have you got what we asked for?"

"Indeed Ma'am. Three Armoured Personnel Carriers for your squad in case the locals get a bit crabby with you, and I've also got a water cannon and another dozen SWAT guys to back you up. Four of those will remain with the plane in case anybody wants to play silly games."

"But aren't you under the command of the State Governor, Captain? I'm surprised he has allowed this action."

"He's a politician, Ma'am. He has presidential delusions. The Dallas Vatican nonsense wouldn't help."

She couldn't help laughing at the cool, laconic way in which he spoke.

"Then let's get going," she said.

* * *

An hour later, the convoy pulled up outside the huge glass tower that was the new American Vatican. The water cannon vehicle remained across the parking lot while the armed troops leaped out, two remained guarding the vehicles, the rest lined up by the entrance as the agent calmly walked up with the National Guard Captain.

"Quietly, I think, Patrick," she said and he nodded.

"Can I come in with you?" he asked. "I'd love to see this."

"You are most welcome."

They walked in through the front door, accompanied by two of the FBI armed squad to be met by startled faces.

"Where's his office?" asked the agent of a young man staring at them, open-mouthed.

He pointed down the corridor at a huge, ornate door and the four of them continued, opening the door without warning and entering. Maguire was seated behind his enormous desk wearing his ceremonial white robes and the astonishment in his face was vast.

"What the hell is this?" he demanded, pressing a buzzer on the desk. "Do you know who I am?"

"Joseph Maguire, I am arresting you for conspiracy and incitement to commit multiple murders," said the agent.

"You're doing WHAT? And you will address me as Holiness. Now get out of here."

"Sorry, Maguire, the party's over," said the agent. "You're coming with us to Washington, so I suggest you get out of those silly robes, put on something suitable and be ready for a long flight."

Behind them, the door flung open and three men in clerical garb rushed in, stopping short when they saw the armed men.

"Ah, good," said Captain Halloran. "Just in time. Go and get Joseph's casual wear, pack a suitcase, tooth brush and shaving gear."

Almost catatonic in shock, the men left.

"Now, Joseph, what are you wearing under that ball gown?" asked the agent.

Maguire was spitting in fury.

"You fools have no idea what you are doing," he grated. "The whole country will turn on you when they hear of this."

"Unlikely," said the agent. "When we show them the images of the slaughter you ordered and then how you told Alvaro to do it. The safest place you can be then is in our cells under armed guard."

"What do you mean, show them images? Nobody has those images."

The agent sighed.

"You really don't know anything do you? That's the technology you tried to ban and now it's turned and bitten you on the ass. Now take that silly dress off. I hope you're decent underneath!"

Maguire seemed to deflate. "I need help," he muttered.

At that moment, the young men reappeared carrying a small suitcase.

"Good," said the Captain. "Help Joseph out of his prom dress, will you?"

It took fifteen minutes before Maguire was revealed to be wearing boxer shorts, a vest and black socks, remarkably thin, hairless legs and looking anything but Papal. His embarrassment was acute and the agent struggled to control her laughter. He quickly dressed again in a pair of trousers and a golf shirt with black slip-on shoes.

"Good," said the agent. "Far more comfortable for the flight. Let's go."

As they walked out of the building, the silence was striking. They saw nobody in the building and when they reached the parking lot, there seemed to be a lot fewer cars there.

"Like cockroaches after somebody had sprayed the place," said one of the troopers waiting for them. "I've not seen a crowd leaving so fast since the last day of the school year."

Maguire was shown into a seat in one of the personnel carriers. There was no fight in him at all, so handcuffs were left off. An hour later, they were at the steps of the Gulfstream.

Captain Halloran advanced and gave the agent another salute.

"Thank you so much, Ma'am," he said. "I haven't had so much fun since I first took a girl to a drive-in movie when I was sixteen."

The agent tried hard not to giggle.

"Thank you, too, Patrick. You certainly added an extra dimension to the day."

She climbed up the steps behind the last of the armed squad who had already taken Maguire and strapped him into a rear seat, the door closed and five hours later they were in Washington.

* * *

The evening news broadcast from BBC America was well watched, as word had spread that the three journalists had been addressing the problem for a long time. Few of the American channels had addressed the issue, perhaps fearing mass public reaction.

"The final report from the FBI shows conclusively that Joseph Maguire literally ordered the hit on the Mormon Church in Dallas two months ago, resulting in over a thousand dead," said Deborah James.

"We know that the indictments have been filed in the DC court and they include the unusual charges of Crimes Against Humanity and Incitement to Commit Crimes against Humanity," said Peter Cahill.

"And we understand that the leader of the attack Terence Alvaro, has already been charged with Crimes against Humanity, found guilty and sentenced to death," added Brad Hollingsworth. "Normally, I'm against the death penalty, but in this case I find it difficult to object to it."

"And we have been told that the remaining shooters are all due for trial over the next few days," said Deborah. "It appears that new laws have been rushed through Congress and they follow the pattern of the British judicial system that came into effect some years ago and are now standard throughout the British Commonwealth and Western Europe. As it is apparent that DNA images both from the FBI agents among the shooters which allowed identification of the killers, and from the killers themselves have absolutely proved the guilt of all the shooters, we can expect guilty verdicts for all of them immediately. The Washington DA has requested the death penalty for all of them and the new laws allow for very early application of the penalties, within a few weeks."

"A statement from the White House said that the President will not consider any pleas for mitigation," said Peter. "I think he is planning to show any possible copy-cat killers that they will be found, tried and executed without any possibility of getting away with it."

"And it may be working," said Brad. "Reports from all over the country indicate that more and more Catholic Churches that had followed Maguire as the new Pope of an American Vatican have abandoned him and returned to the Roman Vatican and acceptance of the new theologies."

"How about those other churches that had joined in with Maguire?" asked Peter.

"Much the same. The Southern Baptists' membership has almost collapsed since news of Maguire's arrest and the evidence of his crimes has been released. All the others have firmly announced that they have no connection to the American Vatican."

"Not unexpected," said Deborah. "And the Church of Latter Day Saints, the Mormons?"

"Membership has soared," said Brad with a smile. "Some of that is, of course, sympathy with the horrible events, some because of their resistance to Maguire's operation and some because many people still want to hold onto the original theologies of a divine Jesus Christ."

"It appears that the American Catholic Church has just about collapsed," said Peter. "Donations have dried up to nothing, the organisation is almost bankrupt. I give it no more than another three months."

"And I consider that a very good thing," said Deborah. She turned to face the camera.

"And this is BBC America's News Hour signing off for tonight."

Chapter 32

"I've got an invitation to observe a hand surgeon at work," said Garry, putting down his mobile phone.

"What's brought that on?" asked Mary.

"Really no idea. But that was the John Hunter Hospital and they seemed keen on having me watch something crucial."

"So it must be something to do with what we've done in recent years. When?"

"Two days. I've never watched a surgeon at work, so I hope I don't throw up."

"Stand next to the door," said Mary with a wide grin.

'This is experimental," said the surgeon. She was tiny, barely a hundred and fifty centimetres tall and the dimensions of a schoolgirl. Her dark brown eyes glowed with amusement at Garry's concerns. Doctor Anne Rahbari was the daughter of an Iranian heart surgeon and a Welsh obstetrician and as she had told Garry earlier, there was never any career choice for her but surgery.

"Somehow, it became hands and wrists," she said. "And that's where I've specialised."

According to the nurse who had taken Garry to the surgery, Anne Rahbari was more than a specialist, she had the reputation of one of the top hand doctors in the world.

"I still don't realise why you asked me to watch this," said Garry, charmed by the elfin features and wide smile of the tiny woman.

"Let's get you scrubbed up and then you'll see," she replied.

During the lengthy process of scrubbing his hands and arms, having a surgical coat fastened around him and then a hat and mask to finish off, she broke the silence.

"Actually, this is going to become unnecessary," she said. "And we don't really need it today unless the experiment fails."

"I can't say I understand that," he replied.

She nodded at the far wall and Garry began to comprehend. Carefully being inserted into a plastic bag that had been sterilised was another of the suitcase-sized machines developed by Bill to enhance the telekinesis power of a capable user. A nurse in fully sterile cap and gown and gloves wheeled it into the operating theatre.

They entered the theatre to see three nurses and another doctor surrounding a woman laid out on the table. One arm of the patient had been stretched out to one side and a large device was placed just a short distance above the wrist and hand. Above her head was a computer monitor that showed an enlarged image of the hand.

"The patient is the principal cellist of a major European Symphony Orchestra," said the surgeon. "Two weeks ago, she fell on the steps of the concert hall and badly damaged her left hand. The general consensus was that she would never play again. I was asked to look at the damage and I believe I can fix it. But with the technology that your team has developed, I believe I can do it without cutting into the hand. If so, everything will heal better and she should recover full use and mobility. You can imagine what this means to a professional cello player."

"She's under," said the other man that Garry assumed was the anaesthetist.

"Thanks, Greg," said the surgeon. "X-ray, please."

The large monitor was filled with an image of the skeleton of the patient's hands from the wrist to just the base of the fingers.

"About a year ago, I discovered that I was rather good at this telekinesis thing," said the surgeon. "But I couldn't do anything useful with it. When your enhancer came on the market, all sorts of opportunities opened up. This is the first time I'm going to try doing a full repair work without cutting into the hand. If it doesn't work, then I'll just have to return to conventional surgery, so let's cross our fingers, eh?"

She turned to the patient and looked at the screen. She picked up a small electronic device and pointed at the image.

"The main damage is to the Hamate," she said and a red point appeared on a large bone. "It has split down about two thirds of its size, one part has been driven up against the bone above it and the other part has been crushed against the large Capitate next to it, There is similar damage to the Scaphoid bone and Trapezium next to it. Now I'm going to try and fix these bit by bit."

She concentrated hard, focussing at the hand, not the image.

Garry stared, fascinated at the monitor. The first bone she had pointed out changed at a microscopic rate. The shaft driven up into the bone above it was slowly moving down and fitting itself back into its position next to the remainder. And that part then began to crawl back away from the Capitate. Garry looked up at the clock and was startled to see that half an hour had passed.

Anne sat back and looked at the monitor. She studied it carefully for a few moments and then said, "Enlarge." Instantly, the image doubled in size and Anne continued her careful examination.

"Enlarge," she repeated and the image again doubled in size, showing only the area in which she had worked.

"Some tiny bone fragments there," she said and used the red dot to point out microscopic fragments of bone. "And now I can see where they belong."

She concentrated on the hand again and Garry watched as the tiny white fragments slowly moved into position against the Hamate bone.

Anne looked up at the monitor again and smiled.

"It seems to be working," she said. "Let's focus on the Scaphoid and Trapezium."

Once again, Garry was entranced as he watched the bones moved slowly and gradually were repaired and repositioned. Then Anne sat back again.

"You know what, I think I've done it! Have the wrist fixed and absolutely immobilised. We'll have a look in a couple of weeks and see how that's worked out, but I do believe she'll be playing the cello again in a month or two."

Garry looked at the clock. More than four hours had passed since he had entered the operating theatre. He took a deep breath.

"That was amazing," he said. "Will you let me know how that all works out?"

"Of course," she said. "Ladies and gentlemen," she said to the room as a whole. "I think we've made history! Will you all join me for a drink this evening?"

There was a round of applause and Garry removed his sterile clothing and left to return to the office with the news of yet another extraordinary change that had been effected by his team.

Chapter 33 – July, 2028

"So what are you up to?" asked Avram, staring intently at his monitor.

"I'm back to 37,912 years ago," replied Penny. "How about you?"

"A bit further back," said Avram. "39,535 years. Bill?"

"About the same as Penny," said Bill. "Just passed 40,000 years."

Conversation stopped again. Ten minutes passed.

"What have you chosen in the sweepstake?" asked Avram.

"I reckon we'll get past 100,000 years," said Penny. "You?"

"That means you think we'll be seeing all Neanderthal samples?"

"Yes, I do," Penny replied. "What's your thinking?"

"I'm betting this all started with Cro-Magnon man. That means nothing further back than 50,000 years. I've picked 48,500 years ago when this thing was implanted in humanity."

"Bill, how about you?" asked Penny.

"I'm with Avram," said Bill. "I think it all started with Cro-Magnon, so I picked 46,555 years ago."

Conversation stopped again.

"Okay, that's it for me," said Avram after another fifteen minutes. "I can't just sit here watching numbers."

"Agreed," said Bill. "A couple of hours a day, that's as much as I can take. Let's go for lunch. They've got roast beef and Yorkshire pudding on the menu."

"Sounds like a plan," said Penny and all three left the room.

* * *

"What we've done," said Avram, "is load up over 100,000 samples of DNA that we've got over the years. It includes the very first samples taken in England, all the ones from the Middle East that were taken during the study in Israel and hundreds more from all parts of the world."

"And the computer has copied them all into its innards?" said Mary. She had joined them for lunch.

"And we got a lot more from the Max Planck Institute in Germany," said Penny. "They've been analysing Neanderthal DNA for many years so they sent us some samples, plus quite a few really good bone samples that we were able to use and extract more DNA. Some of it was too badly decayed, but we did get some excellent specimens and they've gone into the belly of the beast, also."

Mary laughed. "The beast? A good name for something that cost us over a hundred million dollars."

"Now, in the first phase," continued Penny, "the beast is going through every sample, switching to the parents of each individual, going back and back and eventually we expect to hit a point where there's nowhere further back."

"And that will be Day One?" Mary was obviously

fascinated, even though this had been explained to the Second Foundation group before.

"We believe so," said Avram. "Whether it's the same day for every individual or whether the implanting is done over an extended time remains to be seen."

"And you sit in front of the monitor watching the numbers mount?"

Avram laughed. "Not all day! We tend to spend about an hour, sometimes two doing that, but it gives me a major headache. I'm doing a lot of looking at images of ancient people, early Cro-Magnon, how they lived. It's fascinating."

"So how back can this go, do you think?"

"We're divided on that," replied Bill. "Avram and I think Day One was in Cro-Magnon times and that's believed to be from about 50,000 years ago."

"And I'm in the Neanderthal camp," said Penny. "That's possibly as far back as 250,000 years ago up to about 40,000 years ago when Neanderthal man disappeared."

"And how will you know when you reach Day One?"

"When the scan sees no dots on the DNA record that will mean that's when the system was implemented. What we expect is that every one of the records will record the same thing as happening on the same day and that will be Day One."

"And that's when we start the second phase," said Avram.

"Which is?" Mary looked intrigued.

"The really big processing job," said Avram. "By then, we'll have every specimen copied into the beast and the computer will now start reading in full every single day of every life and recording it. So we'll be able to look at every day lived by over a hundred thousand people and all their ancestors back through maybe 50,000 years or more."

"That's quite incredible," said Mary, obviously affected by the concept. "What a gold mine of information we are producing for science."

"I'm almost frightened by what we will find," said Avram.

"And how are you going with the Rosetta Calendar?"

Bill looked smug.

"Pretty well done," he said. "I set up a routine that extracts the time symbol as the computer reads each daily record. Then it adds that to the calendar. But as we can count back each day in normal fashion, we know what that symbol shows in the number of days counting back from when we started. So as the computer reads back in time, we're building up a complete calendar of each day and the symbol it refers to."

"That's clever," said an obviously impressed Mary.

"Actually, it's more than that," broke in Avram. "Now that we've tracked several million days, we can finally see the logical progression of the symbol. We know how it works."

"You've worked out the mathematical logic?"

"We have. And I have to tell you Mary, this is nothing remotely human."

Mary stared at all three of them and took a deep breath. "I'll leave you to it," she said, standing up and picking up her tray. "The Board is meeting the Russian Science Minister this afternoon."

"Good luck with that," said Avram.

* * *

"What the hell?" exclaimed Bill. The others gathered at his monitor.

"No further ancestry," said the legend on the screen.

"Good grief!" said Penny. "Does that mean..?"

"Day One? Possibly," replied Avram. "What's the date showing?"

"It's 46,271 years ago," said Bill studying the computer monitor. "That's actually sixteen million, nine hundred thousand, four hundred and eighty-three days, allowing for leap years."

"What are other screens showing?" said Penny and moved to hers. "Oops!" she said. "On the last sample recorded and tracked back as far as it can do, I've got the same message."

She tapped a few keys and stood up, excitement showing in her face. "46,271 years ago," she said. "And that's sixteen million, nine hundred thousand, four hundred and eighty-three days, again allowing for leap years."

"Mine's still going," said Avram. "It's showing 46,009 years, coming up to sixteen million, eight hundred thousand days."

"Let's check all the others," said Bill. No emotion showed in his face at all. He sat back at his terminal and started reading through all the other twenty devices attached to the Cray computer, all doing the same process. The other two stood behind him as a line of data appeared for each device.

"Twelve of them showing the same Day One," said Bill, some excitement finally showing in his face. "The others are still reading."

"But look at those three," said Avram, pointing at the screen. The others peered closely.

"Uh-oh," said Penny.

"We may have a problem," said Bill.

* * *

"We've hit a very strange place indeed," said Penny.

"Explain," said Garry.

"We've examined over a hundred thousand samples," continued Penny. "And that means we have gone back through several hundred million days, recording the time symbol for each day, just as we planned."

"So what's the problem?"

"The problem is that we seem to have reached Day One for the majority of our samples, but not all."

"I don't understand. Clarify that for this dumb engineer, would you please?"

"What that means is that for over ninety percent of the samples we've gone through, the earliest date when finally there were no two dots representing parents' time lines was 46,271 years ago. All of them appeared to stop on that date and on the exact same day, a bit under seventeen million days ago."

"Good grief!" Garry leaned forward in his seat.

"Indeed," said Bill. "So then we looked at the records of every scan that had been in process. We hadn't really expected this to happen so early, so we'd only been looking at those scans showing the results on a monitor."

"And?" said Garry.

"Ninety-one percent of the scans had been completed, all showing the same result," said Avram. "Day One appears to have been sixteen million, nine hundred thousand, four hundred and eighty-three days ago. The others are still running, though they haven't reached the same date yet."

"That's huge, isn't it?" asked Garry. "We've discovered something critical, surely?"

"We have, yes," replied Avram. "It's some of the others that have given us a problem."

"In what way?"

"They're still reading and scanning and they are well past that number. It looks like Day One is only Day One for most of the people, but not all."

"We have more work to do," said Penny.

* * *

"The Max Planck Institute in Leipzig has been great!" said Avram. "They've been working on Neanderthal DNA for some years and they've sent us some first-class samples to work on. So one thing we've learned is how to distinguish between Neanderthal DNA and that of Cro-Magnon."

"And that's what is driving this project now?" Garry kept his emotions firmly in check but inwardly shook with excitement at the amazing story being unfolded.

"It sure is," said Avram. "The only theory we can come up with to explain why Day One has been identified with our samples so far is that these samples are Cro-Magnon DNA without any trace of Neanderthal at all."

"But we already know that the time lines of the two species overlapped," said Penny. "And it seems almost certain that some interbreeding took place. So those times that go further back are probably where Neanderthal DNA has mixed with Cro-Magnon DNA and we've started to reach back into Neanderthal times."

"So what now?" asked Garry.

"Quite a few things," replied Penny. "One, we let the computer read through every single remaining

DNA record back to the beginning and see what we have."

"Two," continued Avram, "we start calling for every new DNA sample we can get from people all over the world. I think we should set up collection centres in as many countries of the globe as we can, collect samples and send them here for processing."

"And then we feed those into the computer," said Penny. "Pretty soon, we'll have a historical record of millions of lifetimes from every location, right back to the beginning."

"Are you two some sort of comedy turn?" asked Garry, suppressing a smile.

Avram looked at Penny and they both laughed.

"We've been working on the same thing for years," he said. "We pretty well know what each of us is thinking."

"Include Bill in that," added Penny. "It's a sort of intellectual threesome!"

"But just think what we'll be able to do with that massive pile of information," said Avram when the laughter had stopped. "Universities will be able to track the migration of people from Neanderthal onward, follow the developments of languages, confirm or update almost every historical event. It's a world changer."

"Just as Karen said she would," said Garry. "Okay, what do you need?"

"Get those collection centres set up," said Penny. "And put out a call to every government that will listen to agree to them."

"Can I ask for something?"

"Of course, Avram."

"I know that all our research staff have complete freedom to do whatever they want," said Avram. "But I have this deep thought that the transition period between Neanderthal and Cro-Magnon could answer a lot of questions. So would it be possible to ask for anybody who could help to start looking into that period of time?"

"I'll report back to the board," said Garry. "And I'll ask for volunteers. So why are you two still sitting there? Get back to work!"

"Yes boss," said Penny and blew a loud raspberry in Garry's direction.

* * *

"Good grief!"

The explosive astonishment came from Declan Holloway, a genetics doctorate from Melbourne University who had joined the company less than a year ago. He was one of those who had offered to help the review of the several thousands of years between the final generations of Neanderthal humans and Cro-Magnon. He was a short, stocky man with a head of bright red hair that grew in wild profusion and seemed impossible to control.

Every head in the research area turned toward him. He was staring at his monitor in almost a trance. Several others got up from their cubicles and came to see what had caused the reaction.

After a minute of silent observation, one of them said quietly, "Declan, put that up to the main screen. I'll get the others."

The research area was crowded. Everybody in the organisation who was in the building had been advised that something critical had been observed. Garry stood at the back of the room with others of the Foundation board.

The image on the huge screen on the far wall showed a number of Neanderthal men and women, some children sitting in an orderly arrangement of three lines, all facing the eyes of whoever was observing. Their seats appeared to be carved blocks of stone, all of the same dimensions. They had their heads down, their hands folded on their laps. No sounds came through the speakers.

For several minutes the scene looked frozen, no different from the group watching.

Then the sound began. It started as a low hum that grew in volume as each of the individuals joined in and then changed into a low growling chant that was still oddly rhythmic and musical.

"Throat singing," whispered a young woman standing in her cubicle. "Just like in Tibet."

The almost hypnotic sound went on for another five minutes while the observers stood silent, some of them holding their breath.

Without warning, a second sound was added, a higher pitched, melodious song coming from at least two or three of the group of ancient people in the image.

"I think that's two voices from the same throat," whispered Penny. "Just like we saw in Stonehenge." She had tears in her eyes.

"It's a religious service," said another young man watching the event of perhaps fifty thousand years ago. "We must be seeing this from the viewpoint of whoever is leading it."

The researchers fell silent again, almost overwhelmed by what they were seeing. The scene changed as the leader of the service began to move to the side of the building, or enclosure where this astounding religious service was taking place. The rough surface and uneven shape of the walls at last indicated that this was happening in a cave and light was coming in from one side which faced the exterior.

The surprises were not over. The watcher began looking at the walls of the cave and pictures began to appear. These were not primitive art, these seemed to be sophisticated images of people and animals in brilliant colours. As the observer moved from one to the next, his arm became visible, reaching out to touch the edge of each painting with a reverential, gentle touch while the extraordinary throat singing continued from what was now obviously a congregation. There were ten such paintings and as the observer touched the last, the singing stopped abruptly.

He continued to stay in this position but turned to face the centre of the cave and his congregation rose and began to file out in silence. When all had gone, the remaining man returned to the original position, turned to face the wall and the shifting perspective indicated he had sat down or sunk to his knees, nothing became visible but the floor and then blacked out as the man closed his eyes.

"Stop it there," said Garry softly. "Declan, that is an amazing find. Have you any idea where that took place?"

"None at all," said Declan. "I just stumbled on that scene while I was surfing the thread. But I'll go back to see how this group formed and then follow it after and see if the shaman or priest or whatever he was goes anywhere that might be identified."

"If you can't see it, call the University here in Newcastle, see if anyone in the geology section can help," said Garry. "If not, come back to me and we'll send out calls for help to other Universities around the world. Somebody may recognise the shape of the landscape outside. And record the time symbol at the start of the day. We'll find out how long ago that took place."

"Will do," said Declan.

As Garry walked out, he heard a woman's voice saying softly, "Play that again, Declan. It was astounding."

Penny and Avram joined Garry as he returned to his office and they sat around his desk, visibly moved by what they had seen.

"Holy *Cow!*" said Avram softly. "That will open some eyes in the history departments around the world."

"It could have been a church congregation anywhere and anytime in history," said Penny. "And the multi-voiced throat singing, that had started thousands of years before we heard it at Stonehenge, and that was what, five thousand years ago?"

"But those paintings!" said Garry. "I don't think anybody has ever thought there would be such works of action and colour. We sure have to find that place. If somehow it got closed off, we may be able to find it again."

"It's a pity we heard no speech," said Penny. "It will be fantastic if we ever find some form of language from those times."

"I'm sure we will, some day," said Avram. "We've got several of our people reviewing these times and the people at the Max Planck Institute have requested some of the records. They have our equipment, so I'm sure we'll hear speech before long."

"Meanwhile, we've got a massive task," said Garry. "Samples are coming in from all over the world, most just as swabs with a note to say what they are. I'm hiring a small army of technicians to prepare slides and the catalogues so you can feed them to the Cray. I think we'll have a couple of million before too long."

"And the beast is working up a good sweat going through the ones we have," said Penny with a smile. "One day soon, we'll discover when Day One happened with Neanderthal Man."

"How far have you gone back so far?" asked Garry.

"Over sixty thousand years," replied Penny. "And no sign of Day One yet."

"Talk about hunting for the Snark," said Garry. "That's how I thought about my job when I first started. I could never have guessed we'd be going back tens of thousands of years and still be looking for it."

"Let's go and see if Declan has found an outdoor scene yet," said Penny, rising to her feet.

Avram nodded and they both left Garry to his thoughts.

* * *

"That scene in the cave occurred 73,823 years ago," said Avram. "That's twenty six million, nine hundred and sixty-three thousand and eight hundred and fifty-one days ago, allowing for leap-years."

"Good grief," said Garry. "No sign of Neanderthal Day One yet?"

"Still counting," said Avram.

Chapter 34 – July, 2028

"I'm glad that we both have secure lines," said Cardinal Eamon Jackson.

The call had come to Garry's office late in the afternoon and Garry felt a surge of delight at hearing the Cardinal's North England accent. Becoming friends with this extraordinary man had been one of the greatest benefits of the work he had been doing for so many years.

Garry laughed. "The privacy will last as long as it takes for somebody to get some of our DNA," he said. "But Eamon, what has caused this unexpected call? I imagine life has been frantic for you since publishing Vatican III."

"You could say that," replied Jackson. "The reactions of the breakaway Eastern Orthodox Churches have been a shade heated."

Garry could hear the smile in the Cardinal's voice.

"And of course, the events in Dallas were a cause for some intensive discussions," said Jackson. "As you might imagine, there was no great distress shown at the collapse of the Dallas Papacy."

"That I can believe," said Garry with a smile.

"But Garry," continued Jackson, "I need to advise you of some upcoming events that will make Vatican III somewhat reduced in importance. We've been able to keep this under wraps for a few days, though it could break at any time. But so far, nobody seems to have accessed any of the DNA of people in the know, so it's all still hush-hush. But I'd like you to know now, seeing as all this is your fault."

Garry laughed, despite the surge of curiosity. The Cardinal's very British sense of humour had always been in tune with Garry's own.

"I'm intrigued," he said. "What am I to blame for now?"

"Garry, the Pope took ill a few days ago and his condition has deteriorated severely. He could die at any moment."

Garry was silent. He recalled that he had seen the Pope on television news broadcasts only a week or two ago and there had been no signs of anything wrong.

"Cancer of the stomach," continued Jackson. "We had known about it for a while, but the condition took a sharp turn for the worse. His pain was terrible and he asked to be placed in an induced coma, knowing well he would die before anything productive could be done."

"Eamon, this is dreadful," said Garry. "Things must be distressing in Rome."

"Actually, we all seem to be handling it rather well," replied the Cardinal. "His Holiness displayed a remarkable calming influence on us all and we are just working on the continuation of the Church's work."

"So when will you call the next convocation?" asked Garry.

"I've been told by many of the Cardinals here that everybody has already decided on the next Pope," said Jackson. "The gathering of the Cardinals will be very short."

"Do you know who the next Pope will be?" asked Garry.

"That would be me."

"Eamon, there could not be a better choice," said Garry in delight. "And I'm not surprised. I thought I'd see that some time. Congratulations!"

"Well, thank you, Garry. But here's the thing."

Garry waited for a second, recognising that something earth-shaking was about to happen.

"I'll be the last Pope," said the Cardinal.

* * *

"I'll take the name of Leo the Fourteenth," said Jackson. "That's only because I was born in early August, so that's my star sign."

Despite the shock he was still feeling, Garry could hear the laughter in Jackson's voice. Finally, he felt able to make his voice work again.

"Eamon, this is stunning. I think you'll make the greatest of Popes. But why the last?"

"That's the other thing, Garry. I got back early this morning from a quiet visit to meet somebody in England. There was no publicity, nobody knows about it yet, though of course, we can't keep these things secret for long any more. But I had a long and highly informative meeting with a man in London."

* * *

"It's been some time since our predecessors met," said the Archbishop of Canterbury. "And it was all rather more colourful than this time!"

"It was 2013, and in Rome," said Cardinal Eamon Jackson. "And of course, your predecessor met the Pope, I'm just a Cardinal."

"And I was just a lowly Bishop when it happened," said the Archbishop with a smile. He was a tall, slender man with an imposing head of grey hair and a deeply lined face in which hugely intelligent eyes seemed to shine like lanterns. Peter Collins had been appointed to the position only a few months before.

"I am grateful that you have told me what is happening in Rome," he continued. His accent was slightly south-west England, just a trace of his childhood and upbringing in Dorset. "I am truly distressed that the Pope is so close to death, but the fact that you will almost certainly succeed him gives me great hope."

The two men sat in a comfortable lounge room, each in an armchair. Neither wore any form of religious clothing, instead dressed in casual slacks and sweaters.

"No difficulties getting here?" asked Collins.

"None," said Jackson. "A business jet chartered from a local company brought me here, and we had arranged for us to land at Farnborough rather than at a major airport. I used my own identification of course, but British Customs and Immigration didn't seem too interested in my reasons for visiting."

"I'm grateful you accepted the invitation," said Collins. "It was becoming critical that we meet."

"if you hadn't invited me, I'd have issued my own invitation," replied Jackson.

"Then let's get to the meat of this, Eamon," said Collins. "It's obvious this had to happen soon."

"Indeed," said Jackson. "Since all the amazing revelations of historical accuracy, both our organisations have adjusted considerably. There's almost no difference at all now between us."

"Certainly there are few doctrinal differences remaining," said Collins. "But we are both committed to improving the world by following those teachings of two thousand years ago. I suppose the only issue is the one that led King Henry the Eighth to break away and create the Church of England."

"Our supposed authority over you?" Jackson smiled. "Negotiable, I think, Peter!"

"That's a good thing," replied Collins. "Because I'm not letting you lord it over me, not nohow!"

Both men laughed. They had obviously felt at ease with each other from the beginning.

"No, I would never expect that," said Jackson. "And I don't think we can expect our churches to merge again in such circumstances. But here's what I think will work."

Both men settled back in their armchairs. Nobody looking at this simple scene of two men relaxing in a comfortable room could have imagined the enormity of what was being discussed.

"Once installed as Pope, I intend to begin a firm process of liberation policies," said Jackson. "I'll start with the celibacy of priests. We both know what a mockery that has been for decades and the revelations of appalling child abuse have made me deeply ashamed."

"You're not the only one," said Collins. "There's much shame in my people as well."

"So priests will at last be able to marry," said Jackson. "That whole idea has been modified in recent years as the Church has allowed married men to become priests in some circumstances because of the huge shortage in the clergy."

"That will help," agreed Collins. "I've always felt that priests should be married anyway. They better understand families that way. I've always liked the policies in Judaism which expects that Rabbis will be married."

"I'm with you on that one," said Jackson. "Then

we'll continue what is already happening, a de-mystification of the religious services," he continued. "That's proceeding well already. The whole Eucharist thing has faded sharply almost everywhere."

"So, much as is happening here," said Collins. "Church services have become far more informal, more group gatherings for support, information exchange and commitments to leading good lives, helping the less fortunate. It's been a major source of astonishment and pleasure that congregations have been steadily increasing with this change."

"And you're doing the same as us in another area," said Jackson. "The cross remains a potent symbol, but all those ghastly crucifixion statues have gone. I've always hated that image of a hideous torture representing a love of humanity."

"Just about all gone," said Collins. "We've also started a program of selling off all the gold and silver things, all those chalices, jewels and stuff. They were of no use to us except to symbolise the wealth and power of the Church. Now we'll use the money for proper programs."

"I heard that," said Jackson. "It inspired us to start a similar process. None of all that richness and pomp would have been in the minds of those original young rabbis."

"What about confessions?"

"Purely voluntary," said Jackson. "The process can be very therapeutic for some. So what I will initiate is considerably more training for priests in psychological counselling. They'll become genuine mental carers and offer proper, professional assistance to those who need it. No more penances, Hail Mary's and all that stuff, but just a chance for unloading and getting help."

"But what if somebody confesses a crime, such as murder or rape?" asked Collins.

"I believe the sanctity of the confessional remains, just as the professional relationship with a psychologist would forbid a counsellor revealing a crime to the police," said Jackson. "But the perpetrators will be given all encouragement and assistance to go to the authorities themselves."

"It all sounds good," said Collins. "Do you believe your people will follow this lead?"

"I think so. Vatican III indicated this path and it hasn't caused too much upheaval and the power of a Papal statement remains."

"And your own position?"

"It seems firm. Every one of the Cardinals has indicated their sincere wish to put me in the hot seat because they really want to see this new form of religion. They have also expressed their wish for some sort of alliance between us."

"So is a merger possible? Can we revert back to a time of a single church? Me, I rather doubt it. Not yet, anyway."

"I agree," said Jackson. "That's not on the cards for years, yet. But I believe that this new form will gradually become the standard, as will the changes in the Anglican Church until there is simply no discernible difference between the two and all the boundaries between them will fade away."

"And an actual merger may never happen, anyway," said Collins. "It will be more like the differences between various Christian sects, more traditional than based on actual doctrinal differences."

"I think so. We should just let history and society follow the usual developments and see what happens."

"While I've always had my doubts about the Freemasons, they do have one message that may be the way we're heading," said Collins. "It came from an Austrian diplomat who developed the libretto for Haydn's great work, *"The Creation."*

"Ah! Baron van Swieten!" said Jackson. "It's one of my favourite works."

"Mine too," agree Collins. "One writer has given the term "Pantheistic Humanitarianism" to the philosophy Swieten expressed and the Masons appear to have adopted. It's the idea that the nature of God is expressed not in the doctrines of the Church but in the manifestations of nature and that humanity should really promote the brotherhood of man, not preach dogma."

"That would certainly seem to reflect the message we are both trying to send," agreed Jackson. "And as we see an apparent rise in agnosticism around the world, I believe fewer and fewer people will even relate to any concept of an actual God and just concentrate on being people. Maybe it's time for the Judeo-Christian God to follow all its predecessors into the realms of myth and legend."

Collins laughed, a real bellow of relief and joy.

"Your future Holiness, I think we can do business! We've been doing much the same, a gradual liberation of religious dogma. Once you've made your changes as Pope, I believe there will be a gradual growth in the idea of reunification. I suggest we set up a couple of working parties to develop the idea and an operational plan to follow. Now, fancy a spot of lunch before you head home?"

"Indeed, Peter. I've brought along a couple of bottles of the very best Australian Cabernet Merlot from the Vatican cellars. Let's drink to the world's health!"

Collins got to his feet.

"Henry the Eighth will be spinning in his grave," he said.

Chapter 35 – August, 2028

History repeated itself that morning.

Garry was standing in the lobby of the building when he saw through the front entrance the line of cars approaching along the road and stop outside the high security fence. He watched as four men climbed out and began laying packages along the base of the fence. He felt a shiver of anticipation, a flash of memory of a dreadful moment and when he saw that more of the men getting out of the cars were carrying heavy weapons he hit the emergency button on the receptionist's desk, one of several installed around the building.

Immediately, a loud crash resounded as a steel barrier shot up from a concealed space in front of the entry door, completely covering the entrance.

Simultaneously, the rattle of the steel coverings rolling down from similarly concealed spaces above every window on the upper floor broke out. Within seconds, every point on all walls was protected. A similar steel barrier dropped across the loading dock at the rear of the building.

At the same time, heavy explosions rocked the air and shook the ground and one section of the fence collapsed to the earth. Broken shards of steel from the fence flew in all directions.

A large monitor came to life above the receptionist's desk and similar monitors switched on all around both floors, showing the scene outside.

Six cars had arrived. Garry counted at least fifteen men, most carrying automatic rifles, two of them holding somewhat larger devices which Garry recognised from his briefings by Sir Connor Shackleton as grenade launchers.

The men separated, running around the building until all four sides had attackers facing them. There was a massive crash as an explosion hit the barrier in front of the entrance but nothing broke. All round the building, there was an outbreak of metallic clattering as the armed men opened fire at the steel shutters before every window, but again, no damage could be detected.

Sir Connor's work appeared to have proven itself, though Garry. He pressed the loudspeaker button on the desk.

"Everybody, this is Garry. The crazies have struck again, but we're far better prepared than we were before. Stay calm if you can, help will be on its way soon. But you will have noticed that signs everywhere are now pointing to the nearest emergency exit. As you know from our emergency briefings, these lead to three different escape tunnels that will take you quite a long way from the building before coming out on the surface. For this attack, we'll be better off staying where we are. You can see what's happening outside, so hold tight and wait for the cavalry to arrive."

Feeling a lot calmer as he saw that Shackleton's building design was proving itself, Garry studied the scene outside. One thing he noticed was that all the licence plates on the vehicles had been covered up. So the fact that the entire action was being recorded would not have that indicator to the identity of the attackers. All the men had balaclavas over their heads. Finding them might be a bit problematical, Garry thought.

The noise of bullets hitting metal faded and Garry watched as all the men returned to their cars. It seemed they had realised the futility of what they were doing and were making a rapid retreat. Within seconds they had vanished. The whole thing had lasted just three minutes. And only two minutes later, the cavalry arrived, as Garry had promised.

Six trucks arrived, doors were flung open and yet again, hordes of men carrying weapons surged out. But this time, Garry knew they were the Tactical Operations Group of the State Police. He pressed the second button the desk and the barriers to doors and windows slowly retreated back into the shells.

Once clear, Garry walked out of the entrance and advanced on the first officer to approach. He had three fabric stars on his shoulder indicating his rank of Inspector.

"What kept you?" asked Garry innocently, struggling to control the incipient hysteria that was threatening him. He recognised that this was a common feature with people who have narrowly escaped violent, life-threatening danger and the hysteria subsided.

The officer raised his face mask.

"Had a spot of bother, did we?"

The wonderfully understated comment nearly shattered Garry's self-control again, but he fought it and shook the Inspector's hand.

"You missed the party," he said. "I think they've moved down to the pub up the road."

The officer grinned cheerfully. "We'll find them," he said. "Let's have a look at the videos."

Inside was a loud roar of conversations as people recovered from the events and shared comments, all talking far louder than normal, another reflection of the after-effects of violence avoided. A few minutes later, as the Inspector studied the videos, he pointed at one man.

"I know that bastard," he said. "Face mask or not, I know that shape, the way he moves, everything. We've come up against him before. Tommy Richmond, general-duties thug, right wing fanatic, we've done him for Grievous Bodily Harm, robbery with violence and I'm sure he's killed a couple of people. When we find him, we'll take his DNA and that will give us all the bastards involved. They won't see daylight again. But it will be interesting to find out who put them up to this."

"I'll send the film over to your office," said Garry.

"Do that," the officer said. "I'll let you know as we round them up."

He turned and realised almost the entire staff of Blueprints was standing in the lobby.

"All right, you lazy bastards," he said loudly. "Why are you all standing around like a bunch of whores on their day off? Get back to bloody work!"

He walked out to a roar of laughter and loud applause.

* * *

Garry gave the Council two days to recover from the violence and return to normal before calling a meeting.

"Two things to discuss and a recommendation," he said. "The first thing of course is the attack. We came out of it quite unscathed except for some scorch marks on the front door barrier and a few scrapes on the window coverings from the bullets. I'd like to send a letter of commendation to Sir Connor Shackleton for his design."

Nods of approval ran round the table. Signs of strain were still evident in a couple of faces, Garry noted. Only Ben Fuller and Mary Hennessey looked normal.

"The second thing is the computer data we have," Garry continued. "Since we installed the Cray with effectively unlimited storage, we've started receiving huge amounts of DNA data from all the universities, corporations and government departments around the world who have installed our equipment. There are now well over a thousand such installations and to date we have over thirty million DNA samples. That number is rising significantly every day. Isaac Asimov once told Karen that such data volumes allowed both incredible research potential but also represented danger if misused. We hired an excellent man before, but he has left us for family reasons. I doubt he could have coped with the new dimensions of the task. So because of the recent events and hugely increased data volumes, I believe it's time we hired a top notch security specialist."

There was an immediate buzz of approval round the table.

"It's a job requiring serious abilities and experience with top-secret installations," said Garry. "Mary, do you still have some connections with ASIO?"

She laughed. "Like I told you before, Garry. Once a spook, always a spook. Of course I do. I'll talk to some people."

*　*　*

Only three days later, Garry was at his desk reading some reports from universities about their installations when the phone rang on his desk.

"Garry!" His receptionist sounded agitated. "There's a woman here, she refuses to give her name and she's demanding to see you."

"I'll have a look," said Garry and switched his computer monitor to viewing the lobby area.

The woman standing before the bullet-proof partition in front of the reception desk smiled up at the camera and waved her hand.

"I hear you're looking for a security chief," said Alana Shimova. "You've just found her."

* * *

They stood in Garry's office, too tense to sit down.

"Alana, this way over my head," said Garry. "Obviously, I'm delighted to see you, but something doesn't feel right about this."

She moved nearer to him and looked him in the eye.

"I can't hide anything from you, Garry," she said. "And yes, there are some levels about this. But can I start with telling you I wanted to come back and be with you? And I really did want to retire from public service. I've had enough."

"But you said several levels?" Garry was feeling confused and stressed, despite her reassurance.

"I did. The Israeli government needs to keep a close eye on what is happening around the world and when it was obvious I was ready to retire, they suggested I take on this role."

"So once Mossad, always Mossad, eh?"

Finally, she smiled warmly.

"As you say. But this can have great advantages for you."

"Tell me."

"It's clear that the Second Foundation is becoming the global advisor on the changes happening around the world. You will have contacts with officials in governments from almost every country. I can promise you, my government has the best inside information on anyone who is anyone. I can help you in this process."

"And the issues of security?"

"Do you know of anyone who knows more about protecting people, buildings and assets than Mossad? My gang has already talked to the Tactical Operations Group that arrived here. They knew the ringleader and they've been working on him, but we saved them some time and brought in the others. They're all behind bars now."

Garry felt himself relenting, realising how badly he wanted to believe her.

"What about data security? We have tens of millions of sensitive records on our computer."

"Same thing, Garry. Do you think there's anyone better in the whole world than Mossad? I'll have all the support I need."

"And what does ASIO think about this?"

"All done with their approval."

"One more question. Where are you planning to live?"

She took his hand. "I recall that you have a very nice house, Garry. I'm sure it's big enough for two."

"Welcome to the Second Foundation," said Garry and took her in his arms.

Chapter 36

Alana Shimova had no difficulty being accepted into the Second Foundation. Her background and experience immediately qualified her and the ease and rapidity with which she received permanent residency status in Australia surprised no one. Her value as Security Chief was made obvious almost immediately.

"I've implemented some recent developments in the computer systems," she said one morning.

"Can you describe them?" asked Mark.

"Not really. But they are the same ones used by my government for their security forces."

"Your government? Mossad, I assume?"

Alana smiled. "Nobody at all will be able to hack into our systems. And nobody will be able to enter the building without our clearance."

Murmurs of interest and some humour ran round the room.

"And all of you will be seeing building contractors coming to your homes in the next few days," she continued. "New technology will indicate anyone approaching the building and will conduct face recognition. It will also scan the person for possible weapons. Anything or anyone suspicious will trigger an alarm at the police station and the response will be fast."

"Ah yes," said Mary Hennessey with a grin. "More Mossad. ASIO has just been able to acquire the same thing for certain high-value personnel. It's good stuff, I assure you."

"When you say face recognition, can you tell us more?" Robert Swann looked interested.

"Again, we can take the benefits of the Israeli security teams," said Alana. "We have the faces of almost every known terrorist in the world. As a result, few of them have been able to enter Australia because this same system has been acquired by Australia's Border Security Force. But there's always the risk. And of course, between our two countries, we also have the details of all potential security issues in Australia."

"Seems to be a most useful international cooperation," said Robert. "I'm all for it."

"And now we have a request for help from overseas," said Garry. "I believe our two most recent acquisitions will be of critical assistance."

He looked round the table. He had everybody's complete attention.

"The European parliament has requested assistance in what will be the biggest political change in history. We don't have the details but we will receive the report on the plan when it is documented. With your approval, I recommend that we send Jennifer as the team coordinator. Her reputation as an international legal expert qualifies her well."

Murmurs of interest and approval ran round the table and Jennifer smiled with delight.

"And with the other qualifications of our two most recent personnel, I propose to send Alana. She has the inside knowledge of almost every critical person in Europe and what she doesn't have, Mossad and ASIO will supply. And I'd like to add Galina to the team. Her multiple language skills will be invaluable."

"Any idea what they're planning?" asked Ben Fuller.

"They've given us no indications at all," said Garry. "But it sounds enormous. Obviously, we'll get the first developments."

"I've always liked Brussels," said Jennifer. "When do we leave?"

"As soon as you can pack," said Garry. "But I think we're about to see another of Karen's forecasts coming true. The world is changing."

Chapter 37– April, 2028

"We had an interesting report from Egypt," said Garry as he sat at lunch with Ben Fuller and Mary.

"We sold them a few systems a couple of months ago, if I remember," said Mary. "Wasn't that to Cairo University?"

"It was," replied Garry and took a mouthful of lasagne, chewing it carefully and then swallowed. "To the Department of Archaeology, to be exact."

"I can imagine just how incredible they might find the system," said Ben. "Lots of mysteries to be revealed in their thousands of years of history. So what the gist of their report?"

"Enough to blow the minds of much of the world," said Garry. "And it appears to be just the beginning."

* * *

Doctoral student Halim Khalifa peered at the monitor, not able to identify what he was seeing. He had not got over the excitement of looking back through time through the eyes of people dead for years, centuries and now millennia. The University had spent months gathering the DNA of several thousand Egyptians and searching through the thousands of hours of life records had been long, intensive but always enthralling work.

This was his first "deep dive" into ancient history and he had spent the last three weeks deliberately following the lifelines of people going further and further back in time. Now he knew he was back at least two thousand years and his heart was pumping with excitement as he looked at the scene in the monitor and heard the voices of ancient Egyptians. He couldn't identify the language, so he looked around the research room where several other students were performing similar tasks to his own. One of them he thought might be able to help him.

"Mohamed!" he said softly. "Can you come and help me here?"

The young man staring at his own monitor looked up and smiled. They had been friends since high school and had been delighted when they both got places to work on their doctorates after graduation two years ago, Halim in archaeology, Mohamed in ancient languages.

Halim beckoned and Mohamed rose to his feet and walked the short distance to Halim's cubicle.

"What's the problem?" Mohamed said, standing by his friend's shoulder and looking down at the monitor. "Where are you?"

"I'm sure it's Egypt, the scenery looks about right and this is about two thousand years ago. Whoever this person is, he's in a crowd. I can hear people talking, but what's the language?"

Mohamed bent down closer to the monitor. "How about I use the earphones?" he said and put the large headset on, turned up the volume and listened intently, his eyes closed.

"Oh man!" he exclaimed after a few minutes. "This is incredible! At first I thought it was Coptic, which would be logical for that time and place, but it's not quite. My guess is it's Sahidic, a dialect of Coptic. How about I get my supervisor to come and listen?" He took out his mobile phone, spoke briefly and put it away.

A few minutes later, a young woman entered. She was about thirty and dressed in European style. They all greeted each other and then Mohamed handed her the earphones.

"Vana, I think it may be Sahidic."

She put on the headset and listened the same way her student had done, eyes closed, concentrating hard. She remained that way for a full five minutes before opening her eyes and removing the headset.

"Well done, Mohamed. I agree with you, that's Sahidic. Can you believe it, we are the first modern humans to hear that dialect actually being spoken. Some of that pronunciation was different from what we have believed. Halim, amazing discovery! Can you give me a copy of that scene? My colleagues are going to be shaken up!"

"I'll send it right way," said Halim.

Vana bent down and looked at the monitor.

"Any idea where this is?" she asked.

"I'm pretty sure it's Egypt," said Halim. "And I get the occasional glimpses of ocean and a wide river, so I'm wondering of this is Alexandria."

There was silence as the three of them looked at the changing scene as the long-dead subject walked along the street. The picture opened up into a huge plaza. The first half of the plaza was made up of massive white tiles with many people walking around. From the eyes of the long-dead Egyptian, it appeared to be at least a hundred metres on each side. At the back, a wide flight of stairs led up a short distance to an elevated plaza. On either side of the top of the stairs was a tall white building fronted by high pillars, resembling the Acropolis in Athens. The scene was hugely impressive and beautiful.

Vana gasped in shock.

"I think I know where this is," she said in excitement. "It's a bit like some of the drawings we've got. I believe we're looking at the Great Library of Alexandria."

"Good grief," said Halim. "And I do believe our subject is going in there!"

Vana stood up. "Halim, I have a lecture to give. But this may be the most important thing we have discovered yet. You have all this documented?"

"Of course. You can get back there yourself, I'll send you a copy of the DNA and my record of how I got to this point."

"I can't wait to see it. I'll tell the Director about it and we may have a group viewing."

She walked away, looking back at the monitor as if reluctant to leave.

"I've got a schedule, also," said Mohamed. "I'll have to leave this with you, but I agree with Vana, this is probably earthshaking. Congratulations, your doctorate is guaranteed!"

Halim nodded, staring at the monitor, barely hearing his colleague's words or noticing that he had left. The subject was indeed entering the huge building. Almost immediately, Halim saw a large circular area with light flooding in through the ceiling openings. On both sides there were storage areas filled with scrolls, several of them being lifted out by individuals and taken to tables to unroll.

Halim was already certain that he was seeing the Great Library of Alexandria. The facts about it raced through his mid. Built in the third century BCE, Before the Common Era, destroyed by fire and by military assaults in 30 BCE, destroying the greatest repository of human knowledge in the world, it was considered the greatest tragedy of mass loss of science, art and history in the world ever since. He shivered with anticipation, knowing that much of the rest of his life might well be spent studying what he might find in this sample of DNA, taken from a young man in an Alexandria hospital just a year ago.

He watched as the observer talked briefly with a young man at a desk and was then led to a collection of scrolls. The short discussion they had sounded similar to the Sahidic Coptic language that Mohamed had identified earlier and then the young man walked away. Somehow, Halim was sure the observer had asked a librarian for the location of specific scrolls. In growing excitement, Halim watched as his subject took down a scroll from one of the shelves, carried it to a table and sat down, opening up the scroll carefully.

Even with the building tension inside him, Halim gasped loudly as the first data appeared on the scroll.

He knew exactly what he was seeing.

* * *

The auditorium was full. Every seat was taken, all standing space was crammed. The level of noise from the conversations taking place all round the massive hall was almost a roar, such was the degree of excitement and anticipation.

The noise subsided rapidly as the speaker in the middle of the row on the stage rose to his feet. He was a tall, slender man, nearly reaching two metres with a hawk-like face under a completely bald head. His suit was of classic western design and great cost. He cleared his throat.

"Minister of State of Antiquities, Doctor Galal El-Sabaawi, other members of the Government, members of the Board of Governors at the University of Cairo, ladies and gentlemen, I am Maneer Hassan, Director of the Department of Antiquities and I bid you all welcome."

He paused and took a sip of water from the podium, clearly betraying his nervousness.

"Today, we announce a major discovery that has a serious impact on our understanding of Egyptian history and may reveal even more astonishing results as we look further into what we have found."

A small wave of sound ran round the auditorium.

"As you know, the University bought several systems for investigating human DNA some months ago, technology that allows us to look back in time through the eyes and ears of our ancestors. All of you know of some of the extraordinary discoveries that have been made, discoveries about languages, historical events, the movements of people and so on. Now I can tell you that one of our doctoral students, Halim Khalifa of this Department of Antiquities found scenes taking place in the Great Library of Alexandria, including being able to see the contents of some of the scrolls. The very first one he was able to see through the eyes of a scholar in the year one hundred and thirty seven, BCE was written in Greek and contained a number of drawings and technical diagrams."

He paused for dramatic effect.

"The subject matter and the drawings were of the Sphinx," he continued. "And as a result, we must change much of what we know about that extraordinary construction."

This time, the murmurs round the hall grew loud, with many gasping with shock, others laughing with delight at being about to hear new information about one of the most famous historical monuments in the world.

"As you know," continued the Director, "the conventional wisdom has always been that the Sphinx was constructed during the reign of Pharoah Khafre who ruled Egypt between 2520 and 2494 BCE. But the drawings and the descriptions of the monument in that scroll showed that Khafre had not constructed the Sphinx, he had merely restored a much older building."

He took a longer drink of water as the hubbub through the hall rose to a level that nothing else could be heard for a few minutes. When the noise had died down again, the Director resumed.

"We knew that the Sphinx was built on a base of heavy stone. But what we have now learned is that the base goes down over fifty metres. At this stage, we have no idea just how old the monument is, the scroll we have been able to read through the eyes of an ancient scholar has not yet provided that information, who actually built it. But we have some new information that has shaken us all."

The Director was a natural public speaker with a great sense of timing and dramatic effect. He deliberately paused again and waited for the murmurs to die down.

"You will all remember the amazing 'ScanPyramids' project launched by the predecessor of our current Minister of Antiquities some years ago in

2015. The technology was new science, using muon radiography which scanned the Pyramid of Giza and revealed new chambers which we had no idea existed at all. We are still investigating a means of getting to those chambers without damaging the pyramid itself.

"So it is a privilege to announce to you that our Minister of Antiquities, Doctor Galal el-Sabaawi who I introduced earlier gave his consent a few weeks ago to a similar project to study the base of the Sphinx and already we have discovered two chambers present in the base. They are obviously artificial and built for a purpose. The next project is to find some way of penetrating the solid rock base and gaining access to those chambers. In parallel with that project, the doctoral student who made this discovery, Halim Khalifa will undertake as the core of this thesis work to look further for the readings completed by the scholar who worked in the Great Library and found the scroll that gave us this information. It is likely that this ancient scholar was also reviewing the subject so it is likely that by following his lifeline, Halim will see more scrolls on the subject."

This time, the noise level grew even beyond anyone's ability to hear what the Director had to say. Recognising this, the Director smiled, waved at the audience and left the stage.

* * *

"Quite incredible," said Mary. "Any idea of how long it will take to get to those chambers?"

"The Director told me it could be months," replied Garry. "They'll have to excavate all the way down the side of the base which is about fifty metres and build a barricade to stop the sand caving in. That's thousands of tons to be removed before they can start work on penetrating the rock. They're still using the muon technology to pinpoint the exact location and dimensions of the two chambers they've identified and then they'll drill a few holes to send cameras in and see if there's anything there."

"Bloody amazing!" said Ben, a wide grin on his face. "Times like this I know we've really accomplished things that change the world, just as Karen always said she would."

"I doubt even Karen would have forecast the extent to which she succeeded," said Mary. "Every day I wake up, excited about what astounding developments we'll hear about when I get to work. Could anyone have a better job than we do?"

"Impossible," said Garry. "Anyway, back to work. Let's see if anything astounding has come in while we were feeding our faces."

* * *

There was.

"I don't understand what's going on here," said Declan. "I just found this scene while I was going back through the sample of a friend of my mother's. She's fairly new to Australia, so I expected to find scenes from Britain, but this one is strange."

"Put it on the monitor," said Garry.

On the large monitor on the wall, the scene showed three men sitting in armchairs.

"The viewpoint must be an ancestor of Barbara," said Declan. "She said she comes from a long line of civil servants, so this seems to be one of them acting as secretary."

All three men were dressed in clothing that appeared Victorian to Garry. The room was decorated in similar, old-fashioned style.

"Got the date?" asked Garry.

"Some time in 1875," said Declan.

One of them spoke. His face was a powerful one, showing a man of some considerable age and experience who had exercised authority with ease. Garry estimated his age as in the seventies.

"I do not understand why you have been able to achieve this meeting, Mr Harrington," he said. "But for some reason, Mr Cross here seems convinced you have important information for my government."

"Hold it there, Declan," snapped Garry. "Somebody, check who was Prime Minister of Britain in 1875?"

It took only a few seconds.

"That's Benjamin Disraeli," said a voice from behind Garry. "He's aged seventy-four at this time. That other bloke will be Richard Cross, the Home Secretary."

Garry felt a weird sense of déjà vu as he recalled the meetings he and Karen had attended with the British Prime Minister and Home Secretary more than twenty years before. He nodded at Declan who resumed the image.

"I am grateful that the Home Secretary was able to persuade you," said the third man in the room. "I believe that what I have to tell you could influence British international policies for centuries."

"That sounds most unlikely," said Disraeli with an edge of contempt.

"Then let us see," said Harrington. "Prime Minister, the British Empire is at the height of its powers. You control significant portions of the world."

"This I already know," said the Prime Minister.

"You share some similarities with the Roman Empire in that, unlike many other great powers, you introduce British standards of education, government, infrastructure and civilisation to all your colonies."

"Still nothing we don't know," snapped Disraeli, his irritation obviously growing.

Harrington seemed unmoved.

"One might say that your government, those that preceded you and presumably those that come after will continue to play this role of mentor to less advanced civilisations."

Disraeli seemed to melt a little.

"This is the greatest global authority the world has ever seen," he said. "The British Army and Navy are the finest military forces in history. Nothing will change that."

"All empires decline and fall, Prime Minister. Nobody at the time saw the possibility of Rome falling as it did. There was a time when Britain was a small, insignificant part of the Roman Empire. Right now, the British Empire seems immortal, but history is against it."

"If you are going to insult the British Empire, you can leave right now," said the Prime Minister, the volume increasing. "You said you had something valuable to tell us. Now tell us and then get out!"

Harrington showed no reaction to Disraeli's outburst.

"The Roman Empire covered a relatively small part of the world," he said. "The Chinese Empire covered a much greater portion of the world and then declined suddenly. The British Empire is much larger. It will eventually decline, though I suspect it will continue to play a major role in world affairs and global culture for an unforeseeable future."

"Yes, and so?" Disraeli's irritation had not declined.

"Now I would like you to consider a future time when the territory of an Empire far exceeds that of yours today."

"How can that be?" snapped Disraeli. "That would mean the whole world. That's impossible."

"Much more than this world," said Harrington.

There was a moment of silence in the room.

"Explain this nonsense, man," said Disraeli.

"Do you think this is the only world in the Universe where intelligence lives? Do not think that there might be other civilisations living under other suns?"

"Now I know I'm dealing with a madman," shouted Disraeli. "Cross, get this lunatic out of here! Other civilisations on other planets? What garbage! I should have you hanged for this."

"I think you should listen, Prime Minister," said the Home Secretary. "If I may quote the Great Bard, *There are more things in heaven and earth, Horatio, Than are dreamt of in your philosophy.*' Mr Harrington may be telling us about some of them."

Disraeli looked at his Home Secretary in astonishment.

"You believe this nonsense, Richard?"

"I think it may be critical, Prime Minister."

Disraeli subsided in his chair, still looking astonished, but he gestured to Harrington to continue.

"There are many such civilisations, Prime Minister," said Harrington. "Most are very primitive, not yet even showing speech or any facility with tools. Some are more advanced, roughly at the level where this world is today. But just as you have shown guidance and mentorship to less advanced peoples in your empire, somebody is required to show the same leadership to less developed worlds."

"Are you trying to tell us that you are one of these advanced people trying to show us how to progress?" Disraeli looked stunned, staring at Harrington with wide eyes.

"That is exactly what I am telling you."

"But why?" asked Disraeli. "If you are so advanced, why bother with us at all?"

"For the same reason that the British Empire has not just exploited its colonies for wealth, but has also brought education, political stability and processes and culture to them. Unlike some others, you see it is simply the right thing to do."

Disraeli stared at him. "Then where are you from? Under what strange sun does your civilisation live?"

"That I can't tell you," said Harrington. "There would be no point. Your astronomers have not seen far enough to see our sun."

"And so why are you here, then?"

"There are several civilisations that might be able to resume this mantle of leadership and mentorship at some future date. Mine has been in this role for many centuries. But our time is coming to end. We are trying to identify who might take over from us in the next few hundred years. When we have, we will make ourselves known and provide training and guidance to them, just as you have done with your colonies."

"So why have you come here today, Mr Harrington?" Disraeli seemed calm, listening with fascination.

"Your Empire is a force best placed above any others we know so far, for pushing the whole of Earth to the level of maturity where we could consider Humanity as a possible new leader. I am telling you this now, so that you will try and continue as the world leader and help all countries progress to that point."

"How many others are under that consideration?" asked Disraeli."

"Just four," replied Harrington.

"And how do we rate in that list?"

"Right now, you are failing," said Harrington. "That's why I'm here today to try and get you to work on yourselves, your Empire and the rest of the world. You have the power to influence all other countries. Do this right and the Empire could last some centuries yet. If you fail, you will end up as a minor species, governed by another Empire."

In dead silence, Harrington rose to his feet.

"Prime Minister, Home Secretary, I bid you good morning."

Through the eyes of the secretary, Harrington walked out of the door. Disraeli looked at the secretary, as if staring at the camera and the people watching in the office.

"That will be enough, Miss Mitchell," he said. "Please leave us and type the report. It will be classified as top secret, for the eyes only of Mr Cross and myself."

* * *

"I think I'd better tell the Board about this one," said Garry.

Chapter 38 – October, 2028

"While Ben and Mary and I were at lunch the other day, we commented on how we have so many days when absolutely astonishing things have been discovered using our technology."

Garry looked around the table at the members of the Second Foundation and all were watching him intently. These meetings usually only happened when important matters had to be discussed and resolved or new announcements made.

"The first one updated the discovery our researchers made a few weeks ago when Declan saw a religious service in a cave with a group of Neanderthals. It was an astonishing sight, not just the service and the evidence for religious practices about 70,000 years ago, but also the beautiful art painted on the walls. What we didn't know was where that cave was. Yesterday, I got this...

The Northern end of the Grand Saint Bernard tunnel between Italy and Switzerland was an unholy mess. Vehicles were backed down through the tunnel as essential repairs were conducted very close to the Swiss exit. A large subsidence had occurred in the road a few days earlier and the crews had been working day and night to repair this heavily used road.

"Jean-Pierre, something odd here!" called the man operating the ground penetrating radar device. It looked much like a simple garden mower, but no blades were obvious and it operated in silence.

The foreman came over from where he had been checking the last stretch of repairs.

"What is it, Gunther?"

"There's quite a gap about a metre down. I think it's pretty spacious. It might cause another subsidence."

The foreman looked around the work site. The reported space was well to the side of the roadway, almost against the tunnel wall, right at the edge of the repair work that was now complete. Quickly, he ordered all the warning signs lifted, the diversions removed, leaving only a reduced width of one lane where the problem existed. A smaller sign blocked that off. Traffic immediately began to speed up. The foreman called over the drill operator.

"Mario, drill down that, will you. Gunther says it's about a metre down, could be a big space and could cause another subsidence. We'd better be sure."

Nodding, the workman fired up the drill and began working on a circular area about a metre wide. He was joined by a second man and the crew stood around watching. A major space under the roadway could cause massive problems.

An hour later, a hole had been drilled out. Jean-Pierre took a small stone and dropped it down the hole. Two or three seconds passed before they heard the sound of the collision with the ground.

"That's about ten metres," said Jean-Pierre. "That's one hell of a space under here. Somebody drop a ladder down there, I'm going cave-exploring."

A few minutes later, his helmet light switched on, he began descending the rope ladder. Fifteen minutes passed in silence as his crew became increasingly nervous but then they saw the movement of the ladder as the foreman began the ascent. When he lifted his head above the road surface, the shock and sheer wonder in his face was more than anyone of them had ever seen.

"Guys, call the police. Get a secure barrier round this hole and cover it up safely. You won't believe what I found down there."

Garry smiled round the table.

"It was the Neanderthal place of worship. The University of Zurich is sending teams to examine it and the engineers are designing another entrance through the rock to allow full use of the road. They're also reinforcing the ceiling to prevent any collapse of the road. It might be a year or two before we hear the full story of what they find."

A few minutes of excited discussion went on as the foundation members reviewed the extraordinary find then Garry called for attention

"And now, even more," he said. "You've all seen the reports of the discoveries made in Egypt regarding the Sphinx and I know we're all very eager to see what happens next," Garry continued. "But that may take some months. However, something possibly even more world-changing came in this morning."

He looked down at the single sheet of paper before him.

"A couple of years ago, we sold a few systems to Peru's National University of San Marco in Lima. I feel ashamed to admit I knew almost nothing of this University, but it has an impressive history. It was founded in 1551 and it's the oldest university in the Americas. It has over thirty thousand undergraduate student and over four thousand graduate students with a remarkable list of famous alumni. Like almost all universities, our systems were bought mostly for history and language research and this one is no exception. This report came in overnight."

* * *

Professor Abigail D'Angelo of the Linguistics Department watched the monitor with delight, then took off her headphone and picked up her phone.

"Oscar," she said when a voice answered. "Can you get in here? I think this will get your blood moving!"

She didn't look up when a very large man entered the room, having to duck as he came through the door. He pulled up a chair beside her and it creaked in protest as he sat down. She handed him a set of earphones and he had to extend them to the maximum in order to fit over the unruly red hair of his oversized head and even then, the phones didn't cover the ears fully.

"What have you got?" he asked.

"It's just about fifty Before Common Era," she said. "It's in a city, not sure yet where. Listen to these two men talking."

For more than fifteen minutes, both of them listened carefully.

"It's Quechuan!" said Oscar Roncal. "It took a while to tune into it but it does have the echoes of the modern version. This is astonishing!"

"But do you hear anything else?"

For another ten minutes they listened as two men engaged in a discussion that took place over two thousand years ago. Through the eyes of the subject observer, the other man looked quite elderly, with a lined face and deep-sunk eyes. His clothing was not rich, merely a blanket slung over one shoulder and simple trousers could be seen under it. But the blanket was colourfully woven with lines of red and blue adding some variation to the coarse woven cloth. But he smiled often, so the conversation was most likely between friends.

"Some of those words," murmured Roncal. "They're different, not pure Quechuan. Could they be..."

"Akaro-Jaqi, yes!" said Abigail, her pony tail shaking violently as she nodded her head enthusiastically. "It looks like the influence of the earlier culture remained quite strong."

* * *

Garry looked down at his sheet of paper.

"Abigail asked me to give you a very brief summary of some of the history that she's referring to," he said. "The Nazca culture of Peru lasted from about 100 BCE until it finally collapsed around 800CE or AD as it used to be known. An earlier culture, the Paracas existed from about 800BCE to 100BCE but their languages were similar, the main family being Quechuan with one sub-group being Akara-Jaqi."

"Nazca?" asked Ben. "That's the people who drew the outlines on the Plains of Nazca?"

"Those famous and mysterious drawings, extending many miles, yes," said Garry.

"Wouldn't it be amazing if we saw some of those drawings being done?" said Mary "Now that would shake up a whole library of theories!"

* * *

"I'm starting to tune in fully," said Roncal. "These two men seem to having a very simple discussion about the price of fish in the market that morning! Both seem a little upset."

"Indeed," said Abigail. "But it's giving us a whole new batch of words from Akaro-Jaqi that will help me build up the dictionary."

"I hope we can see some more of the physical location so that we can identify where they are," said Roncal.

"Keep watching! I think my subject is moving on."

The scene changed as the man began walking after a short exchange of what was probably a friendly farewell. Structures began to appear.

"Pyramids," murmured Roncal. "I wonder if...?"

"That's one, two, now a third," said Abigail, her excitement growing as the view expanded as the man swung his head around.

"And four... and five," continued Roncal. "I'll bet the mortgage there's a sixth one."

"Caral-Supé," said Abigail. "I was there last year doing some digging around. My God, the oldest city in the Americas, all five thousand years of them! Just look at this beautiful place!"

For the next twenty minutes the two linguistics professors stared at the monitor as their ancient and unwitting guide took them round the historic old city. Many people appeared, most dressed like the man they had been seeing earlier, but the crowds were quite large, indicating a prosperous town. Occasionally, one or the other exclaimed in shock as a new voice was heard.

"That's Topara!" said Abigail at one point. "I have no idea what it meant and the accent was something I have never heard, but I'll go back and examine it more."

"And that's Huangascar!" said Roncal some time later. "Same as you, no idea what it meant, but it'll get my full attention later. Good heavens, Abigail, this sure proves the numbers of people coming to this city and staying. Some of the old cultures and languages survived a long time."

"This is a gold mine," agreed Abigail. "Who ever thought we'd be able to hear two thousand year old speech and languages nobody has heard spoken aloud for centuries?"

"Only crazy people," said Roncal. "But now that you've found this stuff, I believe we'll step up the research. I'll talk to the Rector, get a budget for taking a few hundred DNA samples from indigenous people and start looking back through time."

"Do that," said Abigail. "I'm going to write a summary of all this and send it to the people in Australia. I think they'll be fascinated."

* * *

"That was just the start," said Garry. "Not much of great interest there for anybody but linguists, but already they were able to confirm theories of tribal movements and the effects of language and culture."

"But obviously there's more to come," said Annabelle Calvert, the historian. "Mind you, I found that development quite fascinating already, but that's my job!"

"I think you've got our interest," said Mary. "What came next?"

"Something big," said Garry.

* * *

"I have no idea at all where this is," said Roncal. "I've been looking at the sights of this city, but nothing is remotely obvious."

"When is this?" asked Abigail.

The two of them had developed a great friendship over the last few weeks as they had built a small group of graduate students who had offered their help in the project to look back at Peru's ancient history. Both of them spent almost every working hour at the laboratory, going back through time through the eyes of generation after generation of Inca people.

"About a thousand BCE. What's bothering me is that it's obviously a big city, but there's not a single feature I can find so far that could tell me what it is."

"Any idea who it is?" Mary studied the monitor. The ancient Peruvian had been walking along a city street, rarely speaking to others, but those who had spoken were all apparently elderly and of a low social level, judging by the clothing, traditional Inca garments of coarse material with bright colours woven into the cloth.

"A woman," said Roncal. "Not a high person, she's been buying some vegetables and fish from street traders."

"And the language?"

"Quechua," said Roncal. "With some accent variations from our previous samples."

"So not Machu Picchu?" said Abigail.

"Definitely not. This is a lowland city, no mountains to be seen."

"And not Chavín de Huántar? Those walls look pretty impressive."

"No, I was there last year," said Roncal. "I know the layout fairly well. I don't think this is anywhere I know at all. Nothing you can see that might be familiar?"

"Not so far."

"I'm going to stay with this subject. She might move further afield and show me some scenery that I might recognise, but somehow I doubt it. This is getting interesting."

Abigail laughed at the understatement. Both of them realised they could be on the verge of something critical.

"It looks like this is late afternoon," she said. "It could be interesting to see if she returns home and what that looks like, maybe some family, so there could be some conversation about where she's been."

Roncal nodded and stood up, stretching. "I'll get the coffee," he said. "Anything you want?"

"Bring me a bowl of ceviche," she murmured, staring at the screen. "The canteen does a nice one."

"I might do the same," he said and walked out.

For two hours, they took it in turns watching the monitor while the other attended to the usual administrative requirements of phone calls, emails, communications with doctoral students and examination of budget documents, and then both watched together as the woman from three thousand years ago returned home to a small hut on the outskirts of the unknown city.

"Husband, two kids, one boy, one girl," said Abigail in some amusement. "The traditional nuclear family hasn't changed much in three millennia!"

They watched as the family ate a simple meal of fish and vegetables and talked the way families have talked throughout time.

"They seem to get on with each other," said Roncal at one point.

"Looks like she's going for a wee-wee," said Abigail

as the woman rose to her feet and went out through the single door. Outside it was pitch black with only a sliver of new moon showing.

They waited in some embarrassment as the woman squatted in the grass for a few moments returned upright and smoothed down her clothing. Then she stared up at the night sky that was aglow with the magnificence of the Southern Hemisphere stars.

"Aha!" exclaimed Roncal. "This may be the answer. We know what day it is from that symbol on the record, we know approximately what time of day it is. Now we know how to find out where this is."

* * *

Garry consulted his printout of the report from Abigail.

"They took a snapshot of that night sky and sent it to the Planetarium and Observatory Morro Solar in Lima. The geniuses there were able to identify the key stars and their locations and from that, they triangulated down to the Earth's surface and pinpointed the location of the area to within fifty kilometres and sent the position to Abigail. She and Roncal checked that on the map and made an interesting discovery."

* * *

"There's nothing there but jungle!" said Roncal in disappointment. "Those guys must have got it wrong."

"Come on, Oscar, I'm sure they know what they're doing. What if they're correct?"

Roncal's irritation subsided.

"Cities have been discovered after many centuries in that jungle," Abigail continued. "What if there's another one hidden under hundreds of years, maybe a couple of thousand years of jungle growth?"

They smiled at each other, both suppressing their excitement at the implications of what might be happening.

"This is where we exploit the huge reputation and power of this university," said Abigail. "We call the military, we get high flying ground shots, we ask the Americans for some satellite shots and we employ ground penetrating radar to cut through that heavy growth."

"Could take a while," said Roncal. "I'll get onto it right away."

* * *

Garry looked around the table. Everybody's attention was riveted on him. He smiled.

"The news will break any day," he said. "They wanted to be certain of this, but they found a new city. It looks enormous. Several archaeologists have been dropped into the region with teams of workers and facilities to live for some weeks while they cut through the jungle. The first buildings were found just a few days ago and are now being uncovered. And you know what they have decided to call it?"

He grinned at the faces round the table.

"Petrova," he said. "In honour of our very own founder, Karen."

He sat back, poured himself a mug of coffee from the pot on the table and relaxed as the celebrations began.

Chapter 39 – November, 2028

Doctoral student Halim Khalifa felt distinctly nervous as he was lowered down the solid rock wall that was the base of the Sphinx. The University had borrowed the cradle used by the window cleaners and Halim felt unsteady as the cradle rocked and swung as it descended. Beneath him was a drop of over fifty metres and he had never had a head for heights.

He was also claustrophobic. On the other side of the rock wall was a massive steel mesh curtain supported by a framework of girders that had been built down the side of the rock wall and that kept a solid wall of sand away from Halim and the other three men in the window-cleaner's cradle. The headphones felt clammy in the morning heat and sweat was already running down his cheeks.

The cradle stopped as it became level with a rectangular shape marked out on the wall by a previous team who had precisely calculated a suitable area for drilling based on the muon pictures that had been developed by the technologists.

Hiding his discomfort, Halim nodded at the engineer next to him and all four of them covered their eyes with Perspex shields lowered from the safety helmets and put on masks over their noses and mouths.

The engineer picked up his powerful drill and switched it on. The roar filled the small space between the rock and the steel barrier, increasing Halim's discomfort but he suppressed it under the excitement of perhaps finding an earth-shaking discovery some time soon. The scene became almost a motionless picture as the engineer drilled his way through the rock, watched intently by the others.

After twenty minutes, the engineer stopped the roar and withdrew the drill. He carefully took off the drill bit, added an extension rod before placing a new drill bit on the end and inserted it into the three centimetre hole.

"Thirty centimetres," said Halim.

"Acknowledged," said a voice into his ears. Even that single word in his earphones expressed tension and excitement.

Half an hour later, the engineer repeated the process with a longer extension and resumed the drilling. Halim saw that rock dust had appeared on his face mask and all over his overalls. He wiped it off the Perspex.

"Seventy centimetres," he reported.

"Acknowledged,' said the same voice as before. The tension had not died down.

When Halim reported one point five metres, the tension grew further in all of them. The muon pictures had indicated the chamber was about that distance from the edge of the wall but with no greater accuracy than that.

Once more, the engineer added an extension and replaced the bit. Drilling resumed.

"One metre seventy," said Halim, just as the engineer's hands jerked forward.

"Breakthrough," said Halim.

Carefully, the engineer withdrew the long extension and drill bit and began disassembling them. The other two men began work on their large case, extracting a long cable with a tiny camera at the end. The cable was attached to a large box. One of them began threading it through the three centimetre hole.

The other one lifted up a computer monitor that was also attached to the box, switched it on and intently watched it as his colleague gently eased the cable forward. At the one point five metre mark, he touched another switch and the screen came alive as the camera's light came on and showed the tunnel through which it was moving.

Halim no longer felt the sweat, the claustrophobia or the fear of heights. His breathing came faster.

"Are you getting this?" he asked into the microphone.

"Affirmative," said the other man on the edge of the cliff above them.

Centimetre by centimetre, the camera was gently pushed forward. Hardly able to breath, Halim moved to stand behind the technician at the monitor and stared at the image. It had changed from being a dark hole at the end of a tunnel and now lit up a large volume of space. The technician used a small lever and carefully rotated the camera around an arc to look at each part of the chamber that had been revealed.

"Oh my God!" exclaimed the man above them.

"Allah be praised!" echoed Halim.

He was looking at racks and racks of scrolls. All he could think of was how was it going to be possible to get to those scrolls and see what was in them that somebody in the Great Library of Alexandria had decided should be saved from the catastrophe that had destroyed the others.

* * *

Three weeks later, Halim was back in the window-cleaner's cradle with three different technicians. In that time, the bore had been drilled out to ten centimetres. As the cradle stopped with a slight jerk that caused Halim's stomach to react with slight nausea and made him tighten his grip on the rail, the three technicians opened up their crates and extracted the latest in micro-drones that the University had purchased recently. They also lifted up their controllers, switched on the drones and gently placed them in the tunnel. There was almost zero clearance for the drones to move, but the expert handling by the technicians let them move slowly along the tunnel until they reached the chamber.

With their remarkably strong lights and minute cameras, the drones began exploring the open space.

"Ahmed, will you focus on the scrolls?" asked Halim. The technician nodded and slowly moved his drone to the stacks of scrolls. Halim began counting. This would be slow, because he had already seen that two walls of the chamber contained shelves of scrolls.

"What on earth is that?" said the second technician, Hazem as his drone focused on the top right hand corner.

"Can you wait a while?" asked Halim, carefully counting the scrolls. It took a few more minutes before he completed the count. There were eighty-five scrolls on the shelves and he felt overwhelming excitement at one day being to read them and see what made these so important that they had been moved to this secret and secure location. He noted the details and then turned to the monitor image of Hazem's drone.

The sight of the image felt like a punch in the gut. It was a diagram. Two lines branched down from a common point, a curved lined extended to the left, turned down and crossed the two straight lines. On one side of the right hand line was a dot. Halim knew exactly where he had seen this diagram before.

It was the symbol in the DNA images that indicated the day the human watcher had experienced the sights and sounds of his or her life.

*   *   *

The Second Foundation members had watched the recording of the drilling and the entry into the chamber deep in the rock under the Sphinx. The silence had been intense.

When the image of the symbol appeared, there were deep sounds of shock through the room.

"This is just not possible," whispered Salmaan Basrai. Jennifer stared wide-eyed, her hands over her mouth. The rest looked pale. Only Ben Fuller seemed calm.

"We passed that image to Bill's team as soon as we received it a few hours ago," said Garry. "They calculated that the symbol represented a date six thousand, three hundred and twenty years ago, or approximately the year 4510BCE. Just what the symbol means is not clear. It could mean the date when the chamber was built, or when the Sphinx construction was started or maybe ended. We just don't know yet and everybody in Egypt is hoping that they'll learn more from any more scrolls they manage to read from the Great Library or from those secret hidden scrolls. But current theory has been that the Sphinx was built during the rule of Khafre between 2520BCE and 2494BCE. But this discovery dates the construction about two thousand years earlier. It's causing some excitement among Egyptologists."

"I imagine it is," murmured Mary. "Look what it's done to us."

*   *   *

The discovery of a date symbol on the wall of the chamber was not the only shock for Halim that day.

"Hey! Look at this!" said Medhat, the third technician. The other two brought their drones to positions alongside the third and shone their beams on the wall.

"It's a passageway!" said Medhat. "Pretty narrow, but enough for one man to walk along carrying a scroll."

Without being asked, he took the drone slowly along the passage and the other two followed. It went straight for about three metres, suddenly turned left for another metre and then met a solid wall.

Medhat touched his microphone button.

"Move us along to your right, about three metres," he instructed the crew atop the rock wall.

Slowly the cradle inched its way as Medhat hit a switch on his drone controller.

"I've set the beeper going," he said to Halim. "It will get louder the nearer we get to the drone."

Halim nodded, feeling his tension increasing again. The small beep on the controller got louder and louder and then began to fade.

"Back again, very slowly," Medhat said to the crew.

The cradle moved just a few centimetres and Medhat was satisfied.

"It's just seventy centimetres away," he said. He

took a chalk stick from his overalls, leaned over and marked a cross on the wall. "That's the entrance," he said. "Break in there and you have your passage to the chamber."

Halim remembered to breathe again.

"But we have a problem," said the technician. "We took a sample of the atmosphere in there, thinking there could be dust or fungus or something that might cause breathing problems. What we did find was mind-blowing."

Halim stared at him.

"Nitrogen," said the technician. "Clever, because a nitrogen atmosphere would help preserve the scrolls, but leaves a question."

He paused, sensing a dramatic possibility.

"How the hell did somebody know that four thousand years ago and how the hell did they make it?"

* * *

"The Director told me it could take a month to get government approval for the excavation," said Garry. "But then we might get a chance to discover what those scrolls contain."

"But that date symbol," said Mary. "The fact that it's the same symbol as we have found in the DNA records is mind-blowing. I just cannot imagine what it might mean."

"And the question of how nitrogen filled the chamber," said Ben. "It's impossible to know now how the ancients knew about the gas and certainly how they could make it.

"It's getting curiouser and curiouser," agreed Garry. "Alice in Wonderland has got nothing on what we're discovering here."

"They'll have to fit an airlock on the entrance and ensure anyone going in wears breathing apparatus," said Ben.

The Foundation members were silent as they left the conference room. All of them were deep in thought.

Chapter 40 - An Ancient Mystery

Professor Abigail D'Angelo had got used to spending over twelve hours a day at her computer terminal. She had become totally addicted to seeing the history of her country through the eyes of people dead many hundreds of years and each day brought fresh new jolts of delight and excitement as she worked through hundreds of generations of ancestors of people now living in Peru.

The scene she was looking at didn't seem too exciting, but something about it made her call her friend and colleague, Oscar Roncal for a second opinion.

"Where and when are you?" he asked as he took a seat beside her. The huge mass of humanity next to her made her feel like a child, but she had got used to it and found that it gave her a sense of security.

"It's about 70 BCE, but I haven't worked out where yet," she replied.

"Whose sample is it?"

"A woman working in the government offices. She volunteered a sample last year when the big call went out after our initial discoveries."

Silence reigned for a few minutes as they studied

the image. The scene appeared to be a flat plain with no obvious features. At least two men were in the vision of the subject, both dressed in the style of ancient Inca people of middle class.

After a few sentences were spoken, Roncal nodded.

"Quechuan again. And the accent, the speech intonation, that matches the time period."

The subject's head swung round as another speaker was heard.

"Looks like five people in total," said Abigail. "And one of them is holding something like a scroll in his left hand. This could perhaps be a training session of some kind?"

"Could be," agreed Roncal. "And, hey! What are those poles lying on the grass at his feet?"

As the ancient Inca focused for a few moments on the holder of the scroll, they also saw four large vessels of some kind like ceramic pots and several small bags that contained bulky, hard shapes inside. Behind them was a cart with a donkey harnessed to it, obviously the transport for the materials.

"This is all a bit strange," murmured Roncal. "Somehow, this looks like a teacher is going to run a practical class of some sort, but I can't see what yet."

"Let's try and tune into the speech," said Abigail. "It should help clarify the situation. You're the expert in ancient Quechuan, go for it."

Roncal leaned forward and picked up the headphones by the monitor, leaned back and concentrated on the images of the five men. He began translating as the men spoke, hesitantly at first but with increasing fluency as he tuned into the ancient conversation.

"You will work in pairs," said the man holding the scroll. "Manko, Abik, you will take the south side,

Hakan, Samin, the north side. Report back to me at noon."

"I think our subject is Hakan," murmured Roncal. "These are genuine Inca names of that era." He resumed his concentration on the monitor, translating as the men spoke and commenting on the process they were following.

"Samin, here is your exercise," said the teacher and handed over a scroll. "Your starting point is the red stake over there."

Hakin and Samin walked over to the cart, lifted two poles and several of the bags. Then they walked a few metres and stopped at a red, wooden stake protruding from the ground. Samin partially unrolled the scroll and studied it.

"I wish we could see what he's looking at," said Abigail. "We have no idea at all of what they're doing."

"I'm sure all will be revealed in time," said Roncal with a smile.

They fell silent as Hakin held one pole vertically at the site of the red stake. Next him, Samin took something from his pocket, laid it on the ground and studied it. Hakin looked down as well.

"It's a compass!" exclaimed Abigail. "That's a magnetised piece of iron on a pivot! This is incredible!"

"We've always known the Incas had some process of determining compass directions," said Roncal. "Look at all the examples where they built structures pointing perfectly due north. Now we know how they did it!"

On the monitor, Samin marked the ground where the compass was, then a second mark at the due north as indicated by the instrument. He put away the compass and extracted a round disc about twenty centimetres in diameter with a hole in the centre. As Hakin watched, Samin carefully placed the disc on the ground with the central hole on the mark of where the compass had been and then appeared to line up a point with the second mark indicating due north.

"Good grief, it's a protractor!" said Roncal "You can see the marks indicating degrees all round the disk!"

"This certainly explains the accuracy of many of the old structures," said Abigail. "And you know what? This is a training session for surveyors!"

"I think you're right," said Roncal. "Let's see what they do next."

As they watched, Samin moved the protractor to the red stake, laid it down and aligned it with due north and marked off an angle that he had read off in the original location. He said something to Hakin.

"Twenty-two something," translated Roncal. "Whatever word that was, I had never heard it before and it must be equivalent to a compass degree."

"Forty poles," said Samin. Hakin lifted the pole he was holding, laid it on the ground and carefully aligned it with the mark Samin had made. Samin took the second pole and with equal care, laid it at the end of the first pole, checking that the direction was the same.

Five times they did this, each time taking a small wooden stake from one of the bags they had carried with them and marking the line. Then they switched jobs, Hakin taking the compass readings and marking the direction.

After twenty such positioning of the pole, things changed. A new direction was set with each pole and gradually a curve developed.

"That's it for now," said Hakin. "The workers can now sweep the top layers away and reveal the line in the white layers underneath. Let's have a look at the plan."

Samin took out his scroll and opened it. Both men studied it and finally Roncal and Abigail could see what was there. But it was not very informative. The scroll simply showed a diagram of what the two men had marked out on the ground.

"Those are the instructions," said Roncal, "the direction of the long line, the degree of curvature, the distance in pole lengths, nothing more."

"So it was probably just a surveyor's exercise," said Abigail. "Well, at least we've see the Inca compass and found that they used a protractor, so it's been a valuable session."

The two Incas picked up the poles and bags of remaining stakes and began walking back to the instructor. When they arrived, the other two men were there.

"When I have examined your work, I will give you the results," said the instructor. "Now, let's see what this is all part of." He lifted his scroll and unrolled it on the ground. All four surveyors looked down.

Abigail and Roncal took a deep breath in anticipation, looked at each other in disbelief and then burst out in uncontrollable laughter.

* * *

Garry looked round the table.

Mary was staring wide-eyed at him, just the hint of a laugh on her lips. Mark Craymer was head down, his shoulders heaving in laughter. Ben Fuller was leaning back, laughing loudly. The others simply looked stunned.

"That's right," said Garry. "Those two professors in Lima have solved a problem that has plagued humans for decades. The enormous and beautiful diagrams on the Plans of Nazca were not landing strips for alien space-ships, they were not offerings to the gods. They were just graduation tests for several generations of surveyors."

Chapter 41 – February, 2029

Garry was sitting with Bill, Penny and Avram in the main research area when the next shockwave hit. They were discussing some of the discoveries made by the Egyptian students in Cairo and the potential for even more critical revelations if more of the scrolls in the Great Library could be read.

"It's all such a lottery," said Bill in frustration. "Finding the one scroll about the Sphinx was stunning, but now we know there are all these thousands of scrolls and all we can do is keep looking back through people's DNA and hoping and praying that eventually we find somebody reading another scroll."

"I agree," said Penny. "We can see thousands of scrolls in the shelves through the eyes of this one man, we know that they contain almost all the knowledge held by almost the entire world and we can't get to them."

"I feel like a kid looking through the shop front window of the cake shop," said Avram. "All those goodies and I can't get my hands on them!"

Their quiet laughter was interrupted by a gasp of shock from one the researchers in his cubicle. They looked over to see one of the newly-hired graduates staring rigidly at his monitor. Garry sorted through his memories and recognised him as Kieran Wells, a doctorate in Genetics from Sydney University.

Everybody in the room was looking at him, but Kieran seemed transfixed. Garry got up and walked towards him.

"What have you got, Kieran?" he asked as he approached. Kieran had his earphones on and didn't hear, so Garry gently touched his shoulder. The young man started, stared up at Garry and then removed his earphones. His eyes were wide.

"I... I think this is important," he stammered.

"Put it up on the main screen," said Garry. "Rewind to where you first saw this."

Kieran nodded and a moment later the main screen came alight.

The scene showed a group of people settling down on the ground. The observer through whose eyes they were seeing it was behind most of the people, so only their backs were seen, but as some of them turned to speak to a neighbour, their faces appeared brown-skinned, dark-eyed, the women with red shapes painted on the foreheads between their eyes.

"Indian sub-continent, I would say," murmured another researcher. "Any idea of timing, Kieran?"

"About 60 Common Era," said Kieren.

The observer looked down and rearranged brightly coloured clothing, arms decorated with decorative bangles.

"And a woman," added the other researcher. "So, Kieran, what caused your reaction? Any idea what's going on?"

"Just wait," replied Kieran. He appeared to have regained his composure.

At that moment, the observer turned her head as

another person sat down beside her and this was another woman, similarly dressed. The two spoke like friends.

"We're going to have to get help identifying the language," said Penny.

"No we don't," said Bill.

The others looked at him in astonishment.

"Remember that time I found some monks talking about the death of Buddha just a few days earlier?" said Bill. "I reckon that's the same language. It's Magadi Prakrit, a form of Sanskrit spoken by the lower classes because Sanskrit was spoken by the educated elites. This is India all right."

"How did you confirm it?" asked Garry, his eyes on the monitor. The crowd was growing but nothing had yet happened to indicate what was drawing them to this spot.

"I called the Ancient Languages people at Cambridge University," said Bill. "They identified it and translated for me. They should be able to do the same here."

"Let's see what it's about first," said Garry. "It's obviously shaken Kieran."

On the monitor, the crowd was stirring, most of them rising to their feet. The woman through whose ancient eyes they were seeing this was blocked from full view of what was happening at the front, but it looked like a man was walking in from one side, accompanied by a small person. But as the crowd subsided again, it became clear.

A man stood in front of the audience. He looked middle-aged, possibly in his forties or early fifties. He wore the same colourful style of local garb that the others wore but he was not Indian. His hair was long but his beard was neat and well-trimmed. His complexion was more Middle-Eastern than Asian. His right hand rested on the shoulder of a small boy, perhaps nine or ten. His face was different, too. Not quite Indian, not quite Semitic.

"Good grief!" exclaimed Penny. "Haven't we seen this man before?"

"We have," said Garry, feeling his astonishment increasing. "Years ago, when Helen Macauley told us of her research into the origins of Christianity. She told us then that Jesus really was just one of several young radical rabbis preaching the Christian messages. We saw this young man in the scenes she displayed. He was one of those young men."

Several people around overheard and turned in astonishment.

"You don't suppose this could be...?" said one of the women.

Garry smiled at her then returned his gaze to the monitor. "It's possible," he said. "But unless he gives his name sometime and hasn't adopted a local name, we may not be able to be sure."

On the monitor, the man began to speak. His voice was strong and carried well to the woman at the back of the crowd. Occasionally, she looked around and this showed that the crowd had grown to well over a hundred people.

Despite the inability to understand what was being said, the group in the room stayed deeply engrossed throughout the forty minutes that the man spoke. When he stopped and began to move away, the room let out a collective sigh.

"Bill, will you call Cambridge at a suitable hour this evening, see if you can contact the Sanskrit expert?"

"No problems," said Bill.

* * *

At seven that evening, Bill called Garry at home just as he was preparing a meal of roast chicken and potatoes. It was his turn to cook and Alana was about to open a bottle of wine. He hid the irritation at this break in what had become a wonderfully close, warm and intimate evening routine, knowing that calls to his home usually were seriously important.

"I got through okay," said Bill. "At least, I got to the office. The real expert in Sanskrit and also in Magadi Prakrit is a bloke called Gerald Finlay, but he's away right now."

"Bugger," said Garry. "Nobody else who could help?"

"Not really. They were pretty well shattered when I told them what we had and they said that if we sent them the recording, they'd probably be able to translate in a couple of weeks, but really we needed Professor Finlay."

"And when does he get back?"

"In about six months. He's on Sabbatical."

Despite the calm voice giving this disappointing information, Garry felt that he could hear a trace of a laugh in Bill.

"Bugger again," said Garry. "Can he be reached?"

"I already have," said Bill. "I spoke to him about ten minutes ago."

"You what? Bill, where is he? Can he get here?"

"He's already on his way, driving up the motorway. He's spending his Sabbatical in Sydney, doing some work at the University of New South Wales."

This time, the laughter in Bill's voice was bubbling out strongly. Garry echoed it.

"He's staying at my place," continued Bill. "I'll

bring him in for nine o'clock. I think we're really going to rock the joint."

* * *

Professor Gerald Finlay was a short man, rather overweight and his light blond hair was thinning badly. Garry thought he was about forty. He wore blue jeans, a black golf shirt and sneakers. But his dark eyes reflected significant intelligence.

"I can't really believe what you have here," he said after the social amenities had been completed. His voice was a strong baritone, reflecting a fine singing ability. "I was pretty gobsmacked when Bill first called me and showed me the Buddha preaching, his death and the funeral rites. And of course, some of the people who worked with Helen Macauley on her earth-shaking discoveries are my colleagues. They're all eager to hear what we find. So can we get started?"

Garry laughed and led the way to main work area.

"Ladies and gentlemen, let me introduce Professor Gerald Finlay. He helped us before with this language when we found astonishing scenes of the Buddha and I'm certain he will leave us astounded this time. Kieran, can you start the display?"

A few second later, the scene appeared as several people began gathering and the woman took her seat on the ground.

"Pretty fascinating already," said Gerald to the room. "Some of our historians will want to study this to examine the turbans being worn, different styles and colours. It means there were social strata already in operation two thousand years ago."

He went silent again, listening intently to the conversations coming over the loudspeakers.

"Definitely Magadi Prakrit," he said. "Simple

conversations about food prices, kids, the weather. The accent and intonation has changed from what I heard in the Buddha scenes, but they were about five hundred years earlier, so not a surprise. I really look forward to studying then more for my current research program."

His silence resumed as the crowd gathered but Garry could see his tension rising as the people rose to their feet and the newcomer arrived with his son.

It took just a few seconds before Gerald took a deep breath. "Can you stop it just there?" he asked. His voice was shaky. He took a deep breath.

"He just said, 'Welcome all here. My name is Yeshua. This is my son, Shimon.' I think you have just answered another of the great questions of the last two thousand years."

He took another deep breath.

"That man is Jesus. He has a son called Simon."

Chapter 42 – Lima, Peru, March, 2029

"The shocks keep coming, it seems," said Garry. "I've had a new report from Lima."

*   *   *

"The clearing is going well," said Roncal. "I just had a report that they've opened up a wide street moving straight to what appears to be the heart of the city we've called Petrova. The crews are clearing away the debris of all the trees they've cut away and they're filming the results now."

"This should be interesting!" said Abigail. She settled back to watch the monitor. "They're using a drone?"

"Either that or a helicopter," said Roncal. "Looks like it's about a thousand feet over the area."

For several minutes they watched in silence as the sides of the wide avenue became clear and then opened up into a square region. Bulldozers and other machinery attacked the piles of trees, bushes and smaller branches that had been cut down and slowly, the expanse of cleared buildings became clearer and clearer.

"What's that in the middle?" asked Abigail, leaning

forward in her seat. The city square had been cleared from the end of the avenue to just past what appeared to be the centre, but a small patch remaining in the middle.

"Could be a statue?" suggested Roncal. "That could be illuminating if it's a statue of the great leader or historical figure."

"I don't think it's high enough," said Abigail. "Maybe it's just a small decorative garden or something."

"Could be," said Roncal. "They've just turned the water hoses on to it."

For another ten minutes they watched as the high pressure water hose blasted away the greenery that covered the small patch. Then both of them let out a deep sigh as the object became clear.

* * *

"Bill has calculated that the alien symbol in the middle of that lost city in Peru gives a date of eleven hundred and twenty years ago," said Garry. "That's the second such symbol we've found recently. I wonder how many more there are."

"I'm starting to think there's a pattern," said Mary into the silence that held the room where the Second Foundation was gathered. "First, Karen Petrova's group finds the records hidden in our DNA. Then we start discovering more and more of our past and where we have been so wrong about our conclusions. And now we start to find this alien symbol. So far, only two, but Garry may have a point. Are we going to start finding more? And what are they telling us?"

Nobody in the room had an answer.

* * *

"If we haven't found enough to blow our minds into small fragments, this will complete the task," said Abigail as Roncal walked into her office. She had called him as soon as she could after seeing the latest developments on her monitor, though it had taken her a few minutes to recover her composure.

Roncal didn't smile, he too had experienced such severe shocks of discovery in the last few months that he was certain nothing else could ever surprise him again. He took a seat next to her and looked at the monitor.

"I'm certain this is taking place in the huge building that got uncovered last month in Petrova," said Abigail. "The shape and the dimensions seem to indicate it. I'm only back about fifteen hundred years after following the ancestry of an architect in Lima. He gave us his DNA after I talked to him at a faculty lunch."

Roncal studied the scene which was now frozen. The hall was huge, and appeared to be almost full of people. The centre was clear, however and against one wall was a low platform about a metre high with a large metal throne. Seated on that was a man in ornate robes and two armed soldiers stood on either side of him.

"Definitely some sort of royalty gathering," said Roncal. "It will take some time to discover just who this is. And the people are commoners, judging by their style of dress. Maybe one of those mass gatherings where the people can petition the king?"

"It looks like it," agreed Abigail. "Let's roll on and you can translate better than I can." She touched a key and the scene came alive.

Initially, nothing critical happened. There was a loud buzz of conversation around the hall and the king on the throne was deep in conversation with a man who had walked onto the platform, clearly a trusted advisor or assistant, judging by the way he held the attention of the king. Then the man stood up, bowed and walked off the platform. The buzz of conversation fell silent and a voice rang out from the rear of the hall.

"Definitely Quechuan," murmured Roncal. "He just called on the king to admit a stranger from a far land."

At the rear of the hall, a huge double door was opening and a man walked through. He was alone and he walked up the empty space to the throne platform with an easy assurance and pride. He looked considerably taller than anyone else in the hall.

"That's no local," said Roncal. "His clothing is nothing like anything else around and he's physically quite different."

"That's what got me interested," said Abigail. "This is no commoner petitioning the king for a redress of something."

The stranger stopped a couple of metres before the platform and bowed. But it was no bow of obeisance, it was more a gesture of courtesy towards an equal. He spoke a few words.

"Great King, I greet you," said Roncal in translation.

"What brings you here?" asked the king. "You seem to be from a very strange country a great distance away."

"Further than any man of this House of the Gods, Great King," replied the stranger

"You speak strange words that seem to have no meaning," said the King. He showed no hostility and the way he sat forward on the throne indicated interest.

"Think you that this world, these shores, these skies are the only House that the Gods have built?" said the man.

A brief murmur of soft conversation ran through the hundreds present in the hall.

"We know of no lands beyond our western coast," said the king. "Your home must be from a great distance indeed if they are beyond the great ocean."

"Further than that, Great King," replied the visitor. "So distant are they that other suns shine down on the land, men stand in the light of those suns but have not the likeness of Man such as you would understand."

"These are words beyond my comprehension," said the king. "What brings you here? Have you a request of my lands? Or do you bring a message from these other Houses of the Gods as you call them?"

"A message, great King. It is one that my people are spreading throughout the world, to other nations, to other people, to other Kings like yourself."

"A message? This is curious. How are you able to travel across such voids as the great ocean? There are other nations? Other countries? Other kings? And what is the message?"

Abigail studied the king's face. Fortunately, the long ago observer was fairly close to the throne and she could see that the king was uncomfortable, his body seemed tense.

"We have ways of travel," said the stranger. "They allow us to move over the whole world. One day, you will learn these ways."

"Do I have reason to fear you?" asked the king. There was anger now in his face and the other man shook his head and raised both hands in a placatory sign.

"There are very few of us, Great King," he said. "All of us could fit inside a small room and we have no weapons. We only bring a message."

The king sat back, seemingly reassured.

"And that message is?"

"One day, the men of this House of the Gods may be asked to play a role of leadership, teacher, perhaps protector to the men of other Houses. There are a few of them, hidden now among the stars. For now, my people play that role but we will not last forever and somebody else must take our place. The men of this House may well grow so far that they could take that role, but there are a couple of others. We only ask that you consider this, you and the kings of other lands in this House and try to grow to full adulthood so that you may be the ones chosen for the great role."

"What would you have me do?" Abigail thought the king's anger had faded to be replaced by intense curiosity.

"Pass this message to your sons as they grow," said the visitor. "Tell the people of this nation. When you or your successors meet other kings and other people, tell them of this. Over time, the whole world may understand the task facing them and try to grow to meet it."

"Few will believe it," said the king. For the first time, a smile broke his severe face.

"I will leave a sign in the city square," said the man. "It may puzzle many, intrigue many, perhaps one day people will realise what it is and remember the message."

The man bowed again, a little deeper this time and walked out of the hall, leaving silence behind him.

Roncal let out a deep sigh.

Chapter 43 – Cairo, June, 2029

"The Cairo people have been putting a huge amount of time looking for more students who studied at the Great Library of Alexandria," said Garry to the circle of Second Foundation members. "By sheer luck, they found four more scrolls being read by people in the Library. And the shocks keep coming, it seems."

* * *

Moneer Ragheb had thrown a small party for his family when he found the images of an ancient student opening and reading scrolls in the long-destroyed Great Library. He knew that he had opened a path for many years of research and a sure route to his doctorate and he could barely contain his eagerness to start full-time work on looking for scrolls being read.

His first one didn't disappoint him. He watched through the eyes of an ancient student as he located a scroll and took it from the shelves to a table, unrolled it and began reading.

Moneer switched on the recorder that was a standard piece of equipment and watched intently. He knew from the alien images on the DNA extract that the year was 54BCE. The script was Greek, the language of the very few scrolls they had been able to see so far. Excitement building, he watched as the reader carefully read the opening sections. They were very short but the opening sentences were startling;

"As air flows over a curved form, the density of the air is reduced. The density below that form remains the same and this creates an upward force on the form."

WHAT? Moneer stared at these words until the reader moved his gaze further down the surface of the scroll. This was the basic principal of an aerofoil in a wing that allowed an aeroplane to fly. How could it possibly be described in this ancient document? He continued reading but was initially baffled by the many lines of hieroglyphics that followed and none of them could he understand. But the reader remained studying them and slowly, Moneer realised that these were a form of mathematical symbols.

When the script returned, so did the astounding discovery.

"We made a form in which the upper surface was curved and the lower surface flat. We placed it before a fire on which we put a load of reeds that smoked when lit and then had four servants fanning the fire energetically so that the smoke passed over the form.

Equally astonishing was the drawing that followed this paragraph. It looked exactly like the diagrams in basic books on the principles of flight, with smoke passing over an aerofoil.

The ancient student from fifty four years before the modern era continued to unroll the document.

"We have watched different birds in flight and concluded that those birds which can fly for extended periods with their wings open and not moving have a different shape from those birds which must flap their wings most of the time. The hawk is the best example and the shape of the hawk's wing is more like this."

Then followed a diagram of the profile of a hawk's wing.

"But in order to make such a shape which would take advantage from air passing over it, we felt that a simpler form would be necessary and we designed this one."

Another diagram followed and Moneer gasped in astonishment. The shape shown was almost exactly the familiar and beautiful ellipse that had been the defining characteristic of a World War II Spitfire.

* * *

"This is quite amazing," said Professor Hazem Yehia of the Department of Mathematics. "I have never seen such glyphs before, but they are absolutely decimal in logic. There are only ten shapes. Now, our conventional wisdom is that the decimal Hindu–Arabic numeral system with zero was developed in India by around 700CE. The development was gradual of course, spanning several centuries, but the decisive step was, we have believed, provided by Brahmagupta's formulation of zero as a number in 628CE."

He shook his head as if to clear a generation of knowledge away.

"But here you have shown that the decimal Arabic system was in use in 54BCE and probably well before. And just as amazing is that the zero was invented at least seven hundred years earlier than we had believed. I took those glyphs and after playing around, I confirmed that they are equivalent to the digits we use and I constructed a conversion table, but I have never seen them before in any documents we have known about."

"Can you identify what the lines of numbers represent?" asked Moneer.

Professor Yehia smiled.

"It's a pretty good guess that they are aerodynamics-related. Based on what they're describing, I'd be fairly confident that they're the ancient equivalent of Bernouilli's equations on fluid dynamics and how they relate to the theory of flight. But you'd better talk to the aviation people."

"I'll do that," said Moneer.

"Is there any more in that scroll?"

"I haven't gone further yet," said Moneer.

"I'd lay odds that those ancients designed an aeroplane," said Yehia. "In fact, I wouldn't be surprised if they actually built one. Nothing surprises me any more!"

"I'll get back to you on that," said Moneer, laughing.

The following day, he returned to the scroll being read by an ancient student in the Great Library. To his relief, the student continued to read along the document and it revealed an even greater event than Moneer had thought possible.

We realised that we had no way of increasing the speed of the airflow over the form to see if enough upward pressure could be created. So we built a small structure that had the wing shape on either side and pulled it to the top of a small hill with a steep incline down a grassy slope. Then we pointed the structure down the hill. It slid quite rapidly and then to our delight, it lifted off the surface into the air. There was much rejoicing.

But the structure was not stable, it did not fly like a hawk but instead twisted in the air and crashed to the ground. We have since further watched birds in flight and realised that they appear to use their tails in some way. We will consider adding a similar tail to our rebuilt structure.

They had flight! Moneer was having trouble breathing. This civilisation, whatever it was, had discovered the technology that allowed an aeroplane to fly! Unfortunately, the scroll ended at that time. Moneer marked the time and prayed that the student would return to the study of aviation very soon and locate a sequential scroll that would tell more of the astounding story.

* * *

Sabri Nassif, assistant professor in the Department of Antiquities was also as thrilled as a child receiving a present he had dreamed of for years when he was granted permission to search for ancient students at the Great Library of Alexandria.

But so far, the work had been frustrating. Starting with dozens of DNA samples from Egyptian people, he had spent many days going back to the times when the Library had existed, hoping to find somebody who had entered the place of learning and examined scrolls that had been destroyed hundreds of years ago. So far, he had not been successful.

There had been interesting episodes, however. As a historian, he had been fascinated by seeing life in ancient Egypt, simple discussions between people on the streets, family interactions and disputes and he had received a severe shock to his system when the subject he was studying had killed several people but never appeared to have been found out. He had experienced nightmares for some days at the sight of savage blows with an axe to three defenceless men and one woman.

But one morning, he took a deep, shuddering breath of anticipation when he saw through the eyes of a young woman the impressive shape of the Great Library and the vast square before it.

Could she be entering the Library? Would she take a scroll and read it or was she just a worker there, perhaps a cleaner? Sabri prayed softly that his search would at last pay off with a sight of a scroll being unrolled and open for his inspection through the eyes of this long-dead woman.

But as she walked through the entrance hall, Sabri saw smiles of welcome from other students and officials and one or two murmurs that sounded friendly and he began to feel hope that the woman was a genuine researcher and academic.

To his delight, she took down a scroll, laid it on a table and began opening it slowly. Sabri found it almost impossible to believe what he was seeing.

"That is a stunningly accurate diagram of every bone in the human body," said the surgeon. He had taken nearly an hour examining the detailed drawings that Sabri had copied through the computer and brought to the hospital. "Somebody has conducted extraordinary research, almost certainly cutting up a cadaver and noting every bone. Look, he or she has even named every one of them, even the tiny bones of the hands and feet. And this is over two thousand years old?"

Sabri nodded. "The student was reading this in the year 102BCE, that I can tell from the symbols in the DNA track. But I have no idea when the drawings were made."

The surgeon took a deep breath and turned to the second drawing.

"And this one shows every major artery as well as the heart. Even some of the smaller capillaries are shown, though not all. This is far more detailed and accurate than anything done before the modern era of medicine. And he has even examined the heart, shown every section, the valves and the blood flow direction. He clearly understood the pumping function."

He looked up at Sabri and shook his head.

"We have always known that the destruction of the Library took away so much of human knowledge, but nobody could have imagined that there was so much data that was ahead of even the science of the nineteenth century. Are there any more such scrolls?"

"I don't know, but I hope so," said Sabri. "As soon as I saw this one being put back in the shelves, I brought the copies to you. I will continue to follow the lifeline of this woman's DNA and hope that she will look at other scrolls."

"Let us pray so," said the surgeon. "Given this degree of knowledge and research, we must believe that there are more diagrams of the human body, perhaps the other main organs. What a tragedy this is! Imagine if the world had access to this information when it was first produced! How much further would we be today?"

Sabri had no idea how to answer that one and with a polite comment, returned to his laboratory, even more excited by what he would find over the coming weeks.

Chapter 44 – July, 2029

"Avram, you'd better get down here right away!"

Penny's voice sounded near to hysteria and Avram immediately left his desk and raced down to the Childcare Centre. When get there, the sight of Penny sitting next to four-year-old Jessica against one wall and smiling eased his panic. He sat down, cross-legged across from them. Jessica looked up from her tablet and smiled.

"Hi, Dad!" she said.

"Hello there, little girl," he replied and touched her head. She resumed her study of the tablet on her knees. Avram looked at Penny.

"You sounded terrified!" he said.

"I was shocked."

"What about?"

"Several things. First, look at what she's reading."

Avram leaned over and looked at the screen.

"New Astronomy? She's reading about the planets in a professional journal?"

"That's just the first thing. Jessica, tell Daddy what you just told me."

Jessica looked up with a frown.

"I don't think they should have downgraded Pluto from a planet," she said. "It looks like a perfectly normal planet to me."

Struggling to control his breathing, Avram smiled at her.

"Why do you think so, kiddo?"

"Just look at the data," she replied and proceeded to recite facts and numbers about Pluto's size, orbital time and rotational time. "That sounds like a planet to me," she concluded.

Avram gulped and had nothing to say. He looked helplessly at Penny who looked equally shaken. He regained control of his voice.

"That all sounds very logical, Jessica. I'll have to think about it."

"Okay," said the child and bent her head over the tablet again.

"That's not all," Penny said. "Okay, we might have produced an exceptionally bright kid, but that's not really why I called you down. Jessica, what was that you were telling me before I called Daddy?"

Jessica looked up and laughed. "What, you mean about the first time you met Garry? I don't know if you could tell, but he obviously thought you were very pretty! You could see it in his face!"

Avram felt as if he'd been punched in the gut.

"Is your finger properly grown back, Daddy?" said Jessica, looking up at him.

"Yes, it's all back to normal."

"It was horrible when you lost it," she said with a grimace. "All that blood all over the place?"

"You remember that, do you?" Avram's world was turning over. He glanced at Penny and saw that she was almost in shock.

"Yes," said Jessica. "And you were crying all during the ride to the hospital. And then I remember when it started growing back. The doctor who treated you was really surprised when he took the bandage off and saw the little bit sticking up!"

"You're right, it was all dreadful," said Avram. "Now, little girl, you go back to your reading, Mummy and I want to talk about what we're having for dinner tonight."

Jessica looked down again and seemed to be concentrating. Her parents stood up and walked across to the other wall.

"Okay, I suppose it's no surprise that a couple of high-achieving, super intellects like us might produce a sprog of amazing intelligence," said Penny. "But she's reading our DNA records."

"I don't think anything has shaken me so much in my whole life," said Avram. "What the hell are we going to do? Imagine if she starts reading the DNA of other people and telling them about incidents in their lives?"

"Maybe we can cut that off right here. Let's go back and have a talk with that astonishing little thing we produced."

Sitting back down with Jessica, Penny took the initiative.

"Jessica, it's really brilliant what you did, remember some things from mine and Daddy's life. But while it's all right with us, will you promise us that you won't do that to anyone else? Other people might get frightened."

"Sure, Mum," said Jessica. "I promise. But will you go and get that diabetes looked at?"

"What diabetes? I don't have diabetes."

"Yes, you do, Mum. Just a tiny bit."

"We'll get it looked at," said Avram, seeing Penny unable to speak. "Remember, Daddy's a doctor, we'll make sure Mummy is fine."

"Okay, see you later," said Jessica with a wide smile and turned back to her tablet.

Avram helped Penny get to her feet. "Let's get a pathology test done," he said softly.

Penny was in tears. "There's no history of diabetes anywhere in the family," she whispered. "I get checked every year, there was nothing last time."

"I know. But of that weird daughter of ours says you have it, we'd better get it checked out."

"I don't think Karen Petrova could ever have thought just how much she would change the world," said Penny. "If this is a sign of how humans are changing, it's blowing my little mind into tiny pieces."

* * *

"We had the tests done that day," said Avram seated across the coffee table from Garry. "They confirmed it, Penny has very early signs of Type 2 diabetes."

"I'm really sorry," said Garry.

"It's not a thing that comes from lifestyle and diet and that stuff," said Avram. "Not like Type 1 which is inherited. So she never expected ever to get this, there's never been a sign of it. And there's no cure, it needs a lot of insulin and could get a lot worse, with heart disease, even blindness." Avram had tears running down his face.

"Something I need to tell you," said Garry. "And I know this will help. Remember when Galina joined us? She brought something with her…"

* * *

August, 2022

"G'day, Garry as you Australians say, this is Greg."

Garry smiled in pleasure at hearing the voice of the CEO of Life Technology.

"Yeah, well, we do actually say that, Greg! Good to hear from you!"

"I have some good stuff for you, Garry. We've been working on the cache of data you sent me a few weeks ago and may I say, it has blown our collective minds up here!"

"Nothing about Karen Petrova can surprise me anymore, mate! So what new treasures have you found?"

"There are five new drugs here. We've done a first scan of all the formulations and they all look astounding. But we've decided to develop just one for now. It will take us about a year to make the first samples and then as you know, a long time to get it through the approvals, but knowing Karen and her reputation with the authorities all over the world, I expect no problems."

"So which one are you taking as the first, Greg?"

"One of the worst afflictions for humanity. Karen has invented a drug that looks like it will cure diabetes or at worst, hold it in check."

"Diabetes? Holy shit, Greg, that's incredible! Type 1 or 2?"

"The first one is for Type 2, but the next one on the list is for Type 1."

"Simply amazing! Let me know when you can start licencing it to the major manufacturers."

"You can count on it, Garry. Not that we need it, but it will make us a few more hundreds of millions."

Garry laughed, they chatted as old friends for a few more minutes than he hung up.

* * *

The Present

Avram stared at Garry, hope alive in his eyes.

"There's a drug?"

"It took a while longer to gain international approval than we expected, but the first global release is due from the three biggest manufacturers any day. Greg will send me a year's supply immediately, though he believes that with the early stages of Type 2, you can expect a complete cure within weeks."

"I need to call Penny."

"I have no doubt. But when you've given her the news, get back here and tell me about this daughter of yours. I can hardly believe what you told me before."

"Sure!" but Avram was already out of the door, his phone in his hand.

Chapter 45 – August, 2029

"We have Jennifer's report from Brussels," said Garry. "Rather than reading it to you, here's the written report."

He slid a stack or printouts to the middle of the table and each of the council took a copy.

The room went silent.

Summary of Agreed Developments

Negotiations with a number of countries' leadership have confirmed that the European Community will be expanded to include all the remaining European countries including the major ones, such as Switzerland, Norway, Ukraine and Russia, but all the smaller nations such as Monaco, Belarus, Armenia and others. With the United Kingdom rejoining the Community in 2028, the total membership will be forty-five.

Several non-European countries have been invited to join this new, enlarged Community. These include Australia, New Zealand, Japan, Israel and Canada

All these countries have pledged their continued support for the International Criminal Court.

All of them that were not previously members of the North Atlantic Treaty Organisation have now joined. NATO will now offer policing support to Interpol and provide it with powers of arrest and transport to the Hague for trials by the ICC.

Originally starting in the United Kingdom, protocols for the use of DNA evidence in all crimes have been adopted by all the Community nations and trials before the ICC will use these protocols.

In other parts of the world, this growing cooperation is also evident. The ten nations of the Association of Southeast Asian Nations (ASEAN) have expanded by one to include Papua New Guinea. This organisation will strengthen its ties to the European Community, its support for the ICC and will provide support to NATO if required.

In the Americas, the USA has renewed its support of NATO, including the enlarged version, the ICC and Interpol. Discussions are taking place with all the South American nations to join the European Community which is now considering a change of name to reflect its new scope.

There was a collective sigh as all the Foundation members finished reading the summary.

"A changed world indeed," said Ben. "How splendid that our members have been instrumental in achieving this."

Chapter 46 – Cairo, August, 2029

The cradle had been replaced by a permanent structure built into the wall under the Sphinx and a staircase constructed that led down to it from the top. The original cradle was still in use, but now for equipment to be lowered down or taken up again as needed.

Because of his role in discovering the secret of the ancient structure, Halim had the privilege of being with the small crew of engineers on the platform against the wall. Over the previous four days, they had drilled down two vertical lines about a metre apart and two metres long and then two horizontal lines at the top and bottom. Little was left to do now but carefully tap against the oblong shape and collapse the remaining stone to open up the doorway into the tunnel that led to the chamber containing the ancient scrolls.

Halim stood in the corner away from the work and watched, feeling tension rise in him. Two engineers worked on the doorway, one with a wooden mallet with which he hammered hard on the wall nearest the drill lines. Occasionally, he nodded at his associate who picked up the drill and cut away small obstructions.

"The wall is just seventy centimetres thick here," said the man with the mallet, looking back at Halim.

His voice was muffled under the face mask he wore. But I can tell from the vibration whether there is a clear cut. That's the last one. So now the big guns come out."

The two men put down the drill and mallet and picked up two heavy sledgehammers. In well coordinated alternate movements, they swung hard on the wall, aiming at the edge of outlined area. Twenty minutes later they stood back as one large block of stone fell away. It was big enough for a man to walk through and one of the engineers waved at Halim.

"Your honour, I believe," he said. "Be the first man in several thousand years to enter."

His heart thumping, Halim put on a breathing mask, stepped over the broken blocks, switched on the light on his helmet and walked through the tunnel, turned at the corner and found himself in the secret chamber. He slowly moved his head to illuminate the walls and again saw the racks of scrolls neatly stacked on the shelves. He turned and walked back out.

"Okay, it will take us a day to clear this entrance, and get lights installed," said the engineer. "Then you can start collecting the loot." Both men had removed their facemasks and were grinning cheerfully at Halim. "Go home and somebody will call you when we're ready."

Not sure of his ability to speak, Halim bowed his head and turned to the staircase for the long climb to the top.

* * *

The following morning he was back just as the engineers were wrapping up their gear. They didn't seem surprised to see him so early.

"Lights installed, doorway cleared," said one. "We put an industrial fan in there and extracted the nitrogen and tested the air again, so it's breathable and we won't need an airlock like we first thought, nor will you need breathing apparatus. We'll follow the developments with interest."

As they began the climb out, the cradle stopped level with the platform. It was loaded with specially constructed containers for the scrolls, metal, lined with soft material and airtight. A clatter of feet on the stairway indicated the arrival of the ten students from the university, all skilled in the handling of ancient scrolls. Halim greeted them and led the way into the chamber.

There were four lights in the room, none of them very bright but enough illumination for the work. Nobody wanted to risk too much light or heat with these ancient documents. There was silence as the students stared in awe around them. Halim broke it.

"There's only room for four of us at a time," he said. "Each of you, get a case, bring it in, wrap up the scroll and carry it out. It's a narrow passage as you saw, so wait until all four are out before another group goes in."

The room emptied and the recovery began.

Chapter 47 – Cairo, June, 2030

Unrolling scrolls that had been sealed away for thousands of years was a delicate task requiring huge expertise and skill and few scholars had it to the degree required for the task. Specialist experts were invited from around the world and there was no shortage of people offering their assistance. It was another two months before the Director allowed the students to start examining the scrolls, in which time some of the finest experts in the world had been working on unwrapping then unrolling the documents. Many scrolls were so fragile that they were filmed instead and then wrapped away again in atmospheric-controlled conditions.

The times became extraordinarily exciting. Halim was in the room when one student shouted in amazement when his sheaf of photo-copied pages appeared to show maps and drawings of Atlantis. Several experts moved in to try and decipher the entire batch and Halim was intensely curious about what they might reveal.

But it was his own discovery that threatened his mental balance. It was one of the scrolls that had been filmed as it was unrolled and now Halim had a pile of printouts he could examine without the worries of damaging the originals.

As with most of the scrolls so far examined, the text was in Greek but most students of Egyptian antiquity had developed some facility with the ancient version of the language. The words were faint, but some technology had been applied and the texts had been enhanced to reasonable legibility. As Halim read, he felt his breath get shorter and sweat broke out on his hands. It was the report of a conversation between a citizen of a country as yet unidentified and a man, obviously a visitor.

In my studies of the ancient Kingdom of Akkad, I found a tablet written in the time of King Sargon. It is in the language of the time, but I have achieved some understanding of that tongue and this is my translation of the words inscribed in the clay. It was well preserved and clear. This is what was written.

And when I came out of the temple, there was a man standing in the sunlight. At first, he seemed ordinary enough but his clothing, his face, his eyes were not like those of my people and I asked him if he needed help. He smiled at me and I sensed great authority in this man.

"No help is needed, my friend, I am secure in my path."

"You seem like a man who has travelled far," I said. He smiled again.

"You display great wisdom, Child of Man, for indeed I have travelled from another House of the Gods."

I felt baffled by his words and could not understand why he called me Child of Man or what he could have meant by another House of the Gods. But I knew I was before a great man, perhaps a priest, perhaps a teacher or a prophet.

"Other Houses, Teacher?" I asked him.

"Indeed, other Houses." The Teacher waved his arm to encompass the town, the country around it and all the known lands of the world. "Think you that this world, these shores, these skies are the only House that the Gods have built?"

"You mean those far lands of the west and south, Teacher? Few have ventured there and lived."

"Further than that, Child of Man," replied the Teacher with a friendly smile. "So distant are they that other suns shine down on the land, men stand in the light of those suns but have not the likeness of Man such as you would understand."

"You have been to these lands, Teacher?" I asked. I knew that I should have felt ridicule at these extraordinary words that this man was speaking, but something in the depth and power of the his face made me instead feel awe and wonder, a sense that I was privileged, while unknown, unimaginable doors were being opened to me.

"I am of these lands, and others. I have been to them and walked upon them," replied the Teacher. "And the Men of some of those Houses have learned the lessons and discovered the choices that Men of this House have yet to learn and discover."

I felt some fear at these words, wondering if he was perhaps giving me a warning.

"Why are you telling me these things, Teacher? I am but a simple servant of the king, not a man of power as you are."

"I and my colleagues have already told many of the Children of Man and we will tell many more and perhaps the words can be spread. But I have not told you the real message."

I know that I felt some fear again, but the man smiled again and eased my fear.

"Mankind has the chance to achieve such greatness as you cannot as yet begin to comprehend," he said. "Many in those other Houses of the Gods are too young to play their full role in the life of the Universe and they need mentors and guides while they grow to maturity. Some show promise of growing into the role which my people carry out in this time. Mankind is one of them, though you are a long way from being ready. My people will perform these duties for a long time yet, but we will not live forever. Before us, there was another race of men of another House of the Gods and they helped my people grow until we could assume their duties. And then they died as we will one day die and someone else will assume the role."

I felt my head spin with confusion. Was he telling me that other beings lived on planets near some of the distant stars that we could see in the night sky? It seemed so.

"But I must ask you again, Teacher. Why are you telling me these things? As I have already said, I am just a servant of the king."

He smiled and touched my shoulder.

"You are more than just a simple man, my friend. You are a servant of the king as you have told me, but you work in the court and you can arrange for me to be there and request the ear of the king. This I want you to do."

I wondered how he knew that, but I was beyond disbelief and I knew this was an agent of some impossible power.

"I will do that, Teacher. What will you tell the king?"

"I will tell him what I have already told you," he said. "And more. We have identified three other Houses of the Gods where men live who might one day grow enough to become the guides and mentors for the rest," he continued and I struggled to follow him though my mind was feeling overloaded with impossible facts. "Mankind is one of them. We will watch all of you over the coming years and hope that one of you shows the full potential to lead other men of other Houses of the Gods to full adulthood. We will help you. We have implanted in much earlier men the ability that one day you will discover to look back through your history and learn your role in the Universe. At intervals we will come back and look at your progress. But we will only give you three chances to continue your development. If you fail those three times, you will be relegated to being just one of the secondary people."

Halim sat back, sweat running down his back, his thighs and arms. He could hardly even ask the question that he knew was in his mind. Had he just read a conversation between a human being and an extra-terrestrial entity? Was that entity telling humanity that it was the mentor and guardian of a number of other intelligent, sentient beings around the Galaxy? And had it told humanity that several of those beings were being reviewed for eventually taking over the role? And that humanity might fail?

Despite the shock of what he had seen, Halim decided to go further and see if there were any similar references in this scroll.

It didn't take him long.

"Great King, this traveller from far lands desires audience."

The hall was full of citizens for this was the day every month when the King heard petitions and ruled on matters that called for his attention. Already, he had ordered the freeing of prisoners from a camp containing soldiers captured by our armies.

"These were brave men obeying the orders of their lord," said the King. "They had no choice in the matter and I will not punish them for their loyalty. They may remain in the Kingdom if they choose to serve me or they are free to return to their own land. This I command as King."

There had been other matters settled, mostly minor disputes of property or debts and the King had spoken quickly, now looking a little fatigued and bored. That is when one of his counsellors had spoken.

"Let him approach," said the King.

The man who walked from the back of the hall to the foot of the throne looked like no man I had seen before. Taller than most, his complexion was lighter than was usual in our people and he moved with an assurance and pride that signified noble birth. He bowed before the King but it was not the abasement of a subject before his lord, but the acknowledgement of almost equality. The King seemed to recognise it because he showed no anger.

"I greet you, Great King," said the man.

The King nodded. "You have travelled far, I think."

"Further than any man of this House of the Gods, Great King," replied the stranger

"Those are strange words," said the King. His interest showed in his face and the way he sat forward on the throne. "What mean you?"

"Think you that this world, these shores, these skies are the only House that the Gods have built?" said the man.

A stir of interest ran through the hundreds present in the Royal Hall.

"You mean those far lands of the west and south?" asked the King.

"Further than that, Great King," replied the visitor with a friendly smile. "So distant are they that other suns shine down on the land, men stand in the light of those suns but have not the likeness of Man such as you would understand."

Halim sat back with a gasp of shock. These were the same words he had read just minutes before. Was this man addressing the King with such confidence the same man who had spoken to an unknown person outside the temple? Halim had no idea when this conversation had taken place and he could not identify what Kingdom or what King was the centre of this discussion. But the two sections were clearly related.

"We know nothing of such lands," said the King. "What brings a traveller like yourself so far to my Kingdom?"

"Mankind has the chance to achieve such greatness as you cannot as yet begin to comprehend," the stranger said. "Many in those other Houses of the Gods are too young to play their full role in the life of the Universe and they need mentors and guides while they grow to maturity. Some show promise of

growing into the role which my people carry out in this time. Mankind is one of them, though you are a long way from being ready. My people will perform these duties for a long time yet, but we will not live forever. Before us, there was another race of men of another House of the Gods and they helped my people grow until we could assume their duties. And then they died as we will one day die and someone else will assume the role."

Halim was somehow not surprised to read these words again. The rest of the document was too faded to be legible. Still feeling waves of shock run through his body, Halim carefully put the sheets into a folder, his mind racing.

He felt terrified of what this would do if these words leaked out to the world. He looked down at the sweat on the documents where his hands had touched them and decided he would at least talk to the Director.

* * *

"And the director sent a translation to me and that's what you see before you," said Garry. Around the table, the members of the Second Foundation were completely silent in the shock the news had caused.

"The document identified King Sargon of the Kingdom of Akkad when this took place," said Garry. "This would place it at least three thousand years BCE, so possibly the language in which it was originally written was either Archaic Sumerian or Semitic Akkadian, according to the experts in Cairo. But I have no doubt we all recognise the earth-shattering implications of all this. If this text is really true, it tells us that there are other intelligent, technological species in the Universe. That's enough to shake the world to its core.

"The astounding thing is how similar the whole scene appears to be to the scene that Abigail and Roncal found in the recently uncovered city they have named Petrova. The two episodes are some thousands of years apart, but the messages they give are almost identical, even some of the phrases are the same. It must be almost certain that as we continue researching our histories, we will discover more episodes of this nature. Somebody has been trying to tell Humanity something for some thousands of years.

"And some time earlier, we found an episode with somebody giving yet another similar message to Prime Minister Disraeli, as recently as 1874.

"These episodes confirm what we have been thinking for some years," Garry continued. "This whole ability to look back through our timelines has been artificially implanted in humans and we know this happened some seventy thousand years ago in Neanderthal Man and then again in Cro-Magnon Man about forty-five thousand years ago. But we still have no idea who it was that gave us this ability."

Silence rang around the table and then it was broken by Ben Fuller.

"That would be me," he said.

Chapter 48

The room was frozen. Everybody stared at Ben, nobody seemed capable of saying anything.

"Ben?" Mary finally spoke. Her voice was weak and shook slightly. "Ben, that's not a funny joke."

He smiled at her. "Not a joke, Mary. Not me personally, of course, but several long-ago ancestors."

Silence fell again as everybody tried to absorb the shock. Mark Craymer sat back in his chair, his arms folded across his chest in some form of protection. Salmaan Basrai, the statistician was wide-eyed, staring at Ben, his complexion an unhealthy grey. Jennifer Chang leaned on the table, her elbows supporting her and her hands over her mouth. Annabelle Calvert was white-faced, her eyes wide as she stared at Ben. Alana didn't move, but her eyes studied Ben with cold attention. Garry and Mary looked least affected, but both had gone very still.

"You'd better explain, Ben," said Garry after a few moments. "Who or what are you?"

Ben turned his smile onto him. He looked like a college professor running a tutorial with a group of students.

"Not of this Earth, as you have already realised," he said.

"So from where, then?" Garry's voice seemed under control, but the rigidity in his body indicated the shock he was experiencing.

"Elsewhere," replied Ben.

"Where elsewhere?" snapped Mary, shock making her irritable.

"That I can't and won't tell you. If I did, astronomers all over the world will show serious attention to the region and it won't help because whatever they see will be several hundred years out of date."

"This really should be insane," said Garry. "Ben, we've known you for some years, you've been an invaluable member of our group. There is absolutely no reason to believe any of this."

"None at all," agreed Ben. "But...?"

"But somehow I do," said Garry. "And somehow I think everybody else does, too."

In various ways, from small nods to muffled sounds, the rest of the group indicated acceptance.

"So you had better explain everything," said Garry.

"It's what was said in the scroll," said Ben. "There are a number of intelligent races in this Galaxy at various levels of growth. Four of them are at a similar level of technological development. Humanity is one of those."

He paused and looked around the listeners as they absorbed this information.

"One of you will have to grow into the future leadership and mentorship of all the less developed species. In time, you must take over from us."

"And who is us?" asked Mary. The tensions showed in her harsh, strained voice.

"You won't know that until you are appointed the guardians," said Ben.

"And just how did you get to have this exalted role?" asked Mary. Her anger was becoming evident. Ben looked at her.

"Why so angry, Mary?"

"At university I knew who the professors were," said Mary. "I knew their backgrounds and qualifications, I could look them up in public records. In ASIO I knew who the top people were, the ones defining and arranging my life, I knew what training and qualifications they had. When I worked for them or studied under them, it was my choice to do so. But here you are, Ben, telling us you are somehow our supervisors, mentors and perhaps authorities over the human race. We know absolutely nothing about you and we obviously have no say in your appointment. Are you also responsible for our discipline? What punishments do you impose for our failings? Who are you to judge us? Who the hell gave you this power over us?"

Mary was almost trembling with anger.

Startled, Garry looked round the table. He could see in several faces the reaction to Mary's blast and some echoes of her fury.

"It's a fair question, Ben," he said. "Can you answer it?"

Ben was silent for a moment.

"Civilisations have risen and collapsed around the galaxy," he said finally. "Many species have developed technology, become the dominant one on their world, risen to great heights of genius. They developed machines to build amazing structures, science to explain the beginnings of the universe and weapons that could obliterate their world and its inhabitants. What they didn't develop was the wisdom and maturity to manage their technologies. They collapsed and died."

The room was so silent Garry could hear the breathing of each of the people there.

"There was one species that was one of those that was in the ascendant path of technology," continued Ben. "But many of them knew they could be causing trouble for themselves. There were the usual problems, pollution, wars, social unrest, the same stories were common to almost all of the technological species. They lived in constant fear of conflict, disease, possibly even global nuclear war, just as this human race has lived for a century or more."

He was silent again for almost a minute. Nobody moved, sensing that the key part of what he was telling them was yet to be told.

"Then one day, a brilliant scientist began exploring the nature of DNA, something that had been discovered a few decades earlier. And yes, DNA and its characteristics are common to all the intelligent races. As his team of researchers became more and more skilled in what they were doing, as they developed astonishing technologies to help them, they found that their DNA held the visual and sound records of their lives and then also the lives of each of their direct ancestors. They found they could explore the history of their species and this helped them learn everything about themselves. But they also asked the question of why did they have this ability? It wasn't necessary for survival, it didn't help them become and remain the dominant species on their world."

"Just as we have asked," said Mary, her anger fading in the increasing fascination with what Ben was saying.

"Exactly the same. And they came up with the same conclusion that you did, that the ability was installed in their people by some external force for some specific reason. They were correct, just as you are correct."

"And what happened?" asked Garry.

"Their world changed," said Ben. "They became thoroughly knowledgeable about their histories and with that, their understanding of the forces that they had allowed to act on them increased. They transformed from a large number of different groupings, all at war with each other to some extent, to a single group of cooperative people who knew that there could be no more lies, no more subterfuges, no crime, only people with extraordinary gifts of creativity."

"We're not there yet, not by a long way," said Mark Craymer, the first words he had spoken since Ben's revelation.

"And you may never get there," said Ben. "But soon after that moment of discovery, somebody appeared among them who told the people involved in these discoveries something of interest."

"As you have appeared among us," said Mary.

"Yes," said Ben. "He told them of the many civilisations that had reached a similar stage of technology and destroyed themselves. He told them of one civilisation that had somehow avoided that self-destruction and grown so much that it could travel between the stars and had seen how close to suicide the other civilisations were. It learned to become helpers and mentors to these civilisations but without revealing themselves because that could cause massive stress and fear."

"And those mentors and helpers are your people?" asked Mary.

"No," said Ben. "Those people knew that they would one day die out as all civilisations do and they were looking for somebody who could replace them.

My people are the ones they found as potentially able to do that."

"Good grief!" said Mark. "Just how long ago was this?"

"Our discovery of the DNA implants occurred nearly two million years ago," said Ben. "We picked up the baton from our mentors about one and a half million years ago when the last of them died out as they had forecast."

Silence fell round the table as they absorbed this.

"Ben, something here doesn't ring true," said Mark after a minute or so. "When we played golf that day and you showed the telekinesis abilities, you seemed astonished by it, just as anyone else would have been. Why? If you are as advanced as you say, your people must have had this ability for centuries, maybe even millennia. So why did you reveal this in our game? Why reveal it at all?"

Ben smiled at him.

"Because I was genuinely astonished," he said. "I had no idea I had the ability. My people have never shown anything like that, nor have any other intelligent races."

Mark looked unconvinced. "Are you saying that your work with human DNA gave you the ability?"

"It would appear so," replied Ben. "Somehow, spending all those hours studying human DNA, I was taught how to do it. Honestly, Mark, I was as gobsmacked as I seemed. This is a completely new development."

Silence fell again for a few moments before Garry broke it.

"So now what?" he asked. "Will you start some sort of training program to raise us from this primitive state to somehow being able to mentor alien species?"

Ben shook his head. "No need for the sarcasm, Garry. I understand your resentment, all of you, but that's not how it's done."

"So why don't you explain how it's done?" said Mary. Her anger had not faded completely.

Ben looked thoughtful. "One of the basic realities of achieving change is that the person or group being changed must *want* that change. It cannot be imposed successfully by an external authority, not permanently, anyway. My having told you all this is about as far as I go for now. The rest is up to you."

"And can you suggest how we will do this?" asked Mary.

"It won't be easy. As I said, the whole world must want the changes that will be required for you to grow to maturity. But you have made a good start. This foundation is already perceived as a world influence by most countries. You must use that good will. Go to the United Nations and tell them what I have told you. Talk to world leaders everywhere. Explain how maturity comes from knowing where you came from and how you have developed to this stage. Encourage the spread of this technology, refine it until every home has access to learning about their ancestry. Some great strides are being taken already."

"Such as?" asked Garry.

"The great fortune that your friend, Eamon Jackson, now Pope Leo XIV has established a relationship with the other great religion and set in motion a gradual decline of religious forces, that's one significant step towards maturity."

"That's going to take many years, maybe centuries," said Garry. "And other religions are not yet showing any inclination to follow them."

"You have the time," said Ben.

"Really?" said Garry. "Is there some point at which you sit in judgement over Humanity and decide our future?"

Ben looked sadly at him. "You're still angry, I can see. So I must tell you something. Such a judgement has already been carried out once. It took over a hundred years and ended just a decade or two ago. We looked at Earth's history since the start of the twentieth century."

"And?" Garry's voice was harsh.

"You failed," said Ben.

Chapter 49 – Redemption

The silence in the room could be felt.

Garry broke it after nearly half a minute.

"Why?" he asked. "And what does this mean for us?"

Ben looked at him. His expression was sad.

"There are many factors on which a species is evaluated," he said. "But the overall question we have to ask is whether the species has the characteristics needed to act as mentors, guides and teachers to the less developed ones.

"I said we have looked at you for many centuries before deciding that Humanity had at least the potential for the role and that's why we implanted the DNA recording ability. You have displayed many positive characteristics, many negatives and for the last century or so, the evaluation has been intensive as you found yourselves on the shortlist."

"And this where we failed?" Mary's voice was cold, almost contemptuous.

"Still angry, Mary?" said Ben. "I can understand that. But bear with me, please."

He looked round the table. All the faces showed varying degrees of shock and anger.

"Yes," he said. "As Mary asked, this is where you failed. The last couple of centuries have had more wars than any other species we are evaluating. The level of cruelty, inhumanity and lack of concern for others has been quite frightening. The numbers of mass killings by various political authorities of all shades of philosophy, added to the greed that has seriously damaged the planet, all this was enough to remove you from the shortlist."

"So where does that leave us?" asked Mark. "Do you and your mentors now fly away and let us continue the process of destroying ourselves?" His expression was one of somebody who had just witnessed a disgusting sight.

"We wouldn't do that under any circumstances," said Ben. "We haven't been all that successful in preventing the ugliness, but we're still hoping that the ability to look back through your own history will give a boost to self-understanding and improvement."

"Jesus Christ, Ben," broke in Garry. "This makes you sound like the most sanctimonious prick of all time. Do you realise how you are bloody *preaching* to us?"

Ben nodded, his face calm.

"I do understand why you see it that way. But it's the role we were asked to take on and we accepted. I can only report what we have seen."

"So that's it, is it?" said Mary. "We are doomed to remain as the poor students while somebody else is promoted to teacher, guide and mentor? I'd be interested to hear just what this other species has that made them fit for the job."

"Nobody has been nominated for the job, as you put it," said Ben. "But will you give me a few more moments to finish what I was saying?"

"Is it worth it?" snapped Mark.

"I think so," said Ben. "Let me tell you some other things we saw that make a difference to our conclusions."

"A difference?" Alana had remained silent till now, but her anger was still obvious.

"Yes, a difference," replied Ben, smiling at her. Her face remained hostile.

"Two things we have found about Humanity that gave us some doubts," Ben continued. "The first was this astonishing factor of telekinetic powers. We have never seen this in any other species among the dozen or so we know about. And that includes my own. When it showed up in me, I was utterly shocked. Somehow, the human DNA has a teaching capability that we could never have foreseen and that makes you unique. I can't imagine just how it might be transferred to another species or how they would use it, but we are encouraged that to date it has been used for perfectly benign, creative applications."

"And the second?" Alana still looked cold and angry.

"The second reflects one of the main things we look at. A seriously indicative factor in a species is how it treats helpless animals. A second one is how it treats its criminals. Humanity does not rate well in those. A third is the creative ability in the arts. We know of several species that display no such creative talents at all. They are very dull people and could never function as teachers and guides."

He paused and looked round the table again. Some of the hostility appeared to have eased.

"But in you, we have seen the astonishing artistic, musical and dance techniques, even in pre-Christian millennia. Nobody else has developed such features so early in their growth. Those talents vanished for many reasons and remained largely hidden until what you term The Renaissance occurred. In reality, the first Renaissance was what you have been finding in early millennia. The developments of the middle ages are really the Second Renaissance. The fact that humanity could have a second such flowering of the arts, medicine, politics and learning is astonishing. And now you have done it again. You are into your Third Renaissance."

He paused, looking round as if checking for reactions.

"And that was enough to convince us that Humanity did have the potential for massive growth and maturation. You have been returned to the evaluation list."

Chapter 50 – Coda

"So now what?" asked Garry.

The reaction to Ben's words had been severe, almost as severe as hearing of Humanity's failure. There had been no celebration, no calls for drinks, nothing of that kind. Instead, all of the Second Foundation had reacted as if given a reprieve from a death sentence, almost collapsing in their seats as if like marionettes, their strings had been cut. Annabelle was weeping into her hands, Mary was staring at her hands as if studying very vein and muscle. Alana was still studying Ben like a scientist examining the effects of an experiment. Garry had his chin in his hands, his elbow on the table, looking into some unknowable distance. All of them seemed incapable of speech.

"Now you must use your role and your position as the focus of everything that has happened since Garry's people discovered the technology. You should probably start as many of my ancestors did, meeting with the influencers, the leaders and trying to teach them about this and why Humanity must change and mature. Maybe start with the United Nations and some very specific world leaders who have the perception to accept the reality. It will not be easy and you will face opposition and blank refusal to believe. It will take generations. But the signs of potential are there. The probable merger of the two main religions in the world and their changing focus on humanitarian acts rather than dogma is a positive sign. Get them on side, their assistance will be critical."

"How long have we got?" asked Garry.

"About five hundred years," said Ben. "And you will need every minute of it."